Sweet Poison

ALSO BY ELLEN HART

The Mortal Groove
Night Vision
The Iron Girl
An Intimate Ghost
Immaculate Midnight
No Reservations Required
Death on a Silver Platter
The Merchant of Venus
Slice and Dice
Hunting the Witch
Wicked Games
Murder in the Air
Robber's Wine
The Oldest Sin
Faint Praise
A Small Sacrifice
For Every Evil
The Little Piggy Went to Murder
A Killing Cure
Stage Fright
Vital Lies
Hallowed Murder

ELLEN HART

ST. MARTIN'S MINOTAUR NEW YORK

This is a work of fiction. All of the characters, organizations, and events portrayed in this novel are either products of the author's imagination or are used fictitiously.

www.minotaurbooks.com

Library of Congress Cataloging-in-Publication Data

Hart, Ellen.
Sweet poison / Ellen Hart. — 1st ed.
p. cm.
ISBN-13: 978-0-312-37525-6
ISBN-10: 0-312-37525-5
1. Lawless, Jane (Fictitious character)—Fiction. 2. Women detectives—Minnesota—Minneapolis—Fiction. 3. Minneapolis (Minn.)—Fiction. 4. Governors—Election—Fiction. 5. Political campaigns—Fiction. 6. Lesbians—Fiction. 7. Political fiction. I. Title.
PS3558.A6775S94 2008
813'.54—dc22 2008028962

First Edition: November 2008

10 9 8 7 6 5 4 3 2 1

For Elton John,
just because

Cast of Characters

Jane Lawless: Owner of the Lyme House Restaurant in Minneapolis and the Xanadu Club in Uptown.

Cordelia Thorn: Artistic director at the Allen Grimby Repertory Theater in St. Paul. Jane's closest friend.

Raymond Lawless: Defense attorney. Jane and Peter's father. Candidate for governor of Minnesota.

Peter Lawless: Photographer, videographer. Jane's brother.

Kenzie Mulroy: Professor of cultural anthropology at Chadwick State College in Chadwick, Nebraska. Jane's partner.

Charity Miller: Assistant account manager at American Eagle Bank & Trust. Volunteer for the Lawless campaign.

Gabriel Keen: Executive recruiter. Charity's ex-fiancé.

Corey Hodge: Ex-con. Car mechanic.

Mary Glynn: Corey's aunt. Housekeeper.

Serena Van Dorn: Corey's ex-girlfriend.

Luke Durrant: Computer specialist working with the Lawless campaign.

Reverend Christopher Cornish: Methodist minister.

Julia Martinsen: Doctor of oncology.

Neil Kershaw: Doctor of oncology.

A. J. Nolan: Ex–homicide cop turned PI. Jane's friend.

Minds differ still more than faces.

—**Voltaire**, *Philosophical Dictionary*

Sweet Poison

When you return home from hell, people watch you. If you've ever been there and back, you know what I mean.

Your friends, your family, they search for the cracks, the wounds, the inner disfiguring that suggests a deeper, more fundamental breakdown. You look the same. Maybe you even act the same. Eventually, you see them getting tired of the game. That's probably too harsh. For some, it's not a game; they really care. But they get tired of taking your temperature every five minutes, nonetheless. They tell you straight out, "You're back from the brink. You've got your whole life ahead of you. Count your blessings. Get on with it."

You want to give them a little love tap with an ice pick, but there's never an ice pick around when you really need one.

Instead, you take their advice. You get on with it as best you can. But your priorities, what used to be important to you, have altered. You have a passion now, one that, in your wildest imagination, you never dreamed would possess you. It's so sweet, overpoweringly so, that you can't help yourself, even though you know it has the power to destroy everything you love.

So you wrestle with that awhile until you think you really have taken a dive off the deep end. But you're addicted. You're out of control.

Listen closely now, because you're about to hear some truth.

That passion, that sweet poison, is the most intense high you've ever felt or ever will feel. It boils in your veins until your skin catches fire. It turns your eyes to lasers.

And all would be well except that you remember something disturbing that you once read: And if thou gaze long into an abyss, the abyss will also gaze into thee.

You don't know what that means, but in your bones, you know you better give it some very serious thought.

1

Late October

Jane carried two extralarge air pots filled with the Xanadu's gourmet hot chocolate into her father's campaign office. It was Saturday afternoon, one of the busiest days of the week at the club, but Jane had set her priorities the day her father entered the race for governor of Minnesota. She was fiercely determined to do everything she could to help him win the election.

Jane brought food for the employees and volunteer staff several times a week, and spent as much time as she could squeeze out of her busy schedule to work the phone banks, stuff envelopes, knock on neighborhood doors with information about her father's political positions, deliver lawn signs—anything and everything that needed to be done. Time was running short. Election Day was a little more than two weeks away.

The campaign office was located on the first and second floor of the Gussman Building, deep in the heart of St. Paul's Midway district. The most recent polls, including the one the campaign staff had just completed, put her father ahead of his Republican opponent, Don Pettyjohn, by eleven points. Even correcting for error, that was a substantial lead. All signs at the moment pointed to a win. Because of that, Jane couldn't understand why there were so many long faces on the volunteer workers.

Entering the break room, Jane set the air pots down on a long table covered in a red plastic tablecloth. She found a box under the table that was filled with stacks of paper cups and began to set them out along with napkins. As she worked, she noticed a number of volunteers walking past the door, heading for the reception area. By the time she was done arranging the napkins, a couple of the volunteers were actually running.

Seeing Charity Miller, one of the volunteers, pause in the doorway, searching for something inside a file folder, Jane called out to her. "What's going on?"

"Oh, Jane . . . hi." She seemed startled. "I didn't know you were here. You must have come in the back way."

Charity was in her early twenties, pretty, fresh faced, and eager. She'd been donating her time since January, when Jane's father had first thrown his hat into the political ring. Her friendliness and genuine empathy drew her into other people's problems a little too easily, which caused her to waste a lot of time, but her warmth and willingness to do just about any job, no matter how boring, had won her high marks at the campaign office. Jane liked her enormously.

"It's your father," said Charity, biting her lower lip, looking suddenly anxious. "His plane was supposed to land in St. Cloud half an hour ago, but there was some sort of problem."

"What kind of problem? Where is he?" The face of Paul Wellstone flashed through her mind. He'd been a deeply loved Minnesota senator. His plane had gone down in bad weather up near Eveleth in 2002, killing everyone on board. Jane's dad owned a Cessna. He'd been piloting it himself around the state, pretty much nonstop, since the campaign had begun.

"We don't know," said Charity. "But Maria's in touch with the St. Cloud airport."

Maria Rios was her father's campaign manager.

"Come on," said Jane, bolting out of the room, heading straight for Maria's office, which was located directly behind the reception desk.

The crowd of staffers parted as Jane made her way to the front.

Maria, elbows resting on her desktop, one hand holding the phone, the other pressed to her short salt-and-pepper hair, appeared to be listening. Jane wanted to grab the phone out of her hand, demand to know what was going on, but she waited.

"I see," said Maria. She paused, her eyes focused away from those standing in the doorway. "Yes, as soon as you know anything. *Anything*. Thanks." She gave herself a second, then looked up. Seeing Jane, she stood, her eyes registering caution. As she clipped her gold earring back on, she said, "I was about to call you. You've heard the news?"

"Just that my dad's plane hasn't landed in St. Cloud."

"They've requested backup from local emergency responders. So far, we don't know if the plane is down, or simply off course."

"Is Peter with him?"

Peter was Jane's younger brother. He was a photographer who was making a documentary of the campaign.

"No. He's in St. Cloud, on the ground. He drove up with a couple of the staffers this morning."

Jane was relieved to hear it, though it didn't do much to quell the battle of the titans in her stomach. "My dad's an experienced pilot. He knows what he's doing. He wouldn't take off if he thought there was a problem." She said it as much for her own sake as for those standing within earshot.

For her forty-third birthday, Jane's father had given her flying lessons. She often flew the Cessna herself when he wasn't using it—which meant she hadn't piloted it much in the last ten months. But her dad was meticulous about the plane's maintenance. Still, there were so many things that could cause a small plane to crash. Defective parts. Engine failure. Weather. Pilot error. Flight service station negligence. Wind shear.

"Where were they coming from?"

"Bemidji. Your dad's scheduled to give a speech tonight in St. Cloud." Before Maria could continue, the phone rang. She grabbed it, pulled off her earring, and sat back down.

"Yes, this is Maria." She sat forward in her chair, listened, closed her eyes. "I see. You've talked to him, then?"

Jane's heart stopped.

"How long will it take for the van to reach them?" She waited. "Good. And everyone is fine? No one was hurt?" She looked up, smiled. "That's fabulous news, Mr. Nelson. I'll pass the word along." She listened a moment more. "Did he say what kind of mechanical problem?" She nodded. "No, you're right. They're safe, that's all I care about. I'll try calling his cell again in a few minutes. Thanks so much." As she hung up, she sat back in her chair and sighed. "They're all fine. A van will pick them up and take them to a hotel in St. Cloud."

The crowd behind Jane cheered.

"What happened?" asked Jane.

"I'm not clear on that, but your dad was able to land the airplane in a field. Sounds terrifying to me. They were pretty rattled, but nobody was hurt. John Thompson, one of the field coordinators, finally radioed the field."

"What took him so long?" asked Jane.

"No idea," said Maria. "I'm just glad they're all okay."

Jane felt her cell phone vibrate inside the pocket of her jeans jacket. She pulled it out and looked at the caller ID. It was her father. She held it to her ear. "Hi! Where are you? What's going on?"

"I take it you heard about the plane," said her dad.

She sat down in a chair across from Maria, so glad to hear his voice that she felt tears come to her eyes. "You're all okay, right?"

"We're fine."

"What happened?"

"I don't—" His voice cut out.

"You're breaking up."

"We're in the middle of nowhere. Bad cell phone reception. But believe me, I landed by the seat of my pants."

"Sounds serious."

"We're down safely. I'll get a mechanic to come out and look the plane over tomorrow. In the meantime, I just wanted to check in. I . . . I mean, I'm—" This time his words were clear, but he simply stopped talking.

"Are you sure you're okay?" He was shaken up, but she had the sense that, because he couldn't seem to finish the sentence, he was holding something back.

"I'll be in touch. I love you, honey. You know that, right?"

"Of course I do."

"Good. I better call Peter."

She wanted to say something more. Maybe push for a better sense of his emotional state, or a clearer picture of what had happened with the plane. But with everyone standing behind her hanging on her every word, she ended the conversation with a simple good-bye.

Eight years, one month, and twenty-three days hard time.

Sixty days in a halfway house with electronic monitoring.

Six months at home with an electronic curfew and an obsessive-compulsive corrections agent.

Not that Corey was counting.

When he first set foot in St. Cloud state prison in central Minnesota, Corey Hodge was twenty-four years old. A young man. He no longer felt young. He'd been charged with one count of first degree sexual assault, one count of kidnapping, and two counts of aggravated battery. Because he'd never had so much as a parking ticket before, his lawyer was able to arrange a plea bargain in which Corey served the minimum. What amazed him was that no matter how loudly and logically he proclaimed his innocence, nobody seemed to be interested. His lawyer explained that if they took the case to trial, chances were he'd receive an even stiffer sentence.

"But I didn't do it," insisted Corey.

"Doesn't matter," said his lawyer. "They've got a good circumstantial case. You wanna play Russian roulette with your life, that's up to you. But if you want my advice, take the plea."

So Corey had spent the better part of nine years living with convicted rapists, murderers, attempted murderers, arsonists, child molesters, and other dregs of society. He'd been transferred to Lino Lakes state prison a few months after his processing at St. Cloud, and that's where he'd served the remainder of his time. The funny thing was, he discovered early on that he was now a full-fledged member of the great criminal choir, where almost everyone was innocent. That's when he got the point and shut up.

But yesterday everything had changed.

Corey stood in the middle of his aunt's garage working some leather polish into the seat of his '82 Moto Guzzi. It was an old motorcycle, which he'd lovingly restored several years before his arrest. He'd begun working on it again when he was transferred from the halfway house in north Minneapolis to his aunt's home on Sunrise Drive. North Minneapolis felt foreign to him, since he'd grown up on the south side. He would have preferred a halfway house closer to his aunt's place, but there weren't any that accepted a level-two sex offender. He was a marked man now, still getting used to his outcast status, but at least there were no more curfews or sacks of shit following him around, demanding to know what he was up to.

Corey had plans. He'd been a patient man and played the game. Now it was time for his reward.

The cycle had sat unused in his aunt Mary's garage the entire time he'd been inside, covered in a blue plastic tarp. Tonight he would celebrate the removal of the electronic ankle bracelet yesterday afternoon by getting on his cycle and riding. Didn't matter where. Corey still had to check in with his probation officer once a month, but compared to what his life had been like, this was freedom.

His aunt Mary appeared at the door into the garage. "I've got a job this afternoon," she said, hooking the strap of her purse over her shoulder. "If you're hungry, there's some leftover split pea soup in the fridge."

Mary's van was parked on the street. It was too big for the garage, mainly because the garage was stuffed to the gills with years of collected yard sale junk. She needed a van for her cleaning business. She was dressed in her usual work clothes—dark polyester pants, a short-sleeved cotton shirt, and a pearl choker. The idea of cleaning wearing pearls—even a cheap necklace—always made Corey smile.

Mary Katherine Glynn was a short, stout woman. Not beautiful by most standards, but comely, especially as a young woman. *Comely* was a word Corey had looked up in a dictionary once. When he read the definition, it made him think of her. It meant something like pleasing. Wholesome. That was Mary. She was also opinionated beyond belief, had a temper, but was soft in her own way. A pushover for sentiment. He was lucky that she'd agreed to take him in, although he never doubted for a minute that she would. She'd always been there for him.

Corey's childhood had been chaotic. His mother had died when he was ten. Left alone with an asshole father, Corey felt abandoned. A typical day for him—from the time he was ten until he turned thirteen—would start with him fixing himself breakfast while his father slept, then making himself a lunch and walking to school. When he got home in the afternoon, his father was away at work. He'd grab something to eat, then go outside to play with his buddies.

Corey's dad would arrive home around six, fix him some crappy microwaved dinner, and then leave Corey in the kitchen to eat while he retreated to the living room to drink cheap bourbon and watch TV. He made it clear that he wanted to be alone, so after dinner Corey would go up to his room. Sometimes, after dark, he'd sneak out his window and ride his bike or walk to the the mall. His father never caught on because he usually fell asleep on the couch and didn't come up to bed until well after Corey had returned home. Corey and his dad rarely talked.

The summer after seventh grade, Corey's dad brought a woman home. Ann Esseldorn. Corey took an instant dislike to her and never changed his opinion. She was pushy and loud, and made his dad act all stupid and goofy. A year later, his dad married her. Corey suddenly found himself living with three other kids, two boys, one his age and one a couple years older, and one younger girl. He felt lost in the shuffle and had to share a room with the kid his age, who stole from not only him but also the entire family. When Corey pointed this out to his dad, he took the other kid's side and accused Corey of the thefts. Corey began to feel like an outcast in his own home.

A month after his fourteenth birthday, he took off. He hadn't planned it very well. He had only twenty bucks, what was left of his birthday money, and he didn't even think to bring a warm jacket. It was late March, and the nights were cold. He was gone only a couple of days before the cops found him and brought him back. His father and stepmom tried to make nice, tried to smooth things over, but in his mind it was too little too late.

That's when Mary, his mother's elder sister, stepped in and suggested that he come live with her for a short time—a "cooling-off period," she'd called it. He'd always liked spending time at her house, so he agreed to the arrangement.

Corey never went home. Looking back on it now, he knew without a doubt that if Mary hadn't taken him in, he would have ended up on the streets. Mary insisted he go to church every Sunday, eat a good dinner with her every night. She told him that it didn't matter if he didn't get straight A's in school. What counted in life was effort, hard work.

Mary loved books and wanted Corey to read more. When he balked, she read to him—stories that bored him initially, but the more he got into them, the more he liked them. He eventually plowed through all of Tolkien. Heinlein. Dickens. Poe. Twain. And later, Hemingway, Vonnegut, Stephen King, Robert Ludlum, Clive Barker, and other writers his aunt didn't approve of, not that she ever censored anything he brought home.

"What's that funny business on your face?" asked Mary, stepping closer to get a better look.

Mary was old school. Didn't like long hair, grungy clothes, or beards. Corey's hair was ginger colored, like hers, but while his aunt's was fine and curly, his was thick and straight as a board. He'd given some thought to growing a beard in honor of the end of the electronic monitoring but settled instead for an abbreviated version.

"It's a mustache and a goatee." He couldn't use the prison slang that was more familiar to him because she'd come after him with a shovel.

"Not much of one."

"It'll grow."

"I can't understand why such a handsome young man would want to look like a thug."

"I thought it made me look sexy."

She whapped him on the arm.

Mary had a sense of humor, but she also believed in an orderly life. All those years ago when he'd first come to live with her, she'd stated her rules up front. No foul language or raunchy jokes. Home by ten on school nights, midnight on weekends. No drugs of any kind. Keep his bedroom clean and, when asked, help around the house without grousing. She believed in a Catholic God. She believed in kindness. And she believed in Corey.

After his arrest, what Corey feared most was that she'd buy the story the police were telling her. That thought alone almost pulverized him. Amazing as it seemed to him now, she'd never wavered in her support for him, never expressed anything other than complete confidence in his innocence. For that, Corey loved her beyond telling. She prayed for him every night. He figured that if anybody had God's ear, it was his aunt Mary.

"So, what are you planning to do tonight?" asked Mary, pointing at a section of the leather seat he'd missed. "I assume you're going out."

Corey did a quick swipe with the rag, then tossed it aside and screwed the cap back on the polish. He had something important he'd been waiting to do since his first day out of the hole. "Not sure. I'll probably just go for a ride."

"You keep your nose clean."

He grinned. "Yes, ma'am."

"You work in the morning?"

"Nah. It's Sunday." He'd found a job as a mechanic at a car dealership in Crystal. It was close to the halfway house, but it took him nearly an hour in rush-hour traffic to get there now, which annoyed the hell out of him. It paid pretty well, which was good because electronic monitoring wasn't cheap. The state didn't pick up the tab, he did, to the tune of three hundred bucks a month. The head mechanic at the dealership had served time himself, so he was willing to cut another felon a break. His aunt had offered him a job with her cleaning crew, but the last thing Corey wanted was to be released from prison so he could go clean houses and office buildings for the rest of his life. He wasn't about to be anybody's servant.

"You better change your clothes before you leave," said Mary. "Don't wanna go out looking like a grease monkey."

"No, ma'am."

"Put on some of that nice aftershave you bought yourself."

"Yes, ma'am."

"Stop it."

"Stop what, ma'am?"

Her eyes narrowed. Pulling his head toward her, she planted a kiss on his cheek. "If you say 'ma'am' one more time, I'm gonna muck up the shine on your chrome."

"You wouldn't do that." He raised his fists and threw a couple of mock jabs at her.

"Hey, I understand your lawyer is speaking over at your old high school tomorrow tonight. You might want to go hear him. If all the polls I'm reading are correct, he may be our next governor."

"Yippee freakin' skippy."

She regarded him silently.

"Why should I care? What did he ever do for me?"

"He got you the minimum sentence."

"For something I didn't do."

"He gave you what he thought was his best advice. And don't forget, he worked for free."

"Yeah. You get what you pay for."

"Stop it right this minute. I didn't have the money to hire a high-priced lawyer. Neither did you. You could have gone with some overworked, underpaid defense attorney the state provided, someone with so many other cases to work that, even if he wanted to, couldn't give much time to yours."

"And Lawless did?"

"Yes, Corey, he did. I've cleaned that man's house—*and* his daughter's house—for over fifteen years. When I went to Ray for help, he was more than willing to give it."

"You see goodness everywhere, Mary. I don't."

"Well, maybe you should start looking a little harder."

Or you should, he thought, though he kept it to himself.

3

Late Saturday night, Jane and Cordelia lugged four giant pumpkins into the screened porch attached to the back of Jane's house and dumped them next to the wicker couch. Turning to look outside, Jane gazed up at the moon. Harvest moons always reminded her of Humpty Dumpty before he fell off the wall. And that made her think of the book she was currently reading—*Death by Black Hole: And Other Cosmic Quandaries*.

"What are you thinking?" asked Cordelia, catching her breath as she draped her supersized frame across a comfortably padded chaise.

"Humpty Dumpty and black holes."

"Silly me, I should have guessed." Under her breath, she added, "Why did I ask?"

Cordelia Thorn was Jane's oldest and best friend. She was the creative director at the Allen Grimby Repertory Theater in St. Paul, which in her case meant she wasn't much interested in galactic gas clouds, quasars, and being torn apart—atom by atom—inside a black hole. Their common ground was food, theater, literature, film, and a shared history that covered almost three decades.

Cordelia swatted one of the last flies of the year away from her face while Jane leaned over to unclip the leash from her dog's collar. Once Mouse, a frisky chocolate Lab, had trotted into the yard for his evening ablutions, she sat down on the rocking chair.

"I love pumpkin hunting." Cordelia gazed lovingly at the large round orbs. "Almost as much as I love pumpkin carving. Say, changing the subject, your dad sure dodged a bullet today. I don't trust small planes."

"They're usually very safe."

"Yeah, well, but when they're not, you're hundreds of feet above the ground. Doesn't matter, though. He's okay. And he's going to win. Perry Mason always wins."

"My dad isn't Perry Mason."

Cordelia waved away the comment. "When he does, I'll get to say I knew him when."

"When what?"

"Well, for instance, when he taught us how to play tennis that one summer and I sprained my ankle and he carried me home."

"I think you stubbed your toe."

"No, no. It was a sprain. I still have a bad scar."

Jane could have pointed out that sprains didn't leave scars, but Cordelia didn't much care for that kind of corporeal detail. "Where's Melanie tonight?"

Melanie Gunderson was Cordelia's new—old—girlfriend. They'd been together years ago but had broken up because they fought all the time. Last May they'd reconnected in a big way. Since then, Melanie had given up her teaching position at St. Cloud State and was now living in Cordelia's loft, working as an investigative reporter for an alternative newspaper.

"She's on assignment," said Cordelia. "Down in Rochester."

"How come you didn't go with her?"

"Too busy at the theater. You knew I was directing a Nilo Cruz play in January, didn't you? *Anna in the Tropics*. And anyway, she keeps everything she's working on these days a secret. By the way, she may be moving out."

"What?" Jane turned to look at her. "Out of your loft? You're kidding me."

"It's possible. She's found something she likes better."

"Better than you?"

"I said some*thing*, not some*one*. No, we're still an item. But a little space might be good for us. I'll tell you more about it when I have something definitive."

Everything Jane knew about Melanie and Cordelia led her to believe that they were an impossible match. They were both imperious, both know-it-alls, both high-strung and opinionated. On the other hand, when they were able to work through—or ignore—their differences, they had this mad passionate attraction thing going for them, though, in Jane's opinion, it wasn't the best basis for a long-term relationship. Still, when they weren't throwing pots and pans—or verbal grenades—at each other, they seemed happy.

"You know," said Jane, stifling a yawn, "I'm beat. And I've got an early morning meeting at the Lyme House."

"Boring!" huffed Cordelia. "Boring, boring *boring*. What you need is more spice in your tamale."

Right. "Want a beer?"

"Oh, I suppose. One beer and them I'm off. I feel like doing something decadent and sophisticated after spending an evening in the pumpkin patch."

They hadn't actually been in a patch, just a large outdoor market. But for Cordelia, who didn't "do" the outdoors, it probably felt disturbingly rural.

Jane gave the pumpkins a friendly pat, then pulled out her keys to unlock the back door. As soon as she cracked it open, she heard the phone ringing, but by the time she raced through the kitchen, it had stopped. "Damn," she said, hoping she hadn't missed a call from her dad.

She waited for the red light to blink, telling her that she had a message. When it did, she hit the star button, then pressed 98.

"Ah, hi. Jane?" It was a male voice, one she didn't recognize. "I hope

I have the right number. You don't know me. My name's Neil Kershaw. I, ah, I need to speak with you. It's . . . not something I want to discuss over the phone. I know you own a couple of restaurants in the Twin Cities. I'm in Cambridge at the moment—Cambridge, Massachusetts. I do some teaching at Harvard. Among other things." He paused, gave an uneasy laugh. "Look, I'll be arriving in Minneapolis tomorrow. I'll try to catch you at one of your restaurants." Another pause. This one longer. "I guess that's it. Talk to you soon."

She replayed it. When it was over, she whispered, "Why didn't he leave a number? Weird."

"Who was that?" asked Cordelia, ambling into the kitchen. She looked sufficiently ridiculous in her bib overalls and spiky pink hair. She wore the overalls only on their yearly pumpkin hunt. The hair was another matter. After some prompting from Melanie, she'd gone to her salon and had her long auburn curls cut and dyed. The color changed periodically, depending on her mood.

"A guy named Kershaw. Anybody you know?"

"Never heard of him. Where's my beer?"

"In the oven. Where do you think?" Jane grabbed one from the refrigerator for herself and handed another to Cordelia. They drifted into the living room.

"Stop," said Jane, holding up her hand.

"You know, Janey, you might want to turn on the heat sometime before December—unless you like your home to have that nice meat-locker feel."

"Just stop for a minute and sniff the air."

"Why?"

"Do you smell something . . . unusual?"

She looked at Jane out of the corner of her eye. "Give me a clue. Animal, vegetable, or mineral."

"There's a foreign scent in the air."

"Foreign as in . . . Peter Lorre and Sydney Greenstreet foreign? Or are we talking *reallyreally* foreign, like ET or Gort?"

"Be serious. Don't you smell it?"

"No."

It wasn't a scary smell. To the contrary. It was familiar—something out of her past.

"Maybe you sprayed too much Febreze."

"I don't use Febreze."

"Well, maybe you should."

"Are you saying my house stinks?"

Cordelia angled carefully past Jane into the living room. "Of course not."

"Just because you sashay through the world in a miasma of perfume, doesn't mean everyone wants to."

She stared at Jane a moment. "What are you suggesting? That someone was in here while you were gone?"

"Doesn't seem very likely, does it." She checked the front door. "The door looks fine. So did the back. Just stay put. I'll look around."

"Turn up the heat while you're at it."

Jane spent the next few minutes searching the house. The scent seemed strongest in her study, just a hint of something spicy sweet. She looked everywhere but couldn't locate the source.

On her way back to the living room, she let Mouse in the back door. He followed her into the living room and lay down next to Cordelia, who was sitting in one of the wingback chairs by the front windows, her legs crossed, one leg bouncing casually as she sipped her Corona.

"See, he doesn't smell anything out of the ordinary," said Cordelia. "Maybe it was Peter."

"I doubt it."

Jane had hardly seen her brother over the summer. Partly, she assumed, it was because he was sick of arguing with her, although mostly she knew he was buried in work. Peter had been hired as the official campaign photographer, but because he was also shooting a documentary of the campaign, a conflict arose. The campaign didn't have the money to pay for the documentary, so her father was financing it now out of his own pocket. That meant her brother had to cut all financial ties to the campaign.

Last June, Peter and his wife, Sigrid, had moved from their apartment in south Minneapolis to a double bungalow in Elk River, about thirty miles away. Jane figured it was his way of putting some distance between him and the rest of the family. Distance allowed him to hide certain things from their dad that he didn't want him to know. For instance, his marriage was, for all practical purposes, over. After the election, he and Sigrid would file for divorce.

Peter and Sigrid's lives were a chaotic mess at the moment, born of the best intentions. Their little girl, Mia, sat directly at the center of a growing emotional firestorm. Jane feared that a custody battle wasn't far off. The problem was, the battle couldn't take place in a court of law because Peter had purchased forged adoption papers. Thus, they were at the mercy of their anger, frustration, and desire for revenge. It would be months, perhaps years, before that struggle would play out. For now, they were on their best behavior—publicly. Privately, it was all-out war.

"Doesn't your neighbor have a key?" asked Cordelia.

"Evelyn? Oh, sure."

"Maybe she came in for some reason. She's just like me, right? Likes her perfume applied with a paint sprayer?"

Jane closed her eyes and shook her head. "I can't call her until tomorrow morning. She goes to bed at ten, right after *20/20*."

"What about your housekeeper? What's her name?"

"Mary Glynn? She has a key, but she was here yesterday and isn't scheduled again for two weeks."

Cordelia tipped the beer bottle back and took a final swig. "You want my advice?"

"Of course. I think. Maybe."

"Forget about it." She raised her arm and pointed at her glitzy gold wristwatch. "Better hit those bricks if I'm going to get in a little partying before the bars close. Later, babe." She gave Mouse a scratch on her way out the front door.

After Jane's meeting at the Lyme House with her business partner, Judah Johanson, on Sunday morning, she gave her neighbor, Evelyn Bratrude, a call. Jane hadn't slept well and hoped that Evelyn would be able to put her mind at rest by explaining why she'd been in Jane's house the night before. But Evelyn wasn't home. Jane left two messages. By the time she left for a second meeting, she still hadn't heard from her.

Jane had been attempting to get all her ducks in a row before next Thursday, when Kenzie Mulroy, her partner, planned to drive up to spend the weekend. Jane and Kenzie had been together for two years, Jane's longest relationship since her partner of ten years, Christine Kane, had died of cancer when Jane was in her early thirties.

Kenzie taught cultural anthropology at Chadwick State College and lived outside of town in an old farmhouse on twenty-six acres. The land was necessary because she owned horses. The long-distance romance had been working so far, although it had its moments.

Jane and Kenzie had both had busy summers. Kenzie had stayed with Jane for most of June and two weeks in July, partly because she wanted to work at the campaign office, but mostly because summer was her only real free time. Jane was grateful for the commitment Kenzie had made to her father's bid for governor. But Kenzie was like that. When she got excited about something, she was tireless. She'd spent all of August in China on a cultural/history/archaeology tour that started in Beijing, continued to Xi'an, where she was able to view the Terra-Cotta Warriors, and then on to Kashgar, the city that lay at the junction of four branches of the Silk Road.

All along the way, Kenzie had sent long dispatches to Jane detailing what she was seeing and learning. The letters were fascinating, explaining as much about Kenzie as they did about China. Over the period of a month, Jane had fallen even more deeply in love with Kenzie, impressed by the thoughtful way she analyzed her experiences, as well as her writing skills. She'd made her trip come alive for Jane, so much so that when combined with the photos she'd sent back, Jane almost felt as if she'd been there. Kenzie was so absorbed by her August trip that she'd begun taking a class in Mandarin as soon as she got back to Nebraska. She was also writing up some of the notes she'd taken into articles she intended to send to various anthropology journals. As she so often pointed out, as a college professor, she needed to publish or perish.

Due to the length of Jane's morning meeting and road construction on I-94, she missed the brunch rush at the Lyme House. She didn't arrive until shortly after two. The main dining room was on the second level, overlooking the lake. As she came up the stairs from the pub, the cashier, Sandra Cushing, a longtime employee, caught her eye.

"There was a guy here who wanted to talk to you. He stayed for brunch, but left about half an hour ago."

Jane wondered it if was the same man who'd left the message last night. "Did you get a name?"

"I think he said it was Kershaw. Ned or Neil or something like that. He left a note." She reached under the counter and handed it to Jane.

Jane—Sorry I missed you. I'll be in touch.
Neil

"Did he say anything about why he wanted to talk to me?"

"Sorry, nothing. But he raved about the food, and he mentioned that he liked the log walls, said they reminded him of his parents' cabin up north."

"So, maybe he's a Minnesotan." Who taught at Harvard. And who was back in Minnesota for some reason. "If you see him again when I'm not around, try to get a phone number where I can reach him."

"Will do."

Jane spent the afternoon working in her office.

Just after four, Cordelia phoned. "So, was it Evelyn?"

"I don't know," said Jane, tossing her pen down. "I haven't been able to reach her."

"Heard anything more from your dad?"

"No. Why?"

"I assume you didn't read today's *Star Tribune*."

"Did I miss something?"

"Not really. It's just more of the same. A political year." Lowering her voice, she continued, "But . . . there's a drumbeat out there, Janey. It's like we're standing in the deepest jungle with glowing eyes all around us. Headhunters. Lions. Tigers. Everyone's coming after your father with sabers rattling, hammers cocked, bayonets set. And on that note, I think I better go before I start hyperventilating."

"Are you at the theater?"

"Where else? Meeting with a new director in ten minutes. Think Princess Kay of the Milky Way meets Christopher Hitchens and you'd be in the right personality ballpark. Call me later. Ta."

By five, Jane was about to leave and drive over to the campaign office when her cell phone began vibrating inside the pocket of her jeans. She pulled it out and said hello, thinking it was probably her dad. She knew he had a speech in town tonight. It was only an hour's drive from St. Cloud back to the cities.

"Ah, hi. This is Stan Masters at Flying Cloud airport. Is this Ray Lawless's daughter?"

"Yes?"

"We have a Cessna here that belongs to your dad. It was flown in yesterday afternoon—"

"Yesterday afternoon? Are you sure about that?"

"Very sure. Anyway, it's sitting near one of the back runways, and we need to have it moved ASAP. Not quite sure how it got there, but I wasn't working yesterday, so it didn't happen on my watch."

"Who flew it back from St. Cloud?"

"Um . . . Byron Jostein. He logged in at 5:14 PM. You know him?"

"No." Jane couldn't believe the plane could be thoroughly examined and repaired so quickly.

"Well, whatever," said Masters. "We need to get it moved. Your name's on the hangar, too, so I thought—"

"I'll take care of it," said Jane.

"Great. Appreciate it. And hey, FYI, I'm voting for your dad."

"Thanks. He'll be happy to hear it."

That same afternoon, Corey raked his aunt's yard, put away the garden tools in the garage, and finished up by covering her rosebushes for the winter. He spent a few minutes repairing the lock on the back gate and then went inside and took a shower. Mary would be at church until six. Feeling at loose ends, he hopped on his cycle and rode to St. Paul.

As the light began to fade, Corey stood in Raymond Lawless's campaign office, surveying the whirl of activity. He'd talked to a woman at the reception desk and learned that Lawless wasn't around, although his picture was plastered on every wall. If nothing else, it made for a sort of Andy Warhol–esque moment. Raymond Lawless as pop icon. No doubt a piece of irony lost on the enthusiastic minions.

Examining a life-sized cardboard cutout a little more closely, Corey discovered that the great man had grown older and thinner since their last meeting. His silver hair was less shaggy, more styled, although his smile was every bit as phony and high octane.

Corey sucked in a breath. He wasn't sure what he'd expected. It was unlikely that Lawless would remember a guy he'd met only a few times nine years ago. But Corey remembered him. He realized that he was disappointed. He was sorry he wouldn't get to see the next governor in person.

"Can I help you?" asked a female voice.

Corey turned around to find a gray-haired woman peering at him through her bifocals. She was elegantly dressed in a yellow suit, the half ton rock on her finger the exclamation point at the end of an unspoken sentence.

She gave him a friendly smile "Are you looking for information on Raymond Lawless?"

He'd expected a cultured voice, but her tone was pure Minnesotan.

"No, not really," he mumbled.

"Excuse me?"

"I'm . . . um . . . I thought maybe I'd offer to help."

"You want to volunteer?"

"Yeah." He pushed his hands into the back pockets of his jeans. "I'm a Lawless man, one hundred percent."

"That's good to hear, Mr.—"

"Hodge. Corey Hodge. Call me Corey."

Before she could respond, a guy came out of one of the small offices in the back of the main room. He was dressed like a clown—striped cotton shirt, polka dot tie, red suspenders. He introduced himself as Luke Durrant, the IT manager.

"You here to work?" asked the clown.

Corey nodded, introduced himself.

The clown gave him a crooked stare. "Hodge? Have we met?"

"Not that I remember." And I'd remember meeting an asswipe like you, Corey thought.

The clown regarded him briefly, then asked, "Know anything about computers?"

"Me? Not a thing."

"Too bad." Turning to the woman, he said, "He's all yours, Viv."

As he walked away, Corey said under his breath, "Dickhead." Uh-oh, he thought again. Not a socially appropriate thought. What would his anger management therapist think?

"You've got a couple options, Corey," said Viv. "You could work our phone banks, although we like to give you a short tutorial if you're going to do that. You'd have to come back tomorrow afternoon at one."

"Can't."

"Okay, well, then why don't you join us at that table." She nodded to a group of women sitting next to a series of windows. "You could help stuff envelopes."

"Sure. That's perfect."

"Wonderful," said Viv, leading the way through the room. "We'll be getting another delivery of lawn signs next Tuesday. If you'd like to help deliver them, you could come by late in the afternoon—as long as you have transportation of some kind."

"I'll think about it. Is our next governor going to be here before his speech tonight?"

"I'm sorry, no."

"Too bad. I was hoping to say hi."

"Do you know him?"

"Yeah. Well, I mean, we've met."

"He's in and out," said Viv, pulling out a chair for Corey and getting him all set up. "But you'll get a chance if you continue to volunteer, I'm sure of it. He's very friendly, always comes out and talks to us."

Gosh, thought Corey. What a guy.

The woman he sat down next to was young, maybe midtwenties, with a sweet, schoolgirl kind of look, all freckles and straight brown bangs. Very little makeup. He nodded and smiled his most charming smile, the one he reserved for attractive women.

She glanced at him, smiled back.

He introduced himself.

"Charity Miller," she said in response.

"You been volunteering here long?"

"Ever since the campaign began."

"But you have a regular job?"

She nodded. "I'm an assistant account manager at a bank."

He whistled. "Account manager. Very cool."

"It's a living. For the moment."

"You wanna do something else?"

"I'm hoping to go to veterinary school at the U of M. It's a hard program to get into, but my grades are good. And I've been volunteering at the zoo down in Apple Valley since I was sixteen."

"How long you been at the bank?"

"A few years. I like the people but not the work."

His gaze dropped to her hands. She wasn't wearing a wedding ring. "Where is this bank? I moved recently and I need to find one closer to where I live now."

"Nicollet and Sixty-first. American Eagle Bank & Trust."

"Perfect. Maybe I'll come by one of these days and you can set up a checking account for me."

"Sure," she said. "I'd be happy to. Come by anytime."

He fixed her with a smile of great sweetness and warmth. His eyes assured her that she was the only woman in the room worthy of his undivided attention. She returned her attention to the stack of envelopes in front of her, but he could tell she liked it, that she wouldn't forget him.

Half an hour later, Corey felt a tap on his shoulder. He turned to find the clown standing behind him.

"Can I talk to you?"

"What about?"

"It's . . . I just need some information."

Corey had no idea what the guy wanted, but anything was better than staying at the table, listening to two of the women hog the conversation, talking nonstop about their kids. He was about to introduce a different topic—say, body piercings—but Durrant got to him first.

"It'll only take a couple of minutes," said the clown.

Corey shrugged and got up, followed him back to his office.

Durrant closed the door and then dropped down on his desk chair. It gave a loud squeak.

Corey pulled a beat-up folding chair away from the wall. "What?" he said, feeling impatient for no real reason.

"I know who you are."

"Goody. Who am I?" He sat down.

"I thought I recognized your name. It took me a few minutes to put it together. Ray Lawless represented you in a rape case."

"I served my time."

"Yeah, but like most felons, you only served two-thirds of your sentence. Not much time for what you did."

"Thanks to *Ray,* an innocent man went to jail."

"Sure," said Durrant.

"You don't believe me. Fine. Why'd you call me in here?"

"I just wanted to make sure you were him."

"Now you know."

The clown was momentarily at a loss. "Takes a lot of guts to show up here and act like you're just another guy."

"I am just another guy."

"Some people here might not be happy to know they were working alongside a rapist."

"You gonna tell them?"

"I might."

"You want to pick a fight, man, just say the word."

The clown suddenly looked uncomfortable.

"Just to clarify, I was *innocent,* but I served my time, so I expect to be treated with a little Christian kindness."

"I did some research on the case before I called you in. You raped a woman at a rest stop along I-35 up near Duluth."

"*Someone* did. It wasn't me."

"Right. Right."

Corey had just about had it. He stood to go, but on an impulse, he turned back and swept his arm across the clown's desk, sending everything but the computer crashing to the floor. He regretted it instantly. If the clown reported what he'd just done to Corey's probation officer, it could be bad. Then again, it was unlikely the guy even knew he had a probation officer.

"You enjoy torturing ex-cons?" asked Corey, staring him down.

"No," said Durrant, his tone cool. "That wasn't my intention."

"I'm outta here."

Pushing out the glass front door on his way to his cycle, he smiled. He knew Durrant wouldn't report him. He'd seen more courage in a dog's eyes.

5

When Luke Durrant entered his condo later that night, he was immediately assaulted by the smell of burned food. It was just after eleven. He tossed his keys and billfold on the table in the foyer, then followed the smell through the kitchen, past the disarray of dirty plates and glasses, the remnants of an incinerated grilled cheese sandwich, and finally into the large open room that served as both living and dining room.

Over the last few months, he'd developed an instinctive sense for what he thought of as emotional air currents. Tonight the air was thick with tension, so much so that his stomach clutched as he moved across the bare wood floor to one of two matching white leather couches. What upset him wasn't the mess. Messes could be cleaned up. Dishes could be washed. But never knowing what he was coming home *to* was what got to him.

Tonight, for instance, he might be called upon to be a nurse, a therapist, a pharmacist, a cheerleader, a liar, an activity director, or some permutation he'd never considered before. What he wanted to be was simply a guy coming home after a long day of work to the arms of the person he loved more than anyone else on earth.

"Couldn't sleep?" he asked, leaning over and giving Christopher a kiss.

"I tried, but no luck. Charity called, wanted to come over, but I told her to make it another night."

Charity Miller was one of Christopher's best friends. She was also the reason Luke had learned about the job as IT manager at Ray Lawless's campaign. He was between positions at the time. When Charity told him the old IT guy had quit, he applied, even though he was overqualified. Everybody liked her so much that when she'd recommended him, he got an interview the next day. He was offered the job a week later.

Luke pulled up a chair and sat down next to Christopher, picking up his partner's hand and pressing it to his lips. "I'm sorry I'm so late. Was that charred grilled cheese sandwich your dinner?"

"I wasn't hungry," he mumbled, his eyes fixed on the plasma TV hanging on the opposite wall.

Not exactly what Luke wanted to hear. "Let me make you something else."

He shook his head, kept his eyes on the screen. "Don't bother. I'm just glad you're home."

The comment wasn't meant to make Luke feel guilty, but it did. Christopher's six-month medical leave was almost up. Luke figured *that* was partly behind his most recent decent into a deep funk.

Initially, after Christopher got out of the hospital, Luke had encouraged friends to come in during the day to keep him company, but Christopher insisted he wasn't up to it. He was too embarrassed by the scars on his face, too nervous that he'd have to talk about things that upset him, and simply too stubborn to see how desperately he needed to reconnect with humanity. The only person he let in, other than Luke, was Charity.

Luke was grateful that Charity had stuck by Christopher. She was a sweet kid, although she had serious problems of her own. Sometimes their friendship seemed like it was based on nothing more than mutual commiseration. Sure, they had a lot to commiserate about, but still, it didn't strike Luke as particularly healthy.

Luke did his best to hide the anger he felt toward Charity, but every now and then it showed. Christopher was far more forgiving than he could ever hope to be. Maybe it was a strength, but Luke saw it as weakness. That's why he kept his eye on Charity. If she let her big mouth flap again without thinking, he'd be there to shut it.

Tonight, after three computers went down, Luke felt pressured to stick around and get them back up and running. He wanted to come home earlier, but it just wasn't possible. He'd never discussed his personal life with anyone at the campaign office. The fact that he was gay wouldn't have been an issue, but he made the decision when he took the job to keep his personal life private.

"Come on, Christopher, let's get you something to eat."

"Just go to bed. I'll be in later."

Luke pulled him to his feet. "You're angry at me."

"Good Lord, I'm not angry. Truly, I'm not. I'm just . . . tired. Sick and tired of myself."

"Stop it." Luke drew him into his arms. "What you need is some food in your stomach."

Christopher shook his head but allowed Luke to help him to the dining area. Once he was settled at the table, Luke retreated to the kitchen to fix them each a ham and Swiss sandwich. At the last minute, he whipped up two martinis, hoping that a little alcohol might oil their conversation.

Before he sat down, he turned off the TV and replaced it with some soft jazz. Christopher rarely turned on the television. If pressed, he probably couldn't have said what show he'd been watching.

"Hear anything more from the investigative committee?" asked Luke, taking a bite of his sandwich.

Christopher looked down at the food as if it presented an impossible task. "Ring the bell. Close the book. Quench the candle. I'm done for. I knew that last April. This medical leave just put off the inevitable."

"You already know what I think." He hesitated. "Maybe it's not such a bad thing."

Christopher drew in a long breath. "I sit here all day, trying to figure out what I should do with my life. I assumed that conversation was over years ago, but here I am, thirty-six years old and back to square one."

"You can do anything you want. Go back to school, get another degree. Or start a business. As soon as the campaign is over, I'll find a good job. You know how much money I can earn. Enough for both of us."

"It's not a matter of money," he said sharply. Then, looking contrite, he added, "I don't mean to jump down your throat. You've been nothing but supportive. I'll figure it out. I just need a little more time."

Luke sipped his martini. They both knew Christopher was hiding, and frankly, after what he'd been through, Luke didn't blame him. Wiping his mouth with a napkin, he continued, "You know, you need to get outdoors, get some fresh air. Why don't we make a day of it tomorrow? I'm sure I can get the day off. We could walk across the Stone Arch Bridge. That would be good for your leg. And then we could have lunch somewhere along the river. Come on, babe. You haven't left this place since your last physical therapy appointment."

The suggestion earned Luke nothing but a baleful stare. "Let me think about it."

"What's to think about? We need to have some fun together. I mean, all you do anymore is drift around this place like a ghost looking for his shadow."

"How poetic." He brushed a lock of blond hair away from his forehead.

"I get it that you're still recovering. But even so." He knew that when a person was sick, it was hard to see anything other than his own pain. But Christopher wasn't the only one who'd been to hell and back. "Look, I'll say it again. Maybe you should see a shrink. If you're clinically depressed, you can get help. You have people who need you, folks who love you and want to know how you're doing."

A tide of hopelessness washed through Christopher's eyes. "I'm working on it."

His voice sounded so bleak, so vastly lonely. "Of course you are," said Luke, feeling like a jerk for pushing him. "I'm sorry if it seems like I'm always ragging on you."

"No, you're right. I should see someone. I'll get a referral from my doctor, I promise."

After dinner, Luke helped Christopher to their bedroom. He got him settled in bed, pulled the covers up over his chest, then sat down next to him.

"Aren't you coming?"

"I need to work for a bit. I won't be long."

"Sometimes I think you should have that computer surgically implanted."

"If I could figure a way to do it, I would."

Christopher smiled at that. It wasn't much of a smile, but it was something.

"Go to sleep," said Luke, kissing him again, this time more tenderly. "And no more bad dreams."

"I don't know what I'd do without you," said Christopher, his eyes glistening.

"You'll never have to find out."

So Evelyn was never in your house?" Cordelia pawed eagerly through the mound of silk and satin, glitter and feathers on her bed, trying on the clothes as she stood next to a full-length mirror on the back of her bedroom door.

"No," said Jane, who was lying on the bed. "She finally called me back. That smell . . . it was probably just my overactive imagination."

"You drink too much coffee. It's hallucinogenic."

"You drink gallons of coffee every day."

"What's your point?"

Mouse sat on the rug in front of Jane, watching Cordelia fling the glitzy garments in every direction.

"Where'd you get all that stuff?" asked Jane.

"From my friend Michael. We're about the same supersize."

Michael Ensler was a pharmacist and a drag queen. Jane had met him at a couple of Cordelia's parties. Cordelia always gave him complimentary season tickets to the theater, thus, when it came to time clean out his closets, he was in a generous mood.

"He's got incredible taste, don't you think?" She pressed a hand against the front of a black and yellow striped jacket that was solid sequins. Jane thought it made her look like a bumblebee.

"Incredible," repeated Jane, her tone flat.

"Don't get so excited. It's not good for your blood pressure." She held up another dress, tucked it around her breasts.

"What's that called?"

"A pirate wench costume." It was black crushed velvet, with open shoulders, a plunging neckline, a double-laced front, and arm wraps. The skirt was flared and extremely short. "I've got some great fishnet stockings that will be perfect with it."

"And what sort of event would you wear that to?"

She shrugged. "Brunch?"

Jane flipped over on her stomach and laughed.

"Here's the best one," said Cordelia, digging through the pile. "Michael had this professionally made in England." She pulled out a stunning, heavily beaded, fringed jade green gown. The dress ended in a two-foot train. "I'll wear this when your father is crowned."

"Inaugurated."

"You say potato, I say po-tah-to." She stalked over and snapped off the CD player. Barbara Streisand's emotional rendition of "People" ended midwail. "I'm deeply into a Ziegfeld Follies idiom at the moment."

"Kind of clashes with your home furnishings," said Jane.

Cordelia groaned. "Swedish modern is so *unbelievably* boring."

"Then why did you buy all of that furniture from IKEA last year?"

"Boring fascinated me at the time."

"So change it. Bring home part of a theater set like you used to. Something Ziegfeldish."

"Can't."

"Why not?"

"Because I refuse to change anything in the loft until Hattie comes back. It has to be just the way she remembers it."

Hattie Thorn Lester, Cordelia's niece, had lived with Cordelia for two of her four years. Her mother, Cordelia's sister, Octavia, had swooped in a year ago and taken the little girl—"abducted," Cordelia usually said—moving her to England to live with her and husband number five or six. Jane could never keep track. Cordelia had been devastated. She'd tried everything—sweet talk, bribes, threats, private investigators, lawyers—but so far, Hattie was still in England and Cordelia was still miserable.

Jane had been astonished by Cordelia's transformation. Prior to Hattie being dropped on her doorstep by a mother who had little time for a child as she single-mindedly dug her manicured fingernails into the slippery slope of a film career, Cordelia let it be known to anyone within hearing distance that she thought little children—detestable urchins, as she more often phrased it—were all noisy, annoying, sticky, smelly, poorly socialized little brutes and she wanted nothing to do with them. If a child started to cry in a restaurant, Cordelia had been known to leave in a righteous huff. But Hattie had changed everything.

"I assume you've heard nothing new from Octavia. A letter? A phone call? A note via carrier pigeon?"

"Apparently," said Cordelia, sitting down next to Jane, "they don't have modern methods of communication in Northumberland. Don't get me started. It will ruin the entire evening."

"Fine," said Jane. "Let's change the subject." She swung her legs over the side of the bed and sat up. "I stopped by the campaign office on my way back from Flying Cloud this afternoon. I wanted to find out who was on the plane with my dad yesterday when he landed it in that field. I knew John Thompson was there, but it turns out so was Steve Worlander, his press secretary."

"Back up. You drove out to Flying Cloud Field?"

Jane explained about the call she'd received.

"But if the plane had mechanical problems, how could someone fly it back so quickly?"

"That was my question. I've called Dad a couple of times, left several messages, but so far he hasn't returned any of them. Worlander is still up in St. Cloud, and Thompson lives in Bemidji."

"You think there's more to this than your dad is telling you?"

"I'm not sure, but . . . yeah, I guess I do." As they stared at each other, each considering the possibilities, Jane heard the door open downstairs and a voice call, "*Babalu!* I'm HOME. If you don't have my mojito ready, you've got some serious 'splaining to do!"

Cordelia leaped up and thundered downstairs into the living room with Jane following directly behind. She almost knocked Melanie over with a bear hug that could easily have been considered an illegal tackle.

Jane waited for the kisses to stop, then helped Mel with her luggage.

Melanie was wearing her signature tight black jeans and red crew-neck sweater. As usual, she smelled of stale cigarette smoke and looked exhausted. Jane had always been a little in love with Melanie. Everyone had. She was smart and salty, and had an irresistible throaty laugh that she used to punctuate her stories.

"How was the trip?" asked Cordelia, walking over to the drinks cart.

"Long, but profitable." Mel was about to sit down on the couch but changed her mind and strolled over to the floor-to-ceiling windows overlooking downtown Minneapolis. The view was partially obscured by a new building that had gone up across the street. "I can move in this weekend."

"You're really moving out of here?" asked Jane.

"Yup. I've bought a small loft on the fifth floor, directly across from Cordelia's loft. Come here. I'll show you."

Jane walked over to the windows.

"See that single window next to the four bigger ones?"

"Yes?"

"That's the kitchen. The others are in the living room. There's lots of light, beautiful bamboo floors, a skylight in the bedroom. Even a roof garden."

"But—"

"We need space," said Melanie, turning and drawing her arms wide. "A loft of our own, so to speak. There's no reason we have to live like every other couple in the world." She winked at Cordelia. "Come to think of it, Jane, you and Kenzie aren't exactly living the Brady Bunch life either."

"No, but Kenzie would prefer we did."

"Nonsense." Melanie could be as imperious as Cordelia. "Is my mojito ready, babe?"

"You'll have to settle for a martini or a manhattan."

"What are my martini options? Anything fun? Apple? Chocolate? Blue?"

"Gin or vodka."

"Well," she said, sighing, "I'm so happy to be home, I'd settle for a can of your black cherry soda."

Jane winced. It had to be true love.

By ten that night, Jane and Mouse were back at the Lyme House. She pulled herself a beer in the pub on her way to her office, then spent the next couple of hours reading her book on black holes. At one point, she phoned Kenzie, hoping to catch her before she went to bed, but when her voice mail picked up, all Jane could do was leave a message.

Around twelve thirty, she closed the book and looked over at Mouse. "What do you say we call it a night?"

His ears pricked up. He was in his favorite spot, lying on the braided rug between the fireplace and the couch. Jane had worked with the architect who'd designed the building to turn her office into a kind of home away from home. She had not only a private bathroom complete with a shower but also a closet that she kept stocked with clean clothes. The couch and the fireplace made it a perfect place to spend the night, especially during a winter snowstorm when even the few blocks she had to drive to her house seemed like too much effort. She'd spent many nights here, curled up on the couch, reading or writing in her journal. Mouse seemed to love it as much as she did. And if she had a midnight craving for a slice of cold prime rib, there was a fully stocked kitchen right upstairs.

As they made their way through the back parking lot to Jane's Mini, she was struck by what a beautiful night it was, the air crisp and fresh, full of the scent of dry leaves and wood smoke. "Let's walk home," she said to Mouse, crouching down, stroking his fur. "What do you say?"

Mouse was a typical Lab: easygoing, up for anything. They took the stairs down to the lake path and headed west.

On the way, Jane's thoughts turned again to Kenzie. The two of them had exchanged rings a few months back. Kenzie had bought Jane a small diamond last spring, but when they discovered it was several sizes too big, Kenzie took it back. They began to visit local jewelry stores while Kenzie was in town last summer. Since Jane had far more money than Kenzie did, she offered to buy the two matching rings they both fell in love with—one-and-a-half-carat diamonds, emerald cut, set in filigreed white gold bands. Kenzie wanted to drive up to Thunder Bay after Christmas and get married. Jane loved Kenzie with all her heart, but for some reason she hadn't quite been able to put her finger on, she didn't want a marriage. Kenzie, of course, thought Jane was afraid of commitment. It seemed like such a stupid cliché, but if that was her underlying reason for wanting to table the discussion for the moment, then she figured she had a right to it.

Jane had been badly burned awhile back after an affair with a woman who turned out to be a liar and a manipulator, a doctor who was not only deceitful but also dishonorable. Passion might be great, as was the feeling of going a little crazy, of losing control, of thinking that this was true love that would last forever. But that was a package Jane simply couldn't buy anymore. Kenzie was getting the jaded, older, war-weary Jane instead of the young, obstacles-be-damned, give-me-a-dragon-to-slay-for-you Jane of yesteryear. Jane doubted she'd ever feel that way again.

"The thing is," she said to Mouse, as they walked up the steps to her front door, "if I ever lost Kenzie, I don't know what I'd do. She keeps my heart ticking, you know what I mean? My feet planted firmly on terra firma. But marriage . . . I don't think so."

Mouse looked up at her with soulful eyes.

"I know. You don't want to take sides. Always the diplomat."

She bent down and kissed his nose, then straightened up and

pressed the key into the lock. As soon as they were inside, Mouse strained at his leash, pulling her through the dining room into the kitchen. He wanted to be let out into the backyard, and then he wanted his bedtime treat. No deviation from routine was allowed. He was a creature of habit, but then, who wasn't?

She'd just come back into the kitchen when her cell phone rang. Checking the caller ID, she saw that it was Kenzie. "Hey, sweetheart. I was just thinking about you."

"I got your message," came Kenzie's voice. "Hope I'm not waking you."

"I just got home. I'm glad you called."

"I was in town at a movie."

"Anything good?"

"It was a testosterone flick. Not too bad, but not great." She had an easy laugh. "I probably should have stayed home and taken Ben or Rocket out for a ride."

"The horses are going to miss you while you're gone."

"Nah, they won't. They're used to Lee by now. I think they might even like him better than they do me."

"Not possible."

Lee Lundeen was a neighbor of Kenzie's who also owned horses. While she was out of town during the summer, he'd boarded them at his place. He didn't ask for much money because he loved horses and was happy to do her the favor.

"He's more free with his carrots than I am." Another laugh.

They talked for the better part of an hour. Jane checked on Mouse a couple of times. He was chewing on his green tennis ball, lying in the grass, oblivious to the chilly night air.

Kenzie was appalled when she heard about the near plane crash. "Have you talked to your dad since he got back?"

"He's so busy right now he hardly has time to comb his hair. But he'll call."

"Maybe the three of us can get together for a cup of coffee when I'm in town next weekend."

"I wouldn't count on it. Not until after the election."

At one point during the conversation, Jane had turned off the lights on the mantel in the living room. She liked talking to Kenzie in the dark because she could pretend more easily that they were together, not linked merely by a cell phone tower. It was a little before two when they said their final good nights.

"I'll see you around three on Thursday," said Kenzie.

"I'll be waiting with the marching band. Drive safely, okay?"

"I will, Lawless. Love you. See you soon."

Jane sat in the darkened living room, thinking over what they'd talked about—everything from interdepartmental politics at Kenzie's college, to the *Oxford English Dictionary,* to the comic Eddie Izzard, the new Einstein biography, time travel, a breakfast cereal Kenzie liked, the weather in Mongolia, Chinese proverbs, and on and on. They never ran out of topics, it seemed. Jane loved talking to Kenzie because she was so alive, so interested in the world around her. And she had a wry sense of humor that kept everything in perspective.

With soft moonlight streaming in through the living room windows, Jane rose from her chair. She was about to head to the kitchen to let Mouse back into the house when she heard the umistakable sound of a key slipping into the front door lock. Startled, she backed up. Cordelia was the most likely suspect. She tended to arrive at Jane's house at all hours of the day and night, but because Melanie had just returned home, it didn't seem likely that Cordelia would come over tonight. Jane moved back into the living room and, on instinct, picked up the fireplace poker.

The door opened.

The front hall light burst on.

"My God," said Jane, feeling a shock of recognition. She understood now. The scent in her house. It all made sense. "What the hell are you doing here?" She lowered the poker, then changed her mind and raised it again. "Answer me!"

Two A.M. Closing time.

Corey had been waiting outside the bar for over an hour, working on what he'd say when she came out. Serena had written to him at least a dozen times when he was first inside, but the letters had died off after a month. He understood, never blamed her. Serena's mother hated him, simple as that. Every day they were apart was another opportunity for the old witch to bad-mouth him. Nine years and change had given her plenty of time, and the rape conviction plenty of ammunition.

When the plea bargain went down, Serena had only been nineteen, five years younger than him, still living under her mom's thumb, attending the university like her mom wanted. She tended bar in the evenings because it gave her a reason for getting out of the house. It hadn't taken Corey long to find out she was still tending bar, although the location had changed. The Unicorn was a dive in Uptown. It was a big comedown from the fancy place she'd worked at nine years ago. He wondered idly how far she'd gotten with her nursing degree. By the looks of it, not far.

Corey had tried college himself for a couple of years, gone into debt for a piece of paper that he finally understood meant nothing to him. He'd never had much focus. He thought maybe he'd be a writer because he liked books. Stupid idea. His teachers made it clear right off that he didn't have the talent. He'd scribbled some short stories in prison, nothing great, although he liked them. He'd never shown them to anyone. What was the point? He'd been laughed at in college enough to last a lifetime.

It was Serena's mom who wanted her to be a nurse. Mad Marsha had wanted to be a nurse herself before she got pregnant, got married, and ended up with a sick husband who never had the good grace simply to die and let her get on with things. Corey laughed to himself when he realized that maybe Mad Marsha had gotten her wish after all. She'd nursed old Woody Van Dorn until his death two years ago. The only reason Corey knew the old guy had kicked the bucket was that his aunt Mary had written to him about seeing Woody's obituary in the paper. Tough break for Woody. Good news for the rest of the world.

Sitting on his motorcycle, which he'd parked across the street, Corey watched the front door, willing it to open. He hadn't gone in because meeting up with her that way wasn't part of his scenario. He'd done a quick reconnoiter of the building. There was a back door, but from the looks of it, it wasn't used much. That meant Serena would most likely come out the front. It might still be awhile. Bars usually had managers who closed up, but if she was feeling talkative, she might stick around and hang out with some of the barflies.

It didn't matter to Corey how long he had to wait. Eventually she'd come out and he'd walk over to her. And then . . . what? As much as he'd fantasized it, she wouldn't fall into his arms. That would be too easy. And life, as he'd learned, was never easy.

Corey tilted his head sideways, cracked his neck. After a warm, sixty-degree day, tonight was actually chilly, but he'd worn his leather motorcycle jacket and black Dingo boots, so he was plenty comfortable.

And then it happened. The door opened and she came out. She looked both ways down the sidewalk, bundled her thin cotton coat around her, and started walking east.

Corey eased off the cycle. Moving fast, he caught up to her just as she was about to cross Emerson.

"Serena, wait." He felt a sudden lightness in his chest.

She didn't stop, but she twisted her head around. When she saw who'd called to her, she turned all the way around and stood very still.

He raised his hands in a gesture of surrender. "I just want to talk."

Her eyes searched him, first with fear, then with a kind of hopelessness. "Go away. Please . . . just go away."

"I can't."

They were only a few yards apart.

"Why now? You've been out for months."

The fact that she knew surprised him. "I was on probation. Still am. But up until Friday, I had to wear a monitoring device. I couldn't leave the house at night." He fought the urge to move closer. Her shoulder-length reddish-brown hair still slid across her face, covering one eye. She brushed it back behind her ear, her hand lingering as she took him in. The realization that he'd forgotten that one small mannerism opened him up inside. Despite his best efforts to stay cool, he could hear the desperation in his voice.

"If you don't talk to me tonight, I'll just find you again. Until you *do* talk to me."

She folded her arms protectively over her stomach. "Just say what you're gonna say so I can go."

Her tone was so harsh, so bitter. He hadn't expected that. "Have you completely changed your mind about me? You know who I am, Serena. You know I never hurt that woman. It's Mad Marsha, isn't it? She's had all this time to work on you, get you to change your mind."

"I was never really sure about you. It's not just my mom."

"Serena, please!"

She seemed to hesitate. But then, appearing to reach a decision, she swung away from him and crossed the street.

Okay, he thought. Maybe she needed to put some distance between them. If so, fine. He'd give her distance, as long as she stopped. But she didn't. If anything, she walked faster.

"Don't you walk away from me!" he shouted, the words coming out angry. He knew that was a mistake. "I never blamed you for anything. All I ever did was love you."

"Leave me alone," she called, getting into a car parked along the street.

He stood watching, frozen in place, as the engine caught and she pulled away from the curb. When the car passed him, she never even turned her head to look.

Jane's surprise was so total, her jaw dropped. Standing just a few feet away from her was someone she'd known in another life. Or at least, that's the way it felt.

"Your car . . . it's still at the Lyme House. I thought . . . I was sure you weren't here." The woman blocked the bright overhead light with her hand. "Why on earth are you holding that poker?"

The scent of the the woman's spicy perfume told Jane everything she needed to know. "You've been in the house before. Was it just last night, or were there other times?"

"You sound angry. Don't be angry, Jane. I've been gone such a long time."

She'd always been good at changing the subject. "Answer the question. And don't lie to me."

What had it been, four years since the last time Jane had seen Julia? There were a couple of phone calls from France, a letter, and then . . . nothing. The last Jane remembered, Julia was headed to South Africa to work on the AIDS crisis over there. But when it came to her ex, Jane figured she was never getting the entire truth.

Julia Martinsen was a doctor, an extremely wealthy one. For all

Jane knew, she could have been living the high life in Paris all these years, or been in jail. Still, something about the pained look in her eyes gave Jane the sense that this time, she might be telling the truth.

"I've been ill." Her hand jerked to her short blond hair, then dropped to her face. "But I'm better now."

Jane lowered the poker, tossed it on the couch.

In fact, Julia had changed so much that Jane wasn't sure she would have recognized her if she'd passed her on the street. Her former lover's Scandinavian good looks had been refined into something almost ethereal. Her eyes were carved far more deeply into an impossibly pale face. She looked older, thinner, terribly frail. An almost palpable heat radiated from her eyes. It made Jane wonder not only about her physical health but her emotional condition as well. She was holding a small picture frame in her right hand. Jane recognized it immediately as one she'd put away in a desk drawer in her study. It was a photo of Jane and Julia up at Blackberry Lake. A happier time. "What are you doing with that?"

"Would you mind . . . could I sit?"

"No."

Her gaze took in the hallway, the stairway up to the second floor.

"Tell me why you've been breaking into my house," demanded Jane.

Julia looked up sharply. "I didn't break in. I had a key."

"We ended our relationship years ago. It's considered good form to give the key back or throw it away."

"Don't laugh at me, Jane."

"Believe me, I'm not."

"I tried to forget you. Maybe it seems ridiculous, but I couldn't."

"Let's skip the melodrama, okay?"

She pressed her lips together, raised her chin in a show of defiance. It wasn't much of one, not up to her old standards at all.

Jane was angry, but she was also curious. Curiosity might have killed the cat, but Julia was hardly dangerous. Just manipulative and a little free with the truth. "Did you ever make it to South Africa?"

"Botswana. It was my base of operation."

"And . . . what are you saying? You got sick because of your work?"

"Yes," she whispered.

"And now you're back. Where are you living?"

"White Bear Lake."

"So you've been home awhile."

"Three weeks."

"And how many times have you invaded my home without my knowledge?"

"Just last night. I never thought of it as an invasion. I needed to reconnect with you but not face-to-face. Not right away. I didn't want you to see me until I was completely well."

"What exactly is wrong with you?"

"I became infected with a drug-resistant form of TB. I was in Vermont for most of the last year. I'm lucky that the doctors finally found an antibiotic that worked. Don't worry, I'm not contagious."

"Thanks for the clarification."

"I knew it was wrong to take the photo, but I couldn't help myself. I forced myself to come back tonight to return it to your desk." She paused. "Aren't you even a little happy to see me?"

Jane's hands rose to her hips. "Let's see. Happy. Well, you've been breaking into my house—key or no key, that's what it was. You stole from me. What in all that am I supposed to be happy about?"

"The fact that I'm alive? That I still love you?" Her lips parted, waiting for Jane to respond. When she didn't, she forged on. "I learned some important truths about myself while I was gone. Maybe I do manipulate my world sometimes, but I'm not malicious, I never intended to hurt you. I did a lot of soul-searching, Jane. I needed to find out who I really was, needed a chance to make up for all my failures."

"Good. I hope you made some progress. But sneaking in here doesn't make me think you've changed much."

"Listen to me, *please*." She rubbed her forehead with her fingertips. "The conversation we had when I was in Paris and you were in Connecticut, remember? You sounded so cold."

"That's because it was over."

"But you did love me once. I know you did. But sometimes, I don't know if you can understand this, you seemed so fearsomely contained that I wasn't sure what you were thinking. I'm sorry. I really am. I shouldn't have taken the picture."

"That's too easy, Julia. You want a pass for your behavior, just like always. You haven't changed. I don't know why I should believe anything you tell me."

"Because it's true!"

"If you think we're going to pick up where we left off—" She stared at Julia, then shook her head. "Look, I've gone on with my life."

"Have you? I'll bet you're not dating anyone."

"I've been with the same woman for two years." She held up her hand to show Julia her ring. "We're engaged."

Julia's eyes instantly lost focus. "Who is she?"

Jane didn't think she deserved an answer, but she gave her one anyway. "Her name is Kenzie." Which told her exactly nothing.

"And you . . . care about her?"

"You know," said Jane, folding her arms over her chest, "this entire conversation is utterly surreal. You walk in here, out of the blue, out of the past, and seem to think we can rekindle something that died years ago."

"It never died for me."

Jane held out her hand. "Give me the picture."

Julia's expression shifted subtly. She turned and set it on a small table behind her, then met Jane's gaze. She seemed about to say something, but appeared to change her mind. With as much dignity as she could muster under the circumstances, she opened the door and left.

"Unbelievable," said Jane, picking up the poker but resisting the urge to throw it across the room. "Freaking *unbelievable*."

9

By nine the next morning, all the locks on Jane's house had been rekeyed. Because it was short notice, she had to pay extra, but that was a small price to have her sense of security restored. She didn't think Julia would be back, but she wasn't taking any chances. She hoped the conversation they'd had last night would be the end of it.

With five extra keys jingling in her pocket—one for her father, one for Peter, one for Cordelia, one for her neighbor Evelyn, and one for Mary Glynn, her cleaning help—she drove over to her father's campaign office. Before she locked the car, she gave Mouse a Milk-Bone and promised they'd go for a walk as soon as she was done.

Entering the front door a few minutes later, she asked Tanya, the young volunteer behind the reception desk, if Steve Worlander was in.

"He's talking to Maria in her office."

"When he's done, could you tell him I'm here and that I'd like to speak with him?"

"Sure."

Jane walked back to the break room to get herself a cup of coffee. As she was about to take her first sip, Luke Durrant came in. "Hey, Jane. I suppose you heard the news." He held out his mug, waiting for her to fill it. If it had been anybody else, she might have done it. But not for him.

"Your wrist broken?" she asked.

"Huh? Oh." He poured his own coffee.

Jane liked most everybody who worked with the campaign, but she wasn't that fond of Luke. He was generally pleasant enough, but she detected a streak of arrogance in him that put her off. He was in his late thirties, a computer software engineer and business systems analyst who was hired by the campaign last June when their first IT manager quit to take a job in Arizona.

Most of the computers used at the office had been donated and so were in various states of repair. Luke was a genius with both hardware and software. He was a short, thin, sharp featured man with light brown hair and prominent cheekbones. This morning he had on his usual work attire—striped oxford shirt, designer tie, suspenders, jeans, and calfskin dress sneakers.

"What news?" asked Jane, slipping out of her jeans jacket and draping it over her shoulder.

Luke kept his voice low. "One of Pettyjohn's blogger surrogates finally found a hand grenade. We've seen trolls out there in the blogosphere for months trying to find a supernegative with real gut-level traction. They finally did."

"Speak English."

"Sorry. I've gotten so used to the jargon, I figure everybody understands. Let me regroup. What happened today is a lesson in how effective bloggers can be when they're outside the campaign. Candidates benefit most from the netroots when they inspire bloggers to do their work for free. If this information had shown up on the Pettyjohn blog site—or one of his paid operatives'—their campaign would have been criticized for going negative. I mean, you're dad's got a certain infatuation level in the local blogosphere, but I don't know. This will be a hard one to negotiate. With the posting on YouTube, it won't be long before the papers pick it up. The clip's already had over seventy-five thousand hits."

"Pick *what* up? What clip?" There was a reason why Jane didn't like most computer geeks. Luke was exhibit A.

"From the first day of the campaign, your father began taking hits about the fact that he'd spent his life as a defense attorney. But the more the Pettyjohn campaign talked about that, the more your dad talked about making business, government, and our various communities partners in solving our environmental problems, about the need to modernize our infrastructure, about a major new school-funding initiative. In a sense, the Pettyjohn partisans have waged a one-issue campaign—your father's moral corruption—while your dad's been talking about the issues. It's a clever strategy. He counters their claims by ignoring them."

"I know all that. What's the *news*?"

"Well, it looks like someone's done some serious research and come up with the names of all the people your father has defended during his career. They stripped it to include only the worst of the worst, then made a list, adding the type of crime and the release date for those who were sent to prison. Turns out, two murderers, one attempted murderer, two rapists, one child molester, and four gang-related drug dealers are back out on the streets this year, thanks to the work your father did for them."

"Oh," said Jane. She finally got it.

"And this morning, there was a long op-ed in the *Star Tribune* condemning his values, saying sure, maybe his job is necessary for the system to work, but it's also dirty. And because of that, he shouldn't be a candidate for the highest, most honorable office in the state. It's been said before, but it's starting to stick. Speaking of that, one of the rapists who recently got out of prison—one of the felons your father represented—came by the campaign office yesterday to volunteer some of his time. His name was Hodge. Corey—"

"I know him," said Jane. "His aunt has a cleaning business. She's worked for both my father and me for years. My father took the case as a favor to her, so maybe he came by as a way to say thank you."

"Didn't seem all that grateful to me. What he seemed like was a guy with a short fuse. If we get lucky, he won't come back. Anyway, it's all there in today's *Strib* for everyone to see. Couldn't be worse timing, with the election so close."

"I'm sure Pettyjohn planned the attack all along."

"Probably. But if it came from them, they hid their tracks well."

"You think it could have come from someone else?"

"Whatever the case, connecting your father with these specific felons—showing names and faces and the mayhem they caused—is creating a supernegative in people's minds. And yesterday, somebody sent YouTube a video clip of your dad talking to one of the local TV stations about a man, I think his name was Gibbons, who was sentenced to eight years for a violent assault charge back in 1994. Your dad said the case against him was weak, that he never should have been convicted. As soon as the guy got to prison, he tried to kill a prison guard, then he went to work on his cell mate. He's still inside, serving a life sentence now, so he's no threat to the community, but still. Those clips about the attempted murder of the guard are all on the YouTube piece right after your father basically says the guy was wrongly accused. If nothing else, it shows terrible judgment on his part. The blogosphere is buzzing with it."

"Maybe it will blow over," said Jane, knowing her tone sounded less than confident. "You know what they say about the public having a short attention span."

"Not that short. If we can't figure out a way to bury this before the next news cycle, it's not going to be pretty."

Ever since her dad had tossed his hat into the ring, Jane had been afraid something like this would happen.

"The one thing we've got going for us is that none of the people who were released this year have reoffended. That's huge. We put out a press release this morning to that effect. It's up on the bulletin board near the phone banks, if you want to read it. I don't think it's anywhere near strong enough. If we're forced to put out another one, and then another, trying to answer new charges, we end up playing defense instead of making Pettyjohn fight on our terms, the way we've done up until now."

He made it sound like a war. But then, that's exactly what it was.

"You working the phones today?" he asked.

"Maybe later this evening."

"Just remember, when you call people, some of them are going to want to discuss this." He pointed to a stack of papers next to the coffeepot. "Those are the latest talking points."

"Thanks," said Jane.

One of the computer volunteers stuck her head in the doorway. "Hey, Luke, we got another problem on the Web site. It's just one thing after another. The link that takes people to the pledge page is broken."

"Shit," he muttered, shaking his head. "Talk to you later," he said, nodding to Jane as he stomped off.

Jane spent the next few minutes reading through the talking points. She was almost done when Steve Worlander walked in.

"Jane, hi. Tanya said you wanted to see me."

A couple other staffers had wandered into the break room, so she motioned for him to follow her back to the small cubby where the microwave and refrigerator were kept.

Steve was in his late twenties. When she first started working on her dad's campaign, she was struck by how young the staffers were. Most were in college, or were recent graduates looking to gain both experience and credentials for their own political careers. Steve had surfer boy good looks and might one day be a mover and shaker within the state Democratic Party himself.

"I understand you were with my father on Saturday when the plane went down," said Jane, lowering her voice.

He nodded, shoved his hands into the pockets of his dress slacks.

"I'd like to know the details."

"Hasn't your father talked to you?"

"Briefly, but he didn't give me any specifics. I fly that plane myself. I need to know what went wrong."

"I might not be the right person to ask. I don't know anything about planes or how they work."

"I'm sure you issued a press release. What did it say?"

"That the plane had mechanical problems."

"Okay. Tell me what they were."

He leaned back against the counter, folded his arms across his chest. "Like I said, I don't know."

"Then describe what happened."

"Well, it seemed like some of the controls wouldn't work."

"What controls?"

"The steering, I think."

"Then how did my dad get the plane down safely?"

"The engine cut out and then—"

"In flight?"

"Yeah. But then it kicked in again. It was working when we landed."

That's not what her dad had said. "Did my father send a distress call?"

"You know, Jane, it all happened so fast, I don't remember."

"You don't remember."

"Sorry." He gave a weak smile. "Like I said, it all happened so fast. I was in one of the backseats. And I was pretty scared. Don't tell anyone, but I had my eyes closed."

"Were you low on fuel?"

"No, I saw them gassing up the plane before we left Bemidji."

"Were you carrying anything extra heavy?"

"Not to my knowledge."

"You know, a Cessna is a pretty safe aircraft."

"That's exactly what your father always says."

She was being stonewalled. This guy was going to make a great politician one day. He'd given her exactly nothing. "It seemed like you were on the ground for a long time—over half an hour—before John Thompson radioed the tower in St. Cloud that you were okay."

"Was it that long? I don't think so. Although I never looked at my watch."

"Did my dad try to restart the engine after you landed?"

"Yes, but it wouldn't work."

"Wouldn't work."

"No."

"Look, Steve, what *aren't* you telling me?"

He suddenly became innocence incarnate. "Nothing. Honestly. You should talk to your father if you want more specific answers."

"If the plane wouldn't start, if it had serious mechanical problems, how did it get back the same afternoon?"

His eyes shifted sideways. "Did it?"

"Yes, Steve, it did."

"I wish I could help, but honestly, I don't know anything more about it. We were picked up by a van on Saturday afternoon and taken to St. Cloud. That was the last time I saw the plane."

She searched his face.

"You're clear now? We're okay?"

"Is my father expected here anytime today?"

"He's doing a brunch with journalists at ten, a house party at noon, another one at three, dinner with representatives of the St. Paul fire department at six, and then a speech to the American Association of University Women tonight at eight."

"Just another day in politics."

"That about covers it."

For the moment, there wasn't much she could do. "Thanks, Steve."

"No problem. Sorry I couldn't be more help."

Like hell you are, she thought, watching him walk away.

Luke was still working on the problem with the Web site link when Charity sailed through the open door of his office looking flushed and upset.

"What's wrong?" he asked, typing in a couple more keystrokes and then glancing up at the wall clock. It was ten after two. He knew he'd never make it until five. He wouldn't have come to work at all today if he could have convinced Christopher to spend the day having some fun.

"It's Gabriel." She took a quick look over her shoulder. "I was just about to leave when I saw his car. It's parked across the street."

"Is he in it?"

She nodded. "I've got pepper spray and believe me, I'm not afraid to use it, but I thought maybe you'd walk me out to my car."

"You need to get yourself a restraining order," said Luke. How many times did he and Christopher have to tell her that?

"I talked to my parents' lawyer. I'll have one by the end of the day tomorrow."

He picked up a pencil, began working it through his fingers. Charity wasn't in her usual jeans and T-shirt. Monday was her day off, but she was wearing a tailored gray suit, stockings, and heels.

"Why are you so dressed up?"

"It's my grandmother's birthday. Look," she said hesitating, then easing down on a chair, "I wasn't going to mention anything. You'll hear soon enough." She brushed at her bangs. "I found out at church yesterday . . . There's going to be a trial. The church council has prepared a judicial complaint."

Luke wasn't surprised. And yet he hadn't been prepared for how disappointed—no, incensed—he felt.

"You know how sorry I am."

That you opened your big fat mouth, thought Luke. "Don't worry about it."

"I love you guys. You both mean the world to me."

He thought she used the word *love* way too freely. Lots of people did. Like saying it was supposed to cover a multitude of sins. He put his hands on the desk and stood. "Let's get you out to your car safely."

On the way to the front door, they talked about her grandmother. "You met her once, remember? We all had lunch together at Muffuletta in Milton Square? Must have been a couple years ago."

"Yeah, I remember. She was a hoot."

"I always fix a big meal at her house on her birthday, invite the entire family. It's kind of a tradition."

"You're a dutiful granddaughter."

"She's turning eighty and still going strong. She drinks. Smokes. And swears like a sailor. She's taught me a lot."

"About drinking, smoking, and swearing?"

"No, birdbrain. Stuff like how not to be afraid to fight back. And she's got this great bullshit detector. I wish I had one like it. It would have saved me a lot of grief."

"What did she think of Christopher and me?"

"You she liked. Christopher she loved."

"I can live with that. Did she ever meet Gabriel Keen?"

"Oh, yeah. She said he gave her the willies. I should have listened."

Luke placed a hand against her back and maneuvered her out onto the sidewalk. Keen's Saab was parked behind a white van, the window down, his arm propped on the door. "Somebody should put that guy out of his misery."

"A year ago," said Charity, walking quickly to keep up with him, "I would have told you it was wrong to even think that way. Now—"

"Now you'd like to see him facedown in a swimming pool."

"God forgive me. I would."

Luke looked both ways, then trotted across the street. "Get lost," he shouted, balling his hands into fists. As he reached the front of the car, he banged on the hood.

"Kiss my ass, you freakin' faggot," called Keen, laughing.

Luke grabbed Keen's arm, tried to open the door and pull him out onto the pavement, but the door was locked.

Keen started the motor, turned the wheel, and gave the gas pedal a hit.

Luke had to step away or he would have been knocked down. "You better watch your back, Keen. You're not the only one with a hard-on for some outlaw justice."

"You're a joke," shouted Gabriel. As he drove away, he called, "Tell Charity I'll be in touch."

10

Tuesday was Corey's day off.

"What are you planning to do today?" asked Mary, setting a plate of scrambled eggs and toast in front of him.

He grabbed her hand before she could walk back to the stove, pulled her down, and kissed her cheek. "Anybody ever tell you you're the best?"

"Go on with you," she said, though she flushed with pleasure.

"I'm not sure," he said, digging into his food. "I was thinking that maybe I'd open a bank account. I can't keep asking you to cash my checks."

"I don't mind." Mary sat down at the table with her first cup of morning coffee. "You planning to go see your father?"

Corey looked over at her, gave a shrug. "Why should I?"

"I wish you two could put your old grudges aside. He's not a bad man."

Like hell he's not, thought Corey. He's a human skid mark.

"We all have to forgive each other."

"I know we do," he said. He chewed for a few seconds, then continued, "But we're not all as virtuous as you are."

"Don't sell yourself short, honey. You're a fine man. You may prefer a good story to the truth sometimes, like your mom. And you're a little impulsive on occasion, but you've got a good heart."

"You're the only one who sees it."

"No, God sees it. Don't ever forget that."

He smiled at her. "You still praying for me?"

"Every day."

"Will you pray for something else?"

"What?"

"Me and Serena."

Mary seemed surprised. "Have you talked to her?"

"Last night."

"You still have feelings for her?"

"Stronger than ever."

She mulled that one over. "She's a sweet girl. I always liked her. But I hate to see you getting your hopes up if it doesn't work out. It might be easier to start over with someone new."

"You mean someone who doesn't know I'm a felon. Yeah, I thought about it. But I figure with any woman I'd eventually have to tell her. Who knows if anybody—other than you—will ever believe it was all one big horrible mistake? Sometimes I think this label is gonna follow me to my grave."

"Oh, honey, it may take some time—and finding the right woman—but it will pass."

He wiped his mouth with a napkin, then got up to put his dirty dishes in the dishwasher. "I want Serena to be the right woman."

She gave him an uncertain smile. "Time will tell. Just be patient with her."

Flexing his arm muscles, he said, "I'm not patient, I'm too studly. I crush enemies with my bare hands." He gave her another kiss.

"While you're out crushing enemies, would you stop at the grocery store and pick up some milk, a carton of eggs, a sack of apples, and some of that cereal you like? Can you remember that, or should I make a list?"

He pointed at his head. "Memory like an android."

"I'll take it as a no." She got up, rinsed her coffee cup in the sink, then set it in the dishwasher alongside Corey's. "If I don't get going, I'll be late for my first job."

"You have an absolutely fabulous day," he said, clipping on his watch.

"For all your trials, you're sure in a good mood."

"Lots to do," he said, tucking his chambray shirt into his jeans. "After the last nine years, today is full of promise."

Corey spent the next hour wheedling the information he was looking for out of one of Serena's old girlfriends. He needed to know where Serena lived. She wasn't in the directory. He hoped like hell she'd moved out of her mother's place, and as luck would have it, she had.

The girlfriend, Liza Reynolds, stood nervously next to the clothes she was sorting at the BubbleTime Laundromat on Sixty-sixth in Richfield. She was another boring Minnesota blond, and so skinny she looked like a skeleton with a hairdo. She also looked like she'd aged about thirty years in the time he'd been gone. He figured it was drugs. He knew she wouldn't talk to him if he called, so he'd followed her from her apartment. She acted like he was made of plutonium, which both amused and annoyed him.

"I didn't rape anyone," he said, leaning against one of the washing machines, twisting the turquoise and silver ring on his right hand.

"Okay."

"I'm telling the truth."

"Sure, Corey. I hear you. I just think it would be better for everyone if you left Serena alone."

She seemed so jumpy that finally, out of frustration, he grabbed her by the shoulders. "Jesus. Calm down."

"Hey," she said, pushing his arms away, backing up. "Don't touch me."

"I didn't mean—"

"Just leave me alone, okay? I don't want no trouble. I just want to do my wash and go home. You got no right to harass me. I gave you the information you wanted."

He cocked his head. "*How* exactly am I harassing you?"

"Just go, okay. And don't tell Serena I told you where she lived."

He held up his hands, nodded politely, and backed his way out the door.

Corey arrived at the American Eagle Bank & Trust just before noon. He parked his cycle in the lot and entered the building through the side doors. The interior was one long room with the tellers on the right and the rest of the bank personnel sitting at desks to his left. Along the far wall were a bunch of glass-enclosed offices for the bigwigs. He quickly located Charity. She was sitting alone at a desk in the rear of the room, a puzzled look on her face, concentrating on the computer screen in front of her.

Her back was to him, so when he came up behind her he could study the screen for a few seconds without her being aware that he was there. He saw what the problem was right off.

"Press the Escape button," he said, leaning over her, putting a hand on her shoulder.

She turned, looked up at him. "Corey. Where'd you come from?"

"Thought I'd let you open a checking account for me today. But first—" He pressed a couple of keys, then a couple more. He held one down, smiled at her while he waited for a different screen to pop up, did a few more quick keystrokes, then when the main screen appeared, he said, "Type in your password again and you're off and running."

"Thanks," she said, looking amazed. "It wouldn't let me do a thing."

"Now you can take all my vitals," he said as he sat down in one of the chairs in front of her desk and crossed his legs. "Unless—"

"Unless what?"

She was wearing a pretty blue dress. She looked fabulous, professional and sexy. And those freckles—they drove him crazy.

"You have to eat lunch, right?"

"Well . . . yes."

"I bought us some sandwiches at a deli. Thought we could sit on one of those benches in the park across the street. What do you say? One is turkey and the other is roast beef."

"I love roast beef," she said.

"Oh, sorry. That one's for me." He looked serious, then grinned.

She smiled back a little tentatively.

"Let me run outside and get the sack."

Once they'd found the perfect bench with the most sun, they sat down. Corey handed the turkey sandwich to her. "You thought I was kidding?" He gave her a stern look, then grinned again and exchanged the roast beef for the turkey.

"You're a tease, you know that?"

"Me? No way." He'd had a chance to watch her on the way over. She had an effortless sort of posture and a great ass. He was smitten.

"I've only got half an hour," she said.

"Then we better make the best of it."

As she glanced up at the trees, watching two squirrels chase each other around, a hint of sadness crept into her eyes.

Corey figured she was sad about something in her life, or lonely—or both.

"So, you're a real supporter of Ray Lawless?" he asked.

She chewed for a second. "Well, yeah. I don't much like defense lawyers. But I think he's a good man."

"Me, too."

"I think he's made some mistakes, but I told myself this year that I needed to turn over a new leaf. If I didn't get involved in the process, I had no right to bitch."

As they talked, Corey noticed a guy in a three-piece suit saunter into the park. He kept looking their way until Charity saw him.

"Oh, darn." She turned her back to him, fiddled with her sunglasses.

"Who's he?"

"Somebody I don't want to talk to."

The guy walked closer, stood by a tree and chewed on a toothpick.

"Go away," called Charity.

"Not until you listen to me," he called back.

"Who is he?" whispered Corey.

"We used to . . . date. He promised he'd leave me alone. He frightens me."

"Why? Did he hurt you?"

"Not physically. He's just . . . I don't want him anywhere near me."

Corey shot to his feet, walked across the grass to where the man was standing, and stuck out his hand. "Corey Hodge."

The guy studied him openly. Corey had the sense that he was trying to memorize his name.

"That's Corey with a C."

"Who the hell are you?"

He was tall, cocky, and completely tricked out—gold jewelry, diamond ring, flashy silk tie, expensive haircut.

"I'm Charity's new boyfriend. Who the hell are you?"

"She hasn't told you about me?"

"Apparently you're history, man. Not even worth a mention. But I like to know who I'm talking to. What's your name?"

"Gabriel Keen."

"Well, Gabriel, I think the lady over there wants you to move on."

"She doesn't own the park."

"No, man, she don't. But as it happens, I do."

"You think you're funny?"

"Yeah, I think I'm a riot. I'm also a black belt in karate. You wanna have a little . . . conversation with me, I'm happy to oblige."

Keen looked him up and down. "Bullshit."

"You calling me a liar?"

"Yeah, I am."

"Go ahead, then. Hit me." He stuck out his chin. "Right here." He pointed at his goatee.

Keen crunched his right hand into a fist.

"Course, you hit me and I'll have to arrest you."

"You'll . . . what?"

"It's not your day, pal. I'm a cop. Plainclothes. Better run along."

"You are so full of crap."

" 'Fraid not. Bye." He gave a little wave, then turned his back on the guy and returned to the bench. It was a calculated risk, turning away from a man who seemed that tightly wound. But Corey would have enjoyed getting his fancy suit dirty.

After resuming his place next to Charity, he saw that Keen hadn't moved. "Better go peacefully, man. Otherwise, I might have to arrest you for vagrancy."

"Arrest," whispered Charity.

"I'm sorry, Charity," shouted Keen. "But . . . there's no love in my life without you. No hope. I can't just walk away."

Charity lowered her head.

"I'll make it up to you, I promise. I'll call." He glanced both ways over his shoulders, then dropped his toothpick into the grass and stalked off.

"What an asshole," said Corey, picking up his sandwich and taking a bite.

"He's a psycho." She pulled away and looked him full in the face. "You're a cop? For real?"

"I've been working in the criminal justice system for the last nine years."

"Wow. I mean, I've never—" Another hesitation.

"Dated?"

"We aren't actually dating."

"No, but we could be. I wish we were. Unless you've got something against cops."

A smile curled around the corners of her lips. "No, nothing at all."

He chewed for a minute, watched Keen get into a shiny black Saab. "You wanna talk about the dipshit?"

She shook her head.

"Hey, are you planning to head over to the campaign office tonight?"

"No, but I am tomorrow. Luke called, said all the computers are up and running. Thought I'd put in a couple of hours."

"Great. Me too. Maybe when we're done, you might like to go for a ride on my cycle."

"You have a motorcycle?" She brushed some crumbs off her dress. Gave herself a minute to think what to say. "Well, um, maybe. Do you have helmets?"

"I got one for you."

"You don't use one?"

"Nah." He laughed. "I'm made of steel—planning to live forever."

11

Christopher sat quietly on one of the club chairs in the living room, hands crossed in his lap, eyes closed, listening intently to Jussi Björling and Licia Albanese sing a duet from the opera *Turandot*. He was so caught up in the music that he hadn't heard Luke come in. It was a perfect opportunity for Luke to study his partner in an unguarded moment. He felt a little guilty, but then he figured all men were voyeurs at heart.

Luke was home early today, hoping to convince Christopher to go out to dinner. The answer was always no, but Luke refused to give up.

In many ways, Christopher was a creature of the early twentieth century, not the early twenty-first. He tended to formality, not only in his dress but also in his habits. He wasn't the least bit stuffy or standoffish, but he had a sincere appreciation for graciousness, politeness, modesty, and good manners, none of which were particularly important in today's world.

As Luke thought about it, he realized that tonight was very much like the night five years ago when he'd first met the Reverend Christopher Cornish. Falling in love with a Methodist minister had never been high on Luke's lists of things to do with his life. He was entirely nonreligious himself, sometimes vocally so.

As a gay man, Luke was already at odds with a great deal of Christian belief. So was Christopher. And yet, Christopher believed with his entire being in a Christian God, a loving father who spoke to him and helped him daily. How could Luke argue with a belief that was so essentially gentle, peaceful, with a man whose entire mission in life was to help others, not force dogma down their throats.

Luke and Christopher used to argue about religion in the early days of their relationship, but it became apparent pretty quickly that neither one was going to change the other's mind. Luke had never felt entirely comfortable going to church on Sunday, although he liked to listen to Christopher's sermons. His words never failed to touch something deep inside him.

Christopher loved being a pastor. Luke's first impression of Christopher was that his emotional default setting was enthusiasm. He adored working with outreach ministries, visiting the sick and the elderly, and he got along well with everyone.

Back then, Luke had been employed by the tech giant I.A.M., making piles of money, traveling all over the country and enjoying the single life. He liked sex and he liked variety. He had a nice apartment in downtown St. Paul. Lots of friends. And he had no particular desire to settle down, to "nest," as some guys called it. But Christopher changed all that. Luke had never met anyone quite like him before. He was blond, tall, built, athletic—everything Luke wasn't—and he was also Turner Classic Movies handsome. Looks were important, sure, but Christopher had something else, something special that flowed from his eyes. It was a warmth, an energy, a goodness. Luke knew by their second date that he'd be an idiot if he let Christopher Cornish get away.

At the time, Christopher was deep in the closet at Merriam Park United Methodist. The official church policy stated that self-avowed, practicing homosexuals were banned from the ministry. The trick was, you could be gay, you just couldn't have a sex life. It was a policy that pretty much forced duplicity on otherwise honest men and women.

That spring, while Christopher kept his small apartment in St. Paul for the sake of appearances, he and Luke moved into an apartment together in the Uptown area of south Minneapolis. Christopher didn't have a landline at his apartment, just a cell phone, so people who called never knew where he was. Luke didn't like all the closeted sneaking around, but he understood that it was a delicate situation for Christopher and was willing to live with it for a while. Luke was Christopher's first real love. Before Luke came along, Christopher had been almost entirely celibate.

The situation festered for the next few years. In April of 2007, while Luke was on the road, he got an e-mail from Christopher, saying he'd reached his limit. He'd come to the conclusion that this was the moment. He wanted to provide a different voice for the congregation, especially for those he knew who were also in the closet, hiding from the most fundamental truth of their lives. On a gray spring Sunday, he'd come out to the congregation in his sermon. As Christopher had expected, the congregation was bitterly divided.

One week later, at about ten P.M., as he was leaving through the back door of the church, he was attacked. He was beaten viciously with a baseball bat and left for dead. The assailant got away. Christopher was found many hours later and taken to a hospital. Unfortunately, he'd lapsed into a coma before he could tell the police who his attacker was. But the story didn't end there.

"Oh, Lord, you scared me," said Christopher, nearly jumping out of his chair.

Ever since the assault, he'd startled easily.

"I'm sorry," said Luke. "You seemed so into the music that I didn't want to interrupt." His eyes were motionless.

"Something wrong?"

"No," said Luke. "You're here. You're alive. That's all I need."

12

Jane stood outside the front doors of the Allen Grimby Repertory Theater in St. Paul talking to her dad on her cell phone.

"I'm sorry I didn't get back to you sooner, honey. Steve Worlander said you had some questions about the plane. You know, Janey, as it turned out, it was my fault. Pilot error. I was in such a hurry to get to St. Cloud that I didn't have the plane refueled. I thought we had enough, but I cut it too close."

Now she knew she was being lied to. Worlander had said he'd seen the plane being refueled. It was the one thing he'd told her that she actually believed. And beyond that, her dad would never take off without knowing exactly how much fuel he had and how far it would get him.

"Look, Dad—"

"I know, I know. I'll never be that careless again, I promise you. Somebody hauled some fuel out to the plane and it was flown back to Flying Cloud that same afternoon. I've already had it checked out. I put a few scratches on it when we landed, but that's about the extent of the damage." He laughed.

She didn't think it was funny. But this wasn't the time to get into it with him. He was just about to be interviewed on *Morning Edition* on Minnesota Public Radio.

"I'd like to see you one of these days," said Jane, "just to help me remember what you look like."

Another laugh. "My schedule has been insane. But it will be over soon."

"If you know when you're going to have even fifteen minutes free, call me. I'll drive to where you are, and we can have a cup of coffee."

"It's a deal, Janey. Hey, I gotta run."

"I know. Hope the interview goes well."

"It'll be nothing but a nonstop grilling about that op-ed in the *Strib* on Monday. That's all anybody wants to talk about at the moment. The issues are off the table, and my past as a litigator is center stage. Just what I never wanted. Bye, honey. Talk to you soon."

Jane pocketed her phone, then pushed through the glass front doors into the theater. She found Cordelia inside the main stage. "You meditating?" she called, walking down the center aisle toward her.

"I'm hiding," said Cordelia, looking up at the floodlight batten high above her head. "It's been one of those mornings." She paused, her hand sliding along the ornate iron railing as she moved a few paces to her right. "I've been thinking—" She tapped her lips with a finger. "Remember I told you that I'm mounting the production of that Nilo Cruz play next January. I know this is totally retro, but I might use footlights. You know? They were used in old variety shows. They ran around the floor on the front of the stage."

Jane sat down in one of the aisle seats. "Sounds intriguing."

"It could be, if it's done right." She leaned her hips against the railing, thinking for another few seconds, then said, "So, to what do I owe this unexpected visitation?"

"You make me sound like an evil spirit."

"I've been reading a stage adaptation of Poe's 'The Masque of the Red Death' for the last couple of days. We're thinking about mounting it during the 2009 season."

"Will you direct?"

She lowered her voice to its most suggestive register. "How could I resist? You know how much I *love* the macabre."

"Then you'll love my news."

"Macabre news?" She rubbed her hands together. "Tell me everything."

"That faint perfume smell in my house the other night? I wasn't wrong. Someone had been inside."

"Someone I know?" She pretended to think but was much too impatient to give it any serious thought. "I give. Who! Tell me!"

"Julia."

"As in . . . Julia Martinsen? Your old—"

"The very same."

Cordelia looked startled, then horrified, then entranced.

Jane presented her with a brief summary of what had happened. "And," she added, as Cordelia slipped into the seat next to her, "she'd taken an old framed photograph of the two of us but thought better of it and brought it back."

"The woman has no boundaries! She's a crazy person, Janey. I always said that about her. You just wouldn't listen."

"When we were first dating and I was worried that she had an awful lot of secrets, you told me to go for it. That I'd regret it forever if I didn't give it a shot."

"You know better than to listen to me."

"Pardon me? You think you're the reincarnation of Dear Abby."

"Well, as it happens, I am. But Abby and I can have an off day, can't we?"

Jane's eyes rose to the top of the theater curtain.

"You got the key back, right?"

"Doesn't matter. I had the locks changed." She reached into her pocket and pulled out one of the new ones, handing it across to Cordelia. "Besides, she's not dangerous. She's just—"

"Obsessed."

"No, I don't think so. Just damaged."

"If you believe a word that woman says, something's wrong with *you*."

"Should I take that as another ex cathedra utterance from the mouth of the great Advice to the Lovelorn Diva?"

"Are you telling me you believe any of her self-serving twaddle? Like, she's been off being Mother Teresa in Africa. She's consumptive so she needs to be treated with great care. God, it's right out of a Victorian novel. The least she could do was update it. Maybe give us something from . . . like, *Valley of the Dolls*. That's at least part of the last century."

"No, I believe her. She had no reason to lie about any of that. Tuberculosis is making a comeback, in case you haven't heard."

"She gets you spinning around just like she always does. And you buy into it. You stay away from her, you hear me?"

"I doubt I'll ever see her again. I was pretty clear with her last night. She knows about Kenzie. Maybe—"

"Maybe what?" demanded Cordelia.

"Well, maybe I was a little too hard on her."

"Oh, please! The woman lies like she breathes. You know what attracted you to her the first time?"

"What?"

"She was a mystery. You wanted to *solve* her!"

"I didn't come here to be yelled at."

"I'm not yelling!"

"You love yelling. Nor did I come to be analyzed." Jane's cell phone vibrated again. She pulled it out and checked the caller ID.

"You're changing the subject."

"No, my cell phone is." She said hello.

"Is this Jane Lawless?"

"Yes?"

"This is Neil Kershaw. Hey, we finally connected. Whoever I talked to at the Xanadu Club gave me this number. I hope you don't mind."

"No, but . . . what's this about?"

"I'd rather save that for when we meet. It's important. Otherwise,

I wouldn't bother you. I'm wondering if we could get together later tonight. Say around ten at the Lyme House pub? Is that too late?"

Her curiosity had certainly been piqued. "No, that's fine. I'll grab us a table in the back room."

"Great. Thanks so much. See you then."

As she stuffed the phone back into her pocket, Cordelia tapped her fingers against her chin and said, "Who was that?"

Jane shrugged. "Some guy's been chasing me around. Wants to talk to me tonight."

Cordelia lowered her eyes and gave Jane a sideways look. "Anything I need to know about?"

Jane leaned in close and whispered, "If there is, I'll call your cell phone, let it ring twice, then hang up. And then I'll text-message you. I'll use the code name 'NOSY' so you'll know it's me."

"Cute."

"I thought so. I'll be in touch."

13

Where were you this afternoon when I called?" asked Luke. He was sitting in his hole of an office, talking to Christopher on his cell.

"I didn't hear the phone," said Christopher. "I must have been asleep."

Luke was hoping he'd say that he'd gone for a walk, or that he was out getting his hair cut. Anything was better than sitting around the condo brooding.

"Don't worry. I've got lots to do. I'm actually working on a sermon. I'll give it one day. If not at Merriam Park, then somewhere else."

Not what Luke wanted to hear. He'd been hoping that Christopher would give up the ministry, move on in some other direction. "Have you thought any more about the upcoming trial?"

"The bishop has the power to strip me of my orders and toss me out of the church, but everyone on that jury is going to have to look me in the eye to do it. I intend to rub their faces in my scars, my broken bones and body, their egregious moral teachings. Nobody's going to leave that council chamber feeling good about themselves, you can count on that."

While they continued to talk, Luke got up and stepped outside his door. "Oh, crap."

"What?"

"Charity's talking to that guy I told you about. Corey Hodge." They looked so cozy that Luke wished he'd remembered to tell her about him. But the truth was, after Hodge had stomped out of his office the other day, he never expected to see him again. "She really attracts the nutcases."

"She's easy to talk to. Who'd think being kind could get you in trouble?"

Luke continued to study Hodge. "I suppose if you were desperate, you might think he was good-looking. He bounces around a lot, kind of like a boxer. And he wears these tight muscle Ts to show off his pecs." He laughed. "Maybe he's a muscle queen." The fact was, he reminded Luke of a coiled spring.

"You better have a conversation with Charity about him," said Christopher. "She needs to know who he is, just in case he's putting the moves on her."

"I will."

"Or I can call her. Why don't you let me do that?"

"Go ahead. But I think I should say something, too. I know she's your friend, but sometimes she's as thick as a brick."

"Don't be angry with her."

"How the hell can I not be angry? Sure, you came out to the church all on your own, but she was the one who let it drop that you had a partner. And that's what really put you in hot water, according to the Methodist handbook of mortal sins."

"She wasn't thinking."

"That's her main problem," said Luke, "she doesn't think. But hey, I don't want to argue, especially not about her. Actually, I need to get going. We've got another virus. I'm sorry I have to put in so many late hours."

"It won't last much longer."

"Can't say exactly when I'll get home."

"I may be in bed."

Years ago, that would have been a come-on. Now it meant that

Luke shouldn't wake him up if he was sleeping. "Love you," he whispered.

Hodge and Charity were still deep in conversation. He was about to head over and pull her away, give her a good talking to, when he spotted Gail Chamberlain, his supervisor, making straight for him.

"Oh shit," he said under his breath. The sight of her always made his mood go sour.

"Luke," she called, motioning him into his office. "That link is broken again, the one you worked on the other day. And so is the link that takes people to our video page. Drop everything else you're working on and figure out what's wrong."

"I'm on it."

"I've never worked on a campaign before where we had so many problems with the Web site."

"I didn't design the thing. Whoever did, in my opinion, did a crappy job. I can redesign it if you want, but it will take time."

"No, just keep fixing it when it breaks."

Luke spent the next few hours repairing the malfunctioning links. When he finally did get up to go talk to Charity, he discovered that both she and Hodge were gone.

With Charity behind him on the cycle, her arms around his stomach, her body pressed against his back, Corey sped down University all the way to Dinkytown, then cut over the 10th Avenue bridge to Cedar. He gunned the motor each time they came to a light, impatient to get to the West River Road, where there would be fewer cars. He'd packed a pint of Beam and a blanket in his leather saddlebags for when they stopped.

By ten-fifteen, they were sitting under the stars, passing the bottle back and forth.

"I've never been out with a cop before," said Charity, clearly impressed with her good luck.

Corey regretted now that he hadn't told her the truth back at the campaign office, but if he had, he was pretty sure she never would have gone for a ride with him. And now, if he fessed up and she freaked out and ran off on him, it could snowball into an even bigger problem. If they had sex and he told her later, she'd feel like he'd used the cop thing to get into her pants. It was a no-win situation, unless they didn't have sex. But that was like asking a starving man not to eat.

"I like you a lot," said Corey, turning to her, putting his arm around her waist. "Do you mind?" he asked.

"No, I like it."

"That guy I met the other day. Gabriel?" At the sound of his name, he could feel her body tense.

"What about him?"

"How long did you two date?"

"A year or so."

"Was it serious?"

She took a sip from the bottle of Jim Beam. "Yeah."

"Why'd you break it off? I mean, he looked like a successful guy."

"His parents are superwealthy."

"Does he have a job?"

"He's a headhunter."

"A what?"

She laughed. "He works at his dad's company. It's an executive-recruiting firm."

"What the hell does a headhunter do?"

"Look for people to steal away from one company to place at another company for more money. It's legal, and highly lucrative, but it can be sleazy. Technically, Gabe screens, interviews, and then recommends people for executive or senior management positions. He's got a business degree, but he hates business. He was just doing what his father wanted. He liked the job at first, but now he thinks his dad is dishonest. He wants to go back to school, maybe get a degree in art. We used to go to the Art Institute at least once a week. But he's had a lot of trouble with depression. Sometimes he has a hard time even getting out of bed."

"Any reason?" He handed her the bottle again, but she shook her head.

"He thinks he was responsible for his brother's death."

"Was he?"

"In a way. It's a long story."

He could tell she didn't want to get into it. "But you dumped him?"

She seemed to retreat inside herself for a few seconds. "It's hard to talk about. We weren't just dating, we were engaged. But I couldn't go through with it. I thought I knew him, but—"

"You don't have to tell me," said Corey, pulling her closer. "I get the picture."

"I got a restraining order against him yesterday. Maybe he'll finally stop calling, stop following me around."

"I wouldn't count on it."

"Really?"

"Sometimes restraining orders just make a guy mad. Where's he live?"

"With his dad and his dad's second wife. In Tangletown." She mentioned an address.

"Trust me. He tries anything, and I'll be all over it."

Charity turned, looked deep into his eyes. "I think this time, I finally got lucky. I feel really safe with you."

They sat snuggled together for a while longer, talking, laughing softly, looking up at the stars, and then Corey leaned over and kissed her. She didn't resist. Moving his other arm around her, he laid her down against the blanket. "This okay?" he asked.

"Fine," she whispered.

"You're beautiful, you know that? Just the kind of girl I was hoping to meet."

Slowly, he unbuttoned her blouse. Her body rose at the touch of his hand. "I want you," he whispered.

"I want you too," she breathed.

Her words flooded him with desire—and with a kind of gratitude.

Neil Kershaw set his briefcase on one of the empty chairs.

Jane felt the force of a quick, intense appraisal as he sat down.

The back room of the Lyme House pub was softly lit by wall sconces and washed by firelight from a round, copper fireplace in the center of the room. It was a good place for a quiet conversation.

"It's nice to finally meet you," he said, glancing up at a waiter. "Oh, hi. What's your bar scotch?"

"Cutty Sark."

"Great. Make it a Cutty and water. Thanks."

Jane sipped from a glass of sauvignon blanc. She guessed he was in his forties, though he could have been older. He had a strong face, big eyes, big nose, big mouth. All of his features seemed oversized, but taken as a whole, he was mildly attractive. He wore a school signet ring on his right hand, a gold wedding band on his left. His clothes were casual, a plaid flannel shirt tucked into brown cords. His only unusual feature was the long graying ponytail tied with a strip of tie-dyed muslin.

He made himself comfortable in the chair opposite her while his gaze wandered the room. "Thanks for agreeing to meet me. Like I said, I didn't want to talk to you about this over the phone. It seems we have a . . . friend in common."

"And who would that be?"

"Julia Martinsen."

Jane did her best to keep her expression neutral. "What about her?"

He was clearly nonplussed by her lack of response. "There's no reason you should trust me, I suppose. Let me explain. Julia and I first met in Pretoria, South Africa, and then later in Gaborone, Botswana, where she had a small house. I assume you know this, but prior to her time in Africa, she'd been working on HIV/AIDS in the U.S. She left because she felt she could do more good over there."

"How much do you know about her work in the U.S.?"

"Not a lot. She doesn't talk much about her past."

For good reason, thought Jane. She knew a hell of a lot more about Julia than he did.

"I work with Harvard, the University of Minnesota, and internationally with the UN. I've spent the last eight years working on the AIDS crisis in sub-Saharan Africa, mainly Zambia. I'm a Minnesota boy, born and raised. I come back a few times a year."

The waiter arrived with his drink. Kershaw thanked him and took a sip before he continued. "I don't know how much you know about Africa or AIDS. Africa is the epicenter—ground zero for the pandemic. We may think nuclear war or environmental disaster will be the undoing of the human race, but I'd put my money on microbes. I used to think I burned the candle at both ends, but Julia, she had the most fierce commitment to her work of anybody I've ever known. It's what drew me to her. She was utterly fearless. She chose the neediest, the most dangerous clinics. She'd go into the bush, visit villages where she was met with not only total silence but often outright hostility.

"Sometimes I'd visit a clinic where she was working and I'd find that she'd been up for more than thirty-six hours. It was easy to forget about time because the situation is so dire. I'd make her come back with me to where I was staying, force her to eat, to sleep. She'd thank me, but the next day, she'd be back at it again. I worked mainly in South Africa from '05 to '07, so it was hard to keep track of her, but I did my best. I was the one who finally demanded she see a doctor. I don't know if you're aware of this, but she contracted TB a year ago. I knew she was sick, but she refused to admit it. She kept saying it was just a cough, that she was tired because she was putting in such long hours. My worst fear was that she contracted HIV. It often goes hand in hand with TB in Africa. But she was clean, thank God. She's much better now, but . . . well, she's not fully recovered, physically or emotionally. The years in southern Africa and her illness really took it out of her."

"I'm sorry to hear that," said Jane. She had no intention of giving this guy any information until she knew what he wanted. "But why did we have to meet for you to tell me all this?"

"Because you're her friend. She traveled with two photographs that were always with her. One of you, and one of a man named Leo. I assumed that he was an old love, a boyfriend or husband, and that you were her best friend."

What this guy didn't know about Julia could fill a book.

"What I've come to tell you isn't all good news. First, I wanted you to know that Julia's come home to the cities to recuperate, and perhaps to stay. I don't think she's decided yet. And second, I thought you needed to have some perspective on what she's been doing with her life these past few years. I guess, mostly, I was hoping that it might help you understand why she's not in a very good place at the moment. If she hasn't contacted you, she will. It was clear to me that you're one of the main reasons she decided to move back here."

"She talked about me?"

"Enough to know that you're extremely important to her."

"When you say she's not well emotionally, what do you mean?"

He rubbed his jaw. "She's not the same Julia I first got to know. She doesn't seem to have many internal breaks. If she gets something into her head, she can't stop herself from acting on it."

"I think she was always like that," said Jane.

He furrowed his brow. "You probably know her better than I do. But there *is* a difference. She seems more volatile, and at the same time more vulnerable. I feel as if I'm betraying her in some way, telling tales behind her back, but I guess I'm offering this information so that when she does contact you, you'll understand why you need to be gentle with her. She'll get her bearings, I'm sure of that. She's an incredible woman, probably the strongest, most admirable person I've ever known."

"That's quite a statement."

"But it's true. To be around a human being who's that passionate, that good, well, it's like being on a constant high."

"Are you two close?"

"I wish I could say we were, but it's just a friendship." He stared down into his drink. "There's some hidden part of her, something that drives her, that I may never understand. Perhaps you do. Or if you don't, maybe one day she'll open up to you about what it is."

"Do you plan to stay in touch with her?"

He flicked his gaze to her, then away. "Oh, yeah. I'll be there for her if she ever needs me."

Wearing a camel wool jacket, Julia sat on the cabin's front porch, her computer resting in her lap. Bringing up her Web browser, she logged on to Google, and then typed "Chadwick State College NE." She'd spent the last few hours reading though Ray's campaign site, his campaign blog, and checking all the links from his sites to others. She finally discovered Kenzie's name on a blog about a fund-raising party Cordelia had given at her loft last summer. Along with Kenzie's last name was the information that she taught cultural anthropology at Chadwick State College in northeastern Nebraska.

Julia didn't expect to learn much from the college Web site, but at the very least, she hoped to find a photo. She checked through each page, clicked on every link. She learned that the college had a football team, an art gallery, a new dining hall/student center, and two high-rise residence halls. The only information she could find on the faculty were phone numbers and e-mail addresses, which at this point were worthless.

Returning to Google, she typed in "Nebraska State College Faculty." Up popped a list of Web site addresses. She knew immediately she'd struck gold. She clicked on www.kenziemulroy.net and came to a page with a full-color photo, a list of courses, and instructor policies.

The woman staring back at Julia from the screen was leaning against a fence, a horse in the background. Her arms were folded casually across her stomach. She was wearing a black turtleneck, well-worn jeans, and tan cowboy boots. With her long legs and trim body, she was nice enough looking, although she was hardly beautiful. Her hair was more red than blond, feathered across her forehead and over her ears. Julia studied her for another few seconds and came to the conclusion that she looked like an attractive boy. Jane had always gone for the more feminine type, so Julia was a little surprised. The woman in the picture had a great smile, but Julia knew that when it came to looks, she'd win hands down over this cowgirl any day.

Shutting off the computer, Julia closed the lid and looked up at the shards of shimmering moonlight spreading out across White Bear Lake. A song had been nagging at her all day, one she couldn't seem to get out of her head. It was Melissa Etheridge's "Enough of Me." It wasn't the first time the song had taken hold of her, refusing to let go. She'd begun to think of it as her theme song.

Julia had given up everything for Jane. In the beginning, she'd moved halfway across the country. In time, she turned her back on a life that was not only lucrative but also fascinating. She'd worked through the fallout from that life, even when her decision to get out threatened to destroy her. Okay, so maybe she hadn't done everything right. Bang the friggin' gong. Julia Martinsen wasn't perfect.

But she'd done her penance. She'd gone to Africa. She was still a doctor, thank God. Jane hadn't demanded she renounce her profession. With what little she had left, she'd sunk her bare hands, indeed her entire body, into the worst epidemic the earth had ever known.

She'd worked like a demon, given her life utterly in order to burn her soul clean. She'd gone to bed for four years not knowing if she was among the living or the dead. And all she'd wanted in return was forgiveness. Was that so much to ask?

15

With the beat of a Steve Earle tune throbbing in his head, Corey rode over to Serena's house and parked his cycle in the cracked cement driveway next to a black Monte Carlo. He set the stand and climbed off, noticing that the ground was littered with cigarette butts and even a few discarded needles. Serena lived in a poor, rough section of south Minneapolis called the Phillips neighborhood. Ever since her girlfriend had told him Serena had bought a house, he couldn't figure out how she'd been able to swing the mortgage. But now that he'd seen the place, he wouldn't have been surprised to learn that someone had given it away.

Above the front door was a bare bulb that burned hot and bright in the darkness. Inside, he could see a flickering light coming from one of the downstairs rooms. The rest of the house was dark.

He crossed the dry grass and took the steps to the front door two at a time. He hesitated for a moment, going over in his mind just what he wanted to say before she slammed the door in his face, then pressed the bell. When nothing happened, he pressed it again. Figuring it was probably broken, like everything else on the property, he pounded on the door with his fist.

A light burst on inside the hallway. The door drew back and a man, about Corey's age, stood staring at him. He was taller than Corey, with dark hair and a beard, and he was wearing a Hamline University sweatshirt over a pair of gray sweatpants.

"Is Serena around?" Corey asked, thumbs hooked into his belt.

The guy's eyes were lit with alcohol, or something harder. They registered recognition, then turned into small black stones. "Get the hell away from here." He was about to shut the door when Corey stuck his boot inside.

"What'd you say?"

"You heard me. I know you, man. You're the piece of shit Serena used to date. I don't wanna see you within two hundred miles of her—*ever*."

"And you are?"

"None of your goddamn business."

Out of the back came a young voice. "Hey, Johnny. What's taking so long?"

"Just shut up," he called back. "I'll be there in a sec."

"This is Serena's house, right?"

"It's *our* house."

"You her husband?" His gaze slid to the guy's hands. No ring.

"You're bad news, man. Just do us both a favor and get lost."

Corey was sick of everyone having a ready-made opinion of him. Cons had warned him how hard it would be to return to everyday life on the outside. Corey figured that if he was free, he could handle anything. But this was getting really old really fast.

"Listen, dickhead, if Serena's in there, you go tell her—politely—that Corey's outside and wants to talk."

"She's not here."

"You her big manly protector?"

"You got a mouth on you, pal. Yeah, I am. You wanna make something of it?"

Corey smiled. The guy was built like a rubber band and he was drunk. It would be too easy. "She at work?"

"You're not listening." His voice hardened. "It's none of your goddamn business where she is. Stay away from her. You're nothing but poison."

"Shut the fuck up."

"Just get lost."

This time, the kid from the back came out into the hall. "Is the pizza here or isn't it?"

Corey's heart nearly stopped. The boy was skinny, with crooked teeth, a spray of freckles across his cheeks, and red hair like a thatched roof. He was the spitting image of Corey at a similar age.

"Dean, come on. Go back in the living room. I'll be there in a second."

"I'm starving."

"Get the hell out of my face."

Corey was so stunned, he just stood there with his mouth open. "That Serena's kid?"

"He's ours. Now leave."

"How old is he?"

"Five. I'm not kidding, man. Get the hell out of here and don't come back." He slammed the door.

Corey didn't move for almost a minute. The sight of the kid had shaken him. For sure, Serena's new man had lied. The kid wasn't five. He had to be right around eight.

"Ours?" whispered Corey, ready to put his fist through the door. What a pile of bullshit. That kid didn't belong to the rubber band, that kid was *his*. Serena must have been pregnant before he went inside. But she'd never told him. Why keep him in the dark when he would have been so thrilled he would have shouted it from rooftops?

The words "I have a son" exploded inside his mind. He repeated it again and again until the reality sank in.

And the boy's name sealed the deal. Corey's full name was Corey Dean Hodge.

"This time, you're gonna talk to me, Serena," he whispered, returning to his bike. He started the motor. "Hey, asswipe," he called. "That's my son in there. *My* son. Not yours. I'll be back."

After rolling backward out into the street, he gunned the motor and whooped as he roared away. The rush of power beneath him was nothing compared to the rush of power inside him.

"My boy," he yelled to the houses flying past. "I've got a son!"

We're here," called Jane as she entered Cordelia's loft the following evening. She was greeted by the smell of garlic, rosemary, and roasting meat.

"Both of you?" came Cordelia's voice from the kitchen.

"Yup, me, too," said Kenzie, winking at Jane. "Sorry we're late."

Kenzie had arrived in a filthy mood because she'd been involved in a fender bender less than two miles from Jane's house. Her Dodge Ram had a nice new dent on the right front quarter panel thanks to a Goodhue Florist's truck. Rain had been falling since early afternoon, so the world already seemed a pretty dismal place, but Jane had figured out a way to cheer her up. Thus, their tardy arrival.

Jane counted the number of place settings at the dining room table. Four. "Where's Melissa?" she called, setting a bottle of Bordeaux on the table next to a small arrangement of bright yellow daisies.

Cordelia charged out of the kitchen and marched to the bank of windows facing the new lofts across the street. Pushing open one of the panes, she shouted, "Are you coming or aren't you?"

With her head halfway out the window and her hands flat on either side of the glass, she looked, well, ridiculous. Jane wondered if this was going to be her new form of communication with "the girlfriend."

Their fingers knit together, Jane and Kenzie walked over to the windows to watch the scene unfold. It was all so typically Cordelia. Who else would get involved with a woman who moved in, then moved out to another loft across the street? And still they were a hot item.

"Why don't you try cans with a string attached?" offered Kenzie. "It used to work for my sister and me."

Melanie finally appeared. Not her head, just her hand. Holding a cell phone. "I'm talking to my managing editor," she shouted. "Hold your damn horses." The hand disappeared.

"Is this really how you intend to talk to each other?" asked Jane.

Cordelia pulled her head back in. "Why not? Her window is only thirty feet away from mine."

"But the people down on the street," said Kenzie. "They'll hear you."

Cordelia shrugged. "What would you like to drink? I've got iced tea. Cherry, strawberry, and grape soda."

Jane and Kenzie exchanged pained glances.

"A vodka shot might be nice," said Kenzie.

"Make it two," said Jane.

"Hey, Cordelia!" came Melanie's voice.

Cordelia chugged back to the window. "What?"

"There's been a murder in town." This time, instead of her hand, her head appeared. "My editor wants me to cover it."

"Heavens!"

"Sorry about dinner. I'll call you later."

"Love you, sweetie. Be careful."

Cordelia moved back to the drinks cart and poured three shots, passing them around.

"What should we drink to?" asked Jane.

"Let's drink to your little niece," said Kenzie, picking up one of the three dozen photos of Hattie that Cordelia had scattered throughout the living room.

"Perfect," said Cordelia. "To Hattie, may she be home for Christmas."

They touched glasses and downed the vodka.

"Hey," said Cordelia, "let's drink one to my sister's ill health. Let's see. May her face be covered in big black hairy warts. That should be good for her film career."

"Nasty," said Kenzie.

"Octavia steals Hattie from under my nose and *I'm* the nasty one?"

"Let's table that discussion for tonight," said Jane.

They moved the conversation into the kitchen, where Cordelia had been about to put the finishing touches on the osso bucco.

"A little parsley for freshness," she said, placing two veal shanks on each plate and giving them each a sprinkle of parsley. "And we've got garlic mashed potatoes," she continued, scooping out a hefty portion for everyone. "And then rosemary roasted asparagus," she added, pulling open the oven door, removing a flat pan, and using tongs to lay them perfectly alongside the veal. She might love junk food, but that didn't mean she couldn't swing a mean chef's knife. "We'll be very French and do the salad after the main course."

They carried their plates into the dining room. While Jane opened the bottle of Bordeaux, Cordelia filled the water glasses from a pitcher on the table.

"How was the drive up from Chadwick?" asked Cordelia, sitting down and flapping open her napkin, tucking it into the top of her cotton caftan. This one was an orange, red, and yellow geometric pattern. Maybe a five on her flamboyance scale.

"Long. I'm glad it's Jane's turn to come down next time."

"After the election, I'll be able to use the Cessna again," said Jane, tasting the veal. "Really wonderful, Cordelia. You've outdone yourself."

"I guess I'm kind of surprised that Melanie moved across the street," said Kenzie, her eyes searching out the rivulets of rain cascading down the windows. "But thirty feet isn't like . . . all the way to Nebraska."

"Speaking of odd girlfriends, did Jane tell you—" Cordelia stopped midsentence and yelled "Ouch!" Narrowing her eyes at Jane, she said, "Did you kick me?"

"Must have been the cat."

"I thought we'd called a moratorium on kicking me under the table."

"An addendum to the Geneva Accords," said Jane, smiling at Kenzie.

"What were you going to say about old girlfriends before Jane kicked you?"

Under the table, Jane pressed her boot to Cordelia's shin.

"Just that . . . nobody is Ozzie and Harriet anymore."

Nice save, thought Jane. She removed her boot.

Cordelia's phone rang, cutting off any further conversation on the topic. When she grabbed the cordless off a stack of scripts piled on an end table in the living room, she said, "Oh, hi, Peter."

"My brother, Peter?" whispered Jane.

"Yes, she's here. What?" She glanced at her watch. "Sure. But why?"

She moved over to the TV and turned it on, still listening. "Oh, my God!" She switched stations until she came to Channel 5, then motioned for Jane and Kenzie to join her.

They all hovered around the screen as the anchorwoman reported a story about the murder of a young woman late last night.

"Charity Miller worked at a local bank in Minneapolis," said the anchorwoman. "Her body was found outside her apartment shortly after six this morning by another resident of the building. Police were immediately called to the scene. A statement that was issued later in the day indicated that the woman may have been immobilized by a taser and then sexually assaulted. The exact cause of death isn't known at this time."

"Oh, Lord—" said Jane, grabbing the phone from Cordelia. "Peter, this is unbelievable."

"I know. And it gets worse. The way the police found her . . . it was the identical MO Corey Hodge used when he raped that woman ten years ago. Except the first woman lived to tell about it."

"Do you know how she died?"

"The police aren't saying, and there won't be a medical examiner's report for a couple of days. But it's bad, Jane. Really bad. And I'm not just talking about Charity."

It might seem cold to consider the impact Charity's death might have on her father's campaign, but it was impossible not to go there. "Do the police think Corey had anything to do with it?"

"I don't see how he couldn't be their primary suspect. You should get over here. Dad's pretty upset. He canceled his evening speech. Reporters have been calling most of the afternoon, but now they're showing up, demanding a statement. It's starting to look like a circus over here. I think Dad could use your support."

"I'll be there as quick as I can."

Jane and Kenzie put the food away while Cordelia changed into something more appropriate. She came down the stairs from her bedroom a few minutes later wearing jeans and her red and black buffalo plaid hunting jacket, the one she always wore when she needed to feel strong.

Instead of taking the freight elevator to the ground level, they rushed down the back stairs. Jumping into Cordelia's car, they roared out of the back lot. When feeling rushed, Cordelia could be a heavy honker, a barger-inner, a weaver, and a lead foot. She was all of that and more on the way to St. Paul. They arrived in record time, just as a Channel 11 camera truck was backing into a lucky parking space across the street. It looked like Fox News 9 had already arrived.

"I wonder if this was the homicide Melissa was called to cover?" called Cordelia, locking the car.

Jane and Kenzie were already halfway down the block, with Cordelia flailing to catch up.

Jane lowered her head and attempted to make her way past two men from Channel 4 who were working to erect some lights, but before she could reach the steps, a reporter shoved a mic in her face and asked, "Ms. Lawless? Would you like to make a statement about what effect Charity Miller's murder may have on your father's bid for governor?"

Jane wasn't sure if she should answer the question or refuse to comment. Refusing made it seem as if she was afraid to respond. She stopped, hanging on to her umbrella with white knuckles, and said, "I'm stunned by Charity's death. She was a friend, a wonderful young woman, so full of promise. As far as I know, no one has been charged in her murder. When someone is, I'm sure my father will have a statement. But what I'd like to stress is that I believe the people of Minnesota will see any attempt to connect my father to this homicide as nothing more than deeply cynical negative spin. Thanks. That's all I have to say."

She turned and was about to dash up the stairs when she heard the reporter ask, "Ms. Thorn, would you like to comment?"

"You bet I would."

The lights were finally up and running. Cordelia stepped into the spotlight as if moving from a rainy night into a bright summer day.

"No, she wouldn't," said Jane, grabbing her arm and pulling her up the steps. Kenzie followed.

"Hey, I could have helped," said Cordelia, disengaging herself from Jane's grip. She ruffled herself like a barnyard chicken that had just been drenched with water.

"I'm not sure a statement from a woman with pink hair would play well down on the farm or up on the iron range."

"Well, that's just . . . just . . . just—" She sputtered but couldn't seem to decide on a descriptor.

"Un-American?" offered Kenzie.

"Exactly. I am a rainbow!"

You're a lunatic, thought Jane.

Inside, she saw that Peter had been right. The main room was chaos. It looked as if hundreds of her father's friends and political backers had come to show their support. Some were crying, some looked like they were about to burst into tears. Most of these people had known and cared about Charity.

Placing her hand on Jane's back, Kenzie whispered in her ear, "I think I'll go across the hall to the phone banks. Maybe I can help."

Jane was incredibly grateful. She watched Kenzie weave her way through the crowd, then looked around and saw that Cordelia had already found Peter. He had his camera on his shoulder and appeared to be documenting the uproar. It was his job these days, and while this bleak evening might make for an interesting piece of drama for the finished documentary, it wasn't going to be much fun to live through. Standing on tiptoes, she tried to see her father's silver hair, but it was impossible. There were too many tall people in the room. She pushed her way through the crowd toward his office. The door was closed, so she knocked, hoping to find him inside.

"Who's there?" came Maria's voice.

"It's Jane."

When the door swung back, Jane saw that her dad was sitting behind his desk, his tie loosened, glasses on the tip of his nose, reading through a bunch of papers.

Maria quickly shut the door behind her.

"Peter called me," said Jane.

He removed his glasses and rubbed his eyes. "I'm glad you're here. I just got off the phone with Charity's dad. Her mom was so upset she couldn't even talk." Glancing at Maria, he added, "Could you ask someone to get me something to drink? Water? A soda?"

"Of course." Her eyes grazed Jane as she left.

"Sit down," said her dad, motioning her to one of the chairs opposite the desk. "Keep me company."

"Do you know anything more than what the TV's reporting?"

"Nothing. Someone's supposed to fax us a copy of the police report, but so far we haven't seen anything."

"You know Corey better than I do. Do you think he did it?"

He ran a hand down his tie, thought about it. "My memory of his case is pretty sketchy, but from what I remember of him as a kid, he didn't have an Off switch, especially when someone said no. Yeah, I think it's more than possible he did it." He stood, shuffling through the papers on his desk. "Charity was such a great kid. I can't believe . . . any of this. I was planning to use whatever pull I had on the powers that be over at the university to help her get into veterinary school." Suddenly, he face went deathly pale.

"Dad? Are you okay?" She rushed behind his desk as he half fell, half dropped backward into his chair. Bending over him, she put a hand on his shoulder. "What's wrong?"

"Just a little dizziness." His eyes fluttered shut.

"I'm calling a doctor."

"No," he said, gripping her hand. "Just give me a minute. I'll be fine."

He seemed anything but fine. "Have you felt dizzy before?"

He took a couple of deep breaths. Swallowed a couple of times. "Of course I've felt dizzy before. Haven't you?"

"Not like that."

"It must be a stress reaction." He opened his eyes, looked around the room. "I've dealt with the results of homicide all my life, but . . . it's never been quite this close before. Charity . . . it's such a waste. Such a goddamn waste."

"I still think I should call a doctor, have you checked out."

"No doctors," he said, his tone leaving no room for further discussion. He ran the back of his hand across his eyes, took another deep breath.

Jane was relieved to see that some color was coming back to his face. "I worry about you."

"I know you do, honey, and I love you for it. But I'm okay. Just a little tired."

The door opened and Maria came in with a can of Sprite.

"Perfect," said Ray, taking the can and popping the top. After a couple of swallows, he said, "Much better. Thanks." He squeezed Jane's hand. She was still standing next to him. "Are you planning to stick around awhile?"

"Absolutely. Kenzie's here, too. So's Cordelia."

"Good, then I'll have some friendly faces in the audience when I address the crowd in a few minutes." As he rolled up his shirtsleeves, he gave her a confident smile.

If Jane had ever had a hero, it was her dad.

Luke tried to call Christopher several times from the campaign office that night. He wanted to give him the news about Charity before he heard it on TV. Christopher always listened to the local news at ten. But sometimes he turned off the ringer if he went to bed early. Luke left several messages asking Christopher to call him back, but when none of them were returned, he began to get worried. He stewed around for another hour, then left around nine, saying he wasn't feeling well. He didn't give a rat's ass that some of his coworkers gave him dirty looks. Maybe they thought he was a rat leaving the sinking ship.

Maybe they were right.

Luke and Christopher had recently moved into one of the new loft condos along the Mississippi River in Minneapolis. So far, only three of the other condos had been sold. They both relished the privacy, although tonight, Luke wished he'd been able to call a neighbor to check on Christopher.

The loft was dark and quiet. He called Christopher's name, walking through each room. When he reached the bathroom he flipped on the overhead light. Christopher was curled into a ball on the tile floor holding a bottle of brandy to his chest.

"No lights," cried Christopher, his words slurred. Before he covered his eyes with his hand, Luke caught a glimpse of how red and swollen they were.

It wasn't hard to put the pieces together. "You heard about Charity."

"I should have protected her," he said, grimacing, leaning his head against the wall as a stream of helpless tears ran down his cheeks.

Before shutting off the light, Luke pried the bottle out of Christopher's hand. "I tried to call you." The only light came from a wall sconce in the hallway.

"Charity's dad phoned to tell me what happened. I . . . I've been throwin' up." He looked around helplessly, reached for the bottle.

Luke held it away. "I think you've had enough."

"Not, enough." Christopher rubbed his eyes, tried to focus. "I tried. I tried so hard to keep her safe."

"Oh, baby, if anyone's to blame, it's me." Luke had been afraid to tell him he hadn't talked to Charity last night and that someone had mentioned seeing her leave with Corey. "It was Hodge. You're going to hate me, Christopher, but I never—"

Christopher screwed his head around, looked at Luke from an odd angle. "Hodge?"

"The rapist."

"No. Gabriel killed her. He tried to kill me but—" He wiped his mouth. "But he couldn't. So he went after her. He couldn't stand that . . . that we were friends. He told her that. He demanded that she stay away from me, but she wouldn't. He blames me for their breakup. He's furious at her, thinks she picked me . . . *me*"—he pounded his chest—"over him. He's the one who should be dead. Honestly, swear to God, if he were here now . . . I'd kill him with my bare hands. I would. I'd kill him." He looked around wildly.

Luke set the bottle on the sink. He crouched down and pulled Christopher into his arms, appalled by how much he was shaking. "You're freezing."

"I'm . . . scared."

"Scared of what?"

"Gabriel!" He buried his head against Luke's chest.

"Oh, baby. You're safe."

"I'll never be safe. Never again." Christopher clung to him so fiercely it almost hurt. Luke had never seen him this drunk before. "Look, you can't stay in here. Do you need to throw up anymore?"

"I dunno." His eyes swam in his head. He tried to get up but fell back against the wall.

Luke helped him to his feet. "How about a shower?"

"No way."

"Okay. Bad idea. You probably won't remember this tomorrow morning. But man, you're going to have one hell of a hangover."

"Don't leave."

Luke cocked his head. "Why would I leave?"

"You always leave."

The words stung, but he brushed them away, thinking it was just the alcohol talking.

Luke helped Christopher out of his bathrobe, then got him settled in bed. Sitting on the edge, he removed his shoes. He slipped under the covers without undressing. Whispering that everything would be okay, he circled Christopher's waist with his arm, held him tight.

Luke knew it was a lie. He'd been lying a lot lately. What he feared most was that nothing would ever be all right again.

17

With a brandy resting next to her and the desk light on, Jane sat hunched in front of the computer screen in her study searching for information on the rape Corey Hodge had committed nine years ago. She'd known him almost as long as she'd known Mary Glynn. Not well, of course. But from a distance she'd watched him grow from a stormy, troubled teenager into an impulsive, sometimes self-destructive adult. And yet, through it all, Jane could see that Mary loved and believed in him. It was probably that bond that had kept Corey on the straight and narrow—if anything ever had.

Jane didn't know much about Corey's early years, except for the few comments Mary had made. Before he was arrested, Corey was driving a pizza truck, making deliveries of frozen pizza to various outlets throughout the Midwest.

Jane read through various sites until she finally found something that gave her the particulars of the rape charge.

Louisa Timmons, twenty-six, a dental assistant from Bloomington, had been on her way up to see her boyfriend in Cloquet, just outside of Duluth, when the rape occurred. She'd left work at six, gone home to pack an overnight bag, but got waylaid by her sister who called and asked her to help move some furniture and boxes into her new apartment. She assured Louisa it wouldn't take long. That hadn't been the case. She left the cities late, sometime around one A.M. She'd always been nervous about driving alone at night, but she set out anyway, thinking that it would be only a few hours until she'd be reunited with her boyfriend.

According to the account, she stopped at a rest area around two thirty. She drove off I-35 into the parking area, closed and locked the door to her Honda, then headed straight for the lighted building. She said she remembered looking over her shoulder into the truck area and seeing a midsized transport truck with the word PIZZA written on the side. When asked later how she could see that far away in the dark, she said the parking lot was lighted.

She entered the building, found it quiet and deserted. She thought about looking for the maintenance guy, just to make her feel more comfortable, but instead went directly to the women's room. When she came out, she heard a small pop, then felt an intense cramping pain that spread through her entire body. As weird as it sounded, she thought she'd been struck by lightning.

The next thing she knew she was on the floor, and someone was on top of her, taping her hands behind her back. She remembered seeing the man's hands reach around in front of her and tape her eyes shut. He whispered into her ear, told her to shut up. And then he raped her. When it was over, he flipped her onto her back, pulled up her sweater, and wrote something on her stomach. He left her there on the floor. She lay like that until sometime after three, when a man came in to use the restroom. He had a cell phone and called 911.

The maintenance guy was later found outside with a big goose egg on his head where he'd been hit and knocked out. He said he never got a good look at his assailant and couldn't ID him, except to say that he smelled like he hadn't had a bath in several years. The maintenance man had been out changing the plastic sacks in garbage bins when he was attacked.

The word the rapist had written on Louisa's stomach in bold orange lipstick was *justice*. Just that. The one word and nothing else. Jane wondered if anything had been written on Charity's stomach. So far, nobody had said one way or the other.

During Louisa's interrogation, she told the police about the pizza truck. She thought the letters on the side were red but said she couldn't be positive.

Again, Jane felt guilty for worrying about what effect Charity's death might have on her dad's campaign, and yet she couldn't help herself. Maybe there wouldn't be any effect at all. She hoped Corey had nothing to do with it and that it wouldn't become the negative watershed moment, the weight that would finally tip the scales in favor of Pettyjohn. If Corey had done it, it might give the Pettyjohn campaign the magic bullet they were looking for—at exactly the right time. Here was a vivid, real-life example of what Ray Lawless did for a living. He defended rapists and murderers, the kind of man who had just ended the life of a promising young woman. Her dad was hoping the electorate would vote on the issues. Don Pettyjohn was hoping to make the election a referendum on her father's bad judgment and dirty hands.

Jane looked up from the screen as Kenzie moved into the doorway. "I woke up and you were gone."

"I'm sorry, sweetheart. I couldn't sleep."

"What are you looking at?" She moved around behind Jane, began massaging her shoulders.

"That feels so good. Don't stop." She closed her eyes. She wanted to concentrate on the feel of Kenzie's hands working out the kinks in her upper back, but she couldn't quite let go.

"Come to bed," said Kenzie, nuzzling Jane's neck. "All of this . . . it's out of your hands. The police are working on it. They'll figure it out."

"I hope so," said Jane. Instead of helping, the Web search had left her feeling restless.

"And if you obsess about this homicide the entire time I'm here, I may have to drag you back to Chadwick in a horse trailer and keep you captive for a week or two in the barn."

"That sounds . . . interesting."

Jane switched off the computer and stood up to face Kenzie. Drawing her into her arms, she kissed her softly. For a split second, she remembered that Julia had been in the house just a few nights ago. She felt a pinprick of unease that she'd never told Kenzie about Julia. They'd agreed early on that neither of them needed to take a walk down the other's romantic memory lane. But maybe that had been a mistake. All Jane wanted was to sink into the hazy, intoxicating ache she felt whenever Kenzie was around. "Let's go back to bed," she whispered.

"You're slow, Lawless. But you're capable of learning."

18

Corey pulled the pillow off his head and yelled, "What?" He rubbed the sleep out of his eyes and looked over at the clock. Three A.M. His room was in shambles, as usual, his clothes lying right where he'd stepped out of them a few hours ago.

"Corey, it's me. The police are here to see you." There was a quiver in his aunt's voice.

"Don't come in," he called back, not really sure why he should be concerned that his aunt would scold him for the way his room looked when the freakin' wolf was at the door. "I'll be out in a sec."

"Okay. We'll be upstairs in the living room."

He could tell she hadn't walked away but was still outside the door, listening.

He shoved a bunch of his dirty clothes under the bed, along with a half-empty bottle of bourbon. He pulled on some clean underwear, found a pair of rumpled jeans sticking out from under his dresser, and yanked a sweatshirt off the top shelf of his closet. Sitting down on the bed, he pulled on some socks and his white Adidas. As he drew the shirt over his head, he realized it was the one that said, "Cleverly Disguised as an Adult." The only other one he had said, "Boldly Going Nowhere." With no real choice, he stuck with the first.

Finger combing his hair in front of a small mirror, he decided it was time for the goatee to come off. It looked stupid.

He opened the door and found Mary with her hand cupped to her ear.

"Not cool," he said, turning her around and pushing her up the basement steps. "Did the cops say what they wanted?"

She gave her head a tight shake. "Don't you work in the morning?"

"Yeah, at nine."

When he got to the living room, he saw that both of the cops were actually plainclothes, a man and a woman. "Oops," he said under his breath, immediately regretting his sweatshirt choice. After his hair, it was the first thing the woman cop looked at.

"Are you Corey Hodge?" asked the male cop.

"Yeah?"

"I'm Sergeant Emerson, and this is Sergeant Hamill." They flipped him their badges. "We're here to talk to you about Charity Miller. I understand you know her."

He took in their expressionless faces. They weren't going to give him an inch. "We've met." He dropped down on the sofa. His aunt stood in the kitchen doorway, apparently too nervous to join them in the living room.

"We been told you were volunteering at Raymond Lawless's campaign office," said the woman. She wasn't tall, but she was solid, hefty, not the least bit fat.

"That's right."

"And that you and Ms. Miller were quite friendly," she added.

"We talked."

"We also understand that you visited her at the bank where she works."

"I needed to open a checking account. She told me to come by, that she'd set it up. It was close to where I live, so I drove over."

"You still own a motorcycle?" asked the male cop. Emerson.

"Yeah?"

Emerson shifted his gaze to Mary, then over to his partner, and finally back to Corey. "Where were you yesterday morning between the hours of midnight and three?"

"Why?"

"Just answer the question."

"Well, let's see. I was at the campaign office for a while. I left around ten, picked up some dinner at a Burger King. And then I drove over to my old girlfriend's house, must have been close to eleven. I talked to her boyfriend briefly. After that, I drove home and went to bed."

"Can you confirm that?" asked Emerson, gazing over at Mary.

"I, ah . . . I was in bed."

"Did you hear your nephew come home?" asked Hamill.

She shook her head. "His bedroom is in the basement, so he often comes in through the door inside the garage. If he's quiet, and he usually is, I never hear anything."

Corey was glad she hadn't lied for him.

"I take it neither of you listen to the news," said Emerson.

Mary didn't reply, she just looked embarrassed.

"You wanna cut to the chase," said Corey, cracking his knuckles.

Emerson watched him with his tight, cop eyes. "We're homicide investigators, Corey. Ms. Miller was found dead around six A.M. yesterday morning by a neighbor taking out the trash."

Blinking a couple of times, Corey replied, "Sorry to hear it. But what's that got to do with me?"

"She was hit with a taser."

"Tasers don't kill people."

"They can."

"Bullshit."

"You own a taser, Corey?"

"Nope. And if you're coming to me with some bull crap story that I used a taser on her, you can forget it. I was home, *here,* in bed."

"But you have no proof."

"Can you prove I wasn't?"

Both cops stood.

"We're going to ask you to come downtown," said Emerson, fishing for something in the inside pocket of his raincoat. "Sergeant Hamill will stay here and execute a search warrant." He handed Mary the papers. "Two patrolmen should be here shortly to help."

"Search warrant," repeated Mary, looking like the writing was in Sanskrit.

"For Corey's bedroom and his motorcycle," said Hamill.

"Are you arresting me?" asked Corey.

"No," said Emerson. "I just wanna talk awhile longer."

"Does he need a lawyer?" asked Mary, her fingers kneading the middle button on her robe.

"That's certainly his right, ma'am. But like I said, we just need to talk."

Sure, thought Corey. Like he hadn't heard that one before. "It's fine, Mary. I'll go with him. She won't find anything in my bedroom. Just let her do what she needs to do." He kissed his aunt on the cheek, gave her a hug. "I'll be back before you know it. I haven't done anything wrong. You believe me, don't you?"

She searched his eyes. "Yes," she said weakly.

19

Julia came out of the kitchen carrying a newspaper and cup of morning coffee and sat down on the chesterfield sofa in the living room, wrapping her bathrobe around her legs. She'd turned on the gas fireplace across the room a few minutes before and could feel the warmth starting to circulate. A few degrees colder outside and the rain would turn to snow.

October was a time of change in the north country. She could almost hear the ease of summer being locked away behind a door made of ice and snow. December through March in Botswana was the rainy season—also high summer. The climate was lush, hot, and impossibly humid. The only time the weather turned cool was during the dry season, May through September, and even then, it was nothing like a Minnesota winter. By comparison, Minnesota seemed a stingy place, a country of pale humans who grumbled—and also bragged—about living on such hard, unforgiving land but who loved the place nonetheless, as a sailor might love the sea.

The house she was in at the moment suited her needs, but it wouldn't be long before she went looking for something else. It was more of a cabin, really, the interior of which had been renovated so thoroughly, with such a ruthless eye to modernity, that all of the old-fashioned, wood-smoked, dark, creaky, northwoodsiness it once surely contained had been meticulously expunged. Still, it was comfortable, with a beautiful view of the lake. For some unexamined reason, Julia had come to hate inner cities. It would be hard to talk Jane into leaving her house in Linden Hills, but she was sure they could find someplace that appealed to both of them.

Opening the paper, she searched for an article about Corey Hodge. She'd been following the local political blogs as well as the local papers and knew that Ray Lawless had represented him in a rape case many years ago. If what the TV news had reported last night was true, Corey might be involved in a new crime, this one a rape/homicide. The police had finally released a statement today that stated the cause of death. Surprisingly, it was a heart attack. The taser used to immobilize Charity had interfered with her heart rhythm. Julia had heard of other incidents where tasers had caused deaths, but it was rare. Generally, the individual needed to have some kind of underlying heart condition. In Charity's case, she was so young that her heart had probably never been tested beyond a doctor listening with a stethoscope.

Julia smiled, knowing Jane would be all over this. She would already be sifting through the possibilities, weighing how she could help to prove Corey's innocence. It took a rare sort of audacity to think you had the skills necessary to meet that kind of challenge, but Jane was like that. She'd worked hard and, with little help from anyone, had become a successful businesswoman. She'd also been instrumental in solving some fairly high-profile crimes in the Twin Cities. Who wouldn't admire that?

For the few years Julia had been in Africa, she saw to it that the two major Twin Cities papers had been regularly mailed to her. Since both Jane and Ray were reasonably public figures, she'd been able to keep up with some of what had been happening in both their lives. For instance, she knew about the new club Jane had opened a year or so ago. Julia hadn't gone to see it yet, but she would. Jane may have misread her intentions about the visits to her house, but that would blow over in time.

For the moment, it was the presence of one Kenzie Mulroy that worried Julia the most. She intended to focus all her energy on the new woman in Jane's life. Once she was out of the picture, it might not be clear sailing, but at the very least, Julia would be there to help Jane pick up the pieces of her shattered love life.

Hearing an alarm clock go off in one of the back bedrooms, Julia went into the kitchen to start breakfast. She'd just finished cutting up the fruit for the oatmeal when Neil came out of the hallway, freshly showered, wearing a gray shirt and dark wool Dockers. She was still standing at the sink when he came up behind her, placed his hands on her shoulders, and kissed her cheek.

"How are you feeling this morning?" he asked, popping a piece of strawberry into his mouth.

"Better every day," said Julia. "When does your flight leave?"

"Ten. Which means I need to be out to the airport by eight—eight thirty at the latest."

"Do you need me to drive you?"

"No, a friend's picking me up in a few minutes. I packed last night. To be honest, I never entirely unpack." There was a hint of resignation in the statement.

Julia poured them each a glass of orange juice and they sat down at the small glass-topped table to eat.

"I'll miss you," said Neil, sprinkling brown sugar on his oatmeal.

"No you won't. You'll be so busy at the conference you won't have time to think about anything else."

"I wish you were coming with me."

"There will be other conferences, other opportunities."

The fourth meeting of the International AIDS Society would begin in Sydney, Australia, in two days. Julia had thought about attending. Under other circumstances, she might have gone.

"You know, Jules, you'll have to go back to South Africa when the Southern Africa AIDS Council presents you with that award next year."

"We'll see." She stared at her oatmeal, knowing she should eat but fearing her stomach would rebel.

"Oh. I didn't tell you." He stirred some cream into his coffee. "I heard yesterday that there are some rumblings you might be up for an award because of your work with Doctors Without Borders."

"Really." She was flattered.

"You're an incredible woman," he said, gazing at her with troubled eyes.

"Don't worry about me while you're gone. I'll be fine. I'm much better than I was even a month ago."

"You are," he agreed, eating his oatmeal quickly. "What will you do while I'm gone?"

"Rest. Read. Relax."

"That all sounds good."

"Can I make you anything else?"

"No, I'm fine," he said, twisting the wedding ring on his left hand. "I wish you'd wear your ring while I'm gone. Married women don't get hassled as much as single women."

"I can take care of myself."

"Are you sorry you married me?"

"I never lied to you, Neil. All I can offer you is friendship . . . and gratitude."

He nodded. "One of these days you'll want that easy divorce I promised you."

She could read the pain in his eyes, but there was no way she could stanch it.

During the worst point in her illness, Neil had come to her over and over again, pouring out his concerns. He felt she wasn't getting proper care, the right tests, the best medical advice, but nobody would listen to him because he had no formal connection to her. He was told that the only one who could control the direction of her treatment was Julia herself. She'd been half out of her mind with a fever at the time. Her world had retreated behind a foggy curtain that rarely allowed reality in.

Neil had made his case slowly, day by day, holding her hand, telling her she needed to trust him enough to let him help. The only way he could do that was for her to marry him, in the hospital. He pressed her, said he knew people who would help set it up. Once he had the proper papers, he promised that he would have her moved immediately to a better hospital in Johannesburg. He insisted he would do everything in his power to make sure she was seen by the best doctors in South Africa. And he'd been true to his word. When she was well enough to travel, they'd returned to the United States together, to a clinic in Vermont, where he visited her every day.

It became obvious to Julia over time that, for Neil, this unusual marriage was more than just a necessary legal arrangement. Back in Vermont, he told her that he loved her, that he wanted with all his heart for the two of them to stay married. She was up-front with him at the time and on several occasions in later months. She had no feelings for him other than friendship. She would be forever grateful for what he'd done, but that gratitude didn't include living in a loveless marriage.

He was right about her wanting a divorce, but they could deal with that after he got back from Australia.

A horn honked outside.

"That must be my ride," said Neil. He seemed hesitant to leave.

"Better get going," said Julia, rising, holding her coffee cup.

She waited for him to get his bag, then walked him out to the front porch. "Be safe," she said, pecking him on the lips.

"Miss me a little?"

"Of course I will."

He smiled at her, held her close, and then walked out to the waiting car.

20

You should come see the river," called Luke, standing in front of one of the loft's windows. "It's beautiful—all shrouded in morning mist." He held a can of Diet Pepsi in his hand. It wasn't much of a breakfast, but it would have to do. He had an early meeting in less than half an hour, but he still hadn't decided whether or not he could leave Christopher alone.

Christopher shuffled out of the bedroom, leaning hard on his cane, dressed in his bathrobe and slippers. Luke hadn't seen him out of those clothes in days. He looked disheveled. Hungover. Like he needed a shower and a serious shave.

"How you doing?"

"How do you think I'm doing?"

Luke felt a sudden rush of tenderness. "Take some aspirin."

"I did. So far it hasn't helped." He sat down carefully in a chair, as if his entire body hurt. "Can't say I think much of alcohol as a pain reliever."

"You were really messed up last night."

"I know. You deserve an apology."

"Stop it."

Christopher pinched the bridge of his nose. "I've been thinking. Maybe we should call the police. Tell them about Gabriel Keen."

"We can't be sure Keen did it."

"Of course he did it. He's crazy, Luke. I hardly have to prove that to you."

"The cops will dig into Charity's life. They'll find out about him."

Luke had known for a long time that Christopher lived in a far different world from the one he lived in—a landscape filled with invading shadows, with danger behind every door. For the first few weeks after he woke up in the hospital, he floated on painkillers. But by the time he came home, he was being weaned off them. That's when he finally remembered who had attacked him. A month and a half after the vicious assault in the church parking lot, Luke called the police and sat with Christopher as he gave a statement. Based on that statement, the police were able to get a search warrant. They found a baseball bat at the back of Gabriel's closet. It had been cleaned, but blood and hair from Christopher's head were still embedded in it.

Gabriel Keen was arrested. But before he could be officially indicted for attempted murder, the search was tossed. Without the bat, all the police had was Christopher's word, and it wasn't enough. Gabriel had attacked Christopher because he was gay, because he hated homosexuality and couldn't stand the idea that an ordained elder, one who was so clearly loved and respected by members like Charity, was also a closeted faggot. As Gabriel was let go, an investigation into Christopher's "perversion" was being carried out, one that would end in a church trial. Gabriel was a free man, while Christopher was about to be marked, stripped of his holy orders, and removed from his position as pastor of Merriam Park United Methodist.

Once Keen was released, reality hit Christopher with a sickening thud. Christopher reminded Luke of someone who, without the ability to swim, had been thrown into a dangerously cold lake. No matter how much Luke tried to help or promised to be there for him, Christopher was isolated by violent memories that Luke could only guess at. It took awhile, but Luke finally realized how limited and lame his notion of pain really was.

Feeling a deep grief rise up in his chest, Luke walked over to Christopher, handed him his Diet Pepsi. "Let's go back to bed."

"I can't. I'm up now and I need to do some thinking."

"About what?"

Squinting up at Luke, he said, "You don't seem all that upset about Charity."

"Of course I'm upset. But I'm more concerned about you."

Christopher reached up, squeezed his hand. "Just get out of here. You've got a busy day. All this fuss makes me feel like a child."

"Call me later and let me know how your day is going."

"I will. I think I'll go read some psalms," said Christopher, handing the Pepsi back to Luke.

Luke truly didn't understand. Religion had caused Christopher so much pain, how could he look to it for comfort? Crossing into the hall by the front door, he retrieved his wool Pendleton jacket from the closet, then walked back and stood at the edge of the living room. "Call if you need anything."

"All I need," said Christopher, hanging the handle of the cane over his shoulder, "is to figure out a new plot for my life. This one's going nowhere." He said the words defiantly, dry-eyed, with a hint of humor, and completely without hope.

Outside in the parking garage, Luke settled into his Audi. He stuck his key in the ignition and tried to start the car, but the engine wouldn't catch.

"Damn it all," he said, waiting a few seconds and trying again. This was just what he needed—his car to die on him on a day when he had to be all over the city. He thought a minute and came up with a solution.

Fiddling with his key ring, he found the one to Christopher's Volvo, which was parked on the other side of the underground lot. Rushing across to it, he drew back the door, surprised to find an empty bottle of AriZona Tea in one of the beverage cups. As far as he knew, he'd been the last person in the car. Christopher had driven it to the church on the day he was attacked. The car had stayed in the parking lot until Luke had returned from his business trip and moved it to the lot under the building, where it had sat unused ever since. But if nobody was driving it, where had the bottle come from?

The Volvo started instantly. So did the radio, which was tuned to a classical music station. Luke never listened to classical music. His first instinct was to head back up to the loft and confront Christopher. If he'd been out driving around, why hadn't he mentioned it? But as he thought about it, he decided the question could wait. Christopher didn't need anything more on his plate right now.

Four hours after Corey had been picked up by the police, he and Sergeant Emerson were still at it.

"Let's go over it one more time," said Emerson, arms folded across his barrel chest.

Corey was seated at a table in the same sort of utilitarian, bland meeting room he'd been in so many times before, where the smell of desperation hung in the air like the smell of dirty laundry. He hated the impersonality, as if he was just one more in a long line of nobodies, people who didn't even rate a decent color scheme.

"You say you met Charity the first time you went to Raymond Lawless's campaign office. That was last Sunday."

"For the six hundredth time, yes."

"And the next time you saw her—"

"A couple days later. On Tuesday."

"Where?"

"I dropped by the bank where she worked. She opened a checking account for me. It was lunchtime, so we walked over to the park across the street and had something to eat." Corey had said the same words so many times, it was like he'd memorized them. Emerson kept asking him the same damn things over and over again. He knew why. He was looking for even the slightest discrepancy. It was all a game. If they wanted to arrest him, they would, no matter what he said or didn't say.

"Where'd you get the food?" asked Emerson.

"Like I said, I stopped at a deli before I hit the bank. I bought some stuff to eat for after I was done opening the account. I had it in my saddlebag, so I shared it with her."

"And you don't have a receipt."

"I don't save receipts."

Corey was tired, hungover, and so hungry his stomach was about to eat itself alive. They'd given him a cup of coffee. Big fucking deal.

"When did you see her next?" asked Emerson, chewing on a toothpick.

"The next night, at the campaign office."

"Wednesday night?"

"Right." He leaned in toward the table, dropped his head on his hand. "We talked. Maybe I flirted a little. Again, not against the law. And then I drove around awhile on my bike, had something to eat—"

"Where?"

"I told you. At a Burger King."

"And after you went to Burger King?"

"I ended up at my ex-girlfriend's house."

"What route did you take?"

Corey repeated the same thing he'd been saying for four long hours.

"Your girlfriend's name is Serena Van Dorn."

"Right. But she wasn't home, so I talked to the 'new man' in her life for a couple minutes. We exchanged pleasantries. I told you what we said, almost verbatim. And then I went back to my aunt's house. And no, Mary can't vouch for when I got back because she was asleep."

"And yesterday? Take me through the entire day one more time."

"Oh, Jesus."

"Do it."

Corey began again. He told the cop everything he could think of, ending with him going out to a bar with a few of his work buddies to watch a football game and have a couple beers."

"For a workingman, you don't sleep much."

"I don't have a curfew anymore."

"And so, back to the night in question, Wednesday, from midnight until three in the morning, you have no alibi. Nobody saw you after you left your ex-girlfriend's place."

"Nope."

"Come on, Corey. Are you really going to sit there and tell me you didn't do it when we both know you did?"

He shook his head. "No way. I didn't touch that woman."

"You *want* to tell me, I know you do. If you get it off your chest, you'll feel better."

"I didn't do it."

The cop studied him a few more seconds. He seemed to like long pauses, seemed to enjoy watching Corey squirm.

"Let's go over Wednesday night again."

Corey groaned. But before he could begin his answer, a uniformed cop came into the room and handed Emerson a sheet of paper.

Emerson read through it quickly and thanked him. Sitting back in his chair, he sucked on his toothpick.

Something had changed. Corey could feel it.

"Let's go back one more time to Wednesday night. What did you do at the campaign office?"

"I unloaded some boxes from a semi. Had a few smokes. Talked to a bunch of people, and then I took off."

"You talked to Charity?"

"Sure. She was there. I even said I flirted with her."

"And then you left on your cycle."

"Yeah." He looked away, wondering what the other cop had passed him.

"You didn't take Charity with you?"

Corey's trained his gaze on the piece of paper.

"Maybe you better think long and hard about your answer this time."

He pushed back in his chair, crossed his legs. He'd been finessed before. It was best to wait, make them show their hand.

"We have an eyewitness who says she got on your motorcycle and left with you."

"Okay."

"Okay *what?*"

His eyes strayed to the door. "Maybe we did go for a short ride. I figured if I told you, you'd jump to the wrong conclusion. I didn't kill her, man. When I dropped her back at her car, she was alive and happy as a clam."

Again, Corey looked away. What he'd said wasn't precisely true. Thinking back on it, he remembered kissing her good night. But then she got a call on her cell phone. After she was done talking, she couldn't get away from him fast enough. It was like, all of a sudden, she turned cold as stone. He got pretty pissed about it, too. He remembered standing in the middle of the street, feeling like she'd made a fool out of him. Hell, he'd been nothing but nice to her, and she just shut him down like he was nothing and nobody. He yelled some words his aunt wouldn't like at her retreating car, shouted that he'd be in touch.

"How short was this ride?"

"What?"

"How short was the ride? Where'd you go?"

"Oh, God, I don't know. Around. We just drove around."

"Where?"

"Dinkytown. Then I cut back and we ended up on the West River Road."

"Did you stop?"

"Hell, no." He leaned into the table. "Like I said, I promised I'd take her for a ride and we took it."

"You never said you promised her a ride. When did you tell her that?"

"Christ, I don't know. I guess while we were having lunch at the park. She'd never been on a cycle before, so I said we'd go for a ride. It was completely innocent, man. When we were done, I dropped her off at her car, said good night, got some dinner, and then drove over to my ex-girlfriend's place. End of story. I did not kill her. I had no motive. I liked her."

"You liked her."

"Yeah."

Emerson studied him. "You wanna know what I think happened?"

"Not really."

"You were out for a ride with her, getting along real good. When you bring her back to her car, she smiles at you, you smile at her. Neither of you want to leave it at that, so she invites you over to her apartment for a beer, or whatever. You follow her back there, her in her car, you on your bike. But when you get to the apartment, she doesn't come through. She shuts you down. And here you been thinking you were going to have a real sweet evening together. So you get mad. Things get out of hand."

"That never happened, man."

"Or—" He considered it a moment more. "Maybe you really liked her, so when you got back to her place, you took a chance. You told her the truth. But instead of saying it was okay, it didn't matter that you'd been in prison, she freaked. Went fucking ape shit on you. Maybe it happened right there in the parking lot. And you got nervous, thought someone might call the cops, might think you were hurting her. You wanted her to quiet down, but she wouldn't. So you pulled her into the shadows and roughed her up a little, just to get her to calm down. But instead of backing off, she came at you. Got right in your face and told you she was gonna contact your probation officer, get you in some serious trouble. You didn't mean to kill her. Hell, you'd trusted her, told her the truth. Women can be like that sometimes, right? You think they're thinking something, and they're not. They're thinking the opposite. You got mad. And, like always, you had a taser with you. Hey, like you said, tasers don't kill people, not healthy people. It was an accident."

"No way!"

"I can help you, Corey. I can be the best friend you'll ever have—or your worst nightmare. You pick."

"You're so full of shit."

"You tell me the truth, and I promise I'll work as hard as I can to get the county attorney's office to go easy on you."

"Look. I'm telling you the truth, man. How many times do I need so say it? I'm not stupid. If I was gonna go after a woman, I wouldn't do it the exact same way I supposedly did it before."

"Maybe. Or maybe something drives you to do it exactly that way. Only this time, you weren't so lucky. Your target didn't walk away."

"That is fucking ridiculous. I didn't *do* it."

"Do you hate women, Corey?"

"No."

"Do you think they manipulate you? Lie to you?"

"Manipulate and lie?"

"Yeah."

"If I say yes, does that make me a rapist and a murderer?"

"How about anger? Do you have trouble with anger, Corey?"

"No more than the next guy."

Emerson watched him, tapped his fingers on the table. "You lied to me. What else have you lied to me about?"

"Nothing. I swear."

"There's something you're not telling me."

"No." He shook his head vehemently.

"I *know* you did it, Corey. Maybe not exactly the way I suggested, but it comes down to this. You and Charity ended up in the parking lot behind her apartment building. You pulled the taser, and that was all she wrote."

"If you can prove it, then arrest me. Otherwise I've said everything I intend to say. If you're going to keep me here any longer, I want a lawyer."

Emerson gazed at him for a long moment. "You're making a big mistake."

“I’ll live with it.”

Finally, nodding his head toward the door, Emerson said, “Go. But don’t leave town. You hear me?”

The words surprised Corey. He hadn’t expected to be dismissed quite so easily. Then again, he hardly needed any encouragement. “I hear you. It’s been real.”

I wanna be Christiane Amanpour when I grow up," said Cordelia, sighing loudly through the phone line.

"I thought you adored your work," said Jane. She was up in her bedroom pulling on her boots. Kenzie was downstairs, building a fire.

"I do. But imagine what it would be like to be her. Chief international correspondent for a huge news agency, goes to all these exotic places and appears nightly on TV, looking brave, intense, windblown, gorgeous."

"You're only interested in the image," said Jane. "You can't tell me you'd like to hunker down in a hotel that's being strafed by enemy rocket fire."

"Heavens, no."

"Can't have one without the other."

"Of course I can. I'll stay home and be brave and gorgeous. I'll use a fan to make me look windblown."

Jane could always count on Cordelia to cheer her up with something utterly shallow. Cordelia considered shallowness highly restful. It was the light yin to the dark yang of the world. Jane was just grateful for a little mindless banter after what had happened to Charity.

"Where are you and Kenzie having dinner tonight?"

"At the River Port Inn in Stillwater."

"Lovely. Candlelight. Fine wine. Fine food. Yes, please! You don't want to double-date? I could yell over to Melanie and see if she's interested."

"This communication via window is going to get old. Don't you ever spend the night together?"

"We spend lots of *quality* time together, Janey. Not to worry."

"I don't."

"So, how do you think Kenzie will respond to your surprise?"

"I think she'll be as excited as I am."

"Oops, gotta go. Mel's yelling at me. I'll ask her if she wants to double and get back to you."

"Cordelia, no! I'm not inviting—"

But she'd already hung up.

Later that morning, while Kenzie was out jogging, Peter stopped by.

"Where's your main squeeze?" he asked, taking off his Twins cap. He crouched down to say hi to Mouse. The dog buried his muzzle in the palms of Peter's hands and Peter rubbed his ears.

"Out running. I'm glad you're happy to see Mouse, but we haven't had a real conversation in, what, two months? Don't I rate at least a hug?"

"Sure." He put his arms around her and gave her a rather diffident squeeze. "I wasn't sure you'd want one."

She held him tight an extra few seconds, then backed up. "I thought we called a truce."

"If you say so."

She led the way back to the kitchen, where the coffee was still on. "Want something to drink?"

Peter made himself comfortable at the table, unzipping his leather bomber jacket. "No thanks."

"By the way, here's a new key for my front door. I had the locks changed." She removed one from a drawer and tossed it to him.

"Any particular reason?"

"Long story."

Jane was still getting used to her brother's new style—beardless, with the constant two-day-growth, testosterone-poisoned thug look. He'd always worn his hair on the long side, but now it was cut short, not quite shaved but not far from it. The fact that he didn't look like himself anymore only underscored the very real disconnect that existed between the man he used to be and the one sitting before her now. A fundamental change had taken place in her brother, not all of it good.

Peter dropped his hat on the table. "I'm worried about Dad. Have you seen him lately?"

She explained what had happened last night when she'd been in his office, asked if he'd ever seen anything like that.

"Actually, yeah, I have. This morning. At breakfast he turned the color of spackling paste. I think you and me and Elizabeth should all sit down with him and try to get him to pull back for a few days. Even one day of absolute rest would help."

Elizabeth Piper was the woman her father was currently dating. She was also a lawyer who had joined his firm a few years back.

"We won't get anywhere with that," said Jane. "There are only twelve days left until the election."

Peter shook his head. "Okay then, at the very least, let's insist he have a physical. I'd like a doctor's opinion about what's going on. Maybe it's exhaustion. Or maybe it's something worse."

"That sounds a little more doable. I think getting Elizabeth on board is a good idea."

"Let me check his schedule and I'll get back to you."

"How's the documentary coming?"

"I think it's Oscar material. But I'm biased."

She laughed. "How are Sigrid and Mia doing?" It was a normal enough question, but the absolute worst one she could have asked. As soon as the words were out of her mouth, she regretted them.

A slow burn returned to her brother's eyes. "Fine."

Since the topic had been broached, she asked what she really wanted to know. "Are you and Siggy any closer on the custody arrangements for after the divorce?"

"What do you want me to say?" he asked.

Since they were back to arguing, her own stubbornness wouldn't let it drop. "You moved to a double bungalow in Elk River so you wouldn't have to live together, but you'd still be able to share care of Mia. I'm concerned about how things are going."

"We're still working on it."

"I'm sorry, Peter. Truly I am. I know this has been hell for all of you. I just wish you hadn't—"

"Just stop, okay? Can't you ever let anything drop?" He folded his arms defiantly over his chest, looked around the room as if he was trying to decide on something. "You know, you really piss me off."

"The feeling's mutual."

"Are you ever going to forgive me?"

"None of this has anything to do with my forgiving you."

"It has everything to do with it. In *your* mind. Me, I don't think I need forgiveness because I didn't do anything wrong."

"How can you say that?"

He met her gaze. "You know, Jane. You're tedious. You think you're perfect."

"Oh, right. Well, I guess it's fair to say you don't suffer from a perfection complex."

"I don't. Not anymore. It's a disease. And you know what else? I feel sorry for Kenzie."

Now he'd crossed the line. "You and me, we've got some things to work out, but leave Kenzie out if it."

"You love the fact that she lives in Nebraska, don't you? Oh, you bitch about it, sure, but deep down, it's a perfect situation for you."

"You're making this all about me, when in reality it has nothing to do with me. Why won't you talk to me about what happened last spring, Peter? Help me understand."

"What could your little brother know, right? He's incapable of insight. He's bad, you're good. The world is in its proper orbit."

They were like two soldiers staring at each other across opposite sides of a battlefield. The arguments never went anywhere. Nothing they said to each other these days ever settled anything.

"I think you better go before Kenzie gets back."

"Right. Wouldn't want her to see the pity in my eyes." He stormed out of the kitchen, slammed out the front door.

Sinking into a chair, Jane dropped her head in her hands. She felt shredded. She'd always been so close to her brother. "Not anymore," she whispered.

Not anymore.

Luke was sitting at his desk at the campaign office, staring blankly at his computer, when his cell phone rang.

"It's me," said Christopher as soon as Luke answered.

"What's up?" His first thought was about the car, but he felt it was a conversation they needed to have face-to-face.

"I called Charity's mom and dad a little while ago to see how they were. I thought . . . well . . . I thought maybe I could offer some comfort."

Luke was proud of him for making the call, for coming out of his shell long enough to help two grieving parents.

"They asked me if I'd officiate at her funereal."

"They did? What did you say?"

"That I'd be honored to do it."

"Are you positive you're ready for something like that? You haven't been back to the church since the night Keen attacked you."

"I'm ready. I want to do it. It feels right."

"Okay. Then . . . that's wonderful. Except, will the bishop allow it?"

"I'm still a church elder, still employed on paper. In fact, I don't even need to be ordained to officiate at a funeral service. I think they pretty much have to let me do it."

Luke leaned back in his chair, thinking about Charity. He'd been so angry at her. Now, with her funeral only a few days away, he just felt empty. *"Requiescat in pace."*

"Amen," whispered Christopher.

That afternoon, while Kenzie and Jane were lying on the couch together, talking and generally reconnecting, the doorbell rang.

"Only Cordelia has such perfect timing," said Jane, sitting up. She ran her hands through her long, chestnut hair, then stood. "She and Melanie may want to come with us tonight."

"Not happening," said Kenzie, flopping sideways.

Instead of Cordelia, she found Mary Glynn standing outside. "Mary, hi. Come in." The older woman looked like she was on the verge of tears. Jane was pretty sure she knew why.

"It's Corey," said Mary. She was wearing a raincoat, which she pulled tightly around her plump body. "The police stopped over this morning to question him."

Jane led her into the living room, where Mary eased down on the rocking chair by the fireplace.

"You remember Kenzie," said Jane, sitting back down on the couch.

"Sure I do." She forced a smile. "I'm sorry to interrupt you two—"

"It's fine," said Kenzie. "We were just talking about our dinner date tonight."

Taking a tissue out of her pocket, Mary continued. "Two homicide investigators came to my house in the middle of the night. One of them took Corey downtown to talk to him, while the other stayed to search his bedroom and his bike."

"Did they take anything?"

"A black plastic sack. I don't know what was in it. I thought for a second they were going to impound his motorcycle, but after doing all this fancy testing on it, they left it behind. I haven't slept a wink since three A.M. I just feel . . . so jumbled."

"It's all right," said Jane. "Take your time."

She took a breath. "Do you know what happened?"

"Afraid so."

"They're accusing my nephew."

"Did they arrest him?"

"Thank God, no. He called me a little while ago. He was at work. They kept him in a small room at City Hall for hours, asking him the same questions over and over, but they let him leave. For now. I don't think it looks good, Jane. He said to me, 'Mary, I'm not that stupid. If I was going to hurt someone, I sure wouldn't do it the same way I supposedly hurt someone else.' I believe him. But just like last time, it's going to be another railroad job. The police have him in their sights and they're not going to look for anybody else."

"I'm not saying that doesn't happen," said Jane, "but I think you need to give this some time."

"There *is* no time," she cried. "If the real murderer isn't caught—and I mean right away—Corey is headed for prison again for sure. I'm ashamed of myself for coming over here, Jane, but I didn't know who else to turn to. Please, if there's any way you could help—"

"You want me to talk to my father again? He wouldn't be able to represent Corey."

Mary covered her face with her hands. "I feel like such a wretch. I know I'm asking way too much, but . . . maybe—" She wiped her eyes with the tissue. "Maybe he'd know someone who could."

Jane wasn't sure what her father would think about finding a pro bono lawyer for Corey. There could be political fallout if people found out. "I'll see what I can do." She glanced at Kenzie and saw an odd tightness in her face.

"There's more," continued Mary, her hands opening and closing nervously. "You've got that PI friend, Mr. Nolan? I met him once. He seemed very professional. Do you think you could look into it yourself—maybe with Mr. Nolan? You may trust the police, but I don't. If all they do is look for evidence to prove my Corey's guilty, then they'll never find the real murderer. Someone *else* has to look. Will you do it, Jane? I'm desperate. I'd do anything you ask. I'll clean your house and your father's house for the rest of my life for free. I'll clean your friends' houses. Just say you'll help Corey and me."

Mary was so worked up that Jane was afraid she was going to have a stroke right there in the chair. "Of course I'll help." She'd already come to the conclusion that she would do a little digging on her own.

Instantly, Mary was up, pulling Jane to her feet. "Thank you, thank you. You're an angel. I've been lighting candles for you and your father for years. I want to give something back, in my own way. All I really have are my prayers."

Jane took Mary's hands, held them in hers.

"I'm so relieved." This time her smile didn't look quite so artificial.

Putting her arm around Mary, Jane walked her to the door. "Just don't expect miracles."

"Oh, I never expect them," said Mary. "But that doesn't stop me from praying for one."

For dinner that night, Jane had picked a restaurant on the northern edge of downtown Stillwater, reserving a table that faced the St. Croix River. The fog had lifted midafternoon, revealing a chilly, sparklingly sunny day, which turned into a crisp, clear evening.

While they were enjoying their wine and appetizers, Jane had the distinct sense that someone was watching her. Call it survival instinct, but she figured all women had the same kind of sense. She looked around, but nobody stood out. And then, about half an hour into the evening, the feeling disappeared.

"There's something I wanted to talk to you about," said Kenzie, taking a bite of her main course, a slow-roasted pork with a root vegetable ragout. "There's a sixteen-day tour of the major sites in China being offered in December. The college shuts down for four weeks, so I'm free. I was thinking . . . it might be something we could do together. It would be over Christmas. I know that's always a big event for you and your family, but this would be incredible. We'd see the Great Wall. The Forbidden City. The classical gardens in Suzhou and Hangzhou. We'd even spend some time in Shanghi."

She sounded so excited that Jane found herself getting excited, too. "Can I think about it?"

"If we're going to do it, we'd need to book it soon."

"Just give me a couple of days. I need to check a few things at work, talk to my dad."

"But you're interested?"

Jane smiled. "Yes, I'm definitely interested."

Running a finger along the edge of her wineglass, Kenzie continued. "When are you coming down to Chadwick again?"

"After the election. But now, with this new twist—"

"You mean Mary Glynn dumping all her problems in your lap." Her words were suffused with frustration. She almost sounded angry.

"Well, yes, I guess that's one way to put it."

"You're too easy, Jane. People use you."

"I guess I don't see it that way. But back to your question. I know you've been incredibly patient. And you know how much I appreciate all the time you've given to my dad's campaign. It will be much easier for us to get together once the election is over and I can use the Cessna again."

Kenzie reached across the table and took hold of Jane's hand. "It's just that I miss you when I don't see you for weeks. We have so little time together that I'm jealous of anything that might wreck our plans."

"Do you know how much I love you?"

"Yeah, I think I do."

"Just cut me a little slack, okay."

The touch of Kenzie's fingers seemed to linger on her skin long after she'd withdrawn her hand.

When they were finished eating, Jane caught the waiter's eye. A server materialized and collected all the plates and glasses.

"Are you ready for the surprise?" asked Jane.

"Should we order some brandy?"

"Brandy? No, we need to go."

"Go?" said Kenzie, clearly confused.

Back outside, they walked across the road, closer to the St. Croix

River. Jane stopped at the edge of the grass, drinking in the darkness. Pulling Kenzie into her arms, she kissed her, first on the eyelids, then on the tip of her nose, and finally her lips. "How did I ever get so lucky?"

"Where are we going?" asked Kenzie

"Just follow me."

They started to walk north along highway 95.

"It's dark," said Jane, "but there's a moon, so I think you'll still be able to see it."

Roughly a hundred yards on, they stopped. Kenzie stepped away from Jane and walked to the edge of a huge moonlit pit. "This better not be the scene where you shove me into the abyss so you can collect all my insurance money. Just so that we're on the same page, I don't have any."

Jane laughed. The air had cleared her head, sharpened her senses. "No, this is where I tell my brilliant, amazing girlfriend that I'm opening another restaurant." She raised her hands like she was holding up a sign. "It's going to be called the St. Croix Roadhouse. That's tentative. It could change."

Kenzie turned to look at her. "Another . . . restaurant? *That's* the secret?"

"Yes!" said Jane, spinning around. "I've got two partners this time. You know how I've been talking your ear off about the local food movement, sustainability, organic food, pasture raised animals—well, this is going to be the culmination of all of that. And what's more, we're going to build a totally green building. Low-voltage light fixtures, FSC-certified wood, low-VOC caulks and adhesives. And we're going to reuse and repurpose existing materials whenever we can. That's not my expertise, but it's all part of the package. I am *so* excited!" She grabbed Kenzie and spun her around. "I've got the specs back at the house. I'll show them to you when we get home."

"Great," said Kenzie, turning her back to Jane.

Jane waited for a show of excitement, but there wasn't any. "Is something wrong?"

"What could be wrong?"

"What is it?" asked Jane. "Tell me."

"I was just being silly."

"About what?"

"Well, I thought you'd finally come to the same conclusion I had. That we should get married."

Jane realized instantly that she'd made a huge blunder. "Oh, sweetheart, I never meant for you to—"

"Like I said, I was just being silly."

"No, no." Jane stared at her stupidly. "Of course you thought it would be something like that. I should have realized . . . but I was so caught up in the plans—"

When Kenzie finally turned around, Jane could see that an enormous distance had come into her face.

"Honestly, sweetheart . . . I—" She was blathering and she knew it. "I . . . I'm just not sure I want to get married. I love you, you know that. But do you really think it's smart to get married when we don't even live in the same town?"

"Smart? What's smart got to do with it? It's exactly what I said last summer. You're afraid of commitment."

"Just think for a minute. Sure, we've been together for two years, but when you count up the time we've actually spent together—weekends, some longer vacations, a couple long summer stretches—it adds up to just under six months. Not a lot of time."

"And whose fault is that?"

"Fault?" The bitterness in Kenzie's voice passed through Jane like an electric shock.

"In the two years I've known you," said Kenzie, "you've opened a second restaurant, which took virtually all of your time. You told me to be patient, and I was. And then you connected with that PI. If I could drop-kick him off a cliff, I would, and I'd never look back. You're already so busy you barely have time to breathe, but there he is, whispering in your ear every chance he gets, trying to entice you into helping him on this case or that. And now you tell me you're about to start work on another restaurant, which will suck away what's left of your time. And of course, someone drops a crime 'issue' in you're lap and it's, 'Sign me up!' Where do I rate, Jane? When do you ever put me first on your freakin' to-do list?" She grabbed Jane's hand, pulled it between her breasts. "Don't you miss this when we're apart? I do. I ache to be with you."

Jane could feel Kenzie's heart beating wildly. She stumbled over an answer but quickly realized she was in way over her head. The realization of how badly she'd misjudged the situation was starting to sink in.

"What do you want from me?" asked Jane. "Just tell me. Should I back out of the deal?"

"No." She twisted away.

"Then what?"

"I don't know. I just know that I never come first. And it's always going to be that way."

"That's not true," said Jane, closing the space between them, trying to hold Kenzie in her arms.

But Kenzie pushed her away. "I think we better go home."

"We should stay, talk this out."

"Screw that." She pulled off her scarf and stomped back toward her truck.

Jane realized she had to say something, had to make Kenzie understand that she did love her, but at the moment, she was overwhelmed, confused, silenced.

Standing numb and cold under the vast, uncaring stars, Jane looked down into the pit that was soon to become her next restaurant, feeling like a mourner at a grave.

Luke dragged in through the front door of his condo shortly after eleven. He tossed his keys into the brass bowl in the entryway and loosened his tie. Removing his coat, he hung it in the closet next to Christopher's suede jacket. He touched the jacket, pressing the sleeve to his cheek, remembering all the good times they'd had together when Christopher had been wearing it. He couldn't help but wonder if those good times were all gone.

All the lights were off in the loft, but the blinds were open so the lights along the river cast a bleached silver glow over the interior. The dregs of Christopher's dinner—a plate with a half-eaten sandwich—were sitting on the counter island between the kitchen and the dining room.

Luke should have been exhausted, but instead he felt wired. Maybe he'd poured himself one too many cups of coffee over the course of the evening, or maybe, in a rare prescient moment, he was beginning to understand that his life was beginning to come apart.

The tenor around the campaign office all day couldn't have been more subdued, even dismal at times. The flood of support Lawless had been receiving all summer and fall had been reduced, for the moment, to a trickle. The electorate appeared to be in a wait-and-see mode.

Luke had to give the old man credit. He was out there again today, beating the bushes for support, hammering away at his policies, the issues that mattered to him. He wasn't dodging reporters, or off licking his wounds. He'd appeared on two talk radio shows, never ducking a question. Every morning the old guy came out fighting. The demise of his campaign, if it occurred, wouldn't be from any one thing but from an accumulation of negatives in the voters' minds. No matter what the pundits said, neither campaign could feel completely confident until the votes were counted. In the slightly altered words of the poet John Donne, "Never send to know for whom the fat lady sings; she sings for thee."

Because the condo was dark and quiet, Luke assumed that Christopher had gone to bed. He'd talked to him once more in the late afternoon, long enough to find out that the church had given its okay for Christopher to officiate at Charity's funeral service. Luke assumed the Miller family had put some pressure on the powers that be at Merriam Park United Methodist and that was the only reason he'd been granted the go-ahead. He seemed to be taking it all in stride.

Tiptoeing past the darkened bedroom, Luke went straight into the study. He switched on his desk lamp, then glanced at Christopher's laptop and saw that, as usual, it was buried under papers, magazines, and a few books. His interest in computers would never be anything other than utilitarian.

As Luke sat down at his desk, he noticed that his bottom left-hand drawer was slightly ajar. He opened it and withdrew the only thing he'd ever kept inside—a metal box. Finding the key in the top drawer, he unlocked it and flipped back the cover.

"Oh, shit," he whispered, sucking in a breath.

For years, Luke had carried both a .38 revolver and a taser with him on the road. He felt he needed them for protection. The revolver was in the box, but the taser was missing. Closing the top, he put the box back in the drawer and eased the drawer shut with his foot. And then he sat there, frozen in his chair, thinking about what it meant and what he should do about it.

Rising from the chair a few minutes later, he stripped in the hallway, balled his clothes up and stuffed them in the hamper, then went into the bathroom and took a hot shower. He stood in the spray and the steam, trying to empty his mind and achieve peace. He decided he wasn't any more successful with the Zen of life than he had been with Christianity.

After toweling off, he brushed his teeth and then crawled into bed, careful not to wake Christopher. At least he had the night to think about what to say about both the car and the taser. He'd just gotten comfortable on his stomach when Christopher said, "How was your day?"

The sound of his voice was like the prick of a knife. "Oh, shit, did I wake you?"

"No, I was just lying here, enjoying the sound of you being home."

Steeling himself for the conversation he was dreading, he flipped over on his back, sat up a little. "My day was okay. How about you?" He wanted to start with a few easy questions. They'd made a rule right after Christopher had come home from the hospital. His sleep was so beset by bad dreams, that anything that might cause him anxiety was always left until morning. Luke was about to break that rule.

"I've been making notes," said Christopher.

"About?"

"Charity's funcral. I've still got a few days to pull it together."

Luke cleared his throat. "How will you feel about going back to Merriam Park?"

"I've got to do it sometime. I can't hide here forever."

Waiting a beat, Luke said, "Christopher?"

"Hmm?"

"My car wouldn't start when I left this morning. So I took yours."

"Oh." He laughed. "You must have thought a ghost had been in there."

Not what he'd expected. "Why didn't you tell me you'd been out?"

"Because I wanted to surprise you, you knucklehead." He put his hands behind his head, breathed in deeply. "You want the grisly details?"

"Sure."

"Well, my first time out completely alone was about two months ago. Just for a walk that time. I had an immediate panic attack, which sent me straight back up here. I thought I'd never make it past the doors downstairs. But I tried it again a couple of weeks later, and this time, I walked around for a good twenty minutes before I got that awful feeling in my chest—like I couldn't breathe. I've been working at it steadily ever since. One afternoon, I decided to get in my car. Just sit in it, you know? I touched everything, started the engine. I even turned on some music, tried to remember what it was like when I had a life."

"Oh, baby—"

"No, don't feel bad about it. There was no way you could help. I had to do it myself. And I didn't want to tell you because I'd get to a point, but then I'd regress. I had to do it in my own time and in my own way. The next day I backed the car out of the parking space and took it for a drive. It seemed to help to have music on, sort of normalized things. And before I knew it, I was sailing around Lake Calhoun, feeling pretty good. Not great. Not without fear. It's funny about panic. You get panicked that you're going to feel panic. But the more it didn't happen, the better it got. I even drove around at night a couple times, stopped to buy a special bottle of wine for your birthday next month. That was hard. I felt exposed, vulnerable, but I did it. And I've walked up to Dunn Brothers twice after dark, ordered a pastry and a cup of coffee. Honestly, Luke, I think I'm starting to feel like I've got my life back again."

Luke wanted to ask about the taser, but he also wanted to make this positive moment last. Moving over, he propped his arms on either side of Christopher's body, leaned down, and kissed him. "You're very brave."

"No. I just did what I had to. I did it for both of us. So we could get our lives back on track." He pulled Luke down against him and whispered, "I love you so desperately. I'm sorry I've been such a trial."

"Shhhh," said Luke, pressing a finger to Christopher's lips. "No more words. Show me how you feel."

23

Corey sat on his bed, completely dressed, his door partly closed, listening to Mary upstairs in the kitchen. She'd arrived home a few minutes before and turned on *Car Talk,* just like she always did on Saturday mornings. He could smell the coffee brewing. Around eight, she'd come down and listened at his door, but she hadn't knocked. He'd gotten home late again, and, being the kind soul that she was, she must have figured he needed his sleep more than he needed to be dragged upstairs for breakfast.

As much as he wanted to think otherwise, he figured it was just a matter of time before the cops came calling again. Under other circumstances, he might have split right away and never looked back. But because he realized he now had a son, nothing on earth was going to keep him from getting to know that kid. Not even his goddamn temper. His life had to appear completely normal to the cops, but he'd fake them out—and everyone else—when it became necessary. His goal was to keep things going as long as possible. He knew what he needed to do. He was actually looking forward to it.

Corey had staked out the Unicorn bar again last night hoping to talk to Serena without her new boyfriend around, but when she walked out, she had three people with her—all guys who looked lit and loaded for bear, so Corey hadn't approached her. He drove home depressed and alone.

But this morning, when Corey smelled the bacon frying, he understood that Mary had trotted out the big guns. He'd never been able to resist bacon. In Corey's lexicon of the way the world worked, a person had to be just plain weird not to like the smell of frying bacon.

Tramping up the stairs, he stood in the doorway to the kitchen. "You look tired, Mary."

She lifted the last piece of bacon onto a plate covered in paper towels. "Nothing a good breakfast can't fix."

"Did you wait up for me last night?"

"Well, no, but—"

"You waited up."

She turned, smiled softly.

"You're too good for this rotten world."

"Don't say things like that. Hey, you cut that silly goatee off your face."

Corey felt the skin on his chin for the first time in over a week.

"Why don't you come to Mass with me tomorrow? And confession—"

"I know. Confession is half an hour before Mass."

She nodded, her back to him as she dished up their plates. "Will you go?"

"I'll think about it." When she set the plate in front of him, the sight of it almost made him cry. She'd made pancakes. Pancakes were for special days, home-from-school days, snowstorm days. He raked an arm across his face. He didn't know what was happening to him, wearing his heart on his sleeve the way he'd been lately. He had to get a better grip. "This looks fabulous."

"I thought we could both use a treat." She sat down next to him, put her hand on his arm.

"Listen, Mary—" he began, picking up the paper napkin and

beginning to shred it. "There's, um, there's something I need to tell you. Something I learned a couple of nights ago. I think it may be the best thing that's ever happened in my life, other than you."

She looked up into his face with those soft blue eyes of hers. He could tell she was steeling herself for the worst.

"I've got a son, Mary."

Her eyes widened.

"Serena had a child shortly after I went in. She never told me back then, but I saw him the other night. He's the spitting image of me. Crazy red hair. A mass of freckles. His name's Dean. She even named him after me."

"Serena told you all this?"

"No, but when I was over there meeting the new boyfriend, I saw him. Serena's playing hard to get at the moment, but she'll talk to me now that I know about Dean. She has to."

"Oh, Corey—"

"Isn't that, like, the greatest news?" He smiled, felt his chest expand with pride.

She didn't return the smile, but she didn't launch into some Catholic prayer for forgiveness either.

"I'm a father, Mary. I've got a son!" He poured syrup on his pancakes, tucked into them greedily. "Aren't you a little happy?"

"Honestly? I don't know what to say."

"Well, I do. I'm walkin' on air. And you can take this to the bank. I'm getting to know that kid, one way or the other."

"What's that mean?"

"With or without Serena's permission." He winked. "But I think I'll get it. She's not mean-spirited. She'll want Dean to know his real dad."

"Corey, honey, listen to me. You're not being realistic. Until Charity Miller's murder is cleared up, you're in no position to demand anything from Serena."

He thought about it. "We'll see."

They sat at the table for a few minutes, listening to the radio.

Some woman was talking about fried food, how it wasn't as bad for you as most people thought. It was probably bullshit. You had to be a complete moron to believe the experts since there were so many of them and they always seemed to be changing their minds.

"Corey," said Mary, finally, pushing her plate away, "you should know that I talked to Jane Lawless yesterday."

He stopped chewing. "I don't want her help." He pointed his fork at her. "I don't want her father's help either. You stay away from them, you hear me?" As quickly as his temper flared, he regretted it. "Oh, God, I'm sorry. I don't mean to yell at you. But I meant what I said. I don't need anybody's help."

She looked up at the clock on the wall, tried to keep her face neutral, but he knew he'd hurt her.

"I'll get us some java," he said, pushing away from the table. "Really, I shouldn't have jumped at you like that. I just don't want anything to do with that family."

"But why?" asked Mary. "If you dislike them so much, why are you donating time at Ray's campaign office?"

He shrugged, set two filled mugs on the table. "I was curious." He could tell by the look on her face that she didn't buy it, but that wasn't his problem. As he reached into the refrigerator to get out the half-and-half, he saw a folded piece of yellow paper sticking out from under the Saturday paper. He picked it up.

"Don't read that," she said. She was up in a flash, grabbing it out of his hand.

He grabbed it back. "Why? What's it say?" He opened and read it out loud: " 'Block meeting tonight. For those of you who haven't heard, a level-two sex offender has moved into our neighborhood. If you feel, as we do, that this should never have been allowed, and want to brainstorm ways to have the man removed, please come tonight for a neighborhood discussion. Seven P.M. at the home of Dave and Kelly LaForge, 5924 Sunrise Drive.' "

Corey crumpled the paper. He was so angry, he was shaking. "Where'd you get this?"

"It was under my windshield wipers when I left for the grocery store. Corey, now, just calm down. Getting upset isn't going to solve anything."

He tossed it in the trash and headed for the door.

"Please!" she pleaded. "Think about what you're doing for once!" She rushed out after him. "Just leave it alone," she called. "It will all blow over if you don't stir things up."

"Like hell it will," he shouted back. He was already across the street. He ripped a flyer off a Chevy Astro. "Do you know them?" he yelled over his shoulder, looking around for more.

"Yes," said Mary. She came down off the steps, followed him as he continued to remove the flyers from trees, cars, telephone poles. "They're good people. They just don't understand. Let me talk to them."

Corey ignored her. The yellow signs were everywhere. Grabbing them one by one, he ripped them into small pieces and tossed them in the air.

"Stop it," said Mary, stamping her foot. "Stop it this minute!"

"Stay out of this, Mary. Go back in the house." He zigzagged down Sunrise Drive, hands balled into fists. Each time he came across another flyer, he ripped it to pieces. Cars honked at him for darting out into the street. He gave them the finger and kept going.

"You listen to me, young man." Mary was furious now, her face was crimson. She pointed at him. "You will stop this right now or you will leave my house and never come back."

By the time he'd reached the LaForge place, a few people were standing on their front steps, watching both him and his aunt. He banged on the front door, rang the bell a bunch of times, then banged on the door some more. He saw the curtains move in the living room. "Come out here and talk to me," he demanded, kicking the door with his boot. "You goddamn fucking cowards. Come out here and face me!"

"Corey, I mean it! This is it," yelled Mary. "I've reached the end of my rope."

"Go home," shouted Corey.

"I will not!" She stood her ground halfway down the street.

When he turned around, he saw that everyone who'd come out to watch them had retreated into the safety of their houses.

"You all listen to me," he screamed, jumping over the railing and landing in the center of the LaForges' front yard. "I served my time! I'm a free man now and I can live anywhere I damn well please!" He took a breath, walked out to the edge of the sidewalk, pointed his finger at every house on each side of the street. "None of you know what really happened. I'm innocent. I never hurt that woman. I never should have been sent to jail! You motherfucking morons want to condemn me for something I didn't even do!"

He charged back to Fifty-ninth, past his aunt, letting her outrage slide off him. He was sweating, shaking, seething inside. "Fuck you," he screamed at nobody in particular, turning at the end of the block and heading back to the house.

Mary rushed up behind him. When he turned around, she slapped his face hard. "You're a disgrace."

"You can't expect me not to fight back," he shouted, wiping the sweat off his forehead with his forearm. Opening the garage, he walked his motorcycle out into the drive. "I'm so goddamn sick and tired of people passing judgment on me."

"Where are you going?"

"You just threw me out."

"Nobody pushes my buttons the way you do. You drag me down to your level and I won't have it!"

He lifted his head at the sound of a siren. Climbing on his bike, he started the motor. When he looked at Mary, he was instantly sorry, but he took off toward Penn, heading for the Crosstown freeway.

Jane and Kenzie hadn't said much in the truck coming home from Stillwater. It wasn't that Jane didn't want to talk, but Kenzie had cut her off, saying she was too angry to have a rational conversation. She needed time to think. Jane would have preferred to deal with the problem right away. As it was, she got little sleep and was up early, kicking around the house, trying to figure out what she should not only say, but do.

Jane had barely seen her father during the last nine months. She'd been looking forward to Christmas when the family would finally have some time together. She had hopes that she might even get a chance to mend some fences with her brother, but if she needed to give that up to make Kenzie happy, she would. Kenzie didn't have any family in Chadwick. Her older sister was in prison, and she didn't get along with her older brother. Both of her parents were dead. Family didn't mean as much to her as it did to Jane. But again, Jane was more than willing to give on that point, if only Kenzie would talk to her long enough to find out.

Kenzie came down as Jane was cleaning the refrigerator. She'd spent the night in the guest bedroom.

"I'm going out for a run," she said, bending over to give Mouse a good morning rub.

Jane couldn't read anything from her expression. "Will you be gone long?"

"I'm taking my truck. Think I'll drive over to Lake of the Isles and run over there."

"Before you go . . . just tell me you don't hate me."

A hand rose to her hip. "No, Lawless, I don't hate you."

"But you're still angry."

She stood in the doorway a few seconds, then said, "I'll see you when I get back."

Jane finished cleaning the refrigerator. By ten she'd calmed down enough to sit on the couch in the living room with a magazine. She hadn't calmed down enough to read it, just to hold it open. She sipped from a cup of tea, wishing it was a shot of bourbon, and eventually drifted into her office, where she worked until she heard Kenzie come back.

"I'm taking a shower," called Kenzie, her feet thumping up the stairs to the second floor.

"This is ridiculous," Jane said to Mouse. The slow torture routine, if it was meant to soften her up, was beginning to produce the opposite effect.

When Kenzie finally came down, Jane was back in the living room. Kenzie was carrying her suitcase and overnight bag. She set them in the foyer. She was dressed in a blue silk shirt, brown leather vest, and worn jeans, her reddish-blond hair spiking in every direction because it was still wet. All Jane could think of was that she wanted Kenzie in her arms, not halfway across the room. She wanted things back the way they were yesterday, before she'd taken her to Stillwater and lit the bomb that was about to blow up her world.

After a few tense seconds, Jane stood and said, "Are you . . . just going to leave?"

Kenzie's gaze floated around the room. "I think so, yeah."

"So, is this it? We're over?"

She looked down at her cowboy boots, then up at Jane. "Honest to God, Lawless, I don't know."

The silence that descended felt vast. Arctic.

Jane spoke first. "This is all because you think I'm a workaholic. That I never have any time for you."

"That's part of it."

"The new restaurant pushed you over the edge?"

"I wouldn't put it that way. Maybe it's what helped me finally understand something important about you."

Jane's eyes narrowed. "I'm a businesswoman. I'm ambitious. I can't just tread water and make it in the restaurant world. I don't think any of that makes me a bad person."

"You're right. It doesn't."

"You have interests, too, that take you away."

"I do."

"Then . . . what? What's so wrong with us? With me?"

"Time," said Kenzie. "Time and love."

"You're saying I don't love you because I'm pursuing a career? Because I'm busy?"

Kenzie moved out of the foyer and leaned against one of the living room arches. "I'm saying that you have these boxes in your brain, Lawless. I'm in one of them. You open it every now and then and pull me out, talk to me a little, show me some affection, but you've got way bigger, more exciting boxes than mine."

"That's not true."

"From where I'm standing, it is."

"Sure, you're not the only thing, or person, that's important to me. But I love you. I want to make a life with you."

"How?"

"How? What have we been doing for the past two years?"

"Missing each other."

"That's too easy. From the beginning, we knew a long-distance relationship would be difficult."

"But I thought . . . oh, hell, I don't know what I thought. I hoped you'd move to Chadwick, or that somehow, I could move to Minneapolis. But it hasn't happened, and at this point, I don't think it ever will."

"You're angry, or you're hurt, so you're taking the negative side."

"There are lots of negatives, Lawless. For instance, your father buys this plane. You learn how to fly it, and I think, yeah! This will be the ticket. You tell me it will make it so much easier for us to get together. But you're always so busy that you can't fly down. And then your father runs for governor and he's using the plane all the time."

"That's not my fault. You can't blame me for that."

"That's just the point. I'm not sure anyone's to blame. It's not a matter of does this trump that?"

Now Jane was confused.

"Listen to me, Lawless. What I'm telling you is my truth. Maybe it's not yours, but it's the way it looks to me. See, there's me on one side. On the other, there's always something pulling at you. Your restaurants, or a friend who needs you, or Nolan and his wacky idea that you're going to chuck everything become some idiotic shamus.

Or your dad's campaign. Or your brother's marital problems. Or there's Cordelia's having a meltdown and you have to spend time with her."

"I have friends and family that mean the world to me. You're part of that."

Kenzie just stared at her.

"Look, I . . . I don't know what to say."

"Maybe there's nothing to say."

"You mean, this is it? You're breaking up with me because I'm busy? Because I have friends and a family?"

"I understand you have a life, Lawless. You get to have one. But what I have to ask myself is, is what's left enough for me. It obviously is for you. But maybe you're more independent than I am. Maybe I need more than you do. More of *you,* of your time. I need to be a bigger part of your life."

"You're a huge part of my life," said Jane, moving toward her.

Kenzie held up her hand. "Just stay there for a damn minute. That's what always happens. We start talking and then we get sidetracked. We make love and I lose my train of thought. Don't you get it? I don't think either of us is wrong, or to blame, or . . . the bad guy. I think we're just different, that we want different things."

"And so that's it? We're done?"

Kenzie looked down again, only this time her eyes welled with tears. "God this hurts."

"Give me another chance."

"To do what?" she asked. She moved back into the foyer and picked up her bags.

"You're angry with me," said Jane. "I know you are."

"So what if I am?"

"You can't make a decision like this out of anger."

Silence gathered between them.

Kenzie opened the door, but before she walked through it, she stopped and took off her ring. "Here," she said, holding it out to Jane.

"I don't want it."

"I can't keep it. Not now."

"Just . . . just put it back on. Something to remember me by."

Kenzie set the ring on the table in the foyer. Without looking up, she said, "You be safe, Lawless. I'll never forget you."

As soon as Kenzie's truck pulled away from the curb, Julia put her roadster in gear, waited a few seconds so it didn't look too conspicuous, and finally followed at a respectful distance. She suspected that Kenzie might be leaving today but not quite this early.

Julia had trailed them to Stillwater last night, watched them order dinner while she sat in a dark corner of the bar and nursed a glass of wine. They looked very cozy together, talking intimately, laughing, staring deep into each other's eyes. It wasn't something Julia could stand to watch for very long. She was back home in White Bear Lake by eight, sitting in front of the fire with a brandy and the new FDR biography.

Today, she was simply being playful. She thought it would be interesting to follow Kenzie out of town. Maybe she'd stop somewhere and Julia would get another chance to observe her close up—or maybe even talk to her. Her curiosity about the new woman in Jane's life was boundless. She saw it as a way to gain more insight into Jane, which was the whole point of the game.

But instead of taking 35W south or 55 west, Kenzie got on I-94 going east. Driving a good ten miles over the speed limit, she merged onto 280 going north and eventually merged back onto 35W. Julia figured she must have been headed north all along but had simply circumvented the collapsed bridge closer in to the city. At one point, Julia was near enough to the truck to see that Kenzie was on her cell phone. Clearly, this wasn't the way home. And that only ramped up Julia's curiosity. If Kenzie wasn't headed back to Chadwick, where was she going?

An hour later, the truck's right-turn signal began to flash. Kenzie took the Hinckley exit, made another right at the top of the hill, and continued along Fire Monument Road for a mile or so. Julia was a quarter of a mile back when she saw the truck slow and come to a stop. And it stayed stopped for almost a full minute, until her roadster moved up behind it. Only then did Kenzie make a final right onto Lady Luck Drive, where she pulled into the parking lot of Grand Casino Hinckley, one of the many Ojibwe-owned gambling casinos in Minnesota.

Now Julia really was stumped. Parking behind a van and to the left of the truck about ten spaces, she waited for Kenzie to get out. It took a few minutes because she appeared to be on her cell phone again. When she did finally climb out, she stretched her long legs and glanced around the parking lot with a wary look on her face. Slipping on a pair of dark glasses, she took off her vest, stuffed it behind the driver's seat, and replaced it with a zipper-front suede jacket. Pulling the collar up around her neck, she adjusted the sunglasses and finally made straight for the main entrance. Julia gave her a minute to get ahead of her before she got out of her car and followed.

The interior of the casino was much like the others Julia had seen: all tacky Las Vegas clones with bright lights and garish colors, yet still dim enough to feel like perpetual night. A flyer boasted that Grand Casino Hinckley had more than 2,000 EZ Play slots with payouts of a million dollars a day. There were twenty-eight blackjack tables, large bingo rooms, pull tabs, poker, four restaurants, a lounge, and an attached hotel. And that was just at the casino complex. Beyond that was another hotel, cabins, a golf course, and on and on. Not bad for a small town in the middle of nowhere.

By the time Julia entered, Kenzie had disappeared. Moving slowly through the gaming floor, Julia finally spotted her in the Silver Sevens lounge, still wearing her sunglasses and jacket, sitting alone at the bar, talking to one of the bartenders. Julia made herself comfortable at a table across the room. When a waitress with dyed red topiary hair arrived to take her order, Julia asked for a glass of chardonnay. The woman suggested she run a tab and Julia, operating now on instinct, agreed.

Kenzie appeared to have ordered something harder. From Julia's vantage point, it looked like a double vodka shot. Kenzie swallowed it in four neat sips, one right after the other, and asked for another.

This was growing more interesting by the minute. When Julia's wine arrived, she thought about bringing it up to the bar and attempting to engage Kenzie in a conversation but decided on more of a wait-and-see approach.

Once the second double vodka was gone, Kenzie slapped some cash on the counter and walked out of the lounge. She seemed jumpy, fussing with her sunglasses as if she was afraid someone might recognize her. The fact that she hadn't taken them off made her look even more conspicuous, but she didn't seem to notice or care. She lingered at a few of the blackjack tables and finally chose one. Julia left her untouched glass of wine on the table and wandered out into the crowd. She chose a different blackjack table behind Kenzie so that she could watch without being observed. She played with little enthusiasm but noted that Kenzie had grown far less nervous, no doubt due to the alcohol working its way through her system.

Forty-five minutes later, Julia left the table she was at and moved to Kenzie's. She stood next to her, acting like she wasn't quite sure how the game was played. From the looks of Kenzie's winnings, she was doing more than okay.

"Mind if I watch?" asked Julia. "I'm kind of new at this."

"I suppose," said Kenzie, giving her a sideways glance.

Not terribly friendly, thought Julia. She liked a challenge.

As the afternoon wore on, and as Julia began to do some playing herself, Kenzie seemed to warm to her presence.

Close-up, Julia found Kenzie quite attractive. She had lovely skin, a wonderfully engaging smile, and a dry sense of humor.

Kenzie's small fortune went up and down all afternoon and into the evening. By seven, she admitted out loud that her luck seemed to have deserted her.

"Why don't we take a break?" asked Julia. "Go have a drink, or something to eat. It's on me."

"I'm not that broke."

"Oh, come on. You've taught me more about cards today than anybody ever has. Let me repay you."

Grudgingly, Kenzie allowed herself to be dragged back to the Silver Sevens lounge, where they ordered roasted turkey sandwiches. Kenzie asked for another double shot of vodka, which she downed.

"Boy," said Julia, sipping from a glass of wine, "you seem hell-bent on having one real train wreck of an evening."

"You think?"

"Did you break up with your boyfriend?"

"Something like that."

Julia tried not to react, but inside she was elated. "I'm sorry to hear it."

"It's what happens when you fall for that pathetic pipe dream called true love."

Bitter, thought Julia. Even better. "My name's Jules."

"Kenzie."

"Let's leave it at that."

"What happens in Hinckley *stays* in Hinckley," Kenzie deadpanned.

Julia couldn't help but laugh. "Exactly. You know, you've really got some serious gambling chops."

The waitress with the topiary hair set Kenzie's second double vodka down in front of her. This time, Kenzie let it sit. "I haven't been in a casino in eighteen years."

"Any particular reason."

"Yeah, but I'll spare you the after-school special."

"Hey, I loved those after-school specials. Come on, tell me."

Kenzie hesitated but then relented. "Okay. But it's nothing new. It's not something I've thought much about for many years because I thought I'd beat it. When I was in college, during my junior year, I started gambling, just for fun. Friends were all doing it and so I went along for the ride. Casino stuff. Twenty-one. Slots. I thought it was just a casual thing until I woke up one day and realized I'd lost almost everything. I was on the verge of being tossed out of my apartment. My car had been repossessed. I was flunking out of school. I got some help, thank God. I promised myself I'd never gamble again. And I didn't. Not until I met . . . someone. I gambled, and I lost."

"That's a sad story."

"Sad stories and vodka go together like rice and . . . and—"

"Hot fudge."

Kenzie laughed. "Perfect."

"Where are you from?"

"I drove up from Minneapolis."

"There's a casino a lot closer than here. It's just south of the cities."

"Yeah, but I like poison with my poison." She held up the shot glass. "Can't drink at Mystic Lake."

"Ah."

"I'm making every bad decision in the book. And I'm gonna enjoy every last minute of it."

"And tomorrow?"

She hoisted the shot glass and downed half of it. "This is tomorrow."

The alcohol made Kenzie garrulous, which couldn't have been better. Julia sat back and listened, trying to get a sense of who Kenzie Mulroy really was. She eventually came to the conclusion that Kenzie was well educated, but what stood out was her fundamental lack of cultural underpinnings. She was a hayseed at heart who'd bettered herself, but she remained a small-town girl with small-town attitudes and aspirations. She was rough and essentially ordinary, not right for Jane at all, though she'd probably made for an interesting interlude.

As Julia sipped the wine, she arrived at a quiet revelation. "Will you excuse me for a few seconds?"

"Take your time. I'm not going anywhere."

Heading out of the lounge, Julia made straight for the casino hotel's reception desk. The hotel was conveniently connected to the gaming floor. She booked a suite, paid for it with a credit card, and then stopped one of the bellmen and handed him two one-hundred-dollar bills. "I don't have any bags, but I want you to go up to my room"—she told him the number—"and bring up a fifth of good vodka. Armadale, preferably. But Grey Goose would be okay. I also want a tray of fruit and cheese. Oh, and make sure there's ice and something other than plastic glasses. And while you're at it, if there are any windows to open, open them. If you can find some fresh flowers, bring those, too. Whatever you have left over is your tip. You got all that?"

"Yes, ma'am," said the young man.

"I may be here for a couple of days, so there's more where that came from, if you do it fast and right. What's your name?"

"Jason. And don't worry. I'm on it."

"Good man."

By the time she returned to the lounge, the sandwiches were on the table, but Kenzie hadn't started eating. Good manners, thought Julia. She's halfway to heaven on vodka shots and she still has good manners.

As Julia made herself comfortable, a middle-aged guy with a comb-over and a beer gut, smelling of booze, sweat, and Aqua Velva, dragged a chair away from another table and pulled it up next to Kenzie.

"Hate to see two beautiful gals all alone." He smiled at both of them, but his eyes lingered on Julia.

"Who knew this would be the day my prince would come?" said Julia, taking a sip of her wine.

"You ladies like another round?" He pointed at their drinks.

"Now that you mention it, I would," said Kenzie. She held up her shot glass and caught the waitress's eye.

"It's on me," said the guy, grinning like he'd just struck the mother lode.

"No," said Julia, tapping the table in front of him. "Actually, it's on me."

"Now, don't argue with me, pretty lady."

"Look, whatever you name is," said Julia, "my friend and I are both married."

"So?"

"Where are your Midwestern morals?"

"Left them home tonight." He grinned and leered at the same time.

"You might as well move on. Try the woman over there in the corner, the one with the disgraceful makeup."

The guy turned to look. "Nah, she's not my type."

"Seriously," said Kenzie, "we're not interested."

"Oh, well," he said, with a long, disappointed but tolerant sigh. "Okay. If you change your minds later, I'll be around. The name's Phil." He winked, took one last appraising look at Julia, and then shoved away from the table.

"I'm not really married," said Julia after he'd gone.

Kenzie's eyes were starting to look a little glassy. "Me either. Actually, I'm gay."

"But . . . you said you'd just dumped your boyfriend."

"Girlfriend."

The waitress removed the empty shot glass and replaced it with a full one.

Julia waited a few seconds, then said, "You're very attractive."

Looking surprised, Kenzie leaned into the table. "You trying to pick me up?"

"What if I was?"

"Is this for real? You're a dyke?"

"Bi."

She seemed to be thinking it over. "Hell," she said finally, a sly grin on her face, "if I sleep with you, on top of the booze and a major gambling loss, I will have hit a friggin' trifecta of mortal sins all in one night."

"I've got a suite at the hotel."

"You do?"

"And a bottle of vodka, just waiting for us." Julia felt that, for the first time tonight, Kenzie was really looking at her.

"That guy was right. You are beautiful."

"I bet you say that to all the girls."

Kenzie pressed a fist to her mouth.

Julia realized instantly that being flip was the wrong approach. She might not have known Kenzie was crying if she hadn't noticed that her shoulders were shaking. Dipping her hand under the table, she slipped it over Kenzie's knee. "Let me help. Just for tonight. Let me make it better."

"There's no way you can," said Kenzie, using the napkin to wipe off the tears on her cheeks.

"Maybe not," said Julia, stroking Kenzie's knee, moving her hand slowly up the inside of her thigh. "But what else are you going to do for the rest of the evening? Loose what's left of your shirt?"

"I lose no matter what I do," said Kenzie, closing her eyes, starting to give in to the sensations. "Okay," she said after another few seconds. "Why the hell not?"

Jane was loading another log into the copper fireplace in the back room of the pub when Cordelia breezed in, dressed all in black with the exception of a glittering silver lamé turban. It was going on nine. Jane had spent most of the afternoon and early evening trying to stanch the flow of grief by losing herself in work. She hadn't succeeded.

"Not at the theater tonight?" asked Jane, clearing some dirty dishes off one of the bar tables and taking them over to a bus pan on a standing rack in the corner. She carried the bus pan behind the bar, opened one of the dumbwaiters, and sent it up to the kitchen.

"I stayed through the first act," said Cordelia. "Mel's at home, working on a story, so until eleven, when Mel said she'd take a break, I'm footloose and fancy-free."

Jane turned to look at her. "What's that under your arm?"

"Oh, you haven't met Tallulah yet. Jane, meet Tallulah."

Jane patted the little creature's head, scratched under her chin. She seemed very friendly.

The dog was one of the cutest creatures Jane had sever seen. It was tiny, kind of scruffy, with a mixture of gray and tan hair, soft ears, a black button nose, and dark eyes. It seemed content, almost serene, tucked under Cordelia's arm. "She's half Yorkshire terrier and half toy poodle. You remember Mel's cat died."

"The one that looked like a white bat."

"The Cornish rex, right. A friend of hers is moving to Spain and couldn't take Tallulah with her, so Mel inherited her a few days ago. She's the perfect apartment dweller, manages to get all kinds of exercise just running around Mel's loft, getting lost under the sofa, leaping tiny objects with a single bound. But she whines when Mel is on the computer, so I'm taking her out for the evening."

"How much does she weigh?"

"Seven pounds. She's an adult, completely house-trained. Mel's in love. Actually, so am I."

"Except for the computer thing."

"Well, right."

Jane led the way to her office.

As soon as Cordelia walked across the threshold, Mouse jumped up and skirted around the couch, standing on his back legs with his paws on her stomach, his nose working to understand what fresh horror he was being subjected to. If Cordelia and Mel were included in Jane's family, and of course that's how Jane thought of them, there was a veritable flotilla of animals for Mouse to welcome into his pack.

"Better let them fight it out," said Jane, sitting down behind her desk. Her eyes suddenly welled with tears, as they'd been doing every hour on the hour since Kenzie had walked out her front door.

When Cordelia set Tallulah down, the little critter emitted a sharp bark. Mouse started, backed up a couple of inches. In a spirit of intense but careful inquiry, they began sniffing each other, paying particular attention to each other's nether regions.

"Get it *over* with," cried Cordelia, flopping backward onto the sofa. "Sweet Jesus. You'd think they were proctologists."

With the examination finally done, Tallulah hopped to the rug in front of the fire. Mouse followed at a slower pace. Tallulah chose her spot, fell forward on her front paws, crossed them, then let her hind end sink. Growling softly, she allowed Mouse to curl up a few feet away.

"I guess we know who the alpha dog is," said Cordelia.

"Mouse could eat her for breakfast."

"But he won't. He's too kindly."

"What's Mel working on?" asked Jane, staving off the inevitable—telling Cordelia about the breakup.

"Get this," said Cordelia, pulling off one of her large, silver clip-on earrings. "You knew she was covering the Charity Miller murder."

"I assumed."

"Well, she told me before I left this evening that there's something new in the wind. A new suspect."

"Not Corey?"

"Definitely not Corey. The police are being very tight-lipped about it."

"And you have no idea who it is?"

"None." Apropos of nothing, Cordelia asked, "Do you like my turban?"

"Fabulous."

"I thought so, too. Mel bought it for me." She draped an arm dramatically across her forehead. "I don't suppose—" She let the question trail off, as if she was too weak to finish the sentence.

"Let me guess. You're either hungry or thirsty."

"I could eat. What's on the menu tonight?"

"What are you hungry for? Soup? Appetizers? Dessert?"

"Why don't you choose?"

"Fine. You'll love our whole stuffed cuttlefish."

Cordelia sat up so quickly her turban fell sideways. "On second thought, just run the specials by me."

"You'd probably like the salad special. A poached pear stuffed with Stilton and served with garlic croutons, walnuts, and a sherry vinaigrette. Or there's the light foie gras mousse with candied pistachios and fried garlic bread."

"The second, I think."

"For the main course, why don't you try the pan-seared duck breast. It comes with a special cherry brandy sauce—we make the cherry brandy here—and it's served with sauteed radicchio, baby spinach, and baby bellas drizzled with citrus butter. It may come with something else, too. I can't remember. Maybe a Yukon Gold fondant, or a barley risotto."

"You don't know for sure?"

"I've had kind of a hard time focusing today."

"Really."

She said the word with such force that Jane knew she was in for a grilling. But first things first.

"You can tell me about that in a minute," said Cordelia. "What about a wine selection?"

"I feel like Armagnac. That okay with you?"

She waved her hand. "I am in your hands."

Jane called up to the kitchen and ordered Cordelia's food. She hadn't felt like eating all day but figured she'd better put something in her stomach if she intended to drink Armagnac. She ordered a bowl of the pub's mushroom-barley soup and a baguette and butter. She also asked that a bottle of twenty-year-old Dartigalongue Armagnac be sent to her office with two glasses.

"Ah," said Cordelia, hands stuffed behind her head, "I love the cosmopolitan life. It was fate that my best friend would become an eminent restaurateur, with all the world at her feet."

Jane said nothing, mainly because the comment was so off the mark it was laughable.

"So, now that *that's* out of the way, tell me about your lack of focus."

"You've never been unfocused?"

"Don't be coy." She sniffed the air like a mouse about to leave the safety of a wall crack. "Let me be more specific. What did Kenzie think of your surprise last night?"

"Loved it."

"That's great, Janey. For a minute there, you had me worried." She closed her eyes with a satisfied smile on her face.

"She left me because of it."

"Good. Good."

"You're not listening, Cordelia. I said Kenzie called it quits this afternoon. She left me. We're finished."

Her eyes popped open. "Jane," she said, sitting forward, her voice full of wonder. "No."

"Seems it's all my fault. I'm not spending enough time with her. I'm too busy with my restaurants, my friends, my family. She needs more of me, and there's not enough to go around."

"Oh, dearheart," she said, rising from the couch.

"No, stay there," said Jane, holding out her hand. "If I start crying again, I'll never stop. It took me two hours to pull myself together enough to leave the house." She looked down and saw that Mouse was sitting next to her. She reached down and stroked his head.

For once, Cordelia seemed to be at a loss for words. But it was only momentary. "Maybe she'll change her mind?"

Jane shook her head.

"What . . . I mean, what set this off?"

All the details came rushing out, everything that had happened last night, as well as what Kenzie had said before she left the house earlier in the day. "Maybe it is my fault, Cordelia. When I look back on it, I had the same problems with Christine. It's always been the same old refrain. I spend too much time at work. I get too wrapped up in other people's problems."

"Kenzie actually said she'd like to drop-kick Nolan off a cliff?"

"Direct quote."

"Uffdah."

"I don't know what to do," said Jane, slouching forward against the desk, resting her head in her hand. "If I try to pull out of that restaurant deal in Stillwater, I'll lose my shirt."

"You can't do that. Clothing is mandatory, though hardly essential."

"For the first time in my life, I've got plenty of money. I thought about buying a used Piper Archer. I could probably get one for under a hundred thousand."

"Lord."

"We could keep it down in Nebraska. I'd get Kenzie flying lessons, and she could come up anytime she wanted."

"Did you offer that as a way around your problems?"

"At this point, I'm not sure she'd be willing to listen."

A knock on the door interrupted them.

"Come in," called Jane. She rose and took the bottle and two glasses from one of the bartenders. "Thanks, Connie," she said, closing the door after her. Sitting down on the sofa next to Cordelia, she opened the bottle and poured them each a drink.

"Janey, I'm just . . . astonished. I thought you two were really making a go of it."

"It's all the stuff that never gets talked about that sinks you in the end."

Cordelia got a faraway look in her eyes. "I know," she said softly. "Sometimes I wonder how anyone negotiates a lifelong relationship."

"Lack of imagination?"

"Should we drink to that?"

"I'd rather not."

25

By two in the morning, Corey was seated on the hood of a gray Chevy Metro, half a block from the Unicorn bar, just a few cars back of Serena's red Ford Tempo. He'd gone over what he wanted to say a million times in the last couple of days. This was round two, and this time he wasn't going to blow it.

At two ten, Serena came out of the bar alone. She walked quickly across Emerson with her head down. Corey stood as she reached her car.

"Serena?" He said her name as gently as he knew how.

She squinted into the darkness. When she saw who it was, she shoved her key into the door lock.

Corey rushed up. "Just give me two minutes, okay? That's all I ask."

A car drove past. The headlights lit up Serena's face.

"My God, how'd you get the shiner?" The shame in her eyes told him everything. "It was that guy. Johnny. Why'd he hit you?" He touched her face.

She pushed his hand away. "If you have to know, it was because of you."

"Me?"

"Because you came by the house. We got into a fight about it. He thinks I've been seeing you behind his back."

"How long have you been dating that dirtbag?"

"A few years."

"Has he ever hit you before?"

"None of your damn business."

She tried to yank the door open, but Corey pressed his hip against it. "You deserve so much better than him."

"You mean you?" She brushed her hair defiantly away from her face. "I shouldn't even be talking to you. My mother warned me you'd come back, that you wouldn't leave me alone."

"Are you still taking your marching orders from that old hag? Is she *still* controlling you?"

"Nobody controls me. Not my mother, not Johnny, and for sure not you. I mean, shit, Corey. I can't even believe you're here talking to me. I read all about what you did in the papers. You tried to rape another woman. But this time she ended up dead."

"I never touched her," he shot back. "It was a setup. It had to be. Somebody heard I was out of prison. They figured they could put the screws to her and foist the blame on me."

"Listen to yourself. You're not making sense. I suppose next you're going to tell me you didn't even know her."

"No, we'd met. I've been donating some of my free time over at Raymond Lawless's campaign office. Charity was, too. I talked to her a few times, but I never touched her, Serena. Look, I'm not stupid. I know asking you to believe in me is asking a lot. But you loved me once, just like I loved you. Think about it. Was I ever even the least bit rough with you?"

"You've got a temper," she said grudgingly.

"So do you."

"Yeah, but your temper is different. It's like striking a match. It just . . . erupts white-hot in an instant." She tried again to get in the car, but Corey moved in front of her, grabbed her arms, looked her square in the eyes.

"I blame your mom," he said, trying to rein in his fury. "Somebody must have talked you out of telling me about Dean." He could feel her body go rigid. "It was her, wasn't it."

"You don't know anything."

He pulled a snapshot and a small flashlight out of his jacket pocket. Shining the light on the photo, he said, "Look at that. Who is that little boy?"

She took the picture from his hand, studied it for a few seconds. "It's—"

"It's Dean."

"Yeah. No," she said, looking up into his eyes.

"You're right. It isn't Dean. It's me when I was his age. We could be twins. Dean's my kid, isn't he." He saw in her eyes that he was right. "You can lie to me all you want, but he's my boy. And that's the truth."

She dropped her chin to her chest. "I don't know what to do. Who to believe."

"Believe *me*," said Corey. "Believe that . . . that ever since I saw Dean the other night, I've been walking on air. A son. I've got a son!"

She looked up at the stars, as if she was searching the sky for answers. "Okay, yeah," she said finally. "He is our child. I found out I was pregnant right after you were arrested. I wanted to tell you. I almost did once. But then you took that plea bargain. Everyone said that meant you were guilty."

"No, no. Listen to me. My lawyer didn't think I'd have a prayer of getting off if I went ahead with a trial. If a jury found me guilty, I might've had to serve a whole bunch more time. It was my choice. Maybe I made the wrong one. But I had to take someone's advice because I didn't know what else to do."

"Why didn't you ever tell me any of this?"

"I did. I wrote you a ton of letters."

Her head flicked back like a startled bird. "I never got any letters."

"You were living with your mom. I sent them to you at her address."

"I never saw even one of them."

Corey turned, slammed his fist against the hood of the car. "Do you see now why I hate her? She did everything she could to undermine us. I never raped that woman, Serena. I took the plea bargain because it was the best I could do with a raw deal."

She still didn't look completely convinced, but her resolve was beginning to crack. "If there was only some way you could prove it to me."

"I can't prove it any more than I can prove I love you. Did you feel like I loved you all those years ago?"

"Yes," she whispered, her lips barely moving.

"I still do. I want a second chance. Don't you think you owe me that? And I want to get to know my son."

She nodded but didn't say anything.

"That guy you're with—Johnny?"

"What about him?"

"He's not good for you or Dean. Does he own the house?"

"No, I do."

"Then toss him out."

"It's not that simple."

"Why?"

"Because . . . because—"

A faint breeze tinkled the wind chimes on a porch a few houses away from them.

Corey couldn't stand her weakness. He tipped her face up. "I'll get rid of him for you."

"Corey, no."

He held up his hands. "I won't hurt him. I'll just make it clear that he needs to stay away. For good. Tomorrow . . . what time could I come by when he's not around? I'll help you move his stuff out."

"He's not working tomorrow. He'll probably stick around and watch old movies."

"Boy, you sure as hell found yourself a winner."

"Shut up."

"How about Monday or Tuesday?"

"Tuesday he'll be gone in the afternoon and evening."

"Okay. I'm gonna give you my cell number. You call and tell me what's a good time."

"I don't want Dean around when he comes back."

Corey felt momentarily jealous. "Does Dean actually like him?"

"Hell, no. Dean can't stand him. I just don't want him around if there's going to be . . . you know . . . any problems."

"Is there someplace he can go?"

"I can take him over to my mom's, give her some excuse."

"This is beginning to sound like a plan." In the moonlight, her hair looked so soft it was all he could do not to touch it. "I'll be there when you break it off with him. If he tries anything, believe me, he won't try it again."

"You promised you wouldn't hurt him."

"Not unless he starts something." He closed his hand around hers. "I won't pressure you, babe. We'll take it slow. But I would like to start seeing you again. And . . . of course, there's Dean. Maybe, after a while, you'd let me take him to a movie or something. We don't have to tell him right away that I'm his dad. I just want another chance at the life that was stolen from me."

Drawing her against him, he kissed her. Softly. Just a whisper. She felt so right in his arms. He could tell she still had her doubts, but with time, he was confident he could erase them. Just like he was about to erase Johnny.

26

It was a case of too much liquor and too little sleep.

Jane stayed in bed late on Monday morning, her head aching and her emotions raw. She should have been up at six, to work by seven, but here it was, nearly ten, and she was still in bed. All she wanted was to stay right where she was until everything stopped hurting. She figured she'd passed through the seven stages of grief about five times since Kenzie left. She seemed to be alternating at the moment between guilt and anger with denial pretty well out of the way and flat-out depression beginning to settle in like a bad case of the flu.

When the phone rang, her body jerked. Her first thought was that it might be Kenzie calling to say she'd changed her mind, that she'd given it some thought and decided to give Jane another chance. But that idea carried with it its own kind of aggravation. Was Jane the only one who'd failed? The question circled in her mind until the ringing stopped. She could have looked at the caller ID, but the fact was, she didn't feel like talking to anyone at the moment, not even Kenzie. She waited until the red light blinked, indicating that someone had left a message. Reaching over, she hit *98 and then clicked on speakerphone before dropping the receiver back on the hook.

"You have one new message," said a perky female voice. "First message."

"Jane, hi, it's Mary."

Jane groaned, rolled away from the phone and pulled the blanket up over her head.

"I was wondering if you'd had a chance to do any digging into Charity Miller's murder? Maybe you've talked to your PI friend? If you know anything, could you call me? Corey had a terrible day on Saturday. One of the neighbors posted a bunch of flyers all over the neighborhood. Seems some people called a meeting. There's talk of trying to oust him from my home. Can they do that? Corey saw the flyers and got terribly agitated. Actually, so did I. I'm just so upset I don't know what to do with myself, Jane. Corey left for work a couple of hours ago. He got home late again last night. He never says where he's been, and I worry about him almost all the time now. I thought about going to Charity's funeral this morning. I hear it's at eleven, over at a Methodist church in Merriam Park. I'd like to pay my respects, but it seems kind of wrong for me to go, don't you think? I'm feeling a bit muddled at the moment."

"Join the club," mumbled Jane.

"Call me when you get a moment."

Sitting up, Jane swung her legs out of bed and ran her hands through her badly tangled hair. As soon as Mouse saw that she was still alive, he jumped up from his bed in the corner and trotted over to give her a good morning lick.

"Oh, Mouse," she said, kissing the top of his muzzle. "I feel like shit." She rested her cheek on the top of his head. He seemed to have a pretty good sense of when a lot of activity would put him in the doghouse, as it were. "But I suppose you need to go outside."

He whined, lifted a paw. "You know, I wouldn't say this to anybody but you, but I think I like dogs better than people."

She moved to a standing position, careful not to jog her head. "Let me get myself a couple of ibuprofen and then I'll let you out." She eased her way down the hallway, hand pressed against the wall to steady herself, and finally made it to the medicine chest in the bathroom, where she downed three pills. After letting Mouse out into the backyard, she started some coffee brewing, then returned upstairs for a shower. She was glad Mary had said something about Charity's funeral. Even though she would have preferred to spend the day sleeping, ignoring her responsibilities and proving to all who cared to take note that she could be as derelict and undependable as the next person, she was deeply curious about who would turn up at the church. If she was going to start doing some investigating, that seemed like a good place to begin.

Since the thought of eating made her stomach lurch, she was able to leave the house in record time. The ibuprofen had pretty well silenced the jackhammer in her head. Unfortunately, it had no magical power over the ache in her heart. Still, after two cups of strong black coffee, she felt confident that she could pass for a reasonably put-together human being. This was another example—she'd been collecting them lately—of pretense oiling human interaction and thus making sanity possible. A dark thought for a dark day.

After looking up the address, Jane drove over to St. Paul, finding a space in the back parking lot. She entered through the arched double doors, looking around to see if she recognized anyone. She did. Almost everyone who'd ever worked with Charity at her father's campaign office was there. The organ inside the sanctuary piped a suitably gloomy dirge over the assembled crowd. Spying her father standing in the vestibule next to Elizabeth, Jane edged her way toward them. She was once again reminded of how tired her dad looked, which reminded her of his dizzy spell on Thursday night as well as the conversation she'd had with Peter on Friday. She wondered if Peter had had a chance to talk to Elizabeth yet. To get her dad to see a doctor would take a united front. Maybe even a couple of thugs with guns.

"Janey, hi," said her father, giving her a hug and a kiss.

Elizabeth put her hand on Jane's arm. "Good to see you, honey." Elizabeth had joined her dad's law firm several years ago. She was an attractive woman in her late fifties with a brilliant legal mind—in her father's opinion. She'd spent the last ten years involved in appellate law, but when Jane's dad had left to run for governor, she'd been made a full partner and was now working directly with defendants during their initial trials. Another lawyer her father had worked with for almost a decade, Ted Kaplan, had also been made a full partner several years ago. And thus, the Lawless Law Firm had morphed into Lawless, Kaplan & Piper.

"I didn't know you'd be here," said Jane.

"It would seem pretty callous not to be," said her dad, trying for both friendliness and seriousness, the kind of weird facial contortion a politician learned to project.

Jane's gaze traveled across the crowd. "Have you heard anything more from the police?" She didn't say Corey's name, but she didn't need to.

"We finally received the police report."

Leaning a little closer and lowering her voice, she added, "I'm curious. Was anything written on Charity's stomach?"

"Yes," said Elizabeth. "It was apparently a carbon copy of the rape Corey Hodge did years ago. With the exception of the outcome. The first woman didn't die."

"They're asking us to move into the sanctuary and take our seats," said Ray, slipping his arm through Elizabeth's.

"Why don't you sit with us?" asked Elizabeth, giving Jane a suitably sad smile.

Jane was about to say yes when she spotted Melanie come through the front door. She wasn't sure how long she'd stick around afterward, and she wanted to talk to her, so she said, "Thanks, but I promised to sit with a friend. I'll see you both later."

Skirting her way back through the crowd of mourners, Jane waved at Mel and finally got her attention.

"Didn't know you'd be here," said Mel, switching her purse from one shoulder to the other. "Although I guess I'm not surprised."

"Is Cordelia with you?"

"Are you kidding? She's not a fan of funerals. They remind her she isn't God."

Jane suppressed a smile.

"Let's sit in the back," said Melanie, glancing around to get her bearings. "That way we get the best view."

The sanctuary was one of the loveliest Jane had seen in the Twin Cities. While those around them studied the program, Jane and Mel studied the audience. "The Millers are sitting in the front pew on the left side. The mom has gray hair, the grandmother white."

Just before the service started, Jane noticed a young, dark-haired man enter from the side door. He looked unsteady as he sat down on the front pew opposite the Millers. Mrs. Miller leaned forward to look at him, then turned to the man next to her, visibly upset.

"Who is he?" asked Jane.

"His name is Gabriel Keen. He and Charity were engaged to be married. From what I've been able to find out, she broke it off with him several months ago, but he kept hounding her, so she filed a restraining order. I spoke to her parents briefly yesterday morning. They think he's responsible for her death."

"Have they talked to the police about their suspicions?"

"Oh, you bet. And from what I'm told, the police have heard the same thing from other people, some of them asking to remain anonymous."

"Cordelia told me the police had another suspect. Must be him."

Mel nodded.

"Keen had a motive, I suppose. The jilted lover. Speaking of motive, what do you suppose the police think Corey's motive was?"

"I'm not sure he needed one," Mel whispered back. "At least in the way we normally think of a motive. If he's a serial rapist, what drives him is his anger, the need to control, to dominate, to humiliate. Oh, and get this. Charity's mother told me that Corey told Charity he was a cop. She had a date with him to go for a ride on his motorcycle the night she died."

If that didn't make him sound guilty, nothing did. Jane groaned. "Why would he say that?"

"Because he's a liar. I met him last week at your father's campaign office. The guy is as charming as hell when he wants to be. But he can turn it off just as fast as he turns it on. If I was a bettin' woman, I'd put my money on Corey Hodge."

Jane understood that it was impossible to look someone in the eye and have any sense at all who he was or what he was capable of. Mary believed Corey was innocent. What she had was faith. Some might think faith was just a different form of proof, but Jane wasn't one of them.

"Listen, do you know the address of Charity's apartment building? I'd like to go over, take a look at where the murder happened."

Melanie looked it up in a notebook, then wrote it down and handed the page to Jane. "The police report said she'd been taking out the garbage when she got dropped by the taser. They found the sack in the Dumpster. Inside the apartment, the garbage can was empty. She'd set out a clean plastic can liner on the kitchen counter but never came back in to use it. When they entered, they found two cats, one curled up in the sink, the other sitting on the kitchen table."

"What's going to happen to the cats?"

"They were Charity's babies, both rescue cats. Her parents are planning to keep them." Leaning closer, she whispered, "You think you're going to find something at her apartment building the police didn't notice?"

"No. I just want to take a look." She sat back and tried to get comfortable in the pew. Not an easy proposition for someone who rarely sat in one.

The service was all laid out in the program. Everyone stood for the first hymn, "Abide With Me." Jane remembered many hymns from her childhood. Her mother was English, high Anglican, in fact. Jane had attended services in a number of Anglican churches around the south of England, where her mother was born and where Jane had lived for the first nine years of her life.

When the hymn was over, the minister, a blond, handsome thirty-something man in a black pulpit robe and green damask broad stole, stood up at the front and looked out over the congregation.

"Let us pray." He bowed his head. "Oh God, whose mercies cannot be numbered, accept our prayers on behalf of your servant, Charity Ann Miller, and grant her an entrance into the land of light and joy, through Jesus Christ our Lord, who lives and reigns with you and the Holy Spirit, one God, now and forever. Amen."

While everyone sat back down, Charity's brother got up to read one of Charity's favorite psalms.

After another song, there were more readings, mostly poetry. Jane only half listened. Her gaze roamed over the crowd and then lifted to the soaring height of the pitched roof. Merriam Park United Methodist was an amazingly beautiful piece of architecture, full of large, colorful stained-glass windows and beautifully carved wood. Jane had concluded long ago that her reaction to Christianity, in fact to religion in general, was essentially aesthetic. She loved the majesty of the architecture, the sense of reverence and quiet that a church like this gave to a world full of shouting voices. She loved the beauty of the old hymns, the choral music, the grand sound of a pipe organ, and of course, she would always be drawn to the King James Bible because of the language, part Shakespeare, part Milton. But when it got down to doctrines, to the nitty-gritty of religious beliefs, all of her appreciative feelings vanished.

After the readings were completed, the minister entered from the right side of the altar, and with the help of a cane, made his way slowly to the pulpit. His eyes were filled with an unsettling stillness as he looked over the crowd.

"I knew Charity well," he began. He had a gentle, deep, affecting voice, the kind that lent an air of nobility to his words. But the tone was thicker now, full of emotion. "We'd been close friends for several years. She saw me through many hard times, and I trust that she could say the same about me. I never had a sister, but if I had, I would have wanted her to be just like Charity.

"We all suffer in this life, but we make a mistake if we think that suffering is what life is about. Many of you know that when I was attacked"—he stopped for a moment here and gazed around the audience again, looking this time at specific individuals—"my doctors predicted I would not survive. I've always believed that God has a plan for each of us. That belief was sorely tried this past year. But, standing before you now, I realize that I cling to it still.

"We all know that there are many forces at work in this world of ours, so many that it's hard to see a reason behind everything. Looking for reasons can feel like wandering in the wilderness without a compass. But though it's sometimes impossible to find an explanation, a rationale to put our hearts at rest, we must finally understand that God's purpose informs everything."

He spoke for a few more minutes, quoted several Bible verses, and ended with the words of St. Paul. " 'Neither death, nor life, nor angels, nor principalities, nor things present, nor things to come, nor powers, nor height, nor depth, nor anything else in all creation, will be able to separate us from the love of God in Christ Jesus our Lord.' " He closed his eyes. "Amen."

Raising his arms this time, he prayed aloud: "Father of all, we pray to you for Charity, and of all those whom we love but see no longer. Grant to them eternal rest. Let light perpetual shine upon them. May Charity's soul and the souls of all the departed, through your mercy, rest in peace."

After a final hymn—"Now the Day Is Over"—sung by the choir, and the dismissal, the minister, followed by the pallbearers carrying the coffin, led the way back through the church to the hearse waiting outside the front door. Once the coffin with its spray of white roses had passed, people began to get up and put on their coats.

"Are you going to the cemetery?" asked Mel.

"I think I will," said Jane.

"Wish I could, but I was handed another assignment this morning."

"Boy, that paper really keeps you busy."

"They need about four more reporters, but the coffers are bare."

They said their good-byes under a sullen sky in the church's parking lot.

Jane joined the funeral procession on the way to the cemetery. She stood at the edge of the somewhat thinned-out group as the pastor—she'd learned that his name was Christopher Cornish—said a few words at the graveside on top of the hill. Looking around, she saw that her dad and Elizabeth hadn't come.

As the final prayer was being offered, two women standing behind Jane began to whisper.

"I can't believe the bishop let him come back."

"He took that six-month leave of absence after he was attacked, but that's probably up by now. There will be a church trial, for sure." This woman's whisper held less vitriol.

"You know, Ruthy, it makes my blood boil to see what our church has become. Women pastors. Gay men hiding their sexuality so we don't see who they really are."

"Straight people have all the rights. Gay people just want to be included."

"As if their sins mean nothing? What did you think when he came out in that sermon last April?"

The one named Ruthy didn't answer right away. "Well, I felt betrayed, I guess. Like he'd been lying to us. But then, after he was attacked, I thought that was even more wrong."

"But an elder should be held to a higher standard." The woman was quiet for a few seconds. "Charity was a lovely young woman, didn't you think? A little headstrong, a little too interested in male attention."

"A romantic."

"And perhaps a little too adventurous."

"She was young."

"Such a tragedy. I took a hotdish over to the family yesterday."

"I took one over on Friday."

"I never could understand why Charity and Cornish were such good friends."

"You knew she was engaged to Gabriel Keen."

"I couldn't believe the police thought Gabriel was the one who attacked Cornish. He comes from such a good family. But he was never charged, so we shouldn't judge."

"You're right. It's wrong to judge."

They moved out of earshot. Jane turned to see who they were. Their reasoning processes had nearly brought her headache back, but they'd revealed a story Jane had never heard before.

Standing next to a tree, a cold, late October wind blowing across the dying cemetery grass, she watched a trickle of people come up to Cornish, shake his hand, clap him on the back.

Spotting Luke Durrant talking to Charity's mother, she walked across the grass to the other side of the grave site to offer her condolences. But before she reached them, Cornish stepped right into her path.

"Reverend," she said, extending her hand. "That was a lovely service. My name's Jane. Jane Lawless. My father—"

"I know who you are," he said, pulling his cane in front of him.

Up this close, she could see scars on his face. The longest ran from his left cheekbone all the way down his neck, disappearing underneath the collar of his black robe.

"That was very kind of your father to come to the service," he said, brushing his hair out of his eyes. He was obviously searching for something to say.

"He liked Charity a lot."

"We all did. Well, if you don't mind—"

Jane didn't want him to leave just yet. "I wonder if you'd have just a couple of seconds."

"Forgive me, but—"

"I'm working, unofficially, on behalf of Mary Glynn, Corey Hodge's aunt. You probably know the police think Corey may have been the one who murdered Charity."

"What do you mean by *unofficially*?"

"I'm not part of the police investigation, but I am working with a private investigator." It wasn't true, but it gave her the legitimacy she needed. And if she asked Nolan to help her, he would.

"Wait a minute. I thought you owned a couple of restaurants in town."

"I do. But, as I said, I'm looking into Charity's death for Corey's aunt. She doesn't believe her nephew did it."

"She's not the only one."

"Are you saying you think someone else was responsible?"

"That's exactly what I'm saying. His name is Gabriel Keen."

"I just learned that some people think Keen was the one who attacked you last spring."

"You just learned? Are you kidding me?"

"That surprises you?"

"Nothing surprises me. Now, if you don't mind—" His eyes darted to a man in the distance who was waving at him.

"Did Charity have any enemies?"

"You mean other than Keen? No, not that I know of."

"I'm sorry to hear about the attack. It must have been horrible for you."

The words seemed to stop him.

"Do you plan to continue on as a pastor at the church?"

"I'm about to be stripped of my orders, Ms. Lawless. That's what happens when you're a gay minister in a committed relationship in the Methodist church."

He sounded angry. He had a right to be. "Why do you think Keen attacked you?"

"He told a man in my congregation that he thought all fags should be forcibly castrated with rusted barbed wire. I'm not sure the man disagreed."

"You've been through a lot. I admire your courage."

His eyes remained on her with that same unsettling stillness she'd first noted in the church.

"You know I'm gay, too," she said.

"Yes, I'd heard that."

"I'm not religious—"

"Is this . . . some kind of game with you?"

"A game?"

The man in the distance began waving at him again. "The lunch reception starts in fifteen minutes," he called.

Cornish checked his watch. "I really have to go."

"It was good to meet you."

As he walked away, he muttered, "It's been surreal."

She had no idea what he was talking about.

Looking around, she saw that everyone was leaving, getting in cars and driving off—with the exception of two grave diggers who were standing about a hundred feet away, up on a hill, leaning on their shovels. They couldn't start the real burial process until everyone had left.

Turning back to the grave, Jane noticed a man in a dark blue raincoat sitting with his back against the coffin, sipping from a silver flask. It was Gabriel Keen. She remembered that he'd been unsteady on his feet when he'd come into the church. She wondered how much he'd had to drink.

Stepping up to the grave, she put her hand on the coffin, trying to decide what tack to take with him. This might be her only opportunity to talk to him one-on-one. Unlike a cop, she couldn't just demand that he answer her questions.

"You must have loved her a lot," she said, keeping her hand on the coffin, not looking at him directly.

He eyed her. "You look familiar. Have we met?"

"I don't think so."

He nodded, took a another hit off his flask. "Charity meant everything to me."

Jane waited a moment. She didn't want to make this seem like an interrogation. "Were you friends?"

"Engaged."

"Oh, I'm so sorry."

"She broke it off," he said, covering his eyes with his hand. He was on the verge of tears but seemed to want to talk. Strangers brought that out in people sometimes, especially if the one doing the talking had been drinking too much. "And then . . . then I made every stupid move in the book."

Stepping over to a tree, Jane crouched down, rested her arms on her knees. "It's easy to do."

"Boy, you're telling me." He stared at the flask. "I lost it. I mean, when she first broke it off, I thought, give her some time. She'll come around. But when she didn't, I started calling. Sometimes late at night. But she wouldn't talk to me. She said I scared her."

"Did you do something to frighten her?"

He ground the heel of his hand into his forehead. "I spray-painted a word on her car." He looked up, said, "cunt." Nobody was around now but the grave workers. Not that in his current state he would have cared. "She acted like one. Taking that fag's word over mine."

"Cornish?"

"Yeah, Cornish. And then, last Tuesday, I see her with this new guy. He said he was a cop. Gave me his name, so, hell, I checked him out. Charity wanted to be with a man she could trust. She told me that. Someone she felt safe around. So she hooks up with a convicted rapist. Boy, I nearly laughed myself silly when I found out who he really was."

"Did you want to get even?"

"Yeah. With both of them." He tipped the flask back and finished what was left inside. He wasn't slurring, but he wasn't far from it. Lifting a small, orange plastic bottle out of the pocket of his suit coat, he unscrewed the cap and popped a couple of pills.

"What's that?" asked Jane.

"Vicodin."

"Pain pills?"

"Yeah. I'm in pain. The antidepressants don't work. Nothing works."

"You shouldn't mix those with liquor."

He glanced over at her. "You my doctor?"

She wasn't sure why she cared. There was no reason she should, other than human connection. "Don't take any more, okay."

"What's it to you? Hell, my life is so screwed."

"I know something about pain."

"Yeah?"

"Yeah."

He straightened up, squared his shoulders. "Bet you never killed your brother."

The admission caught her off guard.

Keen pressed the heels of his hands to his eyes, choked back a sob. "God, I'm a useless piece of shit." He didn't move for a few seconds. Suddenly, he threw back his head. "I was sixteen," he said loudly, as if talking to an audience. "My brother was twenty. We were sailing off Bayfield, up on the South Shore. We were drinking, you know? My dad made us promise never to drink on the boat, but that day, it just seemed . . . Andy brought this bottle of rum."

He got up, stumbled around behind the casket. "It was a windy day. I didn't see the boom move until it hit Andy square in the back and sent him over the side. I tossed him a life preserver, but we were moving too fast. He never got to it. I dropped the sail, tried to start the outboard so I could turn around, get back to him fast, but I flooded it." He tossed his arms in the air. "I flooded it, okay! By the time I got it started, I couldn't find him. He was lost. We never even found the body. I killed him, ladies and gentlemen of the jury. Might as well have put a bullet in his chest."

"It was an accident," said Jane.

"No." He shook his head. Looked down. Kept shaking it. "No. Because of me, my family didn't even have a body to bury." He pointed, drawing his arm across the gravestones. "One of those should have *my* name on it."

Jane stood, watched him lean over the coffin, rest his arms on the polished wood.

"Charity always said I had a sad life. In and out of hospitals. Poor Gabriel. He's depressed. Poor Gabriel. He can't get out of bed in the morning. Can't sleep. Drinks too much. Feels way too sorry for himself. Poor, foolish, sad, pathetic Gabriel."

Keen was a horrible, predatory man with a traumatic past. What was cause, what was effect? Jane wasn't sure she cared. Certainly not after what he'd done. And yet, some part of her did feel sorry for him. She looked down when she felt something hit her chest and drop to the ground. It was the bottle of Vicodin.

"For *your* pain," he said, pushing away from the coffin and weaving off into the trees.

27

Luke waited in the church library for Christopher to say his goodbyes to stragglers who were the last to leave the funeral luncheon in the church basement. Christopher had started the day in good spirits, but Luke could tell that as the day wore on, he was working harder and harder to do his pastoral duty and comfort the bereaved. Luke was counting the minutes until he could get Christopher alone so they could talk about the day, about Keen's sudden, unexpected appearance, as well as Christopher's brief conversation with Jane Lawless.

The church library was closed on Mondays, which made it a perfect place for Luke to wait while everyone else was downstairs eating. He cooled his heels, reading *Time* magazine until Christopher came through the door shortly after three. He was still wearing his clerical robes.

Leaning on his cane, he chose a chair directly across from Luke and sat down with a grimace.

"How bad does your leg hurt?"

"Bad enough. Boy, I'm glad that's over," he said, resting his head on the back of the chair and looking up at the coffered ceiling.

"Did you get many comments about coming out last April?"

"A few. Most of them positive. Doesn't change anything."

"Maybe one day it will."

What concerned Luke most was the effect Gabriel Keen's appearance had had on Christopher's mood. "Were you surprised that Keen showed up?"

"Oh, Lord," he said, his hands gripping the handle of his cane. "That really twisted me around. It never occurred to me that he'd have the guts to come."

"He was drunk."

"Yes, I know. At one point, he walked past me and whispered that I should watch my back. That the sky was about to fall."

Luke's body tensed. "What did he mean?"

"No idea. But I'm sure I'm about to find out."

"The guy's like a mad dog. Someone should put him down."

Christopher's gaze came to rest on a painting of Jesus across the room. "He'll have to answer for his acts one day. We all will."

"What did Jane Lawless have to say to you?"

Christopher gave a sharp laugh. "She's something else."

"Tell me about it."

"She made it sound like she knew nothing about what Keen did to me until today."

"You're kidding."

"And get this. She's working with some private investigator, looking into Charity's murder. I told her Keen was responsible. She says she's trying to prove that Corey Hodge is innocent, but I don't believe a word she says. The only thing that woman cares about is her father's campaign. She's not the least bit interested in what's moral or right."

Both men turned at the sound of a knock on the door. The gray-haired woman who worked the office poked her head inside. "I thought I saw you come in here, Reverend." She looked uncomfortable. "There's a policeman outside who wants to talk to you. I wasn't sure if I should bother you, but—"

"It's fine," said Christopher. He pulled himself to his feet. "Did he say what he wants?"

"No, Reverend. Just that he needs to speak with you today if possible."

Glancing at Luke, Christopher said, "Please, Carla, tell him to come in."

A few moments later, a barrel-chested, sandy-haired man in a dark gray suit entered the room. When he saw Luke, he frowned. "I'm Sergeant Tom Emerson, Minneapolis PD," he said, standing just a few feet inside the door, his chilly eyes locked on Christopher. "I'm a homicide investigator." He flipped them his badge. "I was hoping to talk to you, Reverend Cornish. Alone."

"I'd be happy to speak with you," said Christopher, "but I'd prefer that my partner stay."

"It's your call. Do you mind?" He nodded to the chair next to Luke.

"Make yourself comfortable," said Christopher.

Luke could see the deep apprehension in Christopher's face. Realizing that the cop was looking at him, he introduced himself but didn't go beyond his name.

Opening a small notebook and removing a pen from his shirt pocket, Emerson shifted his gaze back to Christopher. "I understand that you and Charity Miller were close friends."

"We were," said Christopher, sitting back down, holding tight to his cane.

"You talked to her a lot?"

"Yes, we talked."

"In person?"

"She came to our condo fairly often, and we also talked on the phone."

"What did you talk about?"

"Mainly the problems she was having with Gabriel Keen, her ex-fiancé."

Emerson studied Christopher a moment. "I understand that you think Keen was the one who attacked you some months ago."

"I know he was. Before he beat me senseless with a baseball bat, I saw him."

"You were the only witness."

"That's right. But the police found the bat in the back of his bedroom closet. It had been cleaned, but there were small bits of my blood and tissue still embedded in it. Unfortunately, the search was thrown out so Keen was never indicted."

Emerson scratched his head, leaned back in his chair. "I talked to Mr. Keen yesterday. He denies he had anything to do with the beating."

"He's lying."

"I tend to agree, except here's the thing. He said that you'd made sexual advances toward him on more than one occasion."

All expression died on Christopher's face. "Are you serious?"

"He also claimed there were other young men, minors, you'd propositioned, but that none would come forward because either they didn't want to get involved in a police investigation, or they had sex with you and were too ashamed to admit it."

"I've never done anything like that. *Never*."

"He went on to say that you were doing everything in your power to destroy his relationship with Charity Miller."

Luke could tell Christopher was drowning. "Keen was doing a pretty good job of that himself."

Emerson switched his gaze. "You were a friend of Ms. Miller, too?"

"Sure. We were both good friends of hers. Keen threatened her. He sent her dog shit in the mail disguised as a birthday present. He punctured her tires. He hounded her after she broke off their engagement until she was so frightened that she got a restraining order."

"Yes, he mentioned some of that. He said he regretted his actions, but that he was deeply frustrated because Charity believed everything Reverend Cornish told her. He said he tried to get her to listen to his side of the story, how the reverend would get him alone, shove his hand between his legs—"

Christopher pushed to his feet. "This is insane."

"He said that you had a 'thing' for him, Reverend Cornish. That if you couldn't have him, you didn't want anyone else to have him."

"It's . . . inconceivable."

Luke felt the accusations hit his body like darts. He had no doubt at all that Keen was lying. But there was no reason the cop would take Christopher's word over Keen's.

Emerson eyed Christopher like a bird eyeing a worm. "How many times a week would you say you talked to Charity?"

Christopher's gaze shifted, drifted around the room as he sat back down. "I don't know. A couple dozen maybe."

Luke had no idea it had been that much.

"On the day Charity died, how many times would you say you talked to her?"

"What's the point? I talked to her a lot. She was deeply frightened of Keen. She often called just so she wouldn't feel so alone."

"Would you say she called you most of the time, or that you called her."

Christopher's gaze grazed Luke, but didn't linger. "I don't understand the intent of your question. We both called each other. We were friends."

"Would it surprise you to learn that you called her thirty-one times during the last week of her life."

"No, it wouldn't."

"That's an awful lot of calls."

"It's a matter of opinion."

"And on the day she died?"

"She called me a couple times in the morning. I called her back a couple times in the afternoon. I talked to her twice that evening."

"What time?"

"I called her around eleven."

"What did you talk about?"

"I wanted her to know that Corey Hodge had raped a woman and gone to jail for it. I thought she should be warned because Luke told me they'd been talking earlier in the evening. I had no idea that she was actually with him at the time I called until she told me."

"You didn't talk about Keen?"

"No."

"Did you talk to her again that night?"

"I asked her to call me when she got home, just to make sure she was safe. When she did, I told her to lock the doors and windows, pull the blinds, and call if she had any more problems."

"You spoke for almost ten minutes."

"It's possible."

"But you never saw her that night?"

"No. What are you suggesting? That I was the one who killed her? Where's this coming from?"

"Did you?"

"Absolutely not!"

"Do you own a taser, Mr. Cornish?"

"A taser? No. Give me one reason why I would want to hurt Charity."

"Maybe she knew something you didn't want to get around. Like, oh, say, that you were sleeping with your parishioners? Maybe you thought she was about to turn you in."

"This is just nuts," said Luke, moving to the edge of his chair. "Did Keen tell you that? He's lying. He's evil. I can't believe anyone would take his bullshit seriously."

"Keen thought your bishop would."

"Then why didn't he tell her months ago? Why didn't he tell that to the police when they were investigating him for attacking me? Why did he save it until now, until he was a suspect in the murder case? Don't you get it? He's manipulating you. Throwing sand in your face."

"It's possible," said Emerson mildly. "But it's equally possible that he's telling the truth."

"I think this discussion is over," said Luke, cutting him off. "If you want to talk to Reverend Cornish any further, you'll need to do it through his lawyer."

"Luke, no. I don't need a lawyer."

Luke fired off a look that silenced him.

Emerson took his time returning the notebook to the pocket of his raincoat. As he got up, he nodded to Christopher and said, "I can find my own way out."

Julia had just pulled into the drive at the house in White Bear Lake when her cell phone clicked through. She heard Jane's voice say hello.

"Hi, Jane. It's Julia." She could picture the contortions Jane's face was going through, not knowing whether she should hang up or take the call. "I wanted you to know that I talked to Peter yesterday."

"Peter? My brother Peter?"

"Yes. He told me all about the concerns you share over your father's health. I've started donating some of my free time at the campaign office—that's where we spoke. Anyway, I wanted you to know that I had a phone conversation with your dad last night. He's agreed to let me give him a full physical in the privacy of his home tonight. I'll draw the blood myself, make sure all the standard tests as well as a few extras are run."

Jane explained what she'd seen in her dad's office the other night. "I don't even want to think this," she added, "but can heart problems cause dizziness?"

"Yes, it's possible. Does he see a cardiologist regularly?"

"Not that I know about."

"Well, okay. I'll bring along a portable ECG. Don't worry, I'll cover as many bases as I can. As soon as the election is over, we can bring him in for further tests if necessary. I'll put a rush on the blood work. I can't promise when it will be back, but I hope we'll have most everything in a few days. Your father's concerns seemed to be mostly political. He doesn't want the public to know he's seeing a doctor because of the conclusions some people might draw. I assured him of my complete discretion."

"You're good at keeping secrets."

Julia almost laughed. "Yes, I am. So, that's all I wanted to say. I hope it will put your mind at rest to know that a doctor is actually looking after him. Talk to you soon, Jane. Bye."

Julia folded her phone shut before Jane could say anything else. She wanted this to be quick. In and out. No strings. Just hi, I'm helping, bye. Jane would be grateful, even if it was a grudging kind of gratitude. But that's all Julia needed. Just a tiny wedge. With Kenzie out of the way, packed off to Nebraska where she belonged, Julia could afford to be patient.

28

Wayne McGill, Corey's floor boss at the Chrysler dealership in Crystal, left the service floor at noon on Monday, saying that he had an appointment for a root canal. He wouldn't be back the rest of the day. Corey didn't know he was leaving until he was ready to walk out the door. That left him with a problem.

Corey liked McGill because he was an ex-con himself and because he'd talked the maintenance supervisor into hiring him on a temporary basis. He'd been taken off temporary status a few weeks before his ankle bracelet was removed. Even though fixing cars would never have been his first job choice, the money was good and so were the benefits. He'd been able to put a fair amount of cash away during the time he'd been out. Mary wouldn't take a dime from him, although he did buy groceries every week. And now, with the possibility of moving into Serena's house becoming a reality, he was glad he had some money squirreled away. First thing on the agenda was to get Serena a ring. But that might have to wait a few days.

The thought made him smile as he knocked on the supervisor's open door shortly before quitting time. "Excuse, me? Milt?"

Milton Cox was a heavily built fifty-year-old-guy who'd worked at various car dealerships around town for the last thirty years. No matter what he was doing, he always seemed harassed. Even at lunch, he'd glare at his hamburger like it had just delivered some bad news. But Milt was generally fair and tended to leave most of the decisions to Wayne. Corey would have much preferred asking Wayne his question, but that wasn't going to happen.

"Yeah?" said Milt, studying something on his computer screen. He had a weak chin. Several of them.

Corey was pretty sure he didn't even know who he was talking to. "I need tomorrow off. I've, ah . . . got some tests that need to be run at my health clinic." What he really needed was time off to get rid of Johnny's stuff at Serena's house.

Milt peered at him over his bifocals. "Kind of last minute isn't it?"

"Yeah, well. Can't be helped."

"You're Hodge, right? The con?" He trained his eyes on the jailhouse tattoos on Corey's upper arms.

"Yup."

Milt examined him for a few seconds, then reached down and picked up one of the local newspapers. "I been reading about you." He held up the paper.

Corey felt his jaws tense.

"Says here the cops think maybe you killed a woman. Last week. What a shocker, huh?"

"Look, if they had anything on me, I wouldn't be standing here."

Cox smiled, let the paper drop to his desk.

Corey could see where the conversation was headed. "So, do I get the day off?"

"Sure. Fine with me. Take the week off. In fact, don't bother coming back at all."

"You're firing me?"

"Yeah. Exactly." Milt licked his lips, eyed him like he was about to take bite out of him. "Clean out your locker. I'll call the business office. You can pick up your final check on your way out."

"This just fucking sucks. I've done my job. Ask Wayne."

"You were late last Friday."

"That's because the cops hauled me in."

Milt held his palms up, shrugged. "Is that my problem? Ever heard of a phone?"

"So I forgot. I had kind of a lot on my mind."

"And you came to work late a few other times."

"It's the traffic. When there's an accident on the fucking freeway, what am I supposed to do?"

"Watch your mouth, boy. Now, if you want to fight about this, I suggest you get a lawyer. In the meantime, take your crap and leave. I don't wanna see you around here after today."

Corey threw his arms in the air. "Fuck fuck fuck," he said as he stomped out, adding one last *fuck* just to make sure Milt felt as harassed as humanly possible.

That evening, Jane came down the stairs from her second-floor office at the Xanadu club, dressed in one of her specially made tuxes. Dinner and dancing at the Xanadu were accompanied by a live orchestra playing twenties and thirties jazz. Tonight, the music hurt her head. She was tired, her headache had returned, and she was in a foul mood. She stayed in the dining room doing her usual meet and greet until she couldn't stand it another minute, finally retreating to her office, where she called Mary.

"The police came back with another search warrant this afternoon."

"Oh, Mary, I'm sorry. Was Corey there?"

"No, he was at work."

"Did they find anything?"

"They wanted his laptop."

"He has a laptop?"

"It was the first thing he bought when he moved back in here. He was always a whiz at computers. Every few months, while he was in prison, he'd ask me to send him this new book or that. He wanted to keep up with the new technology, the new software. Anyway, what bothered me the most was they asked if Corey ever drove my van."

"Does he?"

"Sure, every now and then. But he'd never take it without permission. The police asked if they could look in it, and dumb me, I said sure. They found a tube of lipstick under the passenger's seat. It wasn't mine. I had to tell them that."

"Do any of your female employees ever use your van?"

"Well, sure, every once in a while."

"I wouldn't worry about it, then."

They talked for a few more minutes. Jane finally begged off, saying she'd call when she had something new to report.

Lifting a bottle of brandy out of the bottom drawer of her desk, she poured herself a shot, and downed it. And then she phoned Nolan, her PI buddy. He didn't answer his cell, so she left a message, asking him to stop by the club tonight if he had a chance. If not, she asked him to give her a call tomorrow.

Shortly after eleven, she returned downstairs and wandered into the bar. Monday nights were usually fairly quiet, but tonight the din was almost more than she could stand. She ordered another shot of brandy from the bartender. While she was sipping it, she noticed Nolan come in the front door. He was a big man, African American, powerfully built. Everything about him screamed cop, from the look in his eyes to the way he held his body. She downed the shot in one neat swallow.

"Let's go somewhere else," he shouted, looking around.

"You don't like my bar?"

"The noise level could wake the dead."

"Okay. But you have to drive." She set the shot glass back on the counter and followed him out.

They ended up at a rough neighborhood dive in North Minneapolis, The Tick Tock Lounge, one of Nolan's favorite haunts because of two things: the jukebox stuffed with hits from the fifties and sixties, and the aging group of his old snitches who still hung out around the pool tables.

Thinking she'd had enough booze for one evening, Jane stood at the bar and ordered a tonic water, extra ice, and three olives. The bartender and a few of the patrons turned to check out her tuxedo, but they lost interest pretty quickly.

"You're in a weird mood," said Nolan, asking for a tap beer.

"How is my life screwed up, let me count the ways. First off, my girlfriend left me." She figured she might as well get it over with. He'd find out sooner or later.

"Sorry to hear it. Is it temporary or permanent?"

"The latter, I think."

Nolan paid for the drinks because Jane didn't have her wallet with her. They carried their glasses over to a booth in the back, farthest away from the music speakers.

"So, what's up?" asked Nolan, taking a long thirsty sip of his Leinenkugel.

"There's something I wanted to ask you. Corey Hodge. Know the name?"

"I figured we'd end up there eventually. I been following the Charity Miller murder in the paper."

"You think Corey did it?"

"That would be my theory."

"Do you know anything about his first arrest?"

"Sure. I didn't work the case, but a buddy of mine was the primary. What do you want to know?"

"Do you think he was guilty?"

"No doubt in my mind."

"My dad apparently didn't think it made sense to take it to trial. He must have thought he could get Corey a better deal with a plea bargain."

"That's what I recall."

"I've read some stuff about it—about the young woman who was on her way to see her boyfriend in Duluth."

"She left the state, just in case you were thinking of contacting her."

"No, I wasn't. But what was the evidence against him? I couldn't find that anywhere."

Nolan scratched the back of his graying head. "Well, as I recall, he was working for a frozen pizza producer back then. The plant was somewhere up north. Hodge drove a delivery truck for them. A gas receipt put him close to the rest area where the attack occurred right around the time it occurred. The woman—sorry, can't recall her name—identified the truck in the parking lot of the rest area when she pulled in. She also described his hands, which was the only part of him she saw. She remembered that they were freckled, and that he had a white spot on the middle finger of his right hand, like he'd taken off a ring."

"How did that get you to Corey?"

"We'd been looking at him for another possible rape stemming from the year before. That one took place down near Albert Lea, again along the interstate. Same MO. A taser to drop his victim. There was no word written on her stomach in that case, but he'd drawn the shape of a heart with lipstick. No pizza truck either, but there was a motorcycle parked in the lot. We got lucky on that. The victim's dad owned a motorcycle shop. She'd worked there while she was in college, so she knew a lot about cycles. She was sure this one was an older-model Italian Moto Guzzi. Black and red, with saddlebags and a slightly rounded top case. It's not that common. We matched it to one Hodge owned, but that's as far as we got. The woman didn't remember anything else, so the case went cold."

"But you went back to him after the rape near Duluth."

"We got a warrant to search the pizza truck he drove. Sure enough, we came up with the taser, duct tape, and some lipstick. His girlfriend said the lipstick was hers, and Hodge insisted he had a taser for protection because he was on the road all the time, but taken all together, it was pretty damning. Oh, and by the way, he wore a thick turquoise and silver ring on the middle finger of his—freckled—right hand."

"But there were no witnesses."

"Witnesses are overrated."

"And no actual forensics. No semen. No prints. No fiber or hair."

"It took awhile to get a crime scene unit there. By then, the woman had moved around, washed the lipstick off her stomach. Lots of people had walked around the area. The woman—"

"Her name was Louisa Timmons."

"Right. Timmons. She was so traumatized that the pictures taken at the scene were pretty bad. She refused to be taken to a hospital other than Abbott Northwestern in Minneapolis. She wanted her parents to be with her because she knew that a rape kit was part of the deal. So that's what the police did. Brought her back. To answer your question, yes, a small amount of semen was found, but it was so contaminated by the time it got to the lab it was useless. The crime lab unit did its best but didn't find much of anything. It was a transient place. Lots of fibers, lots of fingerprints. And by the time Timmons was examined, it was all pretty moot. Rapes are hard to prove, even if the woman knows her attacker. So, yeah, you want my honest opinion? When we put Hodge away, we put away a serial rapist."

"You think he was planning to do it again?"

"Without a doubt. The guy's a classic sociopath. Charming. Smart. But completely lacking a conscience. Actually, a few months after Hodge was sent up, we found out about a rape that occurred down in Iowa. It was about a month before the one near Duluth." He counted off the details on his fingers. "Taser, lipstick with the word *justice* written on the woman's stomach. Right off the interstate. Believe me when I say that this time, I hope the justice system locks him up and throws away the key."

Jane tended to trust Nolan's instincts, and yet she knew the police could be myopic when it came to suspects. Taken as a whole, a case against Corey could certainly be made, but it was hardly airtight. Jane wasn't sure that if she'd been on the jury, they would have convicted him beyond a reasonable doubt. "I assume you know more about Charity Miller's murder than I do."

"Not really. Just the basics. Another Corey Hodge special."

"Charity had a boyfriend who'd been stalking her. She got a restraining order against him."

By the scowl on Nolan's face, Jane could tell he hadn't heard any of this before. She went on to explain what she knew about Gabriel Keen, how he'd been implicated in the beating of a gay Methodist minister, a good friend of Charity's. She told him about the conversation she'd had with Keen earlier in the day.

"The lead detectives will follow that up. They'll do their job."

"I'm sure they will."

"Look, Jane, I know you're concerned about Hodge because of the potential impact his arrest could have on your dad's campaign. But I think, when everything is said and done, if Hodge is arrested before the election, it will have a negligible effect on voters. You've got to give people more credit."

Jane nodded, finished her drink. "Maybe."

29

"I thought you were at work," said Mary, coming into the kitchen and setting a sack of cleaning supplies on the table.

"Bad news on that front," said Corey. "I was fired yesterday." He waited for the flood of emotion. He wasn't disappointed.

"Oh, Corey. Honey. Why didn't you say something last night?"

"I promised to take you to dinner and a movie and I meant it. If I'd told you, it would have wrecked the evening."

"Who gave you the ax?"

"The floor supervisor. The delightfully subtle Mr. Cox."

"And he fired you . . . why?"

He stepped over to the refrigerator to get a glass of milk. "He said I was late for work a couple times and that I was late again last Friday."

"You were at the police station on Friday."

"Yeah, well, I didn't call and Cox said that it was grounds for beheading. Oh, come on, Mary. Don't give me that shocked look. It was just an excuse. He's been gunning to get rid of me ever since Wayne hired me. I'm a convicted felon, and because the papers have been printing stories that I'm a suspect in another felony, he decided to be both judge and jury."

"That's so unfair." But her distress turned quickly to wariness. "Your probation officer won't like it. You're supposed to be employed, right?"

"I'll find another job. A better one this time. I've got more money in the bank now than I ever have before in my life. I'm going to look around, sure, but I'm also going to take my time."

With a sigh, Mary eased down onto one of the kitchen chairs. "I wish the police would make an arrest. Then people would have to eat their bad opinions."

"I'll never be off the hook for that rape. I think we both better come to terms with it."

"It's just wrong and you know it," she said, her anger flaring. "I know you don't want to hear this, but Jane Lawless and a private investigator friend are looking into Charity's murder for us. Anything she can do to move the investigation along is welcome in my book."

He stared at her, holding the carton of milk in his hand so tightly he put a dent in it. "Are you nuts?"

"What?"

"How could you do that? The *last* thing I need is more people watching me, digging into my life."

"But you've got nothing to hide."

"Doesn't matter. I'm not in prison anymore. My life is private. Don't you get it? *Not for public consumption.* Call her right now, tell her to back off."

"I can't, not after she was so kind about it."

She was as dumb as a stump. "Goddamn it, Mary. I'm not your personal reclamation project. Stop messing with my life."

"Corey!"

"I hate it that you ask favors of people like Jane and her fat-ass father—almost as much as I hate that you have to clean their houses."

"It's my job. It's how I support myself. And I like cleaning."

"Well, I don't. It makes you their servant. And that's exactly how they treat you."

"How would you know?"

"I helped out a few times when I was in high school, remember? I was so embarrassed I felt like smashing things the whole time I was in those houses. It makes my skin crawl to think of you cleaning rich people's toilets."

"They're not all rich. Some of them are just busy."

"Bullshit. If they can pay you to clean up after them, they're rich in my book."

"Watch your mouth! I will *not* put up with that kind of language in this house. Maybe you think I've gone soft, but I haven't, Corey. I can throw you out now as easily as I could've tossed you out when you were a teenager."

"You won't need to. Serena and I are getting back together. I'll be living over at her house from now on."

Christopher had been so upset by the cop's interrogation after the funeral that he'd talked Luke's ear off on the way home in the car, railing against everything Gabriel Keen had said about him, insisting that it was all a lie. Luke assured him that he'd never doubted it for a minute. It wasn't that Luke didn't have questions of his own. He did. Serious questions. But he couldn't bring himself to start in on another interrogation immediately after the cop had finished.

By the time they returned home, Christopher was wrapped in a moody silence. Luke urged him to go lie down while he made dinner. Later, they ate together in the dining room, both exhausted, both locked into their own solitary misery.

Christopher went to bed early. Luke sat up and watched a bunch of cop show reruns and eventually, after polishing off a bag of potato chips and two beers, fell asleep on the couch. He hadn't even moved when the sun, streaming in through the oversized windows, struck him in the eyes just before eight. Christopher seemed to be resting peacefully, so instead of waking him, Luke showered and dressed, grabbed an apple from the kitchen counter, and headed to the campaign office. But by noon, he felt he'd waited as long as he could. There were questions on the table that demanded answers.

Luke stopped by a Bruegger's and picked up a couple of bagel sandwiches. When he walked into the condo, he found Christopher on the phone, a grim yet oddly resigned look on his face. Luke shook the sack to get Christopher's attention, then tossed his coat over one of the living room chairs and went to the window to watch the river.

"Boy, what a day," said Christopher a few minutes later.

Luke turned around, still holding the sack, watching as Christopher lowered himself carefully onto the couch. "Hungry?"

"Famished."

He tossed him one of the sandwiches. Taking a seat across the room, he watched Christopher tear off the paper and take a bite.

"What is this?"

"Smoked turkey, scallion cream cheese, sun-dried tomato spread, and veggies on honey wheat."

"It's really good." He nodded to the unopened sandwich in Luke's hand. "Aren't you eating?"

"Who was on the phone?"

He chewed for a second, then said, "The bishop's secretary. I've got an appointment to meet with the bishop on Friday afternoon."

"You ready for that?"

Christopher spread one arm across the back of the sofa, thought it over. "Yeah, I am. I thought it was important to take a stand as a gay minister. I still do, but I don't think I'll ever go back."

"You've served above and beyond the call of duty in my book."

Christopher set the sandwich on the table next to him, folded his hands in his lap. "I don't know. I guess I need more time to figure some things out."

"What things?"

"Well, for one, do I want to continue in the ministry. And then—" His eyes shifted to the windows. "I know this sounds melodramatic, but . . . if I'm no longer a pastor, who the hell am I?"

Luke decided just to plunge in. There was never going to be a perfect time to ask his questions. "Listen, Christopher, maybe this isn't the right moment, but there's something I need to ask you."

"What?"

"I was working at my desk the other night and I noticed . . . well, actually I saw that my taser was gone."

"Yeah," he said, nodding.

"Did you take it?"

"Sure."

"Why?"

"Protection. I lied to the cop yesterday because I knew he'd jump to the wrong conclusion. I took it when I first started leaving the house. I needed it. I should have said something to you, but I felt guilty, like a minister shouldn't need a taser to make him feel safe."

Luke breathed an inward sigh of relief. "I wish you'd told me. I would have shown you how to use it."

"I found some instructions online."

"Well, whatever. Do you still need it?"

"I . . . I don't have it anymore."

Luke felt a tiny zap of adrenaline hit his system. "No?"

"No. I . . . gave it to Charity."

"Charity? When?"

"A week or so before she died. That's why the police saw so many phone calls from me to her, or from her to me. Sometimes she'd call me from work to tell me she was leaving. Then she'd call when she got home, when the door was locked and she felt safe. She called like that all the time, to let me know where she was, where she was going. Or I'd call her to check up. Keen was a monster in both our lives, Luke. You of all people should understand that. She knew I had the taser because we'd talked about how hard it was for me to go out in public again, alone. One day she called and asked if she could have it." He held his breath. "God forgive me. I gave it to her."

"Okay. But just because you gave it to her, that doesn't mean it was the one used to kill her."

"Of course it was," he choked out, leaning forward as if he was in physical pain. "Keen must have wrestled it away from her. Maybe that's what gave him the idea to make it look like Corey Hodge had done it. But it's all my fault. I should never have taken that thing out of your desk in the first place. I'm a coward, Luke. Where was my faith?"

"Where was your *God* when you were being beaten half to death?"

Christopher plowed on, indifferent to Luke's words. "It's eating me alive, the guilt I feel over her death. I'm glad you asked me about the taser. I wanted to tell you, but I just . . . I couldn't. Now that you know—" Everything came spilling out. All the pent-up emotion he'd kept trapped inside ever since he'd learned Charity had been killed. "I know how to act, how to cover up my feelings, but the truth is, I see Charity's face in my mind all the time now, see her dying there on the ground all alone. I should never have told her about the taser. I feel like I'm falling, Luke. Like God has forsaken me because of my sins and I'm falling through midair with nothing to hold on to and no one to save me."

"I'm here," said Luke, though he could see in Christopher's eyes that his presence, even his love, would never be enough.

Corey left several messages for Serena, but when she didn't return them, he began to worry. What if Johnny, in a rage at being tossed out, had lost his temper and knocked her around again? Just the thought of that asshole hurting her made Corey want to wedge the guy's head in a vise.

And that's why, on his way down Lyndale, the speedometer on his motorcycle inched up past fifty. He needed to get to her house fast.

When the cop pulled him over and asked for his license, he let loose with a stream of such foul language that if his aunt had heard it, she would have disowned him.

"You on your way to a fire?" asked the cop, standing next to the cycle and writing out the ticket.

Corey thought it was a stupid question, one that didn't require an answer. He took the ticket and stuffed it in his pocket. Before the cop was even back in his cruiser, he was off again.

He arrived just as his digital watch hit noon. Right away he noticed that the black Monte Carlo that had been in the driveway the other night was gone. Serena's Tempo was missing, too.

Setting the stand on his bike, he swung his leg off and trotted across the grass to the front stoop. Pounding on the door long and hard, he stood back and waited, all the while scrutinizing the other houses on the block. None of them were exactly palatial. In the daylight, Serena's place looked smaller and even more dingy than it had the other night. The eaves were all rotted, the screens were either rusted or missing, and some of the windows were broken, the panes held together with tape. Cocking his head at the garage, he had the feeling it was tilted, listing precariously to the left. He was surprised the property hadn't been condemned.

Growing impatient, he banged on the door again. When nobody answered, he walked out to the middle of the front yard and yelled, "Serena! Open up!"

One house over, a woman's head emerged from the front door. "You a bill collector?"

"Me? Nah, a friend."

"She's not home. I saw her drive off a couple hours ago."

"You know when she'll be back?"

"Her kid usually gets home around three thirty. If she can't be here, sometimes her mom comes by to take him, but more often than not she asks me to take care of him until she gets back. She never asked me today, so maybe she'll be home by then."

"Thanks." Corey gazed up at the house, disgusted that his son had to call this dump a home. Head down, he walked back to his bike.

Corey had never been to the Xanadu club before, but he had been to the old Xanadu theater many times in his late teens. Back then it was a pit, a place to hear alternative punk bands, all Nine Inch Nails clones, none of them well-known but each sufficiently loud and agonized to entertain. He was amazed to find that the deco interior had not only been preserved but also restored. Polished brass, lots of beautiful wood paneling, soft lighting. It must have cost a mint to do it. But then, Lawless had a mint. Several mints, no doubt, right at her fingertips.

Catching the bartender's eye, Corey stepped up to the counter. "I'm looking for Jane Lawless."

The bartender, a broad-shouldered guy in a tight yellow Xanadu Club T-shirt, lifted his hand and pointed down.

A second later, Jane popped up from below the bar, a clipboard held in her right hand. "Corey. Hi."

She seemed surprised and a little mystified by his sudden appearance. In person, she looked younger, even a little prettier than the pictures he'd seen of her in the newspapers. He'd met her only a couple of times and didn't remember her all that well. He liked the way she had her hair—kind of twisted into a braid at the back of her neck. But, for sure, she dressed like a dyke—ratty jeans and a gray hoodie.

"Can I help you?" she asked, laying down the clipboard.

"Yeah, you can," he said, pressing his hands against the counter and leaning toward her. "You can stay the hell out of my business."

She motioned for him to follow her down to the end of the bar, where none of the customers were seated.

"Would you care to explain?"

"Sure." He resumed the same aggressive stance. Rocking up on the tips of his toes, he said, "My aunt Mary told me she asked you to look into Charity Miller's murder. I don't need your help."

"Okay."

"Okay?" He blinked. "That's it?"

"Well, Mary thinks you're innocent, but she's concerned the police will come to the wrong conclusion. That's why she asked me—and a friend—to help."

"The private eye."

She nodded.

"My aunt's softhearted. I love her for it, but sometimes she's also softheaded. I'm going to say this one more time. I . . . don't . . . need . . . your . . . help. Stop messing with my life. That clear enough?"

"Very clear."

"You rich people—"

"Excuse me?"

"You think you're better than everybody else."

"Better? I don't believe I've ever had a conversation with you about how I think or feel, so I'm not sure how you'd know that."

"Amusing. You're a real hoity-toity bitch."

"And you're trying to pick a fight. Why?"

"I pegged you years ago. You're one of those people who thinks that because a guy gets in trouble with the law, he's stupid."

"I don't think that. Not for a second."

"Bull*shit*. I didn't do it. I never touched that woman. And I didn't kill Charity." He dared her with his eyes to contradict him. "You wanna know something?"

"Not particularly."

"I've probably read more books than anybody you know."

"Good for you."

Everything she said pulled his strings. "Just stay the hell out of my business. If you don't, believe me, you'll regret it."

"Is that a threat? And before you tell me it wasn't a threat, just a warning, let me say that if that's your answer, I think you've watched way too many crime dramas."

"Jesus, you're a piece of work."

"I'm not sure what you are. The jury's still out."

Before he could dig himself in any deeper, he turned and left. As he reached the sidewalk in front of the building, he felt like putting his fist through the plate-glass window behind him. He had a hell of a time controlling himself when he got all wound up. But he couldn't let go, not the way he wanted to. With all his might, he shook off the anger coiling in his gut and forced himself to walk away.

Serena's Tempo was parked on the street in front of her house when he returned shortly before three. He was still steamed in general and pissed specifically that she hadn't returned his calls.

Banging on the front door, he called, "Serena? Answer the goddamn door." He glanced up at the second-floor windows. One of them looked like a sheet had been hung across it. The sheet was old and dirty, like it had been hanging there since the Civil War. He banged again.

Finally, he heard the bolt being drawn, and a second later Serena appeared. She was wearing a bright green T-shirt and tight jeans. She looked hot.

"So? Can I come in?"

She hesitated. "I'm folding some clothes in the living room."

He walked in behind her, noting that most of the furniture looked like it had come from a garage sale. There was a lot of clutter. After removing a purse, a stack of magazines, and an empty Kleenex box from one of the chairs, he sat down.

"I know the place is a mess," said Serena, brushing her hair behind her ear. "I'm up late because I work late, and then I sleep way too long in the morning. Johnny usually gets Dean off to school."

"Well, I'll do that now," said Corey. "And I can help with the chores. I like cleaning, as long as it's not for somebody else. And I'm even a pretty fair cook, if you remember correctly."

She smiled, but the smile faded before it ever actually bloomed.

"Okay, so . . . should we gather all Johnny's stuff, toss it out on the sidewalk?"

"Look, I—"

"If you don't want to, I'll do it myself. We just need to get it done before he gets back from work. If you don't have any boxes, I know where I can find some."

"About that."

"I know, I know. You probably feel sorry for him. But you've got to see it's for the best. You can't live with a guy who uses you as a punching bag."

"That only happened a couple times. And frankly, I think it was mostly my fault."

"Your fault? How do you figure?"

"Johnny's . . . jealous, you know? Because he loves me."

She hadn't come right out and said it, but Corey couldn't miss the drift the conversation was taking. "You've got cold feet. You don't want to replace the devil you know with the one you don't."

"Yeah. Sorta."

He shot to his feet. "But you do know, me, Serena. You believed I loved you once. You gotta give me another chance. Especially now, with Dean. I've got lots of money in the bank. I can take care of you, both of you."

"You've got a job?" she said, looking at him in that sideways way of hers.

"Yeah. A good one. I work at a car dealership."

"You fix cars?"

"It pays well and I get benefits. We could be a family, babe. I want to marry you—I always have. You'd be on my health insurance, my dental insurance. You'd be the beneficiary on my life insurance, not that I'm ever gonna die." He grinned. "Can Johnny give you any of that?"

She sank down on the couch. "I don't know what to do."

"It's an easy choice. A no-brainer. On the one hand you've got a bum who knocks you around and on the other you've got me, a man who loves you and just happens to be the father of your child."

"You're confusing me. You're a good talker. You always were."

"Baby, what's there to think about? With me it's win-win."

"But Johnny said you're about to be arrested for murder."

"I am so sick and tired of being accused of crap I didn't do."

Looking at the folded clean clothes sitting on the coffee table, she said, "I just don't know."

The front door opened and shut and Dean walked in.

"Hi," he said, glancing at his mom, then giving Corey a quick once-over.

Corey wondered if he was catching the resemblance.

"Who are you?" he asked, chewing his gum.

"Corey Hodge. I'm an old friend of your mom's."

"Hey, Mom, could you take Jamir and me to a movie this weekend? It's at the Riverview, so it's cheap. I'll even fork over some of my allowance."

"What's the movie?" she asked.

"The newest Harry Potter."

"You like to read?" asked Corey.

"Not really."

"I thought maybe you'd read all the Harry Potter books like I did. I think they're terrific."

"I just like the movies," mumbled Dean. "Can we, Mom?"

"Let me think about it. Go get yourself something to eat. Hey, I bought some of those pizza rolls you like. They're in the freezer."

He dumped his backpack next to the stairs and bolted for the kitchen in the back.

"God, what a great kid," said Corey, his eyes glued to the place where he'd been standing.

"Yeah, he is."

"So, come on, Serena. Give me the word and I'll take care of Johnny. You'll never have to see him again. Promise."

"You don't get it."

"Get what?"

"I love him, Corey."

He couldn't believe he'd heard her right. "You're serious?"

She nodded.

"But . . . what about me?"

"You push too hard. I need some time to think about this. It's a big change. You're asking me to turn my entire life upside down."

He didn't see it that way. Not at all. But he could tell he was treading on treacherous ground. "Okay. You got a point. But while you're thinking things over, could I, like, take Dean to a football game or something?"

"I don't know."

"Serena, you owe me that much."

"I don't see how I owe you anything."

He wanted to scream at her, but he didn't want to scare the kid, even though the fire inside him was beginning to build. This was the danger point, and he knew it. "You never told me I was a father."

"I had my reasons."

"Whatever they were, it's not fair."

"You were always so quick to talk about what was fair and what wasn't. Okay, let's talk about that. Was it fair that the man I loved was sent to prison for rape? Was it fair that I was left alone to have a child with only my hysterical, critical mother for moral and financial support? Was it fair that I've spent the last nine years scraping and clawing, working my ass off to make a life for Dean and me just so you could walk in like some king, throw your weight around, and turn everything upside down? You have a murder charge hanging over your head, Corey, and yet you come to me like you're entitled to make demands about Dean."

"He's my son."

"He's *mine.* I gave birth to him. I raised him. I sat with him at night when he was sick, when he was scared. Where were you, Corey? Where?"

"Don't do this, Serena."

"I think you better go."

"You're making this into a war."

Her face flushed a deep red. She pointed to the door. "Get out."

Before Jane drove home from the Lyme House on Tuesday night, she stopped by Charity's apartment building on Colfax Avenue. It wasn't the old-fashioned dark redbrick building so commonplace in south

Minneapolis but something a little more modern—most likely built in the sixties. Three stories. Small balconies for each unit. Modest.

She drove past the building several times before she turned into the short drive on the north end that led to a small parking lot in the back. Most of the slots were filled with cars this late at night, with the exception of the one near the door. She eased into it and killed the engine. She clipped a leash to Mouse's collar, and the two of them walked over to the Dumpster, which sat on the south end of thc lot, backed up into some scrub brush.

"This is where it happened," she said to Mouse, looking around, feeling thoroughly chilled by the knowledge of what had gone down here just a few days ago. "This is where Charity died."

A light was on over the back entrance, and about twenty yards down the alley there was a light high up on a pole, but other than that, the lot was dark.

"I'd hate to meet up with someone out here who wanted to hurt me." There were so many places to hide.

"Who did it?" she asked Mouse, watching him sniff the ground. "You know what? I've been thinking." She crouched down, stroking his fur. "At the cemetery yesterday, I ran into a guy named Keen. Corey lied to him, told him he was a cop. Keen thought he was Charity's new boyfriend, so it was instant dislike. Somehow, he found out Corey had raped a woman. He probably Googled his name, just like I did. What if—"

At the sound of laughter, she straightened up. A woman and a teenage girl had just walked out the back door of the apartment building. They glanced at Jane and Mouse, then got into a van and drove off.

Standing alone in the darkened lot, a wave of unease rolled through her chest. "Come on, boy."

She got Mouse settled in the backseat, settled herself in the front, locked the doors, and started the engine. "Here's what I was going to say. What if Keen found out the details of the rape Corey committed nine years ago? He obviously saw Corey as an interloper. What if he set it up to look like Corey had attacked Charity? He'd get even with her for dumping him and get rid of Corey at the same time. All he had to do was buy himself a taser, some duct tape, and a tube of lipstick, wait for Charity to put herself in a vulnerable situation—just like we were in a few seconds ago—and boom. He takes his shot. But instead of stunning her, the taser interferes with her heart rhythm and she dies. Maybe he's upset, or maybe he isn't. But he's off the hook because it's Corey's MO."

Jane looked around at Mouse. "What do you think? Does that theory hold water?"

He leaned his head close to hers and gave her nose a lick.

"I know. Without proof, a theory's just a theory. Thanks for weighing in."

Late Wednesday morning, Corey found himself sitting in the same police interrogation room he'd been in last Friday. The smell of desperation still permeated the air and clung to his skin like rain-soaked clothes. He'd been here, or someplace very like here, so many times before that, with a certain sense of wonder, he realized that the surroundings seemed oddly reassuring. He knew the drill. He understood the stakes. As much as he railed against it, this had become his world.

Corey sat back, digging his hands into the pockets of his jeans. It didn't take long before Emerson entered and sat down across from him. Watching him, Corey had a flash of insight. Emerson was about to arrest him.

"Now, let's begin again. I'd like you to go through your movements on the day Charity Miller died."

"I've already told that a hundred times."

"Let's try it once more. From the top."

Corey groaned, registered his irritation, then started in once again.

"Back up just a minute," said Emerson as Corey got to the part about taking Charity for a ride on his motorcycle. "What time was that?"

"Jesus. I told you. It was right around ten."

"And you brought her back to her car when?"

"A little before eleven. She got a call on her cell and that's when I looked at my watch. After she was done talking, we said good night, I got on my bike and took off."

"Did you say anything about getting together again?"

"No."

"When you left her, how would you describe her mood?"

"I told you. She was fine. Happy."

"Happy."

"Yeah. I showed her a good time."

"Did she tell you who the call was from?"

"Like I said, no."

"You described your ride together as short."

"Yeah."

"But an hour is a long time just to ride around."

Corey shrugged. "It felt short."

"Did you stop at any time? Get off the cycle and walk around?"

"No."

"Did you come on to her?"

"Hell, no. I've got a girlfriend."

"Serena Van Dorn. But she's living with this other guy at the moment."

"It's just temporary." He could see the smirk on Emerson's face. All cops were sadists.

"So you and Charity never had sex?"

"Of course not."

"You're positive about that?"

Corey caught a look in his eye. It stopped him cold.

"The thing is, we've got your DNA on file. A few hours ago, I received some test results that indicated a semen stain found on Charity's clothing belonged to you. It's an exact match."

He sat up a little straighter. Cops lied all the time in interrogations. As far as he knew, DNA didn't come back that fast. "Arrest me, then. You've got your proof. Why the hell are we even talking?"

"Corey, at this time, I need to read you your Miranda rights."

Corey's eyes opened wide. He hesitated, then shouted, "Do it. I don't care. You got squat."

After he grunted that he understood his rights, Emerson shoved a file toward him. "There's a lot riding on this case. That's why I was able to push to get the tests back fast. I don't know if you can read a medical report, but it's all there in black and white. Your sperm on Charity's panties. You've been lying to me, Corey. All along the way you've been lying. You're guilty as hell and you and I both know it."

He tried to stare the cop down, but in the end, he was the one to blink first. "Look, I just . . . I didn't want you to think we had that much of a connection. I used protection. I didn't . . . I mean, it was no big deal."

"Let me get this straight. You're saying now that you *did* have sex with Charity Miller."

"Yeah."

"Was it consensual?"

"Hell, yes."

"This was her first date with you. She hardly knew you, and yet she had sex with you?"

Corey shrugged.

"Tell me about the word *justice,* Corey. It must mean something to you."

"It means the same thing to me it means to you."

"You like justice? You believe in it?"

"Sure, although I've never seen much of it."

"So you'd say you've seen more injustice."

"Yeah, I would."

"Ever looked up the word *justice* in a dictionary?"

"I don't remember."

"*Justice* has a lot of meanings. Sometimes it means punishment, as in, 'The judge was determined to exact justice.' Ever thought about that?"

"What's your point?"

"You ever feel like you want to punish someone, Corey?"

He didn't respond.

"But you *do* feel like you've been punished for something you didn't do."

"You got that right."

"So, maybe we could say you're concerned with both justice and injustice."

"I'm concerned with getting the hell out of here without being arrested."

"Where did it happen?"

"Huh?"

"Where did you and Charity have sex?"

"We stopped along the West River Road."

"I need the exact spot."

"I can't remember."

"Try harder."

"Who the hell cares? She was fine when we said good night."

"But you lied about having sexual intercourse with Charity because you didn't think we'd find out."

"Yeah. I mean, why tell you something that would make me look guilty when there was a good chance you'd never find out on your own?"

"Find out what? Be specific."

"That I had sex with a woman on the night she was raped and killed."

Emerson's eyes tightened. Corey had no idea what he'd said, but whatever it was, it had thrown the detective.

"What else have you lied to me about, Corey?"

"Nothing."

"Did you follow her back to her apartment?"

"No. I already told you. I had something to eat, then went to my girlfriend's house."

"And afterward you went home."

"Right."

"Did Charity say anything to upset you?"

"Of course not. What would she say?"

"The call she got close to eleven. It was from a minister. He told her you were an ex-con, that you'd gone to jail for raping a woman."

Corey's expression hardened. He didn't reply.

"Charity's parents told us that Charity thought you were a cop. You'd told her that. Is that true?"

Corey's gaze floated around the room. "Yeah. It just kinda came out when I was talking to her boyfriend, Keen. I wanted to scare him, so I told him I was undercover. Charity heard it and asked me about it. I didn't tell her I was lying because . . . well, because I didn't want her to think I tried to con people."

"Even though you do."

Corey glared at him.

"So let's picture this. She thinks she's gone on a ride with a cop. That's probably why she trusted you so quickly. You parlay that into some quick sex and you bring her back to her car. But before you leave, she gets a call from a friend who tells her that not only are you not a cop, but you're a convicted rapist. Are you telling me she said nothing to you about it? She just kissed you good-bye?"

Corey's eyes rose to the ceiling. "I didn't kill her."

"What did she say to you? Did she piss you off? Did you twist her arm? Get rough with her? Did you tell her that people had it in for you? That you were innocent?"

"I *am* innocent. I didn't rape that woman in '97 and I didn't rape and kill Charity."

"*Tell* me, Corey. What did she say to you?"

He looked down at his hands. "She said I was disgusting. That people like me should be locked up."

"And you just stood there and listened?"

"Yeah, I did."

"You didn't think she needed to be taught a lesson? You didn't follow her home?"

Corey was working as hard as he knew how to hold back his temper.

"You drove to her place, waited until she came outside with her garbage, and then you shot her with your taser. You wrote your favorite word on her stomach and left her there, like a piece of trash. Is that what she was to you, Corey? Trash?"

"I didn't do it," he shouted, his fist slamming down on the table. "You should be investigating Gabriel Keen. He did it. He was harassing her. She told me all about it."

"We've talked to Mr. Keen. He has an alibi."

"He's lying. People are lying for him."

"It's hard to know the truth when people lie, isn't it, Corey."

"I never hurt anyone in my life. I'm innocent. How many times do I have to say it before someone believes me? I did not rape and kill Charity Miller!"

Emerson threaded his fingers behind his neck, examined Corey with a weary look on his face. "Don't you ever get sick of saying that? That you're innocent? Nobody's *innocent*. Especially somebody like you who lies all the time. Hell, I wouldn't be surprised if you looked me straight in the eye and told me you weren't in this room."

Corey flattened his hands on the table, waited for the inevitable.

Emerson watched him for nearly a minute. Let the tension build. Finally, he said, "Go on. Get out of here."

31

Julia worked the phones at the campaign office on Wednesday afternoon. Several hours into her shift, a woman asked a question she couldn't answer. The volunteers had been advised not to answer difficult policy questions. Instead, they were requested to hand the phone to someone who could.

At first, Julia had been put off by the campaign's use of cell phones instead of landlines for the phone banks, but in this instance, she could see the wisdom of the decision. Volunteers and staff were walking around talking on phones all the time, occasionally rushing to grab someone with more specific knowledge.

Out of the corner of her eye, she saw Maria Rios come into the room where the phone volunteers worked. Julia pushed quickly out of her chair, waving her free hand to get her attention. After learning what the woman wanted, Maria took the call, and Julia, temporarily without a phone, walked across the hall to the break room to get a cup of coffee. She'd agreed to work from one until five. Checking her watch, she saw that it was just after four. At six, she had an appointment with a real estate agent.

Before Neil returned from the AIDS conference in Australia,

she hoped to be out of his house. She needed a place of her own, where she could live quietly and privately—and where she could entertain Jane without worrying that Neil would return home unexpectedly.

Julia was drawn to the quiet of the country—or the exurbs, as some called it. But exurbia today wasn't just an old-fashioned mill town, or college town, a farm community that housed commuters from the larger urban areas. The houses Julia had been shown were all new American McMansions. She loathed the garish excess, the way exurbia was encroaching on farmland, prairie, and forests, feeding the need for status and luxury with no thought to anything but personal desire and no real understanding—or even a wish to understand anything beyond what CNN or FOX News might report—of what life was like for other human beings in other parts of the world. After all, Americans were blessed by God. The Chosen People. They deserved their wealth and status because God was on their side.

Julia would never be able to get the smell, the taste, the very existence of the slums on the periphery of Johannesburg out of her mind. Poor people living on a belt of toxic waste and unstable soil, contaminated by generations of mining. Everywhere on the planet, poor people were willing to trade safety and heath for a small space they could call their own.

Julia had lived in some of those forgotten areas, worked in villages, shantytowns, in the poorest of the poor clinics all over southern Africa. More than one sick, hungry child had died in her arms. How could her priorities not be forever altered? But then, she'd been guilty of her own kind of hubris.

For a long time Julia actually believed she couldn't die. She considered herself outside the natural order of things—death not only would not touch her, it could not. And by the time it occurred to her that she might be wrong, she was too obsessed to stop. It was impossible to explain, but in pushing herself to the edge, she'd discovered an almost transcendent state of being. For the last year in Africa, she'd worked in a trance. If Neil hadn't stepped in when he had, she would surely be dead by now.

The worst part of her years in Africa often returned to her as vivid images in her dreams. On occasion, they would hit while she was awake, shrieking so loudly that all she could do was sit motionless in a chair and try to shut everything down. She couldn't stand to have anyone touch her or even talk to her during those hours. She had to be alone, in the dark if possible. She couldn't stand any noise, any stimulation. Neil was the only one who knew how bad it sometimes got. She loved him for his care and concern, for saving her from the brutal treatment she was inflicting on her own body and soul, but she would never be able to love him the way he wanted.

As her health returned, Julia was beginning to see that her need to continue to do good work would always be a driving force in her life. But until things were settled with Jane, until Jane forgave her and their relationship was back on track, she had to stay in Minnesota. That was her first priority—her only priority at the moment, now that Kenzie was out of the picture. It might take time, but Jane would come to see that Julia had changed, that she'd walked through fire and been purified by it.

And so, as much as Julia hated the inner city, she couldn't bring herself to look at any more monstrous country extravagances. Tonight, her agent was showing her a new condo development down in Stillwater. At least these lofts were built up, not out. And this one was small. Julia had looked at the floor plan online. It was one bedroom. Almost European in the clever way it utilized space. Perhaps here she would be able to find some peace.

After pouring herself a mug of coffee, she went back into the main workroom, surprised to see Jane standing by the bulletin board talking to one of the staffers. The two of them spoke for a few more seconds and then the staffer took off.

Now that Jane was alone, Julia approached. "Boy, it sure takes a lot of people to run a political campaign," she said, amused by the startled look on Jane's face.

"Julia, hi. I didn't see you."

"I've been working the phone banks. Thought I'd take a break, get some coffee."

Jane was wearing a black velvet jacket with satin lapels, and formal black slacks. No shirt, just a sterling silver necklace against her flawless skin.

"You're all dressed up. Where's the party?"

"I'm working at the Xanadu tonight. I usually wear a traditional tux. This one's new."

Trying not to stare, Julia continued, "I haven't received your father's tests back yet. I should have them soon. He appeared to be in fine shape, for a man his age—with the stress he's been under."

Jane's expression softened. "That was really generous of you. I know Peter appreciates it, too."

"While we were doing the physical, Ray told me all about the Cessna he bought. I had no idea he was a pilot. He said he'd given you flying lessons for your birthday a couple years ago."

"I really enjoy it," said Jane, trying to look like she wasn't studying Julia, when she so clearly was. "Not that I've been able to get much air time this year. Work trumps play."

"Small planes make me nervous," said Julia, taking another sip from her mug. Actually, she loved flying in any form—big planes, small planes, ultralights, even gliders—but figured if she told Jane the truth, she'd assume Julia was angling for a ride.

"They're actually quite safe."

"Is it a two seater?"

"Four."

Before Julia could think of another question to keep the conversational ball going, a woman yelled, causing everyone to turn and stare toward the wall of computers.

"Luke, get out here!" called a man.

Within seconds, everyone sitting at a computer screen had begun shouting, pointing, looking around for help.

Julia turned just as Luke came out of his office.

"It disappeared!" yelled one of the women. "Everything I've been working on all day . . . it just vanished."

"Me too," said the man who'd first called for Luke. "It's all gone."

Luke raced into the room, shoving chairs aside. He hit a bunch of keys. Then more. "Maybe it's a virus," he said, moving from screen to screen. "Shit—" He looked bewildered, panicked, his face deep in concentration as he continued to hit keys, hold keys down, type in words, unhook wires, rehook them. But nothing he did changed anything. The screens glowed but were completely empty.

Jane left for the Xanadu club shortly after the computer meltdown. She wanted to stay and help, but there was nothing she could do. She'd also promised to take the evening shift for one of her managers, a man who'd asked for the night off so he could attend his son's first wrestling match.

Julia, in a rare constructive moment, offered to stick around so that she could keep Jane updated. Jane was a little baffled by Julia's general demeanor. It was almost as if she had entirely forgotten about the night Jane discovered her in her house. Today, she seemed completely normal—except for the surreal fact that she seemed to be suffering from a convenient case of amnesia.

And so, as the evening wore on, Julia phoned with updates. It was strange to hear Julia's voice on the other end of the line. Strange, familiar, and also somewhat disturbing.

According to Julia, everything that could be determined quickly, if not explained, had been. Damages still needed to be assessed. Most of what was lost had been backed up onto disks of one sort or another, but that was only part of the problem. Luke and a number of other tech people had volunteered to work through the night to see if they could get the system up and running again.

Julia also passed along that Luke was pretty sure it was a "nasty trojan."

"What's that mean?"

"He keeps talking about an 'exe.' "

"It's geek language. Incomprehensible to the average computer moron like me."

"Whatever the thing is, it's opened back doors in the system."

"Okay. Go on."

"Luke thought that, given some time, he'd be able to pick out the exact e-mail that was used to infect the system. Others agreed. It was also Luke's opinion that it could have come from virtually anywhere, but most likely the hit was by a hacker attached to the Pettyjohn campaign. When it came down to it, Luke said it could take months and thousands of dollars to find the true source of the attack and prosecute the individual or individuals.

"He said the hackers used an excellent 'rootkit' to cover their tracks. Don't ask what a rootkit is, please."

"I won't."

"Or a webmin bug. Whatever that is was set to detonate at a certain time, and that's why everything died at once. Well," said Julia, sounding weary but upbeat, "that's the last installment. I'm going home."

Jane was on her way upstairs to her office. "I appreciate the updates."

"Glad to help."

Jane could hear a slight hesitation in her voice. They both knew each other far too well to miss a signal like that. "What is it?"

"Huh? Oh, nothing."

"Just say what you want to say."

"It's not about us, Jane. Just something that's been on my mind."

"Do you"—she closed her eyes, knowing she was going to regret saying this—"need to talk about it?"

"Thanks, but no. I just want to go home and get some rest. It's been a long day. See you around the campaign office."

"Thanks again, Julia. Good night." Jane dropped the cell phone in her pocket, absolutely refusing to spend the rest of the evening parsing her feelings.

Jane worked in her office until Cordelia called shortly after ten.

"Aren't you excited?"

"About what?"
"Friday night."
"What's happening Friday night?"
"Halloween!"
"Oh, right." She'd completely forgotten.
"Melanie and I will be over by five thirty. In costume. Don't worry, we'll get all the treats ready to hand out. What are we having for dinner?"
"Candy corn?"
"Tell me you're joking."
"I'm joking."
"What's this year's costume?"
"I think I'll come as a chef. You know, I'll put on one of my chef's coats, wear a pair of old jeans."
"Poor, Janey. I understand. How can you immerse yourself in the revelries of All Hallows' Eve when you've just been dumped?"
"Do you have to put it like that?"
"Don't be grumpy. I'll cheer you up. I'll even come over to your house tomorrow night and decorate the place, just like always. But you'll have to carry the trunk in from the car. Cordelia Thorn does not haul."
Cordelia had a trunk filled with black and orange streamer paper, black and orange balloons, black and orange candles, black and orange jewelry, witches' hats, minibroomsticks, gourds, Indian corn, strings of orange lights, scary rubber masks, magic wands, plastic pumpkins of all sizes, tons of plastic black cats, a rubber severed foot, and two sets of glowing lawn eyeballs. She'd been amassing this treasure chest since she was five.
"Halloween is my favorite holiday."
"I know. Everyone dresses up so you fit right in."
"Was that intended as a put-down?"
"Would I make a nasty comment about your clothing?"
"The world is heavy with complexity, Janey. We humans need to indulge ourselves in a little old-fashioned fun every now and then."

"Old-fashioned?"

"You've heard of the Druids? How much older do we need to go?"

"Okay. I'll make us something suitably Halloweenish for dinner. Eye of newt and bat wing stew."

"I'm hanging up now."

"Toe of frog would make a nice appetizer."

By midnight Jane was tired and ready to go home. She turned off her computer and shut off the desk light. After locking her door, she came down the curved stairway from the second floor, noticing that there were still a few people sitting at tables in the dining room. Food service stopped at eleven on weeknights.

On her way through the Speakeasy bar, she checked in with the head barman. He would be responsible for locking up tonight and running the register after closing. Jane told him she was heading home and wished him a good night.

Turning toward the door, her eyes widened. A familiar form slipped off one of the stools not five feet away from her and stood up.

"Kenzie?"

"I couldn't stay away."

"Am I dreaming?"

"If you are, I am, too. Can you forgive me?"

They fell together, arms surrounding, encircling, hands smoothing, caressing. After a long, greedy kiss, they separated, finally remembering where they were.

Gazing around, Jane realized that the bar patrons had been watching them because they now were clapping and whistling.

"It's a different world," said Jane, her am around Kenzie's waist, guiding her toward the door.

"At midnight in Uptown it is."

Julia was aware of the risk. Any communication she had with Jane at the moment carried with it the possibility of backfiring. As she rang the doorbell at Jane's house on Thursday morning, she worried that if Jane didn't believe what she'd come to tell her, she might decide that Julia was merely trying to insinuate herself into her life. And that would wipe away any of the good feelings Julia had worked so hard to create in the last few days. But she also understood Jane well enough to know that she rarely jumped to conclusions, unlike Cordelia, who was all intuition, instinct, first impressions. Cordelia distrusted reason, and in her case, with a maladaptive brain like hers, it was probably for the best.

It was a bright autumn morning. Frost had formed on the grass overnight but was pretty much gone now, except for the shaded spots under trees and bushes. Julia pulled the collar of her camel wool coat up around her neck. Jane's car was in the drive, which didn't necessarily mean she was home. She could have walked down the hill to the Lyme House. But Julia could smell wood smoke coming from the chimney.

Just as she was about to ring the bell again, the door opened. Jane stood in front of her, still in her bathrobe, wool slippers on her feet, her long dark hair tumbled around her shoulders. Her cheeks were flushed, as if she'd just gotten out of bed.

"Oh, God, did I wake you?"

"No," said Jane. "I've been up for a while. I was in the kitchen making coffee."

"I'm sorry to bother you," said Julia. Actually, she wasn't the least bit sorry. "Could I come in? It's important."

Jane seemed hesitant. "This really isn't a good time."

"It will only take a minute. It's about what happened last night at your father's campaign office."

Reluctantly, Jane stepped back.

Julia hadn't been in the house during the day, only at night. She'd forgotten how lovely the sunlight was as it came in the living room windows, creating a series of paned patterns on the Oriental rugs. And sure enough, a fire was burning in the fireplace.

Jane stood in the foyer, arms crossed.

So be it, thought Julia. Just one more challenge.

"Hey, Lawless, is the coffee ready?" called a voice from upstairs.

Very slowly, Julia's gaze rose to the top of the stairs. "You're not alone?"

"No, I'm not," said Jane.

Julia recognized the voice. Kenzie appeared a few seconds later, wearing a cowboy hat, a rumpled red T-shirt, and jeans that had more holes in them than cloth. She trotted down the stairs, a grin on her face. When she saw Julia, her breath caught in her throat, but she covered by coughing.

"You okay?" asked Jane.

"Yeah, fine." Her eyes registered a mixture of confusion, guilt, and alarm, but she was quick with a comeback. "Maybe I'm allergic to your visitor."

Cute, thought Julia. And well played.

"Oh, ah, Julia, this is Kenzie Mulroy," said Jane. "My partner. Kenzie, Julia Martinsen."

Kenzie held her breath, unsure what Julia would do.

"Nice to meet you," said Julia with a smile.

All Kenzie could work up was a nod.

"You look very familiar," said Julia.

Kenzie's eyes opened a little wider, but it was just for an instant. "I always look like somebody's cousin."

Julia could tell that Jane was as uncomfortable as Kenzie, but for other reasons. Julia's irritation at finding Kenzie back in Jane's life was momentarily tempered by the sheer entertainment value of the situation.

Turning to Kenzie, Jane said, "Julia and I were . . . together . . . for about a year."

"Really," said Kenzie, taking off the cowboy hat and watching Julia with even more anxiety. "How long ago was that?"

"Maybe four years. I don't remember exactly."

"You never told Kenzie about your past?" asked Julia.

"We decided it wasn't necessary."

"That's probably a good idea. Listen, Jane, could we sit down? I won't take much of your time, I promise." She glanced at the fire in the living room. "I'm kind of cold."

"Oh, I'm sorry," said Jane, looking apologetic. On her way into the living room, she called over her shoulder, "Julia's still recovering from a serious illness. She's lost a lot of weight."

"Is that right?" said Kenzie, eyebrows rising. "What kind of illness?"

"Tuberculosis."

She swallowed hard. "But you're better? You're not contagious?"

"No. Not anymore."

"That's good to hear."

"Yes," said Julia, her eyes remaining on Kenzie a little too long, "I imagine it is."

Jane sat down on the couch. Kenzie sat next to her. Julia thought about trying to wedge herself between them but didn't think they'd find it funny. Instead, Julia stood next to the fire and warmed her hands.

"So, what's so important that you had to talk to me right away?" asked Jane.

"It's about yesterday. When we were talking in the campaign office. You remember that Luke came out of his office and rushed over to the computers to see what was wrong."

Jane nodded.

"Well, when that man shouted for Luke to come and help, I turned to his office. He was already in the doorway, looking at the computers across the room. I swear, Jane, for a millisecond, I saw his eyes shimmer. There was even the briefest smile—just the edges of his mouth curling. But in my opinion, it was unmistakable. I think he knew the system was about to fail, that he was standing there waiting for it. And when it happened, he allowed himself just that one brief look, and then he rearranged his expression and rushed across the room."

"You're saying he's responsible?"

"Maybe I'm wrong. Maybe I'm making too much of it, but I had to tell you. At the very least, I think he should be investigated. I've heard from staffers over at the campaign office that the computers and the Internet site have both been hit by an unusual number of problems. I realize I have no proof, just what I saw, but it was there. In that one split second, he looked almost triumphant. I'm good at reading people. You know that. And, well, I've been mulling it over all night."

"Is that what you didn't want to tell me last night?"

"I had to think about it. I know Luke has been working for the campaign for many months. He's a trusted employee."

Jane stared into the fire. "I don't understand what his motive would be."

"Maybe he's a Pettyjohn partisan, a mole in the campaign. I'm sure it happens." She dug into her coat pocket, withdrew a piece of yellow legal paper. "I took the trouble of looking up his address and home phone number for you." She placed it on the mantel. "It's possible I'm wrong. I'm not trying to get Luke in trouble. I like him."

"I don't," said Jane.

Julia tilted her head. "Any particular reason?"

"I think he's arrogant."

"Well, there is that. But he really knows what he's doing."

The fire crackled. Julia had no desire to leave, but if she stuck around and milked the conversation, it wouldn't look good.

"Well," she said, pulling her hands away from the warmth. "That's all I came to say. Take it for what it's worth. Oh, one other thing. I haven't checked on your dad's test results yet this morning, but I will. I put a rush on them, like I said, but sometimes it can take up to a week."

Jane walked her to the door while Kenzie remained on the couch.

"Nice meeting you, Kenzie," called Julia.

Kenzie didn't turn around, she just raised her hand.

"Hey, I think I may know where I've seen you. Do you ever gamble?"

"Never," came Kenzie's voice.

Julia could just imagine the look on her face. A windshield hit by a brick.

Jane opened the door and walked Julia out to the front steps. "I really appreciate all your help. And I'll check on Luke. Thanks for the tip."

"I'll apologize if it leads nowhere. But tampering with a campaign, computer hacking, those are serious offenses." She couldn't help but smile. Just looking at Jane made her happy. "I wish—"

"Wish what?" asked Jane.

"Just . . . that we could be friends. I know it's asking a lot after what I've done, taking that photo, using my old key to get into your house. I have no excuse for my behavior. It's just that I've been struggling—" She couldn't seem to finish the sentence.

"I know you've been through a lot. And I admire what you've done. Let's just take it slowly."

"Really?"

"As long as you understand it's over between us."

"I know that. I wish you two all the happiness in the world, Jane. I really do."

As she walked to her car, all she could think about was Kenzie. Waving with a sunny smile on her face, she got into her roadster and drove off. But she stopped at the end of the block, pulled over to the curb, and rested her head against the steering wheel. It was impossible to believe that she'd gone through hell just to have some pathetic hick from Nebraska take away the only thing she'd ever truly wanted. It was obscene. Vile. Degrading. There had to be an end, a victory, a crown for all her work. Yesterday, she thought she'd glimpsed the finish line. Today she realized she couldn't even find the horizon.

"She's really been through it," said Jane, switching on the dishwasher in her kitchen.

"Do you see her a lot?" asked Kenzie, sitting at the table, playing with one of the frayed rips in her jeans. "You said something about talking to her on the phone last night."

"We're completely over, if that's what you're asking. She's been back in town for a few weeks, I guess, but we're not even friends anymore."

"But she'd like to change that."

It was a subject Jane didn't want to discuss. "Well, yeah, maybe she would."

"She wants to jump your bones, Lawless. If you can't see it, you're as blind as a bat."

Jane laughed. "You're the only one I want."

"Who called it off?"

"You mean when Julia and I broke up? I did."

"Why?"

"She lied to me one too many times. I couldn't trust her. Come on, Kenzie. Don't give her another thought."

"Right."

"Why are you letting her upset you so much?"

"I'm not."

"Could have fooled me. Let's just drop the subject, okay?"

Kenzie nodded. "Yeah, okay."

Jane spent the next few minutes explaining about the computer disaster at the campaign office. She hadn't mentioned it earlier because her dad's run for governor was hardly the first thing on her mind when Kenzie showed up in the bar last night. Everything had instantly taken a backseat to the pleasures of making up after a serious fight.

"That's pretty intense," said Kenzie. "Luke never seemed like such a bad guy to me, although people have been talking about all the computer problems at the campaign since midsummer."

"That's just about when Luke started working for us."

"You really think he's behind it all?"

"To be honest, I don't know."

"Just one more problem for you to work out. Are you still trying to help your cleaning woman's nephew prove his innocence?"

Jane sighed, sat down at the table. "I called Norm Toscalia a couple of nights ago. Before I met Nolan, I could always count on Norm to get me information on various police investigations. He hasn't called me back yet, but when he does, I hope to have a clearer picture." She shrugged. "What I do is listen, learn. I do some digging. I come to some conclusions, then eventually form a theory."

"You really like trying to figure this stuff out, don't you. Crimes. Murders." She shivered. "I don't get it. It scares me. I mean, somebody could get hurt."

"I suppose this is the wrong time to ask you to drive over to Luke's place with me."

"Why don't you just call him?"

Jane pulled her mug of coffee closer. "Sometimes I like to look around myself. You never know what you're going to find."

"Sounds like a waste of time to me."

Kenzie's mood had taken a definite nosedive. Getting up, Jane moved around behind her, began to rub her shoulders. "He doesn't live too far from here. I promise, I won't be gone more than an hour. And then you and me—we can plan the rest of the day."

"Until Cordelia comes over to decorate the house for Halloween."

"That's usually kind of fun."

Kenzie tipped her head back, looked up at Jane. "I love you, Lawless."

Jane reached into her pocket and pulled out the ring Kenzie had left on the table in the front hall before she left. "Here," she said, slipping it back on Kenzie's finger.

Kenzie gazed at it for a few seconds. "I was afraid to ask about it, afraid you'd thrown it away."

"Never," said Jane, leaning down and kissing her.

Jane parked her Mini on the street behind Luke's condo. It was a new building with a façade of copper and brick, three stories tall. Depending on where his loft was located, he had a view either of the river or of downtown Minneapolis. Luke occasionally bragged about how much money he used to make when he was working for private industry. Seeing where he lived made her realize he wasn't exaggerating.

Jane stepped up to the front door and looked inside. She pushed on the bar spanning the glass and walked in. Directly to her right was an elevator that required a key, and the door to the stairway was also locked. There was a common area closer to the river entrance thirty feet away down a hallway, complete with couches, chairs, and a few tall plants, all flanked by solid glass. The walls in the corridor were a textured art stone, the floor inlaid wood. The look was definitely modern but not the kind of modern that shouted. The interior of the building more or less purred.

Across from the maintenance office, Jane noticed a bank of mailboxes. She stared at the left side, moving right. Most of them were blank. She skipped the boxes that had two names on them, but when she didn't find Luke's name, she went back and looked at the double names. He'd never talked about his personal life, so Jane had figured he didn't have one. But there it was. Luke Durrant. And—

She squinted to make sure she was seeing the next name correctly.

Reading out loud, she said, "Luke Durrant and Christopher Cornish."

Luke was gay? And his partner was the minister she'd met on Monday? She hadn't seen them together at the church or the cemetery. It made no sense for Luke to be in the closet. His partner certainly wasn't. There wasn't a gubernatorial campaign in the country that was more gay-friendly than her father's.

So why the secrecy?

33

Corey had memorized the route Dean took home from school yesterday afternoon, after making sure he lost his police tail. That meant today he knew right where to park his motorcycle. It might be the only chance he got to talk to Dean alone, so it was crucial that he make it work.

As Dean came around the corner just after three, walking alone as he had yesterday, Corey was sitting cross-legged on the quiet neighborhood street, working on his cycle.

"Hey, Dean, remember me?" he said, smiling at the kid while he was still twenty feet away. "I was over at your house the other day."

Dean didn't say anything, just kept walking.

"Be a sport and help me out here, will you?" He handed Dean a wrench as he came past. The kid, not quite sure what to do, took it. "Hold that for me while I take this other wrench and tighten this." He pointed. "You like motorcycles?"

"Yeah," said Dean, looking around nonchalantly.

Corey read the stance as nervousness. "This one's pretty old, but it goes really fast. It's called a Moto Guzzi V 1000 G 5. It's an Italian bike. Hey, in fact, I've got some pictures of your mom and me on it. Wanna see?"

The kid shrugged.

Pulling a stack of snapshots out of his leather jacket, he handed one to Dean. "That was me and your mom at the state fair one year. I like cotton candy, but your mom hates it."

"I like it, too," mumbled Dean.

Corey handed him another shot. "That was taken at Lake Harriet. We'd gone there for a picnic."

Dean seemed interested in the photos, so Corey kept handing them over. Pictures shot on a drive he and Serena had taken down the Wisconsin side of the Mississippi all the way to Lake Pepin, photos of the two of them at a motorcycle show, the zoo, a Gopher football game. At one point, Dean said, "Gee, she really looks happy."

"She was," said Corey. "We were in love."

"Then how come you were shouting at each other?"

"Do you ever get mad at your mom? Have you ever shouted at her?"

"Well, yeah."

"Does that mean you don't love her?"

"I love her a lot."

"Your mom and I love each other too, but sometimes we get mad."

Dean scrunched up his face. "If mom loves you, why do we live with Johnny?"

"Do you like him?"

"No." The word came out fast, full of vehemence. "He's a jerk. And he's mean to Mom. And to me sometimes."

"Sit down here next to me," said Corey, patting the grass. "I want to show you a couple other pictures."

"I don't know." He looked around. "I'm not supposed to talk to strangers."

"But I'm not a stranger, am I? My name's Corey, remember? Your mom introduced us. And I've got all these pictures of your mom and me."

"Yeah, but . . . I really should get home. Mom will worry if I'm late."

"Okay," said Corey. "But first, look at this one last picture." He held it up. "Who is that?"

Dean glanced at it, quickly looking away. "Me."

"Is it? Look a little harder."

He continued to stand well back but extended his neck. "Those aren't my clothes."

"No, they're not."

"But it looks like me."

"You know who that is?"

Again, he shrugged.

"Me."

The little boy seemed skeptical. "How can that be you when it looks like me?"

"It's called a 'family resemblance.' You know what that means?"

"That you and me are family?"

"That's right. Look at our hair. It's the same exact color. I think that's cool."

Dean took a peek at the picture again. "How come we never met before?"

"I've been away. As a matter of fact, I didn't even know you existed until a few days ago. But now that I do, I want us to be friends. Would that be okay with you?"

"I guess."

"Look, I already talked to your mom. She says it's okay if we spend some time together this afternoon. I'll have you home before bedtime, promise. You like pizza?"

He nodded.

"Well, then, I thought maybe I'd take you to Chuck. E. Cheese for some pizza, then we could head out to Camp Snoopy at the Mall of America, do some of the rides."

"It's not called that anymore. It's called the Park at MOA."

"No more Camp Snoopy?"

"Nope."

"But it still has rides and stuff."

"Oh, yeah."

"Okay, then we'll go to the Park at MOA. That sound fun? You can ride on my motorcycle, on the back behind me. I've got a helmet for you. You ever had a motorcycle helmet on before?"

"No. But my friend Terrance has one. It's blue and black, kind of sparkly."

"I bought this one especially for you."

"You did?"

"What do you say, pal? Are we on for some fun?" He held up his hand.

Dean hesitated, but then slapped it with the flat of his hand. "You're sure it's okay with Mom?"

"Yeah, it's fine and dandy. She works tonight, so you'd be spending most of the time with Johnny anyway. I figure you'd rather spend it with me." Corey jumped up and took the helmet off the back of the bike. "Try it on."

There was a perceptible gleam in Dean's eyes when he handed the wrench and the photos back to Corey and accepted the helmet.

"See, it's Velcro under here." He made sure it fit snugly. Standing back, he grinned at him. "Very cool." He stowed his tools in the back suitcase, then lifted Dean up on the rear seat, which was a little higher than the front. Perfect for an eight-year-old with a backpack. Lifting his leg across the front seat, he explained to Dean how to hold on to him.

"You ready?" he asked, starting the motor.

"Ready," said Dean, holding on tight.

Feeling like he'd just been crowned king of the world, Corey glanced behind him, gunned the motor, and took off into the cold afternoon sunlight.

Jane and Kenzie spent the afternoon in the St. Croix River Valley, hiking the bluffs around Taylors Falls. It was such a gorgeous day that neither one of them wanted to stay indoors. Jane rescheduled several meetings. Now that Kenzie was back, she was happy to blow off as many days as necessary to make sure Kenzie understood that she was a huge, important part of her life. They still had some potentially dangerous issues to work through, though for the moment, they were both consciously steering away from those topics. With the exception of Julia's early morning visit, the day had felt like a honeymoon. Jane had never felt closer to Kenzie, more sure that they would be able to make a go of their life together.

On their return to town, Jane asked Kenzie if she would mind stopping at the campaign office for a few minutes. Kenzie, who was in a mellow, accommodating mood, said she'd be happy to. Jane called from the road and learned that Luke was still around, that he hadn't been home since the computers had blown up last night. It didn't seem like the actions of a man who was responsible for the computer meltdown in the first place, which made it all the more important to put some hard questions to him.

Inside the office, Kenzie drifted off to the phones. Jane found Luke seated at one of the computers, intently watching the screen.

"How's it going?" asked Jane.

Luke glanced up at her. "If you want a simple answer, go talk to someone else."

Ouch. "No, I'm really interested."

Wiping a hand across his forehead, he said, "Most of the binaries on the server were replaced. For a while, I would delete the virus-ridden files only to see them reappear a few minutes later."

"So it was a virus."

"Yeah. What's even more frustrating is that our computers started sending out tens of thousands of e-mails driving people to our Web site, which overloaded the server. Every time we brought it up, it was impossible to navigate. In the middle of the night, I had to shut off name service to the old address and set up a whole new box. And then we found some kind of date bug on the blog. It reset the dates, making posts and comments look like they were all written last year. Some things are getting ironed out, but this has been one long haul and it's not anywhere near fixed."

"You must be tired."

"Yeah, I must be."

"Look, Luke, I need to talk to you."

"Now?"

"Yes, now."

"Maria Rios wants the system back up and running ASAP."

"It will only take a couple of minutes."

"Jesus H. Christ," he said, pushing his chair back. "I guess what the daughter of Ray Lawless wants, the daughter of Ray Lawless gets."

She wasn't quite sure where all the attitude was coming from. Maybe it was stress, or maybe it was something else. She followed him into his office and shut the door.

"Okay, what's so goddamn important?" He straightened some papers on his desk.

"I intend to keep this just between us, unless you give me a reason not to."

"What?" He frowned, pushing his coffee cup to the center of his desk pad, then his stapler, his Mason jar filled with pens and pencils, and finally his electric pencil sharpener. He lined them up, making a little wall of office supplies between them.

"I have reason to believe that you were the one who created and sent the virus to the campaign's computer system."

He stared at her a moment, then burst out laughing. "Oh, that's rich. Attack the guy who's been here all night trying to help. Maybe I should just leave. Let you people flounder in your own ignorance."

Jane sat down. "You know, Luke, you've never really seemed all that enthusiastic about my dad's run for governor. Why is that?"

"Because I'm not."

"Then why are you here?"

"He's the best of a bad field. That's the way politics works today. You pick the candidate you hate least."

"You hate my father?"

"I sure as hell don't love him."

She had a difficult time not responding in kind. "You're gay, right?"

"Who told you that?"

"Christopher Cornish is your partner. Why be so secretive about it?"

"Because it's my goddamn right. You call it secretive, I call it privacy."

"There's no campaign in this country that would be more welcoming to a gay man than this one."

"I'm not a one-issue voter."

He seemed to have an answer for everything. "I met your partner the other day—at Charity's funeral."

He glanced down at the cold mug of coffee. "He's a great guy."

"I'm sure he is."

"Just so you know, *he* is a one-issue voter. I don't hold it against him."

"You mean gay rights."

"You'd expect that, wouldn't you? Especially after what Keen did to him."

None of this made any sense. "Tell me what my father's done that's so terrible."

"Last I heard, this was a free country. You can't just go around demanding information."

Studying him, she saw something in his eyes she'd never seen before, something that unnerved her. "You really do hate my father."

He didn't respond.

"Enough to manufacture a virus?"

"Of course not."

"We're talking a serious offense here, Luke. The kind you go to prison for."

"Sure, I could've done it. But I didn't."

"Why should I believe you?"

"Because," he said, leaning forward, "you . . . have . . . no . . . proof. You can't just run around slandering people. Even if you are Jane Lawless."

"You hate me, too." She was at a total loss. "I never even met you before last summer. How could I have hurt you?"

"You didn't. Now, are we done?"

"Yes, we're done."

As he walked past her on his way to the door, he stopped. "You say anything to anyone about this crap theory of yours, and I'm out of here. And when I go, the first thing I'll do is hire myself a sleazy lawyer like your father and sue you both for everything you're worth."

"I've got him," said Corey, holding his cell phone to his ear. He was at the Mall of America, standing in the amusement park.

Serena couldn't seem to stop screaming.

He waited until there was a lull, then said, "Have you called the cops?"

"No! I was frantic. I've called all Dean's friends, talked to the parents. He's come home late before, but never this late. I should have known."

"Just listen. You wouldn't let me take him to a movie, or a ball game, so what choice did I have?" Dean was about ten yards away from him, playing in the arcade, having a ball.

"Let me talk to him."

"I can't. He's . . . busy."

"I need to know he's okay!"

"He's fine, Serena. I wouldn't hurt my own kid."

"Bring him home."

"I will."

"Now!"

He knew she'd be upset, but he didn't like all the demands. "I'll make you a deal."

"What deal?"

"You promise me you won't call the cops, and I'll bring him home . . . tomorrow."

"No, I want him home tonight! Right now!"

"You don't get to make all the rules anymore. I'm part of his life now, too."

"Please, Corey. Don't hurt him."

"My God, what kind of man do you think I am?"
"I promise not to call the cops."
"I've got your word on that?"
"Yes. I swear. When will you be here?"
"Tomorrow morning. No, let's make it closer to noon."
"Where will you go tonight?"
"None of your business."
"Corey . . . listen. I need to talk to him. I'll do anything you want, just . . . I need to hear his voice."
He scratched his cheek. "Okay. Fair enough. He'll call later."
"Thank you." She sounded almost breathless.
"Look, I'm sorry. I wasn't trying to hurt you or anything, I just wanted some time with my kid."
"Right. I understand."
She was a liar. He saw it now in a way he never had before. She'd say anything she thought he wanted to hear. He had to make sure she kept her end of the bargain. He had to take it to the next level. "No cops, you got that? I see any cops or hear about any AMBER Alerts and you'll never see Dean again."
"I promise, Corey. I mean it. I swear it on everything I love. I trust you, okay. Just bring him home safely. That's all I want. Corey, please! That's all I want."

Julia had just come out of the women's room when she saw Kenzie cross the hallway in front of her. She was alone. Jane had to be around somewhere, but since Kenzie was all by herself for the moment, it presented Julia with an interesting opportunity.
As Kenzie stood by the bulletin board, reading the newest talking points, Julia stepped up behind her and said, "Looking for the blackjack table?"
Kenzie turned her head ever so slightly. "Go away."
"Why didn't you tell me you were Jane's girlfriend?"
She turned all the way around. "I could ask you the same question."
"I didn't know who you were."

"Same here. What do you want?"

"I like you, Kenzie. A lot. You gave me your phone number when we left the hotel . . . after our night together. And what a night."

"I don't remember."

"I don't believe you." She moved a little closer. "I was thinking of calling you."

"I'm glad you didn't."

"What if I said I thought we'd be good together."

The comment seemed to rattle her. "I'd say you're a head case."

Julia couldn't help herself. She moved in for the kill. "Maybe I should tell Jane about our tryst."

"Go ahead."

"I guarantee she won't like it."

"Nobody holds me hostage. Nothing is that important."

"Really?"

"What's wrong with you? Why are you doing this?"

"I know what I like and I go after it."

"Well, I'm not available. And neither is Jane. So find someone else to chase."

Just then, Jane came through the door. Kenzie was facing away from her, but Julia saw her and smiled. "Hi. I was just getting to know your partner a little better."

Kenzie stepped away from Julia. "Are you done?" she asked, glancing at Jane.

"Yeah." She looked unusually solemn.

"Something wrong?" asked Julia. She saw the hesitation on Jane's face, wondered what was behind it.

"No," said Jane. "But I think Kenzie and I better hit the road. Cordelia's coming over to the house tonight to decorate it."

"Oh, right," said Julia. "I remember. Tomorrow's Halloween, her favorite holiday. Well, you two have fun. Good talking with you, Kenzie." She squeezed Kenzie's arm as she walked away.

Hi, Mom," said Dean. He was sprawled on one of the double beds in the hotel room, still in his swim trunks, the ones Corey had bought him at the Mall of America.

Corey was on the other phone in the room, listening.

"Where have you been?" cried Serena. "Are you okay?"

"Me? Sure. Corey and I been having a great time. We went to the Park at MOA this afternoon, and then we saw a movie. We're staying at this really cool hotel, way high up. And, um, we just got back from swimming. They got this way cool slide and Corey and me slid down it tons of times. I think we're gonna eat pretty soon. Corey said they deliver the food to the room. On a table that rolls. I wanted a burger and fries. Oh, and some hot chocolate, 'cause it's cold out."

"That does sound like fun." She cleared her throat. "Are you being a good boy?"

"Well, I had two candy bars. I told Corey it would make you mad."

"I'm not mad, honey. I just miss you."

"Yeah, I miss you, too. I been riding around on Corey's cycle. I love it, Mom. Can I get a cycle when I'm older?"

"We'll see."

"Corey said he'd teach me how to drive it, and to fix it and everything."

"What are you doing tomorrow morning?"

"Huh? Beats me. Something fun, though. I really like Corey. I wish you'd trade him for Johnny."

Another bout of throat clearing. "I love you, Dean."

"I love you, too."

Serena sounded like she was about to cry. They were saved by the sound of a knock on the door.

"I think the food's here, Mom. I better say good night."

"You're the most important person in my life. You be safe."

"I will. Bye."

"Bye, honey. Bye. I love you."

Corey set the phone back in its cradle. After he signed for the food, he handed the waiter a five-dollar bill.

Dean sat on the edge of the bed as Corey lifted the aluminum tops off each dish.

"Wow, this is so cool."

They ate their food watching a *Simpsons* rerun. When they were done, Corey turned off the TV and sat down next to Dean on his bed. "We better get your pajamas on."

"I'm not cold."

"No, it's pretty warm in here. But you want your swim trunks to dry out so we can go swimming again in the morning."

"Oh. Okay."

"Maybe you should take a shower?"

"Do I have to?"

Corey could tell he wasn't going to be much of a disciplinarian. "No, I guess that can wait." Ruffling Dean's hair, he said, "Look, there's something important I want to tell you. It's serious, so I want you to sit still, stop picking at your toe, and listen."

Dean licked some ketchup off his lip. "What?"

"You remember that photo I showed you this afternoon? You thought it was you, but it was really me when I was your age?"

"Yeah. You said we had a 'family semblance.' "

"Resemblance." The freckles on his son's face, the slight gap in his front teeth, how could they not be father and son? "Well, the reason we look so much alike is because . . . because I'm your father."

Dean looked up at him with curious eyes. "You are?"

"Did your mom ever talk to you about your father?"

"She said he wasn't around anymore. That he'd moved away."

"Well, I am around. And I want you to know that I intend to be a part of your life . . . for the rest of your life."

He seemed to think it over. "You're my dad for real?"

"For real. You know how some of your friends look like their moms or their dads."

"Oh, yeah. Totally."

"Same with us."

Dean grew quiet. After examining his toe again for a few seconds, he said, "I wish you coulda been around when I won that blue ribbon at school."

"What did you win it for?"

"Running."

"Hey, that's great. You like sports?"

"I like baseball. And swimming. And I played bowling once with Johnny and mom, but I wasn't very good at it."

"You'll get better."

He cocked his eye at Corey. "You're really my dad?"

"Yup."

He nodded. "Cool."

In the middle of the night, Corey woke with a start. Blinking his eyes open, he saw that Dean had crawled in bed with him.

"I got scared," came Dean's small voice, muffled by the covers.

"Oh, buddy, there's nothing to be scared of."

"I heard a noise."

"It's a hotel. Lots of people are staying here."

Dean snuggled closer.

"You wanna sleep with me?"

"Yeah."
"You warm enough?"
"Yup."
"Think you can get back to sleep?"
"I think so."
Corey put his arm around his son and hugged him tight. "I won't let anything hurt you. Ever."
"Thanks, Dad."
Those simple words nearly dissolved him.

They were up the next morning by eight. As Dean watched cartoons, Corey flipped through the yellow pages, trying to figure out what they could do until noon.
"You hungry?" asked Corey.
Dean went into a trance whenever he watched TV. Corey did the same thing.
"Well, I am." Setting the yellow pages on the table, he picked up the hotel menu. "Maybe we should go out somewhere. Oh, but we thought maybe we'd swim again. Well, I gotta eat something or I'm gonna starve." He grabbed the phone.
The cartoon changed to an ad. Dean did some channel surfing, looking for something better. Disgusted, he went into the bathroom.
The least he could do was turn it down, thought Corey, grabbing the remote. Glancing briefly at the screen, he saw the words AMBER ALERT flash across it. Moving closer and turning the sound nearly off, he watched as a picture of Dean appeared. A voice said his name and that he'd been missing since yesterday afternoon, when he'd been abducted from his school.
" 'Abducted'?" repeated Corey.
The voice went on to explain that the boy's father, Corey Hodge, had taken him. Hodge was driving a red and black Italian motorcycle. Both father and son had red hair. Any information should be—
Corey snapped off the TV as Dean came back into the room.
"Hey, I wanted to watch that."

"Not now, pal. We gotta hit the road."

"You said we could swim again."

"Yeah, I know, but the time got away from me. They kick you out of here in the morning so they can get the room ready for some new people."

Dean made a sour face.

"But I got lots of plans for the day."

He couldn't believe Serena had gone to the police, not after she'd promised. He'd given her his word that he'd have Dean back by noon. Couldn't she wait *that* long? She'd had him for eight goddamn years. All Corey had asked for was a few hours.

"We both need to get dressed. You can wear your new jeans if you want."

"Okay," said Dean, looking less than enthusiastic.

Corey dressed, then stuffed everything into a small duffel and hoisted it over his shoulder. While Dean pulled on his socks, Corey turned the TV back on, this time to a movie station.

"Shouldn't we turn the TV off?" Dean asked on their way out the door.

"Nah, let's leave it on." He hung the DO NOT DISTURB sign on the outside doorknob. Instead of going downstairs to finalize the bill, he spirited Dean out a side stairway. Corey stuck his neck out the back door and looked around. So far so good.

"Come on, buddy. Let's go find us some breakfast." He glanced at the cycle parked in the lot, then walked away from it.

"Aren't we gonna drive?"

"Nah, let's walk. We need the exercise."

Instead of making a dinner for Halloween, Jane filled the buffet in her dining room with appetizers, wine, a tray filled with local cheeses, French bread, and several of her favorite fall sweets—individual cranberry tarts, a pumpkin-spiced cheesecake, an old fashioned English trifle, and a classic tarte tatin. If they were going to be jumping up and answering the door every few minutes, a sit-down dinner didn't make sense.

Cordelia invited several actors from the theater, some of her poker pals, as well as a few of Melanie's friends from the paper. Jane's neighbor Evelyn Bratrude even put in a brief appearance, as did a number of Jane's friends, mostly other restaurant owners and chefs. Melanie brought Tallulah, and before long the house was filled with laughter and conversation. Everyone was in costume.

Kenzie had gone out and found herself a grim reaper outfit. Jane wore her chef's coat, a tall paper chef's hat, and vampire teeth. Cordelia came as Marie Antoinette, complete with long silver wig and blood dripping from her neck. Melanie was Elvis the vampire in black leather and a cape. There was a Wolf Man; a woman with a hag mask, straw in her hair and a pitchfork; a devil in a red jumpsuit. The only costume that didn't work was the Egyptian mummy. The costume kept unraveling and the woman finally took it off.

Cordelia set out the treats for the kids in big bowls. She took the lead in answering the door and handing out the swill. At one point, Jane noticed that she had tears in her eyes.

"It's Hattie," said Cordelia. "I miss her like crazy. I just know she's going to be home for Christmas this year."

Jane wished she would stop saying that. Cordelia had suffered a "breakdownette," as she called it, after Hattie was whisked off to England a year ago. And now, for some reason, she'd developed this idea, little by little, that Hattie would be back soon. Jane didn't want to burst her bubble, especially tonight, but this was something they needed to talk about. She also didn't want her best friend to suffer another huge crash if it could be prevented, especially if she was away in China with Kenzie when the crash occurred.

Kenzie, for her part, seemed exceptionally buoyant as she carried around the wine bottles, filling up glasses. She and Jane still hadn't talked about any of their problems, but Jane figured they had the rest of their lives to do that.

After stopping by the campaign office yesterday, Kenzie had been quiet on the ride home. Jane began to worry that they were in for another tense evening. But after Cordelia had arrived with her Halloween trunk, Kenzie's dark mood lifted. Still, she had made one thing quite clear. She didn't like Jane getting herself mixed up in other people's problems, especially criminal matters.

And so when the phone rang just before eleven and Jane heard Norm Toscalia's voice on the other end of the line, she took the cordless from the kitchen and went immediately into her study, closing the door behind her.

"You still up?" asked Norm.

"Sure am. What did you find out?" She perched on the edge of the desk. "First tell me about Corey."

"They brought him in on Wednesday morning for questioning. Apparently, they've had a tail on him for the last week, but he lost the guy after he left the police station. They found him again when he returned to his aunt's house that night, but then, after he left there yesterday, somehow or other he lost the guy again. They don't know where he is at the moment. They think he may have abducted his kid after school yesterday. A boy, eight years old. From what I understand, his girlfriend was pregnant before he entered prison. But she never told him about the kid. Sounds like a bad situation."

"Lord, I had no idea," said Jane. She wondered if Mary knew. "Is he still the main suspect in Charity's murder?"

"He was. They found semen on Charity's clothes that matched his DNA."

"Oh, wow."

"Yeah, I know. The police were ready to arrest him. But then something happened in the second interview. Nobody's talking about it, but it was significant."

"Are you kidding me?"

"Well, don't take all of this as absolute gospel. It's second- or third-hand. But I trust these people. Of course, there are still plenty of cops who think he did it. Just not the primary on the case, Tom Emerson."

"So if Corey didn't do it, that means somebody else tried to make it look like he did—used the taser, the duct tape, the lipstick to write the word *justice* on her stomach."

"Her death was probably unintentional. I suppose it could be considered manslaughter."

"What about Gabriel Keen?"

"Yeah, they looked at him pretty hard initially. Charity's parents were sure he was responsible. But he produced an airtight alibi. His dad and stepmom said he was home the entire night, that they were watching a movie together."

"I'd hardly call that airtight."

"Okay, but it's enough to tie the cops' hands. Without some hard evidence, they can't get a search warrant for the house. Not that Keen would be stupid enough to keep the evidence around. On the other hand, he did last time."

"You mean when he assaulted Christopher Cornish. But he was never charged for that."

"It was a bad search. Keen's parents wanted Ray to represent him, but Elizabeth took it. She got wind of the search right away and was able to get the evidence ruled inadmissible. Without the bat, the police had diddly. They had no way to charge him."

"Are you saying Elizabeth represented Gabriel Keen?"

"His father's wealthy and can buy the best. In this town, that's Lawless, Kaplan & Piper."

Jane grew silent.

"Are you still there?"

"What else do you know?"

"Just that Keen apparently took a polygraph. He passed. Doesn't mean he didn't do it, but he's been willing to jump through every hoop the cops have presented him with. No fight about giving a DNA sample. He made himself available anytime they wanted to talk to him. And he never asked for a lawyer. He's been nothing but Mr. Cooperative. That's it. I'll keep my ear to the ground. If I hear anything else, I'll let you know."

"Thanks, Norm. This helps a lot."

"For your dad's sake, I wish they'd make an arrest—and that it wasn't Hodge."

"Yeah, I know."

"On Election Day, just remember what Al Capone said. Vote early and often."

She laughed. "I'll remember that."

After saying good-bye, she got up off the edge of her desk and sat down in her chair to think.

When Cordelia burst in a few minutes later, she'd put it together.

"Why are you hiding in here?"

"I'm not hiding," said Jane. "I'm thinking."

"Can't you think out in the living room with the rest of us?" She adjusted her wig, pulling several strands of the silver locks over her shoulders. "This thing makes me wish I hadn't cut my hair. Maybe I'll grow it out." Hands on her hips, she added, "Okay, tell me what you're thinking about."

"That was Norm on the phone."

"And?"

There was so much to tell her. She explained first about the AMBER Alert, that Corey had a son. She let Cordelia rant about parental issues for a minute or two, then moved on. "It seems my dad's law firm represented Gabriel Keen when he was accused of attacking Christopher Cornish."

"Are you sure? How could your father do that?"

"Technically, Elizabeth represented him."

"But it was a hate crime. Perry Mason's girlfriend doesn't represent sickos who commit hate crimes."

"Maybe *Perry*'s girlfriend doesn't, but my dad's law firm did. Do you remember hearing anything about it last spring?"

"I feel terrible, Janey. I've signed petitions to put more teeth into hate crime laws, written my senators—and I never usually do things like that—even been to the capitol in St. Paul a couple times for rallies."

"I know. I was with you."

"You were?"

"I'm glad my presence is so memorable."

Cordelia patted Jane's knee. "You're very memorable. But what happened to Cornish, that escaped me."

"Probably because Keen was never charged. If it made the papers at all, it was buried on the back page."

"I certainly missed it. Hey, you know why we missed it?"

"Why?"

"When was he attacked?"

"Late April."

"That's exactly when you and your family were having that horrible minicollapse. And I, friend that I am, was right there with you. None of us were tracking very well right around then."

She had a point. "I still feel guilty for not knowing about it."

"Fine. Feel guilty. It's part of a venerable liberal tradition."

"I haven't told you the latest. Julia came over yesterday—"

"Julia!"

"She's been donating some of her time to my dad's campaign." Jane went on to explain why she'd come.

"You think Luke's been the cause of all the campaign's Internet havoc?"

"It's possible."

Cordelia considered if for a few seconds. "Not to change the subject, but was Kenzie here when Julia showed up?"

"Kenzie? What's she got to do with anything?"

"Answer my question."

"Sure, she was here."

"That explains it. She dragged me into your kitchen last night while we were decorating."

"Where was I?"

"Out in the garage looking for a ladder. She wanted to know what I thought of Julia. I told her that she was a manipulative bitch. A beautiful, devious, calculating narcissist."

"Gee, why don't you say what you really think?"

"Kenzie asked if there was a possibility you were still in love with her."

"And you said?"

"Heavens, no."

"Did she believe you?"

"My lips speak only the truth. Everyone knows that."

The last thing on earth Kenzie needed to worry about was Julia. "Can we get back to the subject?" asked Jane.

"What subject? Oh, Luke."

Kenzie appeared in the doorway. "Hey, I was looking for you two. What are you doing in here? Plotting someone's demise?" Her cheeks were rosy from the wine. She held a glass in one hand, tugged at her grim reaper outfit with the other.

"We're solving a crime," said Cordelia.

Kenzie's smile faded. "What crime?"

"Who's been behind the Internet chaos at Ray's campaign."

"And who was?"

"I think Julia was right," said Jane. Moving her attention back to Cordelia, she said, "Christopher Cornish is Luke's partner."

Cordelia's eyes popped. "Luke's gay? What's wrong with my gaydar?"

"See, that's just it. Luke must hate my father for representing Keen. And frankly, I don't blame him." She knew Kenzie didn't understand a word she was saying, but she wanted to make her points with Cordelia first and explain later. For the moment, Kenzie watched stonily from the doorway.

"Your dad didn't represent Keen. Elizabeth did."

"That's a fine point that wouldn't matter to me. I doubt it mattered to him. He must hate me, too. I mean, why didn't I stop my father—or Elizabeth—from representing Keen?"

"Because your father's law office doesn't consult you before they take on a client."

"Another fine point."

"So how do you prove it?"

Jane shook her head. "No idea. But I better call Maria Rios and tell her my suspicions. She can decide what to do from there. Give me a few minutes, okay?" She looked from face to face.

"Take all the time you want," said Kenzie, pushing away from the doorway. "Take the rest of the night."

After she'd drifted away, Cordelia said, "I could be wrong, dearheart, but I think you have one hell of a pissed-off girlfriend."

By midnight, everyone had left, with the exception of Cordelia and Melanie.

Kenzie had taken off her costume. Wearing jeans and an old sweatshirt, she spent the shank of the evening ignoring Jane while drinking too much wine.

"Well, I suppose it's time we clean up," said Melanie, punctuating her statement with an Elvis Presley pelvic shake. She began carrying dishes out of the living room.

Cordelia turned her back to Kenzie, raised her eyebrows at Jane, picked up a few more dishes and followed.

Now that they were alone, Jane wasn't sure what to say. "Are we okay?" she asked.

Kenzie was sitting by the front windows, playing with Mel's new dog. "Right as rain." She smiled, but it was a mirthless smile, even a little resentful.

"If that's the case, why haven't you said a word to me in the last hour?"

Kenzie shrugged. "Lack of perspective?" She lifted the dog down from her lap. "I'm tired. I gotta run out to my truck and get something and then I'm going to hit the sack." Stretching her legs, she stood.

"We need to talk."

"I talk, Lawless. I talk all the time. You just never listen."

She passed Cordelia on her way to the front hall.

As she disappeared outside, Cordelia caught Jane's eye. "What's the deal?"

"It's not good."

"But why? What did you do that was so awful?"

"Not now." Jane was afraid that they were on the verge of falling apart again. She kept hoping there was a way around it, or through it, or over it. They just had to find the right path.

For the next few minutes, everyone carried dirty dishes into the kitchen.

"What's she doing out there?" asked Cordelia, pulling a black plastic garbage sack around the dining room, tossing in paper napkins, drooping streamers, paper plates.

"Maybe she just needed some air," called Melanie from the kitchen. She was loading the dishwasher.

"I should go talk to her," said Jane. She took off her hat and chef's coat and set them on the table.

"Wear a jacket," said Cordelia. "It's cold out."

Jane pulled her jeans jacket from the front hall closet. She took an old leather coat for Kenzie. Pushing out the door, she stood on the steps for a few seconds, letting her eyes adjust to the darkness.

"Kenzie?" she called, trotting out to the truck. But the cab was empty. "Come on, give me a break. Let me explain." She wondered if Kenzie had gone for a walk, but remembered that she had on a pair of floppy slippers and couldn't have gotten far.

"Sweetheart, please. Where are you?"

Thinking that she might have walked around to the back of the house to the screened porch, Jane headed for the driveway. Her patience was just about gone.

"You know, this is a little adolescent. Why don't we cut the drama—" Hearing an unmistakable groan, she froze. She wasn't sure where it had come from. "Kenzie?"

There it was again. She rushed toward the pine tree in the front yard. "Oh my God," she said, finding Kenzie lying on her back, flat on the ground. Her arms were pinned behind her, her sweatshirt pulled up. The word *justice* had been scrawled on her stomach in red lipstick.

Jane's knees hit the dirt. "Are you okay?" She grabbed Kenzie's arms, pulled the tape off her eyes and mouth.

Kenzie tipped her head to the side. Her teeth were clenched.

"What happened?" cried Jane. "Did someone—" She couldn't say the word.

Kenzie rolled over. "I'm okay," she said, breathing hard. "Untie my hands."

Jane removed the duct tape and tossed it aside.

As soon as her hands were free, Kenzie grabbed Jane and held on for dear life.

"It's okay. You're safe now."

She shivered in Jane's arms.

"Tell me what happened."

"I don't know . . . I . . . I heard this kind of sizzling pop and then . . . I felt this pain all over. My legs just gave out. It was so weird. I couldn't move. I felt my arms being twisted behind me. And then I was on my back again." She pushed away from Jane, looked down at her stomach. "Fuck this!" She tried to wipe off the word.

"Don't," said Jane, pulling her hands away.

"Why?"

"Because we need to call the police. It's evidence."

"No, we don't."

"Did he—"

"No," said Kenzie. "He didn't do anything like that."

"Do you think you were hit with a taser?"

"I've never felt anything like it before." She rubbed her arms, then her legs.

"Where were you standing?"

"Just a few feet away." She started to get up.

"Wait."

"For what?" Without a backward glance, she headed for the front door.

"You need to be checked out by a doctor," called Jane.

"No, I don't."

Jane picked up the duct tape, wiping tears from her eyes with the back of her hand. Back inside, she found Cordelia and Melanie standing underneath the living room arch.

"Where'd she go?" asked Jane.

Cordelia lifted her eyes to the top of the stairs. "What happened?"

"She didn't tell you?"

"Not a word. I don't think she even saw us."

Jane took the stairs two at a time. She found Kenzie in the bedroom packing her bag. "You're leaving?"

"You bet I'm leaving. And this time, I'm not coming back."

"Why?"

"You even have to ask?"

"Yeah, I do."

"It's your life, Lawless. I can't take it. You want to mess around with criminals, that's up to you. Me, I need something quieter, less *stimulating*." She zipped the bag and carried it out into the hallway. "I hope you and your crazy ex-girlfriend and your seventeen restaurants and your *Law & Order* cop buddy live happily ever after." She trotted down the steps. "As long as I get away from here with my body and brain intact, I'll consider myself lucky." She passed Cordelia and Melanie without so much as a glance and slammed the front door on her way out.

36

Late the next night, Jane got on the train at the transit station on 38th and Hiawatha. She was alone and didn't have any particular place to go or intent in mind other than to ride the light rail around the city in the dark. She did this occasionally, particularly if she was depressed. Sometimes, just sitting quietly, watching the lights float past, made her feel better. She hoped that tonight, somewhere along the way, she could shed the deep ache inside her. But it was probably asking too much. Too much, too soon.

She'd failed Kenzie. That was the given from which everything else grew. The rule was, no more rationalizations. She was selfish when it came to her time. She was used to having her own way. She didn't always listen well. She heard what she wanted to hear. She'd always thought of herself as a good person, a kind person, but maybe that was just veneer. Maybe she was fundamentally unable to give the kind of time and attention to another human being that a love relationship required. If that was true, she'd better commit herself to some rigid mandate never to inflict herself on another poor, unsuspecting woman again.

Cordelia would say she was being too hard on herself.

Cordelia would say she'd simply hooked up with the wrong woman.

Cordelia would tell her to go home, take two aspirin, and call her in the morning.

Sometimes, Cordelia was right.

It was going on midnight when Jane found herself riding the freight elevator up to Cordelia's loft. She'd spent the entire day floating around, not doing much other than thinking, brooding, moving from place to place. Why stop now?

Trudging down the long hall to Cordelia's door, she realized she probably should have called first to see if Cordelia was home. But when she knocked, she heard a shout. A few seconds later the door flew back and Cordelia yanked her inside. It was Cordelia's usual greeting, so it didn't seem like anything out of the ordinary.

"Where have you been?" demanded Cordelia.

"Here and there. Mostly there."

"You didn't answer your cell phone. I've been calling all day."

"I turned it off."

"You're not supposed to *do* that!" she shrieked.

"Who said?"

"The cell phone police, that's who!" Rushing back to the window, she yelled, "It's Jane. I gotta go."

"I'll be over a little later," came Melanie's voice. "Say hi to her for me."

Jane noticed Tallulah, Melanie's Yorkiepoo, standing on the dining room table, licking out a pizza box. After all the junk she'd managed to steal from people's plates last night at the Halloween party, it was amazing that she wasn't sacked out on the couch, burping, with a doggy bowl of Pepto-Bismol next to her. Jane assumed that Tallulah was over because Melanie was working.

"You look like you just got home from a party," said Jane, nodding to Cordelia's sequined gown.

"Oh, this old rag?" She adjusted the neckline. "So? Did you call the police this morning? Report what happened to Kenzie?"

Jane snagged the last piece of pizza crust while Tallulah was finishing off a blob of tomato sauce. Tallulah snarled.

Chewing slowly, Jane sat down in the living room, lifting her feet up on a footstool. "And what would I say? There was a woman here last night who was attacked with a taser just like Corey Hodge attacked Louisa Timmons and maybe even Charity Miller, except this woman wasn't raped, thank God. But she's not here and refuses to talk about it. And I have no proof except some balled-up duct tape. Oh, and by the way, my dad's running for governor, so it could be a disgruntled citizen, or maybe, again, it was Corey, because the cops think he's a sociopath, or maybe it was Gabriel Keen because he's mean and nasty, but a tortured soul and we should all cut him some slack because his brother died, or maybe it was Luke Durrant who hates me and my dad because of unsavory—but entirely legal and necessary—lawyering practices. Oh, and when you come over to look at nothing and talk to nobody who saw nothing happen, could you check my furnace?"

"What's wrong with your furnace?"

Jane groaned. "Nothing, but give it time."

"Ah, I see," said Cordelia, picking Tallulah up and installing her under her arm. "We've reached the self-pity stage."

"Yes, *we* have."

Fluffing her short pink hair, Cordelia turned on a couple more lights and sat down next to Jane. "Let's change the subject."

"Fine with me."

"Have you heard anything more about Corey and the AMBER Alert?"

Jane shook her hand. "I talked to Mary this morning. She's a basket case, as you might expect."

"Has Corey contacted her?"

"No. Not a word."

"I wonder if the kid's okay?"

Jane laced her fingers over her stomach. "I can't see him hurting a child, but I guess you never know for sure what someone is capable of. By now, they could be ten states away—in any direction."

"It's so scary," said Cordelia, hanging her head. "And so sad. Say, something just occurred to me. Where did you say Luke and the minister live?"

"That new condo over by the river. Luke said they hadn't been there long."

"I thought I recognized the address. The woman who reads my feet lives there."

Cordelia had not only her palms read frequently but also her feet. "How can a woman who reads feet for a living live in a place like that?"

"She married a surgeon."

"And this surgeon thinks it's okay for her to go around to strangers' homes and apartments to read their feet?"

"She also does foot massage, and that thing with the feather."

Jane didn't even ask.

"You reach any new conclusions about Luke—or Charity?" asked Cordelia, brushing crumbs off Tallulah's muzzle.

Actually, she had. "I believe they're separate issues. Luke was responsible for all the Internet problems. I think he was getting even with my father for the part my dad's law firm played in getting Gabriel Keen off the hook for the brutal attack he made on his partner. But here's the thing," said Jane, leaning her head back against a cushion. "Mouse and I went over to Charity's apartment building the other night."

"Without moi? You have to keep me in the *loop*, Janey. Otherwise, how can my superior investigative skills be of any use?"

"I'm sorry. I apologize. It won't happen again."

"See that it doesn't."

"But think about it. Charity has just filed a restraining order against her ex-fiancé. She's terrified of him. And she's just had a date with a guy she thought was a cop but who turns out to be a convicted rapist."

"And?"

"She goes home. And what does she do when she gets home? She takes out the garbage. It's late and it's dark. The back parking lot isn't well lit. She has a maniac after her, perhaps two, but instead of staying inside where it's safe, she decides to take out the freakin' garbage. Does that make sense to you?"

"Well, when you put it that way—"

"That's exactly what we're supposed to buy."

"But you don't."

"Not for a second."

"So who did it? Hodge or Keen?"

Jane had been thinking about it for days. "I think it was Keen. Unlike Corey, he's a guy who does a slow burn. It took him a week to go after Christopher Cornish after he came out to the congregation. And when Charity dumped him, it took him more than a month to begin his barrage of harassment. But when he gets something in his teeth, he doesn't let go."

"You think he attacked Kenzie last night?"

"Yeah, I do. Here's why. When I talked to him at the cemetery on Monday, he said he thought I looked familiar. Asked if we'd met. Just like with Corey, I think he went home and did some checking around, maybe on Google. When he discovered who I was, which wouldn't have been hard, he knew my interest in him probably wasn't just the interest of a simple stranger. He must have been upset, maybe worried that he'd told me too much. So, to get me to back off, he watches my house and attacks the first person he can. I don't think he cared who he hurt. Could have been me. Could have been you. He probably enjoyed it."

"What an absolutely awful man."

"The police know his alibi is crap, but without more evidence, they can't get a search warrant. I think that's the key. I think Keen likes to save little mementos of his conquests. He saved the bat he used on Cornish, and I'll bet he saved something from the attack on Charity. Maybe the taser, maybe something else. But it's there, somewhere, probably not in the house because of what happened with the bat, but somewhere on the property. When he's feeling depressed, which I think he is a lot, he can take it out and look at it and remember that he does have some power in the world."

Cordelia jumped up. "Let's go look."

"You really want to do that?"

"We're a team, Jane. Your brawn and general cerebration, and my infallible instinct. Oh, but I need to take Tallulah out first."

"Bring her along."

"Really?"

"We might need a good attack dog."

Cordelia parked her car along Gladstone Avenue, a block from the Keens' house. Jane had been past the house once during the day. It was a typical Midwestern Prairie School box with a low-pitched roof and overhanging eaves.

Before they left, Jane had insisted that Cordelia put on a hat to cover her hair. Thus, walking along the darkened street, she couldn't have looked more ridiculous in her sequined dress and black wool cape, topped off by a buffalo plaid hunting cap. She maintained that it was the only hat she currently liked—other than her silver lamé turban—and she refused to wear anything else.

Jane held a gloved finger to her lips. "Let's just walk past the place once, see if anyone's home."

Cordelia tugged on the leash and pulled Tallulah and her nose away from a tree.

"That's Keen's black Saab," said Jane. The street was full of cars, no doubt due to the fact that it was a fairly wealthy area with mostly one-car garages. Keen's vehicle was a good fifty yards from the front door.

"I think we can safely assume the cops have already checked the Saab," said Cordelia.

"If they did, it wasn't legal."

"Oh. Dear. Well. Let's both put on our thinking caps, shall we? Now, if you were a crazed lunatic and wanted to hide something, where would you put it?" She raised a finger. "In your car. That's where."

"Too easy."

"Occam's razor."

"What?"

"William of Occam. He was an English philosopher. Occam's razor states that, all other things being equal, the simplest explanation is probably the correct explanation. Thus, what we're looking for is probably in the trunk. Or pushed down into a seat crack."

Jane trotted across the street, bent over, and looked through the driver's side window. Taking a flashlight out of her back pocket, she shined the beam inside. "It's pretty clean. I don't know, Cordelia. Occam might be wrong."

"It's probably in the trunk."

"How do you propose we open it?"

She marched over and reached for the door handle, but Jane stopped her. "If this were my car and I had to park it on the street, I'd protect it with an alarm system. You mess with the door and it could go off."

"Oh. Occam was silent on that point."

Jane was beginning to lose her sense of momentum. "Keen could have stashed the taser, or the lipstick, or whatever he kept anywhere. Or it could all be long gone. But you know—" She looked up. "There are boxes you can buy that attach to the bottom of your car. Some of them can hold up to a hundred pounds."

"You mean like if he was a drug dealer."

"They can hold something heavy, but they're not very big." She crouched down and felt under the car, then flipped on her back and shined the light up under the wheel wells, easing herself along all the way around to the other side. "Nothing," she said brushing the dirt and dry leaves off her clothes. "Let's check out the property."

"What if they've got a security system? Exterior cameras? Why don't *you* go, Janey? I'll stay here."

"I thought we were a team."

"We are. If you get arrested, I'll bail you out."

Setting off across the grass, Jane pointed the flashlight beam up at the eaves, trying to locate a camera. If one was up there, she couldn't find it. Opening the side gate, she slipped into the yard. Directly in front of her was a three-season porch. Nobody appeared to be around. No lights burned at all on the first floor, although there were several on upstairs toward the back. Shining her flashlight in front of her, she made her way slowly into the yard, where a wooden deck jutted off the porch. All the outdoor furniture had been covered for the winter. Orange clay pots had been stacked along one end of the deck. She washed her flashlight over a pile of split logs, stacked and ready for the fireplace.

For the next few minutes, she inspected the yard, turning things over, looking at anything and everything that might be used as a container. She walked behind the deck and opened three plastic tubs but found nothing but gardening tools, hoses, and other summer miscellany. The garage door was locked. It was an obvious hiding place, but short of breaking a window, there was no way she could get inside. She found some plastic sacks half buried under a section of raspberry vines, but they turned out to be empty.

She was just about to give up when headlights struck the opposite side of the house. Switching off the flashlight, she edged along the fence at the other end of the yard until she came to another gate, this one higher. Peeking over the top, she saw that a late-model white pickup truck had just pulled into the drive. Gabriel got out. She watched as Cordelia moved under a streetlight on the other side of the street, nodding pleasantly as she walked past. She was trying to be just another huge woman in a black cape, wearing a sequined dress and a plaid hunter's cap, the flaps now pulled down over her ears, out walking her infinitesimal dog.

"Do I know you?" said Gabriel, standing by the door of the cab.

"Must be the hat," said Cordelia, nodding to him. She kept on walking.

He stared after her but eventually gave up and went inside.

Jane waited until she heard the door latch, then moved carefully through the gate and crouched next to the truck. She assumed it was his father's.

It felt like a lot of effort for nothing, but she reached up again and felt along the underside. She didn't think it was smart to turn on the flashlight this time, so she just slid her hand along, feeling for anything that seemed out of place. She didn't expect to find a magnetic box, so when her hand hit something rectangular in the left rear wheel well, she got down on her hands and knees and pried it loose.

Sure enough, it was just the kind of hiding case she'd mentioned to Cordelia. It was approximately seven inches by four inches by two inches. Probably not big enough to hold one of the bigger tasers, but plenty big enough for the smaller variety.

Scrambling to her feet, she kept her head down until she'd cleared the back of the truck. When she reached the street, she set off at a dead run back to Cordelia's car.

"What's that?" asked Cordelia, already in the driver's seat.

"I don't know." Jane was glad now that she'd worn gloves. She didn't want to leave any fingerprints behind. "Let's take a look." She carefully undid the latch. Inside, a rubber O-ring kept the contents airtight.

"It's a camera," said Cordelia.

It was a very small digital camera with a fairly large screen.

"Turn it on."

Working by the light of the overhead streetlamp, Jane pressed the On button. The camera whirred to life.

"Check to see if there are any photos," urged Cordelia, breathless now that they'd actually found something.

Jane pushed the Menu button, then clicked through the options. "Okay, here goes."

When the first shot popped up, she felt a rush of excitement.

It was a photo of Charity, on the night she died, taken from about five feet away. She was on the ground, curled up in a fetal position right in front of the Dumpster. Her eyes were wide open, staring at the ground, looking terrified. Jane moved to the next picture. Another shot of Charity. This time she was flat on her back, her hands pulled behind her, just as Kenzie's had been. A strip of duct tape had been placed across her eyes to prevent her from seeing her attacker.

Next came a close-up of Charity's stomach, with a word written in red lipstick across it. But the word wasn't *justice*. It was *injustice*.

"Hey, that's the wrong word," said Cordelia, bending closer to get a better look. "Keep going."

"That's it. There aren't any more."

They sat silently for a few seconds, digesting what it all meant.

"We've got to tell someone about this," said Jane. "Give me your cell phone."

"But . . . our search wasn't exactly legal."

"I realize that, but there's got to be some way the cops can use it. Hey, when I put it back, I could leave part of it sticking out. That means it would be plain view. I think the cops can take a look if it's in plain sight."

"Brilliant. But how do we tell the cops about our illegal search?"

It was a good question. "We need to call Nolan. He'll know what to do. As far as I'm concerned, this is as close as we're going to get to a smoking gun. The only person who could've taken those photos was the man who raped and murdered her. If the police can just get over here before Gabriel comes back outside and discovers what I've done, then we're in business."

Cordelia grabbed hold of Jane's hand before she could punch in the numbers. "Charity's clothes didn't look ripped to me. Did they to you? They weren't even out of place."

Jane went back, looked at all three photos.

"I know this is crazy, but could it be . . . is it possible she was never raped?"

"The police said she was," said Jane.

"Did they?"

She had to think. "Yes, it was in all the papers. He must have taken the shots before he raped her."

"Okay," said Cordelia. "I just wanted to make sure we're on the same page. Make the call."

Jane didn't need any coaxing. She pressed the numbers, held the phone to her ear, and waited for Nolan to pick up.

37

The next afternoon, Jane was just about to leave the club and head over to the campaign office when one of the waiters stopped her and said there was a guy in the bar who wanted to talk to her right away. She asked if he was a big black guy with gray hair and a fuzzy caterpillar mustache. The waiter said that just about covered it.

Making her way through the tables to the front of the house, she found Nolan sitting in a booth, enjoying a beer. She slid into the seat across from him. "Have you heard anything?"

"They arrested him," said Nolan, looking up as a waiter set an order of loaded nachos in front of him. "Help yourself," he said, pushing the plate to the center of the table.

"When?" asked Jane.

"Early this morning. He's slippery, but he couldn't talk his way out of that camera. Oh, and I should tell you. Sergeant Liz Hamill, one of the primaries, found a plastic sack buried in a pile of leaves in the backyard. Guess what she found inside?"

"The taser?"

"And the lipstick and the duct tape. Keen's still crying innocent, but then they always do."

"So it wasn't Corey after all." Jane had to call Mary right away.

"Guess not."

"Maybe he never did that rape up north either."

"I wouldn't go that far."

She told him what had happened to Kenzie on Halloween night. "Do you think it was Keen?"

"My God, Jane. I hope you called the police."

"Kenzie wouldn't let me."

"I thought you two—"

"We were, but then we got back together. And now she's gone again."

His gaze dropped to the nachos. "I think I won't keep score."

"Tell me something." Jane picked up a chip covered in melted cheese. "Was Charity raped?"

"No, she wasn't. Emerson played that one pretty close to the vest. The press assumed, but they assumed wrong."

"It didn't look like it in the pictures. Of course Keen could have taken them, then attacked her. But I'm glad she escaped that much."

"I figure her heart probably gave out before he could get to it. The fact that she wasn't raped was apparently the point that caused Tom Emerson to hesitate about arresting Corey. He was all set to, but then Corey started talking like there had been a rape. Of course, he could have been repeating what the news reports were all saying, so that he didn't act like he knew anything special. Whatever the case, Emerson had a gut feeling that he should keep looking."

"I'm glad he did."

Nolan crunched thoughtfully on a chip covered in refried beans and sour cream. "Except, when you think about it, it's possible Corey outfoxed everyone. He could've planted the evidence to make it look like Keen was guilty."

Jane hadn't considered that.

"I think," he said, crunching another chip, "that we've got two highly clever men who both had motives."

"So you're saying I can never feel entirely confident Corey isn't guilty?"

"That's the way I'd look at it. But the cops, well, they want to get the right guy, but they also want to close the case. Arresting Keen makes it all go away."

Not good enough, thought Jane. "The word," she continued. "It wasn't *justice* but *injustice*."

"The police sat on that, too. In fact, they'll sit on it awhile longer, so don't go telling anyone. And make sure Cordelia keeps her mouth shut, too."

"I better call her right away."

"Yeah, you better. I'll stay here, drink my beer, eat my nachos, and enjoy the restaurant my future employee created."

"I'm not going to be a future employee."

"You amaze me, woman. How you stumbled over that evidence I'll never figure out."

"Dumb luck."

"Okay. Maybe so. But I'll take dumb luck over no luck any day. Honey, you gotta work with me sooner or later. And don't wait too long either, or I'll be so old and decrepit that I won't be able to teach you all my secrets. Just come on by some night and I'll show you all my open cases. You can take your pick. Now go call Cordelia."

He had no idea how much she wanted to do just that. "Thanks, Nolan."

He shooed her away, saying, "I don't want thanks, I want *you*."

Up in her office, Jane called Cordelia to give her the news.

After sputtering a few seconds, Cordelia said she was deeply wounded to hear that Nolan thought she had a big mouth. She'd told only Melanie, her neighbor across the hall, a woman at the grocery store who was standing next to her in line, her secretary at the theater—

Jane cut her off, saying she wasn't interested in a list. She told Cordelia to contact the throng and swear them to secrecy. When she was finished, she called Mary.

"Hello?" came an anxious voice.

"Mary, hi. It's Jane. Heard anything from Corey?"

"Nothing."

"Let me tell you the good news I just heard," said Jane, hoping that it would lift her spirits. "Gabriel Keen was arrested this morning for the murder of Charity Miller."

"Oh, Lord in heaven." She was silent for a few seconds. When she spoke again, her voice was thick with emotion. "I've prayed so hard that the police would find the real killer. I knew it wasn't my Corey."

Jane wanted to be happy for her, to feel absolutely confident that the police had the right man in custody, but after what Nolan had just pointed out, she had an uneasy sense that Keen's arrest might not be the end of it.

"Tell me, Jane. Did you have anything to do with Keen getting caught?"

"Maybe a little."

"I knew it. I knew you'd help us."

"Call me if you hear from Corey."

"I will."

"Are you okay? Would you like me to come over? This has been pretty stressful for you, too."

"You've already done much too much. But at least now I have some hope."

Corey stood at the customer phone inside the Lunds grocery store on Penn Avenue and punched in Mary's number. She answered on the first ring.

"Hello?"

"It's me." He glanced behind him. Dean was cruising the candy bars. He looked like a different kid now that his hair was brown.

After catching the news about the AMBER Alert on TV Friday morning, Corey had hot-wired a car. He had to get himself and Dean out of the city fast. He picked up some hair dye on the way to a motel in the boonies. He'd dyed both of their hair last night. He couldn't believe Serena had stabbed him in the back like that. They had a deal. He would have kept his promise to bring Dean back if only she'd kept her part of the bargain. Now he was in deep. Way too deep.

"Oh, honey. Where are you? Are you okay? Is Dean with you?"

"Have the police come by?"

"Yesterday."

"They're not there now?"

"No."

"Go look outside. See if you can see a man sitting in a car. Could be any kind of car."

"Okay. I'll be right back."

While he waited, he unwrapped a stick of gum and folded it into his mouth. He and Dean had ridden the bus to 60th and Penn.

Mary came back on the line. "No, there's nobody out there."

"You looked all over? Up and down both streets?"

"I used the binoculars you bought me for my birthday when you were seventeen."

"Good woman."

"Tell me what's going on."

"I will. I'll be there in a few minutes." He cut the line. "Dean?" he called. "Let's hit the road."

They walked down Penn toward 60th, where they hung a hard right and headed for Sunrise Drive. Entering the house through the side door, Corey found Mary waiting for them in the kitchen.

"What happened to your hair?"

"Not now, Mary." Corey held his son's hand and smiled at her. "Dean, this is your great-aunt Mary." Bending down and straightening Dean's coat, he said, "Aunt Mary raised me, so she's kind of like my mother."

Dean appeared to be struck by a severe attack of shyness. He looked down at his feet, pulled on the brim of his baseball cap, his gaze bouncing around the room, looking at everything except at Mary. "Hi," he mumbled.

"It's very nice to meet you," said Mary. "How old are you?"

"Eight."

"Such a big boy." She pressed a hand to her mouth. "Do you know you look just like your father did when he was your age?"

"Yeah," said Dean. "I saw a picture."

"Come on, buddy. You wanna watch a little TV?"

"Um, okay."

Corey got him set up in the family room, turned on the TV, then the gas fireplace, and finally covered him with a blanket. "I need to talk to my aunt. When I come back, it's time for you to go home to your mom." He figured Dean caught only half of what he'd said. He yanked down the brim of his hat and then trotted back upstairs to the kitchen.

Mary had installed herself at the table with a cup of coffee. He might have been able to read the expression on her face if he'd worked at it, but he didn't have time, so he just sat down across from her and explained where they'd been and what they'd done. Through it all, his aunt remained impassive, hardly moving, never touching her coffee as he described in detail what a great kid Dean was, how they'd connected.

"And now what?" she asked when he was done, her blue eyes searching his.

"I need to get Dean home, but I don't want to take him myself. I need some time, time to figure out what to do." He covered her hand with his. "Would you take him back for me? You can tell Serena I'll call her later. Don't ask me a lot of questions because I can't answer them. Just do me this one favor, okay? I'll never ask you for another thing, I promise. I don't want to leave Serena hanging any longer. I've put her through enough."

"Yes," agreed Mary. "You have."

"Will you do it?" He held his breath. Everything depended on his aunt taking Dean home.

She looked at him with such disappointment in her eyes that he almost lost it.

"All right," she said, finally. "But when I get back, we have to talk."

"Right. Anything you want. I'll go get Dean."

Mary ducked her head inside the van to make sure Dean's seat belt was fastened properly, then she slipped into the driver's seat, started the engine, and drove a little less than a block. Pulling over to the curb, she turned to look at the little boy.

"Dean, I need to ask you a big favor."

"Yeah?" he said, looking at her sideways.

"I know I'm asking a lot, but I need to go back to the house and talk to your father for a few minutes. It won't take me long. I have a good friend who lives in that house over there." She pointed. "Her name is Nann. She has two wonderful little dogs who love to play with kids your age. Do you think you could play with them for just a few minutes? And I'll bet Nann would have some cookies and milk for you if you got hungry."

"What kind of cookies?" he asked, squinting at her.

"Well, I have to admit, I don't know. But she makes all the cookies herself, so I know they'll be good. What do you say?"

He tipped his head to the side. "I think I want to go see my mom."

"I know you do, sweetheart, but I promise this won't take me long at all. Only a few minutes. Could you do me this one huge favor?"

"And then you'll take me home to my mom?"

"Absolutely. I promise."

He adjusted his hat. "I guess."

Corey dug through his aunt's closet until he found an old suitcase. Working quickly, he carried it down to his room in the basement and began packing some clothes. He didn't know what he'd need. He didn't even know where he was going. Grabbing the framed picture off the nightstand, the only photo he had of his mother and Mary together before his mother died, he wrapped a heavy sweater around it and stuffed it into the case. And then he sat down on the bed.

Nothing had worked out the way he'd planned. He couldn't believe what a deep hole he'd dug for himself in such a short time. The way he saw it, he had three options. He could wait for the police to arrest him and toss him back in prison. That really wasn't an option. He was never going back, whatever it took, whatever that meant. He wouldn't survive if he did. The second option was leave the state for good. Or he could buy himself a gun and put a bullet in his brain. But that option had to be reserved as a last resort—if the cops had him cornered or something.

Leaning forward, Corey rested his head on his hands. How could everything have gone so wrong? He'd made a deal with Serena. He just wanted one lousy night. He couldn't fathom why she'd turned him in. Thinking of Dean, of the relationship they would never have, he felt his eyes begin to well with tears. But before he knew it, his cheeks were wet and his nose was stuffed up. He was smart enough to know that he was crying mostly for himself, but also for Dean and Serena, for what could have been.

Pressing his fists against his eyes, he sniffed a few times and then looked up.

He jumped when he saw Mary standing in the doorway. "What's going on? I thought . . . where's Dean?"

"Dean's fine. What are you doing with my suitcase?"

"What's it look like? I'm packing."

"You're running away."

"I don't have a choice."

"You've always got choices, Corey."

He gave a mirthless laugh. "You want me to go back to prison? Kidnapping is a felony. That means I go back and serve the rest of my three-year sentence, and on top of that, I'll probably get nailed for another ten, twelve years."

"You don't know that."

"By the time they let me out, Dean will be the same age I am now."

"So the solution is to run."

"Either that, or I go get a gun and end it."

Her eyes registered shock. "Suicide is against God's law."

"Fuck God's law. Fuck any law that keeps me away from my kid."

A deep crimson climbed her cheeks. "All right. I can't stop you. You're a grown man now, not a boy with a bad attitude. I thought I raised you to respect life—everyone's life, including yours. But I see now that I failed."

"You didn't fail, Mary. It's got nothing to do with you. It's me. I'm the fuckup."

"You will not use that kind of language in this house!"

He turned away, threw a couple more balled-up socks in the suitcase. "I'm sorry."

She didn't speak again until he lifted the case off the bed and faced her.

"Before you go, answer one question for me."

He waited.

"Did you rape that woman up near Duluth?"

The question hit him like a two-by-four. It took him a couple seconds to recover. "Don't, Mary. Don't do that. You've never doubted me before."

"You think I'm just some credulous old lady? Some pathetic old goat that's happy, even eager, to buy anything you have to sell?"

"No, of course—"

She stepped forward with her hand out, like she was going to slap him. "You think it's been easy loving you all these years? Easy keeping faith with a man intent on taking a wrecking ball to his life?"

"No. Of course not. But there's no way I can prove to you that I didn't rape that woman. There's no possible way unless you accept my word."

Corey glimpsed something final in the stillness of her eyes. This was the moment he'd feared the entire time he'd been inside. In fact, fear was what had always driven him. Fear of a personal recklessness he couldn't seem to control. Fear that he'd never amount to anything. Fear that when he went to prison, everyone he knew would forget him. Fear that jail would change him into someone he didn't want to be. Fear that his aunt would start to question his innocence. And now, fear that he could never be a real father to his son.

"The man I thought I knew would never run away from his boy," said Mary. "You understand what that feels like, Corey. Your father did it to you. How can you turn around and do the same thing to Dean?"

"What kind of father-son relationship can I have with him from prison?"

"More than you'll have if you disappear from his life. The Corey I thought I raised would never *ever* put his son through that. That's why I demand that you answer my question. Did you rape that woman?"

"No!"

"Did you?"

He dropped the suitcase, fell back on the bed. "No," he breathed. "No."

He would never forget where he'd been that night. He'd tied one on in a bar the night before, so he was hungover. He'd pulled off the freeway around two and stopped on a dark country road so he could grab a few hours' sleep. He couldn't prove it. Nobody saw him. He'd thought a lot about the concept of proof when he was in prison. There were so many things you couldn't prove. Important things. Like love.

"More lies," said Mary.

"I'm not lying."

She held his gaze. "Then prove it."

"I can't. It's impossible."

"No, it's not. Stay. Turn yourself in to the police. Fight for Dean. Fight to turn your life around."

"I tried. It didn't work."

"Try again."

"I'm not like you. I'm not as strong as you are. I can't go back to prison."

"But if you run you'll never know what you're really made of. If you go, Corey, you leave me no choice but to conclude you lied to me about raping that woman. I may still pray for you, for your immortal soul, I might even still love you, but I will never in this life speak to you again."

Her words gutted him. It was as if she'd reached inside his skin and scooped out everything that made him capable of standing upright. "You don't mean that."

"I do." Her voice shook with anger. "For once in your life, Corey, be a man."

Closing his eyes, he realized she'd called his bluff—that she was the only one who truly could. She'd laid it all out for him. She'd given him a way to prove the unprovable. "Okay," he said, pushing off the bed, his legs nearly giving out on him as he stood. "I'll stay."

She threw her arms around him.

"Drive me to the police station *now,* Mary, before I lose what little nerve I've got left."

38

Let's do lunch," said Cordelia.

"Here? At the Lyme House?" asked Jane.

"And not in the pub, either. In the main dining room. It's on you. You owe me big for pushing you out the door the other night."

Jane sat back in her desk chair and laughed. "You pushed *me* out the door?" Mouse yawned. He was curled up on the rug by the fireplace. It occurred to Jane that she wanted his life, not hers. "So what time do we eat?"

"Well, it's eleven now," said Cordelia. "How about noon?"

"I thought I'd call Merriam Park Methodist, see if Christopher Cornish was around."

"Why on earth would you do that?"

"I don't know. I guess . . . I feel like I should apologize. I need to make more of an effort to follow what's going on around me. Luke indicated that Christopher was probably voting for my dad, so he may not be quite as rabid as Luke is. It's just something I need to do."

"What*ever*."

"I think I'll call over there now. If he's around, I'll stop in, make it quick, and be back by the time you get here."

"Not to worry. If you're not around, I'll start the celebration without you."

"What celebration?"

"Your dad's victory tomorrow, bean brain. I'm starting early. Put a bottle of your finest champagne on ice."

Jane called the church and spoke to the Carla Epstine, the secretary. She said that Reverend Cornish had been cleaning out his office most of the morning but that she'd seen him leave about fifteen minutes ago.

"Why is he cleaning out his office?" asked Jane.

"A bill of charge and specifications has been issued. It's only a matter of time before there will be a church trial. The United Methodists don't allow practicing homosexuals to be ordained elders."

"I see."

"And then there are the other . . . accusations. Of course, we should maintain that someone is innocent until proved guilty."

"Guilty of what?"

A long silence. "Sexual problem with . . . some of the younger men and boys."

"Are you serious?"

"Very serious, Mrs.—"

"Thanks," said Jane, hanging up. She sat for a moment, wondering if this news had any truth to it. "Come on, Mouse. Let's go see if Reverend Cornish is at his loft."

Jane parked her car just a few spaces down from the spot she'd found the other day. She gave Mouse his usual Milk-Bone and told him that she'd be back in a few minutes. If Cornish had left the church fifteen minutes before she called, he was probably just getting home.

Sure enough, she found him at the edge of the drive, unloading some sacks from his trunk.

"Can I help you?" she asked.

He raised his eyebrows at her. His look of puzzlement quickly turned to wariness. "Ms. Lawless. You're the last person I expected to see today."

"I was hoping you'd have a few minutes to talk."

"About what?"

"Could we . . . sit somewhere quiet. I won't take much of your time."

He took off his sunglasses, rubbed his eyes, and thought it over. "Well, I suppose if you're here, you might as well help me carry some of this upstairs." He was wearing a gray herringbone tweed suit with a matching vest. He looked like a very proper English gentleman. He handed Jane two paper sacks filled with books. Before closing the trunk and locking the car, he lifted one sack out for himself. Using his cane, he maneuvered slowly up a ramp to the back door.

They rode up to the third floor in silence. The elevator opened onto a small hallway with three expensive-looking wood-paneled doors. Cornish opened the door directly to her right and stood back so that she could enter first.

"Just set them on the dining room table," he said, leaving his sack in the front hall.

"Would you like me to go down and bring up another load?" asked Jane.

"Luke will do it when he gets home." He took off his suit jacket and hung it up. "Sit down, won't you? Anywhere is fine."

Jane moved into the main living area. "This is a lovely loft." She was surrounded by windows. She sat down next to a large potted ficus tree.

"Thanks," he said, pausing by the kitchen. "Can I offer you something to drink?"

Cornish had far better manners than his partner. "No, thanks."

Pulling one of the dining room chairs away from the table, he sat down just a few feet from her, setting his cane on the floor next to him. "So, what did you want to talk about?"

She moved to the edge of her chair, pressed her hands together between her knees. "I feel that I need to apologize. I should have known about what happened to you last spring. I get very involved in my work and sometimes I forget to look around and see what's happening in the world. That's not an excuse, it's just the way I live my life. But a hate crime . . . I should have known about that. It was probably all over the news, in the papers."

He shook his head. "There was a small article in the local paper. Your father's law firm was able to get the charges against Gabriel dropped so fast that I don't believe any of that even made the TV news."

"But it was undoubtedly covered in the local GLBT press."

"Yes. My story was included in a general article on hate crimes in the Twin Cities, but nothing beyond that."

"Doesn't seem like enough, does it."

"No, it does not."

"Look," she said, feeling uncomfortable, but assuming it was the price she had to pay. "I wanted you to know that my father wasn't the one who represented Gabriel Keen. It was one of his partners, Elizabeth Piper."

"And that should matter why?"

"I suppose it doesn't. I know what you must think of anyone connected to a firm that represents people who commit hate crimes—"

"I'm sure you can guess. And don't trot out the Constitution. I know we need both prosecutors and defenders. I just think, in this case, Keen should have been forced to use a public defender. His father is wealthy and could buy a shark. That's the part that doesn't seem fair."

Jane could hardly argue the point. "It's a different criminal justice system for the poor than for the wealthy. It shouldn't be that way. We're a country of laws. The playing field should be level—for everyone."

"Ah, you're a dreamer. We don't belong in this world."

Jane drew her eyes away. Waited a beat. "I understand you've been accused of sexual impropriety at your church."

His anger spiked. "Keen is out to get me any way he can. He started the rumors, then went to my bishop with the accusation. Any gay pastor who works with young people is an easy target these days.

Of course, I didn't do any of the things he accused me of. The bishop wouldn't be able to prove anything. I . . . I try not to hate Gabriel, but I'm afraid it's a battle I lost long ago."

"You heard he was arrested for Charity's murder."

His body jerked. "No. When?"

"Yesterday morning."

He tipped his head back and burst into a grin. Jane had never seen him happy before. He was good-looking enough when he was sad or serious, but when he smiled, he became almost angelic. "I apologize," he said, unable to wipe the joy off his face. "I shouldn't be so pleased with another man's demise."

"But you are."

"Oh," he said, giving the air a fist pump, "it couldn't happen to a more deserving man."

When Jane saw that his eyes were wet, she asked, "Are you okay?"

"Yes, fine. I just wish Charity could be here to celebrate this moment with me."

"You two were good friends."

"Her loss was . . . it was one of the worst moments of my life. But now, this gives it some meaning."

She wasn't sure what he meant. "In what way?"

His lips parted. "Just that her death brought about his demise."

"Kind of a high price to pay."

"Yes, well, that's certainly true. It was a tragedy. It should never have happened. But, you see, Gabriel thought she'd ended her relationship with him because of me, because of our friendship. In fact, that was part of it. He was infuriated by . . . the injustice of it. I suppose that's why he wrote that word."

"What word?"

"*Injustice.* Didn't you know? He wrote it in lipstick on her stomach."

She looked at him, nodded. He continued to talk, but she wasn't listening anymore. The significance of that one word approached her like a dark figure. In an instant, even though she didn't know how it had happened, she knew the police had arrested the wrong man.

She continued to force a look of interest in what he was saying. He seemed to be soliciting her agreement, so she gave it, nodding, folding her hands calmly in her lap. When he paused, she glanced at her watch. "I've taken up enough of your time. And I need to get back to work."

Jane wasn't sure if she was imagining it, but he seemed to have read something in her face. The silence grew and grew until it was almost volcanic.

And then the front door opened.

"Luke, is that you?" called Christopher, his gaze remaining on Jane.

"Yeah. I bought us some lunch." When he came around the corner and saw Jane, he stopped. "What's she doing here?"

Still watching her, Christopher said, "She came to apologize."

"For what?"

"For . . . ignorance."

Luke grunted.

"Will you two excuse me for a moment?" said Christopher, scooping his cane off the floor.

Jane stood. "I really need to get going."

"No, just stay for another few seconds. There's something I want to show you." He limped out of the room.

Luke glared at her. "You've got some nerve. I suppose you know your dad's campaign manager just fired me."

"Did she?"

He set a white sack on the dining room table next to the bags of books. "Frankly, I'm glad to be out of there."

Jane moved a few feet away from the chair. "I really need to go."

"Fine with me."

Christopher returned to the room holding a gun aimed directly at Jane's chest.

"Jesus, Christopher, what's going on?"

"You've got to help me think this out."

"Think *what* out?"

"She knows. I don't know how—"

"Knows *what*? About the cybercrap I've been doing? So what? She can't prove it. Shit, Christopher, put the gun down." He moved toward him. "Better yet, give it to me. You don't even know how to use it."

"You don't get it," said Christopher, his hand shaking, his eyes filled with a kind of animal terror. "I was the one who killed Charity."

Luke turned to face him. "You *what*?"

"We'd been talking for months about what we could do to get Keen arrested. She wanted him gone from her life as much as I wanted to see him behind bars. So, that last night, when I called her to tell her Corey Hodge was a rapist and that she should get as far away from him as she could, she called me back on her way home. She was angry at Corey. He'd lied to her, told her he was a cop. I explained what he'd done to that woman back in the midnineties. In detail. It was her idea, not mine, to set something up that made it look like he'd attacked her. She asked if I knew where to get my hands on a taser. I said I already had one. She asked how much it would hurt to get hit by one. What did I know? I said it probably hurt, but it didn't last long. So she said, let's do it, let's make it look like Corey had come after her. And then, once we'd set the scene, I'd go over to Keen's house and plant the evidence. That's just what I did. It was her idea to use the camera to link Keen to the attack. We wanted him behind bars. And if it caused Corey some initial problems, she was fine with that, too. He was a rapist, after all. We both thought it was a brilliant plan. Nobody would really get hurt—except Keen and Corey."

Jane watched Christopher's eyes, looking for any hint that he was about to squeeze the trigger.

"You shot her with a taser?" said Luke, his expression full of horrified confusion.

"She had the idea to make it look like she'd been taking out the trash. We went outside, tossed the trash into the bin, and then . . . yes, I did it. I shot her. She dropped next to the Dumpster and I held her until she said she was feeling better. I took the photos. And then I covered her eyes with tape, but not her mouth. That way, as soon as

I was gone, she could start screaming bloody murder, tell the police that Keen had attacked her. But then I began to panic that someone would see us. I told her I had to go. She looked at me kind of strangely. I didn't know how to read it. Maybe her heart was already giving out on her . . . but . . . no, I don't believe that. I think we were both just kind of appalled at what we were doing.

"Luke, you have to believe me. When I left her, she was fine. I swear it on everything I hold holy. We both thought everything would work out just the way we planned. And then, the next day, when I called her, she didn't answer. I got a little frantic. Finally, her parents called with the news. I didn't know what to do. I lost it. I never meant to hurt her. Never!"

Luke's eyes darted nervously to Jane, then back to Christopher.

"If I let Jane go," continued Christopher, shaking now, "she'll run straight to the police. I'll go to prison! Help, me, Luke. I don't know what to do." Beads of sweat had broken out on his forehead.

Inside the pocket of Jane's coat, her cell phone began to vibrate. Slipping both hands into her pockets, trying to make it look casual, she felt for the On button and pressed it.

"Don't judge me," shouted Christopher, his gaze boring deep into Luke's eyes. "You had a hard-on to get even with Lawless and his daughter. I told you I didn't care what you did. I even gave you my blessing. But me, it was always Keen. Only Keen. Since I woke up from that coma, I've had one thought. God forgive me," he cried. "I wanted him dead. Every night I'd go to bed and think of ways to do it. It was wrong! Hate is wrong, Luke. I'm a minister! I shouldn't think like that. But I couldn't stop myself."

Jane could almost see the fuses blowing behind Christopher's eyes. She wasn't even sure he was sane. Thinking that this might be her last chance, she shoved Luke into Christopher and hurtled toward the door.

"Stop!" screamed Christopher. "I'll shoot you. God forgive me, I will."

She almost made it. Turning around, she saw that he was at the edge of the hallway, farther away this time, but the gun was still leveled at her. Even if he was a terrible shot, he could probably hit her before she got out.

"Luke," called Christopher, dropping his cane and holding the gun with both hands. "Get the rope from your camping gear."

Luke was standing a few feet behind him. He didn't move.

"Do it," screamed Christopher. "You tie her up and gag her, and then we'll dump her next door."

"In the empty loft?"

"I've got a key. It's in the kitchen drawer by the phone. We'll leave her there until we decide what to do."

"Christopher, think for a minute," said Luke.

"I can't!"

"People will miss me at work," said Jane. "They'll come looking for me."

"Does anybody know you're here?" asked Luke.

"Yes."

"She's bluffing," said Christopher. "Get the rope."

She pressed her hands into her coat pockets again, hoping like crazy that it hadn't been somebody calling to ask if she needed a new garage door.

Luke rushed up to her and tied her hands. He kept looking at Christopher like he wasn't sure it was a good idea.

"We got any tape?" asked Luke

"Just that clear packing tape. It's in your study."

Luke raced off.

"Christopher, please," said Jane. "Think about what you're doing. It would be so much better if you admitted what happened. It wasn't murder, it was an accident. And there were extenuating—"

"Shut up!"

Luke came back, stuffed her mouth with a washcloth, and covered it with several strips of tape. Opening the door, he peered out into the hall. "Come on," he said, grabbing her arm and pushing her out in front of him. He plugged the key into the lock across the hall and shoved her inside.

"Sit." He pointed to a section of floor in front of a huge stack of plaster board. Unlike Christopher and Luke's place, this one wasn't finished. It smelled of drywall dust, new cement, and soggy spackling paste. She eased down onto the dirty floor. Luke crouched down next to her. "Why'd you have to come over here?" he said.

With the tape over her mouth, she couldn't exactly respond.

"Everything would have been fine if you'd just stayed out of it." Hesitating a moment, he stood. "I won't tie your feet. And I won't let him hurt you, but you've got to stay here until I can talk him down. He's not thinking right. He'd never do this if he was. You stay here and keep quiet and I'll do everything I can to see that you leave in one piece. But if you try to get away before I've handled this, I swear I won't be responsible for what happens."

At the door he turned and said, "Ever since Christopher woke up from that coma, he's been . . . different. I kept hoping he'd pull out of it, but—" He put his hand on the doorknob. "That beating he took. It changed both of us."

After he'd locked the door behind him, Jane scanned the room. Struggling to her feet with her hands still tied behind her, she moved over to the windows, thinking that she might be able to get someone's attention three floors down. But without being able to use her arms or voice, that seemed like too much of a stretch. Instead, she focused all her attention on the rope around her wrists. She didn't know how much time she had, but she assumed it wasn't much. Her heart was beating hard inside her chest. Counting on the kindness of Luke Durrant seemed like a shaky proposition at best.

She wondered about the phone in her pocket as she struggled to free her hands. She quickly made a few straining sounds, hoping beyond hope that someone might still be listening. As she worked at the rope, her wrists began to burn. She jerked and pulled, but the nothing she did made any difference.

Stopping for a moment, she listened to the silence, wondering what Christopher and Luke were talking about. Were they determining her fate, or calling a lawyer? She jumped when she heard a knock—not her door but theirs. Then another knock, this one even louder. A deep male voice said, "Minneapolis police. Open up."

Jane rushed over and flattened her ear against her door, then crouched down, hit the floor, turned on her back, and pulled her legs up to her chest. She heaved them at the door, again and again, making as much noise as she could.

It felt like forever, but the door finally opened. A woman cop stood over her. "What the hell?" she said, bending down.

She pulled the tape off Jane's mouth, pulled out the washcloth, then untied her hands. Jane caught her breath. She quickly explained what had happened. The cop listened, asked a few questions, then told her to stay put. After she walked out, leaving the door open, Jane got up, brushing off her dusty clothes. It wasn't long before a handcuffed Luke and Christopher were led to the elevators by a cop she hadn't seen before. The one she had—she introduced herself as Patrolwoman Patty Heinz—asked if she was okay, if she wanted to be checked over by a paramedic.

"No, I'm fine," said Jane. "I just need a minute."

"We arrested those two guys for assaulting you, but it sounds like there's more to it."

"Much more."

"We'll need a statement. I can take you in my cruiser, or you can drive yourself."

"I'll drive," said Jane.

"You know where City Hall is?"

"I'll be there in a few minutes."

"Thanks."

Jane sank down onto a large plastic container of spackling paste to examine the scrapes on her wrists. Glancing toward the open door, she saw the elevator open and the cop get on. But someone also got off.

"Julia?" said Jane. "What are you doing here?"

Julia rushed in, crouched next to her. She looked terrified, her thin shoulders shaking under her coat. "Are you okay? When I phoned, you didn't answer, but then I heard all this shouting."

"You were the one who called?"

"I finally got the tests back on your dad and I wanted to talk to you. But when you didn't answer and I thought I heard someone say Keen, and then the name Luke, and then someone screamed for Luke to get a rope—it was all so muffled, but I could tell something was wrong. And then your voice said something like 'people would miss me.' You sounded so frightened. I heard someone say 'loft.' I found another phone and called 911, told the police that I thought you were in danger, maybe even being held against your will. I was guessing, but I gave them the address of Luke's loft, and then I drove over."

"I think you just saved my life."

"Your hair, it's full of soot. It looks gray." She touched it. And then she started to laugh. "You look like an old woman."

Jane couldn't help herself. She laughed, too. Laughed until her sides ached and tears streamed down her cheeks. But at some point, the happy, silly tears turned to real anguish. It wasn't just being tied up, it was everything that had happened. Charity's senseless death. Kenzie leaving her. Her concern for her father's health. Her estrangement from her brother. She wrapped her arms around her body and began to rock. She felt Julia's hand on her back, then on her hair.

"It's okay, Jane. Let it out."

It took a few moments, but Jane finally pulled herself together. She stood, wiped a hand across her eyes.

"I'm sorry," said Julia. "I shouldn't have touched you. I should go. I'm just glad everything turned out okay."

"Julia?"

She turned.

"What did the tests show? My dad's tests."

"He's very tired and in need of some serious rest. I'd like to do some follow-up." She paused as if there was more she wanted to say.

"What is it?"

"You should talk to your dad. There's something he needs to tell you."

"Is it his heart?"

"I'm not sure. Like I said, I need to run more tests. But I've fitted him with an event monitor. I hope it will give us the information we're looking for. Don't worry, Jane. He reminds me so much of you—stubborn to a fault. But he's got a good heart, in every way, just like you do."

Jane cleared her throat. "Did you call Peter?"

She nodded.

"Thanks."

"No thanks necessary."

"Why don't you—" A tangle of feelings collided inside her. She wasn't sure if what she was about to say was smart or not, but she seemed to be doing it. "Why don't you join us tomorrow night for the campaign vigil. My father's booked several suites at the top of the Maxfield Plaza. Downstairs in one of the convention rooms, his supporters will all be gathered, watching the TV as the votes come in. It's kind of a big party. He'll give his acceptance speech there—or his concession speech." She wiped her eyes again. "But just friends and family upstairs. There should be lots of food. Wine. We're all going to wait it out together."

Julia looked out the window, then back at Jane. "I'd be honored."

"I'll give them your name at the reception desk. Someone will show you where to go."

"I promise I won't stay long."

"No," said Jane. "Stay as long as you like."

Julia's eyes flickered. "I'll see you tomorrow, then."

Election night brought with it Minnesota's first snowstorm of the year. Six inches had already fallen in the northern part of the state. Four inches were predicted in the cities by morning. The roads were slippery, and many of the citizens, according to the news reports, were staying home.

Jane sat next to Cordelia and Melanie on a couch in her father's double penthouse suite at the top of the Maxfield. The TV had been on for hours. Various staffers controlled the remote over the course of the evening, flipping back and forth between national and local elections. As the returns began to filter in, it looked like Minnesota's race for governor would be close. So far, with just a few precincts reporting, it was a dead heat. The opinion poll the campaign had done a few days ago put Pettyjohn up by five points, which at this point suggested a substantial lead. But no one had factored in the weather.

Jane was sipping from a glass of brandy when her father stepped out of one of the bedrooms and called her name. He was dressed casually, in a green polo shirt and jeans. He'd put on his new suit later when he had to go downstairs.

"Come in here for a sec, will you?"

She excused herself and walked to the end of the room, closing the door behind her.

Her father was already sitting on the edge of the bed. He nodded to a chair a few feet away.

"What's going on?" she asked, still standing by the door.

"I need to talk to you, honey. I need to come clean."

"About what?"

"I lied to you. I lied to a lot of people about what happened a couple of weeks ago, the day I landed the Cessna in that field. Look," he said, rubbing the back of his neck, "you saw what happened to me the other night. That dizzy spell. It's happened before. Once. Only once. But that time, I lost consciousness."

"Dad!"

"It was while I was piloting the plane on the way down from Bemidji. We were never in any danger. The plane was on autopilot. I was only out for a minute at most, but as you can expect, it was pretty hair-raising for the other two guys on board, neither of whom had ever flown a plane. When I came to and realized what had happened, I figured I'd better land while I still could, just in case it happened again. So that's what I did. I had complete power, and although the landing was rough, we set down just fine. By the time we were on the ground, I felt okay. And then we had this big discussion about what to do—what to tell the tower in St. Cloud, what to tell reporters. Whether or not we should call a doctor. I figured it was stress, just an anomaly. That it would never happen again. But it did. The other night while you were in my office. That's why, when Julia came to me, I didn't turn her down."

"Is . . . is it your heart?"

"We're not sure. She's fitted me with a monitor, and if there's another episode, she'll have a better idea of what's going on. She's already set up an appointment for me with a very discreet cardiologist she knows. Quite frankly, Jane, I think she's pretty amazing."

He got up, moved toward her. "Can you forgive me?" he asked, holding out his hand to her.

She'd been thinking about something. She figured she wasn't going to get another chance like this. "On one condition."

"What's that?"

"I want you to find the second best criminal defense lawyer in the Twin Cities and pay him or her to defend Christopher Cornish and Luke Durrant."

He frowned. "Are you serious?"

"Completely."

"But they tied you up, tried to—"

"I know what they did. And I know why. So do you."

"Jane, what Elizabeth did for Gabriel Keen, it was simply good lawyering."

"Fine. So let's get some good lawyering for Christopher and Luke. Paying for a shark would break them financially. I don't want that to happen. I want them to have the best shot possible at getting the minimum sentence."

He bent toward her, cupped his hands around her arms. "If that's what you want."

"It is."

"It will have to be completely off the radar. Nobody can know I'm doing it."

"You can figure that out."

"Yes, Janey, I can."

"Will you?"

"If it will make you happy, absolutely."

When Jane came out of the bedroom, she noticed that Elizabeth was over by the windows, looking radiant in a red suit, talking to some of the women campaign staffers. Jane's brother, Peter, had spent the early part of the evening downstairs, filming the crowd of loyal supporters in the Lindbergh Room, but had returned to the suite a while ago and was now trying to catch a catnap in one of the bedrooms. His wife, Sigrid, and their daughter, Mia, were playing a game of chess at a table near the door to the balcony. It would be hours before anything would be definitive, and even then, there was always the possibility that the election would be so close that there would need to be a recount.

All evening, the suite had been a madhouse, with people coming and going.

By nine, Jane was back on the couch, sipping her second brandy. She hadn't realized she'd be quite this jumpy.

Elbowing Jane in the ribs, Cordelia said, "You're not talking." Her gaze remained fixed on the screen.

"Neither are you."

"I feel like I'm going to throw up."

"I feel like I've got a nest of wasps in my stomach," said Melanie.

Jane took a stiff gulp from the glass. "Ditto."

"So, have you heard anything more from Mary?" asked Melanie. She'd brought along some knitting, so at least her fingers had something to do.

"Actually, I have. Looks like the kidnapping charges might be dropped against Corey."

Cordelia turned to look at her. "Why? He did it."

"Yes, but from what Mary told me, he called his girlfriend the same night he took Dean. They made a deal. She promised that if Corey brought Dean home by noon the next day, she wouldn't call the cops. But when her boyfriend found out, he demanded that she tell the police right away. When she refused, he got physical, nearly broke her arm. So she called. From what I hear, the boyfriend is the one who's going to jail. And if they determine Corey didn't do anything illegal in taking Dean, he may not go back to prison to serve out the rest of his sentence."

"You think he's innocent of that other rape charge?"

"Mary believes he is. I don't know. I guess I'm inclined to agree. If he did get a raw deal, maybe, if he can catch a break, he can turn his life around. I hope that's the case."

"And Keen?" asked Melanie.

"He's still in custody, but if Christopher is charged with Charity's death, they'll have to release him."

"What a shame," said Cordelia.

"It is," said Jane. "But I think that, deep inside where Keen really lives, he must have a hellish existence. I wouldn't be at all surprised to learn that, one day not too far from now, he simply downs one too many drinks to wash down one too many pills."

They all stopped talking when the national election results on TV were replaced with the local races.

Jane took another sustaining swallow of brandy, seeing that her father's outstate numbers had gone down a few points. A collective groan rumbled through the room.

Julia came through the door a few seconds later.

"What's *she* doing here?" hissed Cordelia, nearly choking on her black cherry soda.

Jane smiled and waved. "Over here," she called.

"Move over." Jane pushed against Cordelia's shiplike form. "Make some room for her."

"I will *not*."

Jane stood. "I'm glad you could make it."

Julia's gaze skirted the room. "This is the first large gathering I've been to since . . ." Her voice trailed off.

"Do crowds bother you?" asked Jane.

"It's my nerves. Sometimes I think my emotions are still a little close to the surface."

"Would you like something to eat? Or drink?"

"A glass of wine would be nice." She glanced down at Cordelia. "Your hair is pink."

"How insightful of you."

"You mean you admit it?"

"You know, Julia," said Cordelia, "people would like you a lot better if you had some reconstructive facial surgery."

"For what?"

"Plastic surgeons can do wonders these days removing fangs."

Jane's eyes rose to the ceiling. "Can you two get along while I go get Julia a glass of wine?"

"Not a problem," said Julia, snuggling down next to Cordelia. "We'll catch up."

Cordelia's eyes pleaded with Jane to make it fast.

By two in the morning, the loud buzz in the room had been replaced by a low but steady murmur. Julia excused herself and walked to the bathroom. Inside, she looked to see if there was a lock on the door and was happy to find that there was.

She studied herself in the mirror. She'd had too much wine, so this wasn't the best time to assess damages, but she shrugged and did it anyway. She'd grown older, but then so had Jane. In the last few weeks, her skin had lost some of its deathly pallor and she was beginning to feel less physically fragile. For the longest time, her body had been stiff, brittle, full of aches and pains. But she was finally regaining her strength and, with it, losing the sense of being old beyond her years.

She couldn't quite believe how well things hand gone, and how quickly. But that was because, for the first time since she'd come home, she had a focus, a problem to work on, a goal to achieve. Goals had always driven her.

Running her fingers over the bottles of shampoo, aftershave, gels, toothpaste, and other necessities of modern life that Ray and Elizabeth had brought with them, she noticed a tube of lipstick next to a small bottle of liquid makeup. She examined it, removing the cover, wondering what it would look like if she applied it to her lips.

But then, on a whim, she pulled up her sweater and carefully wrote the word *justice* on her stomach. She stood, her head tilted to the side, regarding her midsection, the word reversed in the mirror but still readable. She traced it a second time, recalling just what it had felt like when she'd pressed a similar tube to the soft skin of Kenzie's stomach—the thrill, the rush, the embracing of risk, the pure shiver of power.

When she smiled at herself, the eyes of a predator were reflected back at her.

And when someone finally knocked on the door a few minutes later, she called, "I'm almost done."

By three, one of the local stations announced it was ready to call the race for governor.

Jane sat rigidly on the same couch she'd commandeered all evening, with Julia and Cordelia as bookends. Melanie was on the floor, her back pressed to Cordelia's legs. Jane's father and Elizabeth were standing in the doorway to the bedroom. Everyone else was gathered around the television screen. Kenzie should be here, thought Jane. It just felt so wrong without her. She wondered if Kenzie was home in Nebraska, watching the returns in the comfort of her old farmhouse.

By now, they were all pretty sure what the decision would be, but her father said he'd wait until one of the stations called it, and then he'd go downstairs to the waiting crowd of supporters.

Jane's entire body tensed as the news anchor on the local NBC affiliate said, "We're getting down to the wire in the Minnesota state governor's race. We understand that Don Pettyjohn is already on his way to talk to his party loyalists."

Jane grabbed for Cordelia's hand. Julia grabbed Jane's other hand.

"It's been a very close race. At this time, we're calling the race for governor of the state of Minnesota. With only seven precincts left to count, the winner is . . ."

Jane looked up at her dad.

"Don Pettyjohn."

The air went out of the room.

Ray kissed Elizabeth, held her close, then lifted his hands for quiet. "We ran a good race. You all did a spectacular job for which I'll always be grateful. We're lucky enough to live in a democracy, something I believe in with all my heart. We fought the good fight and we lost. No shame in that."

Everyone began to cheer, some with tears in their eyes.

Jane had tears in her eyes too, but for different reasons. Hers were tears of joy. Several hours ago she'd come to the startling conclusion that she hoped her dad would lose. Not because he wouldn't make a great governor, perhaps one of the best the state would ever know, but because, selfishly, she didn't want to lose him for the next four years. And even more than that, she was deeply worried about his health. He would push himself too hard if he won, he would put his health and everything else on the back burner, it was just the way he was. Jane was afraid he might not survive his first year in office. She knew her dad well enough to trust that he would always remain engaged, involved, actively speaking out for the causes he believed in. This loss would simply mean he would have to do it without a bully pulpit. In Jane's mind, that bully pulpit came at too great a cost. Not becoming the next governor meant he would get the medical care he needed and thus live to fight another day.

Before he left the room, she walked over and gave him a hug. "You okay?" she whispered in his ear.

"Fine," he whispered back. "Bent but not broken."

"I'm proud of you."

He pressed his lips together, holding back the emotion flooding his face. "That means more to me than you'll ever know." And then, giving everyone one last encouraging smile, he left the room to the sound of cheers and applause.